THE KNIGHTS OF THE COLD WAR AND THE ROAD TO BIN LADEN

A Somewhat Fictional Thriller

Peter Shadowhawk

ISBN 10: 0615976913
ISBN 13: 978-0615976914
Library of Congress Control Number: 2014903774
Peter Shadowhawk, Ventura, CA

Contents

Preface

Within the bowels of every intelligence agency, a few men exist who are far more terrifying and evil than the men they are sent to kill.

They are paragons of excess. They are murderers and sadists who delight in the torture and torment of lesser men; they are creatures of little or no conscience. But they are seen by many in the intelligence community as useful, so they remain.

But in the darkness, there also are "the good dragons." This book is dedicated to those many courageous, selfless men and women who willingly vanish into the shadows and tread into the darkness without care for personal safety.

Nameless, and without glory or recognition, they move silently through the game, for to name them surely would cost them their lives. Though they are nameless, they will not be forgotten.

Who are these fearless men and women who willingly slide into the dark places and fight in foreign lands so the rest of us can live our lives and practice our freedoms in the light?

They are the CIA, and they are America's unbreakable, invisible steel wall; truly, they are "the good dragons." They were without question the Knights of the Cold War.

This book is respectfully dedicated to them, with gratitude for their many sacrifices.

Peter Shadowhawk
Ventura, California; 2014

CHAPTER ONE
The Game of the Hunter

August 9, 1962; Midnight
New York City

From the shadows the Monster grinned, softly laughing in happy chorus with the demons joyfully dancing inside the rancid confines of his twisted soul. Lifting his fedora-clad head a bit above the hedge, he turned slightly to the left and winked toward the black Lincoln Continental and the two emotionless, ice-cool assassins hidden within.

The Monster then lowered his head as he chuckled with glee at the terrified man who sprinted past him. Pulling out his silenced pistol, he gave it a gentle kiss—one could never have too much fun!

The doctor screamed for help as he shot past the hedge and the eyes of the Monster. Approaching the moonlit corner, he shouted again for help as he tried in vain to soften the loud clack of his heavy leather wingtips as he flew across the moonlight street. He knew his only chance was to outrun his pursuers and gain the time he needed to find an out, an escape to anywhere he might find protection.

Dr. Benjamin Waydner, MD, had been such a fool. He never should have called the young Italian student's bluff. He never should have insulted the Mafia, and now, because of it, he was a dead man. His life wasn't worth it; the professor should have altered the test, fudged the little hoodlum's failing grade to a passing one. But he hadn't, and now he would have to pay.

Spotting a gate to his left, he turned and bolted across the lawn; he prayed he could reach it before the Lincoln and the madman with the fedora came around the bend.

Thankfully, the red wooden gate was unbolted and swung easily as he pushed it open and entered. He quickly crouched low and swung it shut. Silently he waited, his heart pounding and his chest laboring for air as he listened for the black Lincoln to creep up the street. A long second passed, then two, then a lifetime. Another few seconds undetected, and he would be safe.

Suddenly Waydner screamed uncontrollably as he bolted upright, the enraged Labrador having left his mark on his left buttock. The doctor tried desperately to remain unseen below the top of the gate as he fended off the repeated attacks, but the black Labrador attacked ferociously, with a purpose that would not be denied and a determination to master its ground. The more Waydner kicked, the more vicious the dog grew. The panicked doctor pushed open the gate and tossed his umbrella at the dog as he slammed the gate shut and then crouched behind some laurel bushes, still listening for the deadly car.

The Labrador was still furiously tearing at the gate. But Waydner gratefully noted that save for that angry din, the street was dead silent. He sighed—he had won; he had survived his gladiatorial match with the black Lab from hell, and it had bought him the time he needed. The Lincoln, he felt sure, was far, far away. The man with the fedora logically would head for Waydner's home, but Waydner was too smart for that. He would return to Georgetown University and sleep on the overstuffed lounge in his office. The police would handle these thugs. In the morning he could return home; the mobsters would be in jail. He would see to that.

With his left ass cheek cold and sticky from his wounds, he dusted himself off as he stood up behind the bushes. He crossed the lawn and turned left onto the sidewalk, retracing his flight from campus. Waydner surprised himself at how well he had recovered from the shock. Moments ago he had been running in terror, with his would-be killer hard on his trail. Now, as he turned the corner, he froze in his tracks. The man in the fedora stood motionless, blocking the path before him.

The dark figure just stood there, dominating the dimly lit street, with a Camel cigarette hanging limply from his lips. His powerful body was covered with a dark-gray overcoat and topped by a crumpled, time-twisted, dark-gray fedora. His eyes regarded Waydner coldly, his lips bent into a sneer. Suddenly he lunged toward the doctor.

"Boo!" shouted the man in the gray fedora, and that was all it took.

Driven by the rush of adrenaline that is the servant of mortal fear, Waydner ran back around the corner. To live, to survive, he would have to outrun this insane Mafia killer. The professor ran as fast as he could in a loud, clacking, cartoonish gait unsteadied by the bouncing of his middle-aged paunch; running as fast as humanly possible, he turned abruptly left toward Washington Street.

To disinterested observers such as you and me, this scene might seem funny—in fact, hilarious! But to Professor Benjamin Waydner, MD, of Georgetown University, it was terrifying.

His blood pressure now dropped to his ankles, and he stopped abruptly because far ahead, he saw the four headlights flash on as the black Lincoln crept out of the shadows. In a flash, Waydner turned around, went back over the lawn, and ran for the gate. At least he knew the danger concealed behind it. He didn't even reach for the metal latch; without missing a step, he crashed through the gate and into the side yard. The Labrador lunged ferociously, but Waydner nailed it with a glancing kick to the shoulder. With another kick into the dog's belly, he sent it galloping and whimpering around the far side of the brick house. Waydner saw lights come on inside as he ran across the yard, jumped its back wall, and entered the yard behind it. He was breathing heavily as the kitchen door to his right opened, revealing a defiant man cocking a shotgun.

"Who is it?" the fellow demanded.

"It's the Mafia. Call the police!" Waydner screamed as he ran right past the armed man and crashed through the rear gate. He blazed past the armed man and onto the street, not even considering that the man might shoot.

Shivering in the center of the street, Waydner stood briefly and gasped, surveying the road for the Lincoln or the madman with the fedora.

The street was clear. With a healthy mix of impulse and caution, he continued across the street. Breathing heavily, he climbed three more fences and passed through two more yards, which brought him one street farther away.

His heart was pounding furiously; there would be no more hesitation and no rest until he made it to the bowels of Jefferson Hall, where he could find safety.

"Boo!" shouted the dark fedora, who had stepped out from behind a poplar tree. Waydner turned and ran screaming into the side of the Lincoln, which seemingly had appeared from nowhere, its front end bouncing as it flew over the curb and onto the sidewalk.

A dark, shadowy figure inside the car flung open the left rear passenger door and slid back to the right seat. The man in the gray fedora grabbed Waydner from where he lay on the sidewalk and tossed him violently through the open door. He then jumped into the car, pushing a dazed Waydner into the middle seat as the car flew off, its enraged tires furiously squealing into the dark, humid night.

William Hampstead kicked his feet up and onto the deserted foreman's desk. His laser-sharp deep brown eyes burned through the open door as he awaited the arrival of his men. "Yes, Mr. President," he spoke into the cracked black plastic phone. "Yes, Mr. President. Thank you, sir. Good-bye, sir." He quietly set down the phone. Many presidents liked to think they kept a tight hold on the CIA, and the CIA always complied by making it appear they were under control, but you know what they say about appearances. And, after all, who was better at deception than the CIA? Even the KGB finished a poor second.

He brushed his tight, curly hair with his right hand and then scratched an errant hair his morning razor had missed on his square jaw. Hampstead had been updating President Kennedy on the Cuba situation, assuring him there was no immediate possibility of war with the Soviets. The president was pleased; he could sleep easier and concentrate on his vision: building a better America. Hampstead, however, as the CIA's director of European operations, considered all such domestic shit hogwash. Until the Soviet Union was destroyed and wiped utterly and undeniably off the earth, America needed no other agenda.

Speaking of agendas, tonight Hampstead had his own: tonight the CIA was embarking on a project that would end the Cold War and obliterate every single Soviet. If the president of the United States knew the director's agenda, he would be furious.

The CIA, working under Hampstead's *sole* authority, was building a research base to engineer the ultimate weapon; not even Hanson Gaines, the director of the CIA, had been informed. After all, he was just another bureaucratic whore. Such idiots came and went at the will and whim of the White House. The director of the CIA had no real power.

William Hampstead, the agency's director of European operations, had moved up through the years to become the third highest-ranking man in the CIA. But the Cold War was centered in Europe, and that made him by default the most powerful man in the CIA. Directors came and went, but Hampstead would be there forever, bravely fighting the good fight, making the world safe for democracy, and padding his own spreading power.

The drama that was playing out tonight had been written, composed, and driven solely by Hampstead's CIA. Tonight, and under his own authority, William Hampstead was going to save the world.

Leo Pagetti strode swiftly into the room, and stopping in front of Hampstead informed him curtly, "We're ready."

"Is the body the same age and weight as the doctor?" Hampstead wanted to make sure Pagetti, who was new, had gotten it right.

"Hey, I'm a professional. I've iced dozens of guys for the mob. He's in the trunk, and he's a homeless bit of garbage. Nobody saw me ice him, and nobody's going to miss him." Pagetti grinned broadly, eager to move up in the CIA.

Hampstead moved his eyes up and down Pagetti's slim, dark, Sicilian body—from the three-hundred-dollar shoes up to his black silk shirt, passing his hawk like nose and stopping at his catlike dark-brown eyes. "Yeah, but you got caught once, Pagetti. If you get caught again, I'll personally kill you. These waters are too deep, and America's future is at stake," Hampstead warned.

"*Paisan*, this is my new home, and you are my *fratello*, my brother. I'd never embarrass or disappoint you. I'm here to stay." Pagetti loved getting paid to kill because it made everything so much more interesting; it made everything a lot more fun.

"OK." Hampstead realized he had to hurry; Emile Beaucroix would be here soon. "But make sure your people get *every* book, *every* scrap of paper from Waydner's apartment. Send the shit to Hogan in Bopolu. Then send Waydner's resignation/suicide letter to the university. Do you know what to do next?"

"Sure. Piece of cake." Pagetti smiled again. "I plant the smelly stiff and torch the apartment, making it look like a suicide. I pay off the coroner, and then I mail his letter." he gave Hampstead a grinning thumbs-up.

"You mail the letter *before* you torch the place, idiot!" Hampstead roared; *his* CIA never made mistakes.

"I know that. That's what I meant," Pagetti apologized.

"Good," Hampstead replied with satisfaction. "Now get the fuck out of here. The doctor will be here soon."

With this Leo Pagetti left the room. He knew full well that if he were successful—if no one questioned the "suicide" of Dr. Benjamin Waydner, MD—he would move up one notch in the close-knit society that was the inscrutable, but superbly efficient CIA of the 1960s.

The black Lincoln rolled down the dimly lit alley toward the old factory. As it entered the dark, deserted lot, two men emerged from the shadows and approached the car. The one wearing a black mackinaw spoke briefly into a radio handset. The car stopped short of the metal doors as the men walked up to it. They peered into the front seat, then the back. Apparently satisfied, the man with the radio put it to his face and said, "OK."

The clanging of heavy chains broke the still night air as the truck door of the factory's IRS-seized machine shop moved up slowly. The car rolled forward, entering the brightly lit interior, and then came to a halt in front of three huge metal-cutting lathes.

The man with the fedora got out first and then quickly opened the rear door. He grabbed Waydner by the coat and yanked him out. When the terrified doctor started to speak, the fedora-headed thug produced an angry pistol and jammed it into Waydner's gut. He grabbed the left side of the doctor's coat, and the driver grabbed him by the right. They led him across the factory floor into the depths of silent machinery, with the other thug trailing behind.

A wide-eyed, panicked Waydner was roughly ushered forward in a state drifting somewhere between confusion and mortal terror as they entered one of the offices on the factory floor.

Sitting behind the dirty oak desk was an elegantly dressed man talking intensely on a cracked black plastic phone. He motioned them in and then, with another wave of his hand, indicated to the driver to shut the door. As he hung up, he rose to greet the party.

"Welcome, Dr. Waydner. It's a pleasure to meet such an intelligent man. I'm Mr. Hampstead." Smiling, the director of European operations extended his hand. He couldn't help notice the crumpled shoulders of the doctor's coat. He shrugged; in his experience, all eggheads were slovenly. Even Albert Einstein had been a pig, rarely combing his hair and often giving lectures without wearing socks, items he simply had forgotten to put on.

Still terrified and visibly shaken, Waydner took a few steps back and refused the director's hand. "Are you going to kill me?" he asked.

"What? No, Doctor. We really are the CIA. Didn't you believe Mr. Beaucroix when he introduced himself and showed you his identification?"

"What identification?" Waydner's terror was amplified his by confusion. His incredulous eyes flew to the fedora and back to the director. *The man in the fedora must be Beaucroix.*

Hampstead looked at Beaucroix, who smiled and shrugged. The doctor probably had been frightened when Beaucroix had flashed his ID. It appeared that Emile Beaucroix had been unable to explain the situation sufficiently, and apparently the doctor had seen one too many spy movies. Hampstead often wondered why so many Americans were afraid of the CIA. After all, the agency did only what it had to do to protect American interests. Hampstead studied Beaucroix; he admired him and needed his skills, but he didn't trust him. He didn't trust anyone;

no good spy ever did. He focused closer on the Monster, who merely grinned as the director searched his square face. He paused at the biting, steel-blue eyes beneath the short, sandy-blond hair. Finding nothing, he turned to Waydner.

"Relax, Doctor." Hampstead grabbed the phone and started to dial. "Do you know who the governor of New York is? He's a friend of mine. I'm going to get him on the phone. You can talk to him. He'll tell you. He'll be happy to confirm who I am."

"No, no. I guess it's all right. You must be who you claim to be, but I haven't done anything. I don't belong to any subversive political parties. I don't even vote; my work keeps me too busy even for that."

Suddenly Waydner became more frightened than ever. Not voting might also be seen as anti-American. He grew more agitated by the second. But still, going to jail was a damn sight better than being killed. Whatever crime he had committed, he happily would go to prison for it rather than face another car ride with a terrifying fedora-wearing asshole like Emile Beaucroix.

Hampstead dropped the receiver and walked around the desk, again offering his hand. Waydner moved a little to Hampstead's left and then weakly advanced to accept his hand. He did this little dance to get as far away as possible from Emile Darwin Beaucroix. The maneuver, however, certainly wasn't lost on Beaucroix, who grinned and tossed the driver a wink.

Waydner released Hampstead's hand and dropped his arm limply to his side.

"Am I under arrest? Do I get a trial? I must tell my department head. There are classes that need to be taught, and he must find a replacement."

Hampstead shot a glance at Beaucroix, who shrugged again and feigned an ignorant expression. Not satisfied, the director shot a glance at the driver, but he was one of Beaucroix's men and wore no expression whatsoever. That man never would cross Emile Beaucroix; he had a family. Hampstead gave up and turned back, tossing his best smile at Waydner. He undertook to set the man at ease.

"Jail, Doctor?" Hampstead shook his head and motioned to the tattered chair in front of his desk. "Have a seat, Dr. Waydner. You're not in trouble at all. In fact, I want to offer you a job. I want to make you wealthy, famous—a national hero. I want you to *save* the world."

Waydner was more confused than ever as he took the offered chair. Hampstead smiled warmly as he returned to the foreman's seat, rolling it up close to the desk and leaning toward the man, ignoring the chair's protesting squeaks.

"I don't think I could be a spy. Too many things frighten me," Waydner explained, and then his agile mind found a sure way out—a reason they must let him go, the one thing that surely would make him totally unacceptable to the CIA. "I can't take pain," the doctor offered, trying to sound as convincing as possible. "If they captured and tortured me, I would talk. Even the suggestion of pain would be enough to make me talk. I can't help myself. I'm a hopeless coward. I would talk."

"No, Doctor. You'll never be in any danger." Hampstead folded his hands together as he leaned back in the chair, distracting Waydner again with its loud, creaky protest. "I don't need you to be a spy." He smiled as he pointed at Waydner's head to accentuate his next point. "I want you to do what you do best: use that phenomenal brain of yours. We need the world's best scientist for a very special job," Hampstead lied, flattering the egotistic pig.

Hampstead actually hated all academics. His high school math teacher had flunked him and gotten him tossed off the varsity football team. He could have been a quarterback, and he would have been better than Jim Thorpe, because Hampstead was a hell of a lot tougher. But that wimp teacher had tossed him, like a broken bottle, out of sports and into the CIA.

Waydner wasn't the world's best scientist; he was simply the one who best fit the necessary intelligence profile. He was a man with few family ties. He was a man who could, with very few complications and little effort, simply disappear. Waydner had many enemies and few friends; it would be easy.

"I'm still scared. What if spies come to kill me?" the doctor protested.

Hampstead waved his right hand around the room, indicating the company present. "This is not *all* we do. The CIA has many duties, many jobs besides cloak-and-dagger espionage. We own—or invest in—fifty-four legitimate companies around the world." He tossed in a wild card next. "We own a company in Toledo, Ohio, that distributes milk. Use your great mind, Doctor. What kind of espionage could we be doing in Toledo, Ohio? How could milk be dangerous? We want you to work for a new company we're starting overseas in a very safe country— a country founded with American dollars in eighteen twenty-one and that has been a friend to America ever since."

"I could still be captured, couldn't I?" Waydner pressed on. "Besides, I don't think I could help. I don't know anything about business. All I know is how to teach pupils and write papers."

"As I said, Doctor, you'll never be in danger," Hampstead assured Waydner, who still eyed all corners of the room nervously. "You'll get the *very best* protection the CIA can provide. Just relax and listen to my offer." The director slapped his hands together and rubbed them vigorously.

He snapped his fingers, and a man opened the door and entered the room. Without a word, he retrieved a briefcase that had been sitting on the floor a scarce seven feet from the foreman's desk. After popping the latches, he opened the case and deposited it on Hampstead's desk, with the open side facing the director. Then he left the room and shut the door quietly behind him.

Waydner was transfixed. Why hadn't one of the other men in the room fetched the briefcase? Why hadn't Hampstead done it himself? Waydner thought this because he knew nothing about the CIA.

Beaucroix worked for Hampstead, but he was too important to do such petty things. It would insult his massive ego if one even thought of asking him to fetch, and insulting that massive ego was a dangerous, deadly thing to do. The driver and the other man worked for Beaucroix, so it would be folly for Hampstead to even try to give them an order. Hampstead had to use an outsider to prove to Beaucroix that *he* also had people—people who could kill even Beaucroix, if Beaucroix ever threatened his power.

Hampstead slowly removed some journals, some magazines, and a newspaper from the briefcase. All were marked with paper clips to quickly access relevant pages. One of the reasons Hampstead had risen so rapidly within the CIA was because he was the best recruiter they'd ever seen; he had recruited both Emile Beaucroix and Maxwell George, a pair of aces who were virtually impossible to beat. Today, William Hampstead would recruit Dr. Benjamin Waydner.

The director was following a carefully orchestrated plan he knew would appeal to any scientific academic: he would stroke the doctor's immense ego, he would offer unlimited funding, and he would offer the academic a tasty revenge.

"Doctor, I have here a series of articles," Hampstead began. "Three in the *Journal of the American Medical Association*, one from the Mayo Clinic, two from Harvard University, and one in the *Boston Globe*. They basically call you a quack, though not in so many words. You doctors have a more polite way of insulting one another, which I find somewhat amusing."

Waydner's jaw dropped. Confused, he started to protest, but Hampstead raised his hand to silence him, clearly indicating he wanted no comment from the peanut gallery.

The director grabbed another paper clip and flipped open the *Boston Globe*. "News reporters, however, are a bit less subtle. This article says you're a fraud. It also calls you arrogant, stubborn, asinine, and opinionated. Your conclusions are false, idiotic, and oblique, and they cannot stand scrutiny. No one has ever been able to duplicate your results given the same laboratory conditions. It calls your so-called research voodoo science!"

The doctor tried to protest, but again Hampstead's dismissing wave silenced him. The director scratched his left temple and then put aside the stack of journals and articles and retrieved two stacks of typewritten documents from the depths of the briefcase.

Waydner jumped as he recognized his own typewritten notes, notes he had been certain had disappeared in a mysterious lab fire several months ago.

Hampstead shuffled through the doctor's property. "I've read your research, and I don't pretend to understand it, but I have here…" He reached into the briefcase and retrieved a folder marked, "SECRET. Eyes only, William Hampstead," and opened it. "These documents are a review by our top professionals. These men are biologists, medical professors, doctors, and chemists who secretly and profitably consult for the US government. I prefer their conclusions to these."

In a coup of showmanship, Hampstead swept the desk with his right arm, sending the briefcase and newspaper and journal articles flying across the desk to the floor.

The only items left on the desk were Waydner's notes and the CIA report. It was a smashingly successful performance; Waydner was smiling.

"After reading your notes, I think you're brilliant, because our analysts think you're brilliant. I want to offer you salvation, a chance at redemption. We're opening a research institute in Liberia in West Africa, and I want you to head that institute. You'll have absolute say and no critics. You'll have complete control, you can do any research you want, and you'll have *unlimited* funding. My analysts are all of the opinion that if you are given substantial material support and are allowed to follow your own direction, you'll make great things happen—you'll make *miracles* happen. Will you join us, Doctor? Will you accept my offer? Yes or no? I offer you what no other man can—an opportunity to redeem yourself."

Waydner looked energized. "I accept! But I'll need a few weeks to—"

"That won't be possible. You'll leave immediately. The plane has been chartered and is on the runway." Hampstead was now curt.

"I need time. What about my classes? My notes? What about my apartment?" the doctor protested.

"We'll take care of everything," Hampstead assured him. "We'll inform the university that we needed you immediately—your *country* needed you. All your notes will be collected and forwarded to you. Your lease will be taken care of, and your possessions will be placed in storage at no cost to you." Hampstead snapped his fingers again, and a man opened the door from the outside.

Waydner pointed at his notes. "Can I have those back?" He made a grab for them, but Hampstead clasped the doctor's hand to halt him.

"No," Hampstead replied, closing the matter. "I'll need these for now, but I'll see that you receive copies." He released Waydner's hand and then rose, announcing that the meeting was over. "Well, I promised you protection. I am sending my best with you to Africa." He smiled generously. "Agent Emile Darwin Beaucroix here will escort you to Liberia. He'll protect you and your work, and he'll be at your disposal."

"Does he have to come with me?" The doctor appeared visibly shocked as he spat out his objection. He felt safe talking in front of Beaucroix right now. With Hampstead present, he felt he was in a friendly camp; he felt he had protection.

"Doctor, Mr. Beaucroix is the *very* best. He will protect you, and he is at your disposal." Hampstead rose to the creaking objections of the foreman's chair and offered his hand. This time Waydner readily accepted it. "It's settled. You'll leave tonight for Liberia. God, I envy you, Doctor. What an adventure lies before you! Within a few years, you'll come back to America with wealth, fame, respect, and a host of exciting stories. Stories to tell your grandchildren. God, I wish I could take your place!"

Hampstead knew full well that Waydner never could return because this project was too important. If the doctor continued to be useful, he would remain in Liberia and want for nothing. If he finished his work, well, one could guess his fate.

William Hampstead was the best recruiter the CIA had ever known because he always knew exactly where the bending twig would break. He could find and exploit the weakness in any man. He was unique in his ability to always succeed, and he really was the most formidable recruiter the CIA had ever known. He was a magnificent bastard!

"You'd better get going," Hampstead said, ending the interview.

The driver gently took Waydner by the arm and ushered him out the door and back to the waiting Lincoln. The other man and Beaucroix turned to follow.

"Just a minute, Beaucroix. We need to talk," Hampstead said, halting him. The second man shut the door as he left. Beaucroix smiled and took a seat in front of the oak desk. "Why was that man so terrified?" The director flavored his question with a dark undercurrent.

"I really can't say, sir. As soon as we identified ourselves, he became unhinged and went to pieces. The whole trip over here, I tried to settle his nerves. I must have talked to him for twenty minutes nonstop, but I couldn't calm him down. I offered to stop to get him a cup of coffee, but he wouldn't respond. He clammed up, so I finally gave up, and we brought him directly here," Beaucroix stated apologetically.

"You're sure none of your people said anything to frighten him?"

"Not a chance, boss. My guys are pros." Beaucroix shrugged again.

Hampstead nodded as he tried to read those cold, shuttered eyes. But the Monster's eyes were, as usual, false shutters and revealed nothing.

"Well, do your best. Try to become his friend and gain his trust." Hampstead noticed the time on the wall clock. "You'd better get going."

Beaucroix stood and headed out the door to the waiting car.

Hampstead leaned back in the chair, grinning with satisfaction at another flawless performance. And why not? All his performances were by nature and by habit flawless.

He rubbed his perfectly cut, tight, curly hair as he pondered the past. With a grimace, he adjusted the crotch-binding wool pants as he scratched and shifted his balls through the tightly woven and itchy fabric. Glancing at the far wall, he noticed a sexy Miss August on the Milwaukee Power Tools calendar and cast her a coy wink as his attention wandered to a time far past when, in the perennially unsure times of youth, he had dreamed of a football career, the chance to be a great NFL quarterback leading a team through many exciting, nail-biting playoff victories and on to a dominating Super Bowl win. He grinned again at the silliness of youth.

But fortunately, time and the wisdom of age had brought clarity to that hazy vision, and, as he grew older, he realized that spending a pitiful retirement sitting in his den with a tarnished trophy and faded glory was not a postscript to a life worth living.

But it would still take a couple more aimless, wandering, wasted years of youth before a drunken, murderous bar brawl gained him eighteen months in prison and the time to ponder his rightful place in the world around him. It was in these long, private moments in isolation that the truth hit him like a hammer. The Super Bowl, the World Cup, the Masters, and the Triple Crown were just sports. They were not real or enduring, and they were certainly not the game.

The true game, the only real game, was the Cold War, the glorious and godly battle between East and West, good and evil, Communist oppression and free will. This was a game in which only the true believers survived. The children of Eric Hoffer and Hoffer alone could understand the dedication demanded by the one true, enduring Game, and now William Hampstead decided he would become a part of it. It was his destiny.

Because in the Game, there were no timeouts, no half times, and no off-seasons. As a player in the masterful and all-encompassing Game, you went to sleep as a spy, you woke up a spy. You ate as a spy, you crapped as a spy, you dated as a spy, and you fucked as a spy; and you knew there were no such things as vacations or days off. Even when you jerked off, you jerked off as a spy.

It was the game, the ultimate game, and it had no equal. It was a twenty-four-hour heroin high played under the most extreme and elegant rules. There were no set penalty calls, no false starts. It allowed for no mistakes, it offered no ten-yard backups, and there was only one rule that was enforced to the core. That rule was failure, and its violation carried only one penalty and no possibility of a referee's review. You got to meet your maker, a final and unappeasable verdict with no reprieve. This was no carrot on a stick but rather the hanging Sword of Damocles that boldly drove your incentive to play the game with a flawless stealth-cleverness and to carry out your assigned role well within the shadows of the shadows, where you could act unsuspected and unseen while working the magic of the game on the world around you.

But forgive me, I did forget to mention the only other violation of the rules of the game, also honored in NFL football, and that is being caught offside. In the NFL that gives you a five-yard penalty and a loss of down. But in the ultimate game, there is a somewhat more severe penalty for being caught offside. It is…well, on second thought, you may have a queasy stomach, so we will not go there. We will simply proceed with this possibly somewhat fictional story. I hope you enjoy it.

And so it was in 1957 that William Hampstead, the wandering punk, convicted murderer, petty criminal, unemployable drunk, thief, and liar, applied to join the CIA. It was a road that small numbers would travel with success. It was a job to which few were called and a great many applied. Most were rejected out of hand as unacceptable and ill suited.

On that miserable, cold, dry, and wind-biting December day in Virginia, the CIA interviewer gave Hampstead little encouragement. The little twerp gave every indication that he had no intention of passing Hampstead's application on; it would die there.

The little asshole had been a stunted, nervous Harvey Milquetoast sort of fellow who squirmed in an ill-fitting discount-store suit with a coffee-stained tie as Hampstead sat and struck his tough-guy pose in the hard oak chair. The interviewer grunted and then frowned as he looked down at Hampstead's extensive and punk-pure juvenile record. The squirrely little man then abruptly stood up and pointed to the left as he ordered William Hampstead to exit the room through the side door. Hampstead's record and demeanor, along with the rumors about him, had gotten him tossed into the club. He was now a player, one of the few, and was soon to be destined for the game.

William Hampstead quickly recovered from the shock of acceptance and made himself an immediate promise: someday he would be the club's one true playmaker. The Cold War was now his, and he knew to the core of his soul that he was the very bastard to win it.

So, in 1957, William Hampstead applied for and won the most dangerous job on earth, a job many wanted but few could do. He knew he had the skills going into this, and his massive ego ensured he was too arrogant to fail.

Because in life, as in the game, there were rules, and in the game the greatest rule of all was the lie, and William Hampstead certainly had what it took, he was a man gloriously devoid of conscience. As a tough guy, punk, thief, and convicted murderer, he was already a proven grand master of the lie. And so the club, the world, and the game would never again see his equal. He was a magnificent bastard!

"Did he have anything to say?" Waydner asked Beaucroix as they walked thru the factory and back to the car. The doctor was feeling a bit more at ease with the man, but Beaucroix only grunted. "I wish I had time to pack. Are there stores in Liberia where I can buy suitable clothes?" Waydner happily chatted because he was energized and excited. "Can we get something to eat at the airport, or will we eat on the plane?"

Beaucroix didn't answer. With a single fluid motion, he drew his Walther PPK pistol from his jacket and placed it, hammer cocked, to the doctor's right temple. "Shut the fuck up!" he demanded as his eye wandered across what he thought was the deserted factory yard. With a jolt, he caught the fat man retreating into the shadows. Damn, the fat man had seen it all.

Frowning, he tossed Waydner into the Lincoln, slamming violently into him and forcing him into the center of the rear seat. He glanced again into the shadows, and then, turning back, he furiously slammed his fist full force into the doctor's jaw and knocked him across the Lincoln's rear seat and into the surprised agent sitting between Waydner and the left door.

"Shut up!" Beaucroix screamed at a dazed Waydner, livid that the fat man, the Shadow, suddenly had entered the game.

CHAPTER TWO
The Gods of Bopolu

One Month Earlier: July 3, 1962
Bopolu, Liberia

The aged chief sat bleeding on the dusty ground with his left arm broken and his forehead slashed just above the left eye. His bright, colorful tribal clothes were painted with the red of his veins and speckled with the brown duff, dust, and mud of Africa. His bare arms and balding head were marked and wrinkled by the passing of time; the numerous hunting scars on his body told the story of a long, brave life lived hard but without fear. The five other village elders sitting alongside him wisely had decided not to follow his example of defiance. Two angry Liberian soldiers with model 1917 US rifles, bayonets fixed, ensured there would be no more trouble.

Five more brand-new American-built jeeps now entered the clearing in a perfect row and stopped in precise military formation in the exact center of the newly cleared compound, thus bringing the legendary Liberian General Kutu and his private staff to inspect the progress of the secret Bopolu medical research center. The old men watched in wonder as the black Liberian officers dismounted the jeeps. To these simple village elders, it was transfixing—how men who looked so much like them could act, talk, and even move like the strange white men who flowed in constant, unstoppable waves into Africa, invading their tribal world.

General Kutu dismounted the lead jeep and then turned to face the whine of two axles and a grinding downshift as one of the CIA's best rounded the corner and entered the clearing. The tall man brought the Land Rover to a squealing halt punctuated by the rattle of the full rifle racks on the right side of the lorry and the bouncing of an enormous antelope carcass tied across the hood.

The tall spy briskly exited the truck and stepped into the dust and mud that was the place called Bopolu. Robert Hogan, just thirty years old, was the CIA's controller, the man Hampstead had sent to work with the locals to activate this base and prepare it for the medical staff.

At a glance, the elderly tribal chief knew this was one of the great men of the legend, the force for good that had been summoned by the gods of Bopolu. The monkeys chattered rapidly in the lively forest nearby; indeed, the gods were excited.

For hundreds of years, the legends of the gods had been passed from father to son. The chief had spent his entire life preparing for this moment. His childhood vision had foretold that he, Chief M'kari, would in his last days witness the battle for the end of the world. Excitedly the chief shouted and motioned for the Poet to come over. He had to know for certain whether this was the right man, the good man of the legend. But he was an old man, and his shouts didn't carry.

As Chief M'kari tried to stand, one of the soldiers raised the butt of his rifle and struck M'kari to the ground, sneering. Noticing this, General Kutu nodded and smiled his approval from across the flat compound.

"Mr. Hogan, how very pleased I am that you found such good hunting." The general extended his fleshy, fat hand in greeting as he beamed his smile to the American. "I do believe that's the biggest antelope I've ever seen." He shook Hogan's hand warmly as he admired the kill. "I personally chose this site for the construction of the facility—not only for secrecy and security but also for the area's excellent hunting. I heard you Americans have a great sporting heart, and I doubt I am mistaken." General Kutu led Hogan to the center of the construction site. Already the living quarters and army barracks were complete.

Hogan stepped in front of the general, blocking his path. "What do they want?" he pointed toward the six village elders, who were shouting frantically to get his attention. Just then two of the soldiers struck the two oldest men with their rifle butts, knocking them to the ground.

"They are idiots…dumb, stupid monkeys," Kutu replied. "They are uneducated old men who believe in hocus-pocus and magic. The sooner such simpleminded old men die off, the sooner Africa can take its rightful place in the modern world."

Hogan noticed their tribal garb. "Why are they here? And why are they so agitated?" Hogan didn't care much for soldiers who beat up old men.

"They have come to see you. They heard this was the best show in town," the general answered with a smile. "It seems you are part of one of their silly ancient legends—quite possibly a legend as ancient as last week. The first week of this month is when they traditionally make the first piss-fresh palm beer of the season. They are probably drunk on it." The general waved toward the far side of the compound, and a dozen more soldiers rapidly moved toward the elders.

"I'd like to hear what they have to say, General." Hogan squared off against Kutu, who obviously disapproved. "Is there anyone who can interpret, someone who speaks their language?"

"Mr. Hogan, let me show you to the living quarters. We just finished them this morning. I think you will find them quite comfortable; they contain all the amenities civilized men such as you and I are accustomed to." The general placed his hand on the American's shoulder and tried to steer him toward the veranda, but Hogan again turned to face him, causing his hand to fall away.

"I don't think you heard me, General. I want to hear what these men have to say." Hogan's hand lowered to touch the flap of his .45-caliber pistol.

General Kutu waved off the guards and tossed a wink in their direction. As he began his silly little game, his men chuckled. "I do as you wish, Massa Boss Man. You lead, and I done do follow."

The general bowed, fully intending that Hogan should notice his insult. Kutu was known for his very special kind of humor. Hogan, however, ignored him and made his way toward the old men. The general followed, walking with an exaggerated, childish gait that made his men roar with laughter. Hogan also ignored this insult as he and Kutu headed toward the elders, who grew even more excited as they approached.

"Massa and I gonna take a silly little walk, sho 'nuff." The general tossed another silly and smug-pregnant wink to his men.

Kutu continued his sloppy, childish walk and then stopped and bowed his cap two paces behind Hogan. His soldiers roared even louder; his corporal laughed so loudly that, losing his balance, he fell from the jeep and landed with a slurping thud in the wet mud of Bopolu.

"Where's the interpreter?" Hogan addressed Kutu in a tone that indicated in no uncertain terms that playtime was over.

"These men are nothing but simple, uneducated trash…nothing more than jungle bunnies." The general had firmly recovered his officer's demeanor. "Nothing such savages say can be worth hearing. Nothing they could ever say would interest educated men such as you and me."

"What about an interpreter, General?" Hogan repeated.

The general seemed not to hear. He stood motionless, his eyes looking at some point beyond the elders.

"General, I will order all construction halted until we get to the bottom of this." Again Kutu ignored him. "Well?" Hogan pressed.

Finally, after talking a slow, deep breath, Kutu turned to Hogan and said, "I can speak their silly monkey garbage, Mr. Hogan." Then, clearly embarrassed, he added, "I also speak German and French. But that hardly makes me a knockwurst or a frog."

As soon as the general spoke in the language of the elders, the scene became very animated. Much shouting and gesturing passed between the general and the tribesmen before Hogan managed to get the general's attention.

"It seems they know you," Kutu told him. "They have come to warn you of the gods of Bopolu and their evil plans. Although they are the holy men and the elders of the tribe, they are full of nonsense, with senile imaginations and probably hung-over from piss-poor beer."

"Why do they want to warn me? I've never met them before," Hogan inquired, regarding the small group with more than some interest.

More rapid exchanges took place between the general and the elders. The old chief with the busted arm nodded toward Hogan and motioned for the general to repeat what he had said in English.

"They have nothing to say!" Kutu was obviously bored with this useless affair.

The oldest man in the group looked at the general and wildly gestured with his wrinkled right hand in Hogan's direction; he clearly he wanted General Kutu to repeat Chief M'kari's words.

"General," Hogan said firmly, "in all my life, I have never once left my house without making my bed first, so I'm not a man who likes to walk away from unfinished business. We're not leaving here until I'm satisfied. And if I go, *ALL* the money goes with me!"

Kutu took a deep breath and then smiled. This white idiot was going to make him rich, so he could afford to pander to the fool's fantasies. "It seems, my friend, that you are a legend, or at least half of one. In ancient times, the gods created many things. They created hippos, lions, monkeys, and man. Most animals—in fact, all animals except man—were content to stay animals. Only man and man alone tried to be a god. Man tried arrogantly and with insult to rule over all life, as if he had created it himself. Most of the gods wanted to destroy man, but not all the gods agreed on this. So finally, the gods of Bopolu agreed on a plan wherein man would decide his own destiny. Meanwhile, the gods disguised themselves as monkeys so they could spy from the treetops and observe the outcome."

Hogan was surprised at the lucidity of their myths; this was certainly a tale worthier of Plato or Homer than a bunch of half-naked tribesmen. "How do I fit into this?" he asked. "Why are they protesting the construction of the compound?"

"They are idiots! They are all stupid monkey-man trash. Nothing they could say is ever worth hearing to educated men such as us." The general was clearly tired of this tribal foray. Africa—tribal Africa in particular—offended him.

Hogan locked Kutu with his stare. "General, if there's going to be any trouble with the locals, I need to know now."

"You are our guest, and I bow to your wishes. Give me a moment, and I will ask these monkey men." The general resumed his rapid-fire discourse with the elders. Completing that, he turned to Hogan and smiled. "It seems the gods have chosen two white men, one very wicked and one very good and brave. They will fight beneath the trees of Bopolu to determine the fate of mankind. The gods, in the guise of monkeys, will watch this contest. Is that enough local color for you, my friend?" The general shrugged; this business was dull and unprofitable. He scratched his swollen crotch. He had a young wife at home, and he badly needed to rock her world with some bow-legged dancing.

"Just one more question: What if the good man wins?" Hogan knew by experience that if you asked questions about local customs, you often gained local cooperation.

Kutu jabbered for some time with the chief. It seemed even he wasn't clear on what the old man was telling him; twice he had to ask Chief M'kari to repeat himself.

"The chief says it doesn't matter who wins, the evil man or the good. If the monkeys aren't pleased with the contest, one of them will reach out and touch the winner. Then all of mankind will perish. See how stupid their superstitions are? They dream of a battle with no winner and a legend with no hero. Let's have an excellent dinner and leave these senile old coots to their mumbo jumbo." The general regained his beaming smile.

But Hogan wasn't finished. "Before we have dinner, there's just one more little thing to iron out." He knew Kutu was getting a lot of US dollars for his part, so he knew just how far he could push things with the general. "Thank these wise men for their information, and tell them it will be of great help when I fight the evil man. Please ask them if they would do me the honor of accepting the antelope on my lorry."

Gruffly the general relayed this information to the elders while he waved his men toward the lorry, directing two of his soldiers to remove the carcass from the Land Rover and bring it over. The elders smiled, then cheered at this generous, unexpected offer.

"Well, bwana, can we eat?" Kutu was back to patronizing him now, but Hogan always knew when to launch a quick counter flank.

"Hold it, General. We're not finished. Two *more* things…" Hogan placed his hand on his Colt pistol, a fact not unnoticed by the elders. "And repeat what I say in the local language as well as English so your soldiers and I can understand it too." The general flinched as Hogan continued. "Tell them their village is now under the personal protection of you and your soldiers. Tell them also that any soldier who kills a monkey in Bopolu will be shot. Tell them. Tell them all."

The general smiled broadly as he relayed the orders first to his soldiers, then to the elders in their own tongue. The elders cheered as Kutu took Hogan by the arm and turned him toward the compound.

"You know…" The general slapped Hogan firmly on the shoulder. "I'm really going to like you. At first I thought you were making fun of me—you know, like I was some dumb black monkey in a general's uniform. But when you pretended to go along with their stupid legend and promised them my protection—that was brilliant, absolutely brilliant! These villagers scour and hunt in a solid ninety-kilometer radius around Bopolu." Kutu waved and smiled as the delighted elders departed with their meat. "Having their village on our side will be like having an extra division. Anything that happens within ninety kilometers will come to my ear first. You, my good friend, are a born tactician, a real Napoleon. Both of us, I think, are going to enjoy great success!"

October 12, 1962
Monrovia, Capital of Liberia

Liberia held two great distinctions among the nations of the world: it was one of the oldest nations, and it was one of the least stable. Formed more than forty years before the US Civil War, the country had been purchased by American abolitionists from the colonial powers of Europe as a home and refuge for freed slaves. These American abolitionists paid for the slaves' journeys back to Africa and gave them enough money and provisions to establish homes, farms, and new lives on their ancestral continent.

But the native Liberian people were suspicious of all things European and all things unknown. They mistrusted the English-speaking freed slaves, with their Western dress and mannerisms. Trouble between native Liberians and the freed slaves began almost immediately and with frequent bloodshed. To outsiders, it seemed as if Liberia enjoyed more revolutions than the British did cups of tea.

Today, Robert Hogan missed his home in the Congo. But that is both a misstatement and an understatement. When away on business, Hogan always missed his home in the Congo because it was his world. It was the only place on earth where he truly felt at home.

Liberia and the Congo were the yin and the yang of Africa because they were two very different worlds. In the Congo, the European powers had left only a framework over the nation. Laws and justice were still basically tribal and African. If a rapist, robber, or murderer was caught, he frequently was beaten to death in the street. To Europeans, this was barbaric, uncivilized, and cruel. But to Hogan, tribal justice was fair and made sense for Africa; to him, tribal justice was basic and practical. If you didn't want to get beaten to death in the street, then you probably didn't want to go around murdering, raping, and robbing people.

Liberia, on the other hand, was like a boxer fighting himself: constantly punching himself with his right hand while trying to defend himself with his left. Liberia was Africa fighting Africa as past, present, and future strove for domination. Each sought to control Liberia's future and tried to marginalize the other two. It was tribal mistrust against colonial corruption, flavored with a rich sauce of ambitious personal greed, which made for the unstable stew that was the wonderfully freewheeling Liberia of the 1960s.

The bouncing, rattling, and jerking of the borrowed American jeep ended as Hogan turned off the dirt track and onto the newly paved road. This road would take him to the crowded streets of Monrovia, capital of the independent Republic of Liberia.

Hogan brought the jeep to a squeaking halt in front of Western Union's telegraph station. He removed the keys, placed them in his pocket, and stretched and yawned. Then he remained in the driver's seat, enjoying the warm African sun. He removed a fresh cigar from his shirt pocket and lit it with a flick of his Zippo lighter as he surveyed the world around him. He leaned back in the hard seat. Lively, bustling, exciting, colorful, and sensual, Monrovia was one of the most beautiful places on earth.

"You dirty little bastard!" a tall Liberian shouted as he kicked a young boy off the sidewalk and into the street. "You filthy hyena! You piece of shit!" he yelled, raising the boy in the air and then slapping his face and knocking him back to the ground.

Discarding his cigar, Hogan leaped from the jeep and landed a full six feet away on the street, only to have his path immediately blocked by one of Liberia's finest. "Where do you think you're going?" the policeman said as he placed a hand on Hogan's chest, barring his path.

"That man is beating that boy to death. You need to stop it immediately!" Hogan looked down at the hand upon his chest.

"I warned you, you dirty bastard!" the African shouted as he kicked the boy again, driving him ten feet farther into the street.

"Take your hand from me, or I'll break it off. Are you going to stop that man from beating that child, or am I?" Hogan challenged the policeman.

"This is an African matter and none of your affair. It is a matter between a father and his son." He removed his hand from Hogan's chest but kept it raised to block the American's path.

"This is the last time you will disobey me, you little turd! I warned you not to disobey me, and now you will pay!" The tall Liberian advanced and cocked his foot to kick the boy again.

"Get out of my way!" Hogan shouted at the policeman.

"This is not your affair. I know these people," the officer said. "The father warned his son many times."

"Warned him about what?"

"He warned him not to go to school," the policeman calmly replied.

"What?" Hogan was incredulous.

"You nasty little bastard. How dare you try to be better than your father?" the Liberian screamed in rage as he kicked the boy again.

"Move it, asshole!" Hogan ordered as he roughly tossed the policeman aside and onto the ground.

The officer jumped up and reached for his revolver but stayed his action as the corner of his eye caught the fat man in the shadows. The fat man raised his index finger and softly wagged "No" as he receded back into the shadows. Confused and afraid, the policeman stayed his hand

and was no longer a player in this human tragedy. A single finger shaken by an unknown stranger had frozen him, removed him from the fray, and, as long as he lived and pondered, he never would understand why.

If it weren't for Hogan's presence, the Shadow absolutely would have intervened. But from the dossiers he had read about Hogan, he knew the matter was well in hand. The fat man departed and faded into Africa's forgiving shadows; he was needed elsewhere and had other roles to play in the game.

The tall Liberian leaned over and grabbed the boy from the dust. Suddenly he dropped the boy as Hogan grabbed him by both sides of his collar and turned his face to within inches of his own.

"I warned you!" Hogan shouted directly into the man's face and then bitch-slapped him, driving him to the ground. "You son of a bitch!" he drove his boot into the man's quivering backside, causing him to somersault into the gathering mass of spectators.

"Stop it! Stop it! Who are you, and why are you kicking me?" the man pleaded from the dusty ground. Hogan again drove his boot into the man's rear end.

"Stop! Please stop! What have I done to you?" the man begged as he formed himself into a defensive ball in the street.

"Go ahead. Roll up like a baby, you piece of pig shit!" Hogan shouted as he kicked the man repeatedly.

"Help! Someone help me! This crazy white man is going to kill me dead," the Liberian pleaded to the crowd.

Hogan scratched a mosquito bite on his forearm as he bent over and grabbed the man, jerking him upright. "Do you know why I'm beating you?" he demanded as he bitch-slapped the man again.

"No, no!" the man answered, trying to shield his face.

"You beat your son because he wanted an education, because he wanted a better future. I'm beating you because you don't deserve such a fine son, but mostly, I'm beating you because you didn't turn out to be a better man than your father!"

With a clenched fist, Hogan struck the man in the face full force, driving him back onto the dusty street. "Feels good, doesn't it?" Hogan bent over the ball of pain, taunting him.

With this, the rapidly growing crowd cheered wildly, and a couple of women slapped their husbands firmly across the face, just in case—just to let them know what might be in store for them after this day, should they decide to be a roadblock to their children's happiness.

Hogan went to kick the man again, but it was too late; the crowd had taken over. Understanding what he had said and taught them today, the assembled and enraged shoes of Monrovia drove the man like a soccer ball up the dusty street and Africa toward a better future.

Khartoum, Sudan
October 17, 1962

Slava Kurnov glanced around as he entered the half-filled hotel restaurant, marking any heads whose ears might be larger than their lifespans; the cautious spy always took care that no bystander should ever hear more than what was in his or her own best interests. With that task now finished, Kurnov helped himself to a seat at the bar and, turning to his left, grinned at Max. "That was very, very funny," Kurnov said as he adjusted his seating in the butt-worn, warped, and cracked leather chair.

Max George grinned back. "I exist solely to amuse you, comrade. It's what I live for!"

"Today the vodka is on me." The Russian snapped his fingers to summon over the bartender. "I really mean it—that was very funny. I mean, telling that poor man the CIA never kidnaps anyone. I am surprised you were able to keep a straight face."

"Kurnov, America, unlike other *Caucasian* countries, is a free nation. We cannot and will not force our citizens to do anything against their will."

"I take it you are cleverly insulting my nation. We both know the Caucasus Mountains are in the Soviet Union." Kurnov shook an accusing finger, but Max merely smiled. "But did you consider this?" He put his finger to his temple. "Since you call yourself a Caucasian, perhaps Mother Russia is your mother too. I have always thought you had too many good qualities to be on the wrong side. Perhaps you should consider coming back to your Russian mother. She would welcome you. She would pay you well."

"What about the Jew? Are you going to kill him, Kurnov? Do I need to recall him and tell him there's no deal?" Max hated murder, especially when a man didn't deserve to die.

"Oh, him…I didn't come here to discuss little matters or little men." Kurnov seemed to consider the matter. "No, people who believe in promised lands are too silly to kill. Israel is but a tiny sideshow to the contest. Such fools are men without science. Besides"—he waved his hand in dismissal—"we care little about the games you play inside Israel. But go ahead and kidnap him; force him to cooperate with you. Torture him, kill him if you want to. You have my blessing." Kurnov smiled again.

"Comrade, we don't do those kinds of things, and you know we don't." Max wondered what Kurnov was trying to pull.

"Then perhaps you should tell Hampstead that such things are not done. He seems to make a habit of it." Kurnov casually lit an excellent Cuban stogie and handed Max one as well.

"What is this conversation about?" Max asked, accepting the smoke.

"Nothing. This conversation is about nothing." Kurnov puffed three pungently flavorful clouds of smoke. "Why don't you ask Hampstead about Waydner, about kidnapping, and about the despicable murder of an innocent homeless man to cover it up?"

"Who is Hampstead? Who is Waydner?" Max lied, although he fully knew the answers to those questions. In the game, one must always play by the rules, and the *lie* was the most common rule of all.

Kurnov stood, brushing an errant ash from his olive blazer. He addressed the blank wall to the right of Max. "We do not approve of murdering citizens, particularly those who are not players. This killing of a poor homeless man—I won't even begin to address how I feel about that. I do not approve of *excess,* and this sort of thing could easily escalate the game and bring us to the *other* set of rules."

Having said his piece, Kurnov rose, left the hotel, and casually melted into the hot, humid African night. Max would talk to Waydner and ask a few questions because Kurnov was good—he was damn good—and he was far too clever to ignore.

CHAPTER THREE
The Baptism of Bopolu

Bopolu, Liberia
January 20, 1963

Cautiously slipping behind the shelves, Hogan silently undid his three lowest shirt buttons, allowing him quick access to the Colt pistol he kept tucked inside his waistband. Moving silently past the last storage shelf, he got his first glimpse into the barracks.

He whipped out the pistol and pulled back the hammer as he stepped over a body that lay spread-eagle on the floor. As he slunk past the latrine, he saw the other soldier hunched over the kitchen table, gently snoring, his steady tempo broken by an occasional burping fart. Hogan carefully searched the barracks to make certain no one else was present. When he was fully satisfied, he strolled over to Sleeping Beauty and shook him violently.

Beauties only response was to plop limply to the floor, snort like a pig, and resume his snoring, scarcely missing a beat. The only indication he gave of objecting to his new repose was an unbelievably loud backfire, which certainly did little to clear the air. A quick examination of the other soldier revealed him to be in much the same state.

Hogan worked his way out of the supply room. From the south corner of the barracks, he saw past the quadrangle and into the laboratory. God, he wished he hadn't parked the jeep right there in the clearing. He didn't dare move it now because he knew that even if no one had heard him drive up, it wouldn't be long until someone noticed the vehicle.

He mulled the possibilities. It could have been General Kutu who had drugged his own guards and captured the doctor. It wouldn't be the first time a foreign general had tried to cash in from both sides.

Hogan retreated quietly into the jungle and navigated a wide circle around the compound, keeping low in order to secretly enter the doctor's hut from the jungle side. As he crouched beneath the window to Waydner's study, he paused and listened for noises from within.

With the expertise of a cat burglar, he vaulted the windowsill and dropped onto the plywood floor without making a sound. He waited quietly, still listening. Then he cautiously crawled forward on his hands and knees to present as small a target as possible. When he reached the canopy bed, he lifted himself slowly from the floor. As the hardwood bed lay crosswise, it blocked his view to the hallway, which marched solemnly onto the veranda and into the compound.

As Hogan's head carefully rose beyond the heights of the mussed bedding, he found himself gazing a scant twelve inches from the surprised face of Dr. Benjamin Waydner, who had been sleeping.

"What the hell are you doing in here, Hogan?" The doctor wondered whether Hogan perhaps had a little too much sugar in his coffee; after all, he never had heard him talk about women.

"Never mind that. What the hell is going on here, and what happened to the guards, and what the fuck are you doing in bed? You have a lot of work to do!" Hogan righted himself and dusted off his tan cavalry trousers.

"A dozen armed Africans came into camp this morning and traded the guard's twenty bottles of jungle rum for a jeep." Waydner glanced down the bed, making sure he wasn't exposing anything. He was still uncomfortable from waking up to find Hogan sneaking up on his hands and knees. "An hour after the Africans left," he continued, "the generators broke down, so there was no electricity in the lab. The soldiers were so drunk that I couldn't get them to fix the problem, so I decided to catch up on some shut-eye."

"You just stood there and let them sell one of *my* jeeps?" Those jeeps were US government property, and Hogan had signed for them.

"The strangers had guns. The soldiers had guns. Everybody but me had guns!" Waydner protested and then, as an accusing afterthought, added, "Where were *you*? You're supposed to protect me! Where in God's name were you? This whole thing is really *your* fault!"

The doctor was right, Hogan thought, but he didn't say it. "I have other responsibilities and other duties also, Dr. Waydner. Get dressed and meet me in the lab, and we'll sort this whole thing out." Hogan turned and strode into the hall, and then across the veranda into the compound.

Waydner was grateful Hogan had left and hadn't waited for him to get dressed. He still felt weird, shaken to have found a man creeping up to his bed. He wondered how long Hogan had been there before he had awoken. As he dressed himself, he couldn't fail to notice his generally sizable organ had retreated a full two inches.

Mental note, thought the doctor, *when General Kutu comes tomorrow, I'll insist on a glass window and a locking door in the hall to the living area.* He would insist, or there would be no more work. Hopefully the general wouldn't press too hard for a reason, because Waydner could never tell him what had just occurred. After all, someone might question *his* manhood, and that prospect terrified him.

Lieutenant Chafa M'butu was leaning over his desk, quietly writing his report to General Kutu. The dented green banker's lamp dimly distorted the pages as he prepared the charges before him. Driven by purpose, he was too occupied in his task to notice Hogan furiously charging across the compound.

Hogan stormed into the study and grabbed the back of M'butu's chair, deftly sending it and the lieutenant rolling across the wooden floor and down the corridor.

"Get your sad, sorry ass over to Waydner's office right now. Move it!" Hogan hated incompetents.

With the composure and aplomb native to a professional soldier, M'butu left the rolling chair on the fly and, following orders, began the march across the compound to the clean veranda that marked the entrance to the doctor's office, where all serious and official business relating to the camp was conducted. Hogan followed him angrily, steering him across the compound with his eyes.

As they entered Waydner's office, Hogan noticed the doctor had made himself a little too comfortable in his normal and official chair. This infuriated Hogan; he couldn't allow these two fuckups to usurp his authority.

"Get the hell out of that chair!" he demanded, pointing to the doctor. "Your asses are in a lot of trouble, and if Beaucroix were here, I don't know if even I could save them. Do you even have a clue regarding the seriousness of what you two have done?"

Clearly exasperated, the doctor rose from the black leather chair and stood near the wall next to M'butu as Hogan commanded the position of authority behind the banged-up hardwood desk.

"Just what kind of idiots am I dealing with here? Would somebody please tell me? Doctor, when they took your IQ in college, did they ever give it back?" Hogan turned to the lieutenant. "M'butu, are there a lot of idiots in the Liberian army, or did I just get jackpot lucky and land the biggest one? Don't you bozos realize how much is at stake here?"

"Mr. Hogan, I am taking measures right now to handle the situation—"

Hogan quickly cut him off. "Just where the fuck were you when your men were auctioning off one of my jeeps?" He shook his finger accusingly.

"I was doing my job. I was working on my daily report to headquarters," M'butu shot back rapidly.

"Your job, you moron, is to supervise your men and protect the security of this compound—not to conduct auctions of US government property!" Hogan held a clenched fist toward the officer.

"What's the problem here, Hogan?" Beaucroix stood framed exactly in the doorway with his cold steel eyes focused on Hogan, his feet spread wide and arms resting on the rough doorframe. He could move like a leopard, silently and without detection, through a herd of antelope. Just like a leopard, he also enjoyed toying with and torturing his prey.

Melodramatic asshole, thought Hogan. "I thought you were in Romania, filling your ticket on fat, ripe communist politicians!" Hogan was pissed. The last thing he needed was more problems. That asshole Beaucroix was *always* trouble, and trouble to an agent was always a problem.

"I killed both of the bastards, the primary and the secondary. So I came to report," Beaucroix stated bluntly and without interest or emotion.

"Beaucroix, I don't care who you kill, boink, or marry. I don't like you much. Besides, Max George is your superior in this theater. You should report to him." *Leave. Just leave*, Hogan silently wished.

"Well, according to procedure, you're also senior, and I can report to you." Beaucroix then proceeded with a sarcastic sneer. "Besides, don't you and George have a *special* relationship? I understand you have a lot of *things* to say to him privately. You can forward my report to him, perhaps between the pillows."

Many psychotic killers, like Beaucroix, were closeted homosexuals, and they bluffed their way through life mortified the world would discover the hidden doppelganger within them. Living in a world filled with self-hate and denial and terrified to face the forbidden urges within themselves, they broadcast their self-hate into the wider world with a rage of accusations of nonheterosexuality toward everyone else. Unloved and unable to express love, they were as close to demons as anything could be and still remain flesh bound in a mortal world.

Psychotics of this flavor all covered up their secrets differently; they all had their own little game they played. To deal with his dirty little secret, Beaucroix had created an entire world for himself in which to hide from himself. He lived in the world of a male lion, a world in which all other male lions were a disposable commodity. He believed all men must consider all others disposable; he had to believe this to validate his world. Further, he believed any man who didn't view everyone else as a disposable commodity wasn't a lion and, by extension, wasn't a man.

"We're kind of busy here, Beaucroix. I'll take your report tomorrow." Suddenly Hogan remembered the two "controls" he had been ordered to provide him with. "Why didn't you send Carson or Helmut Krupp? They could have delivered your report. I'm sure you have a lot of important things to do, hopefully elsewhere."

Beaucroix chuckled. "This was a very difficult mission with a lot of potential complications." The Monster absolutely beamed. "Krupp and Carson were put at my disposal. So after the operation was complete, I disposed of them! Besides, the mission was completed. That's the only thing that matters, isn't it? I was just doing my job, making the world a little safer for democracy." He was grinning because murder fueled the hate within him like the blacksmith's bellows stoked the fire.

Hogan was really pissed; he was especially pissed at himself for having been tricked into sacrificing two good men. There had been no need to kill them. But in the CIA, there were no friendly ears to complain to. The only question they cared about was, "Was the operation a success?" Their usual attitude toward incidental murder was, "Well, shit happens!" Besides, killers of Beaucroix's standing were always hard to find, and to keep the Cold War cold, the CIA needed all the cannons it could get.

"Now, what can I do to help, Hogan? You seemed to be having a problem when I walked in." Beaucroix had had enough fun with the report. It was time to move on. It was time to find new fun.

"It's nothing to light your candle, Beaucroix. Just minor logistical problems that I have under control," Hogan replied.

"We'll see about that." Beaucroix advanced toward Waydner. "Well, Doc, talk!"

Waydner jumped and hit his head against the wall as he retreated in fear.

Beaucroix stood with his hard face inches away from Waydner, who was doing his best to flatten against the wall and not faint dead away.

"It's just…just a small delay, Mr. Beaucroix," he stammered, wishing the Monster weren't stand so close. "I'll work ten times harder tomorrow. Everything will stay on schedule. I promise…I swear."

"Yes, sir. We're just now sorting out the matter," Lieutenant M'butu added in a tone that carried the respect due to a senior officer.

Beaucroix smiled. "Now, Doc, when have I ever pressed you to work harder, eh?" He patted the doctor on the left shoulder then sent his right fist like a hammer into Waydner's gut, folding him like a wallet and sending him crashing to the floor. "When, you son of a bitch, did I ever tell you that you could have delays?" the Monster screamed as he reached down and grabbed the doctor by the shoulders and heaved him across the room onto the sofa by the porch window.

Hogan stepped in. "Hold it, Beaucroix. This man is a US citizen."

M'butu opened his mouth to speak but was cut short by Beaucroix, who was now in an uncontrollable rage as he turned and pulled his pistol, extending it to an arrow-straight line to Hogan's temple.

"Don't you ever dare give me an order," he barked, infuriated. "You don't have Max George here to protect you. You're nothing but a fairy desk-jockey wimp. It'll be fun to watch you suffer and die. Beg me, bastard! Beg for your life." The Monster was an unrestrained whirlpool of spinning rage.

"Put away that gun; you don't scare me, asshole. If you kill me, you'll find out who really is better—Max or you—and Max won't wait for Washington to give him the word, either." Hogan had played too many hands with too many bad men to be scared by this psycho.

"Why would George care if I killed you? Is he your fairy lover?" Beaucroix had cocked the hammer.

Unable to believe his eyes, Lieutenant M'butu was frozen in place.

"You're here to do a job, Beaucroix, so let's see some professionalism." Beaucroix calmed slightly and lowered his gun a fraction of an inch as Hogan continued. "If you don't holster that gun in four seconds, I promise you're a dead man." He pointed to his pistol, tucked inside his waistband, to accentuate his argument. "Either I'll kill you, or you'll kill me and then Max will cash in your chips. Either way, you'll be just as dead."

Laughing nervously, Beaucroix holstered his gun. Then he walked over to Waydner and sat next to the doubled-over doctor on the wicker sofa, which creaked in protest as the Monster put his arm around Waydner's shoulders. "You guys take yourselves too seriously. I was just joking around, having a bit of fun." Beaucroix smiled as he gave the doctor a friendly squeeze. "Now, Doc, take a deep breath, and tell us what the problem is." Beaucroix adjusted and carefully patted down Waydner's collar.

"No electricity," gasped the doctor, who was still short of breath.

"See, everybody?" Beaucroix beamed with revelation as he gave the doc another squeeze. "I knew it was something simple!"

Hogan wasn't about to drop his guard, because he didn't trust this psychotic son of a bitch.

Lieutenant M'butu had seen the spy movies at the theater in town, but he always had dismissed them as fiction because no Western government could possibly countenance behavior that cruel. However, he had just sat for three minutes, frozen to his chair in shock, as this drama had played before him. He honestly believed that if Hogan hadn't controlled Beaucroix, he might never have snapped out of it. Still, he was the sole representative of the Liberian government present, and, given the fact that the doctor was in no condition to talk, he must take charge.

"Mr. Beaucroix, it seems the generators have broken down, and, due to their drunkenness, my men have been unable to fix them," explained M'butu.

Waydner was somewhat recovered now as Beaucroix continued to squeeze the doc's shoulder and smile. Hogan knew Beaucroix was up to something and watched him keenly as M'butu continued.

"It is my duty as their commander to take corrective measures. As soon as they can walk, I will take them back to headquarters, where they will be arrested and punished. Then, tomorrow, I will return with new soldiers who will not drink. As an officer of the Liberian government, I give you my word of honor that this incident will not be repeated."

"Lieutenant…" Beaucroix gave the doc a final squeeze, stood up from the floor, removed his time-twisted, faded safari hat, and dusted off his trousers. "We don't need to go to such extremes. I'll just go have a word with them and see if we can get this whole thing back on track." With this, he strolled out the door toward the barracks.

M'butu was going to thank him, but what he had seen in those hideous steel-blue eyes frightened him, so he merely watched the Monster head out the door.

"Hogan, I am pleased that he is gone," remarked M'butu as he got out of the chair and walked over to help the somewhat unsteady doctor stand. "Does he have to come to Bopolu? I don't think we need him here." M'butu did his best to hide the fear flavoring his question.

"I'm sorry, Lieutenant, but in my line of work, if you tell the director you don't want Beaucroix, they'll think you're afraid of Beaucroix, and nothing is more dangerous than to have them think you're scared. The highest security risk is a scared spy. They send men like Beaucroix to manage security risks. Does that answer your question?"

"Far too completely, but I also think Beaucroix fears this Max George you mentioned. I saw the way he changed when you mentioned the man's name. Do you think this person George will stop him?"

Hogan didn't hear the question because he was now standing at the window, intently watching the barracks across the compound.

"Thank you for saving me, Hogan," Waydner offered. "I'm sure he would have killed us if you hadn't been so brave." The doctor, now completely recovered, was breathing normally. But Hogan, still standing at the window with his eyes focused far away, didn't hear a word of what Waydner had said either. He was the only one who didn't jump when the four shots rang out. He was surprised only that Beaucroix had killed them so quickly. The Monster must have had a meeting he needed to rush off to.

Beaucroix strode casually into and across the room to the telephone. He quickly dialed a number and then fixed Hogan with his cold stare.

Lieutenant M'butu was in shock, unsure whether he should stay there and arrest Beaucroix or go to the barracks to try to figure out what had happened.

Hogan knew that tonight Beaucroix must win this round to satiate his psychotic pride, but he made himself a promise: someday soon, he would kill this vermin. If there was a truly a God, this would be Hogan's ticket to heaven, sending this soulless demon to hell.

"Hello. Give me the general." Beaucroix had made his connection. "Tell him it's his banker...You don't need my name—just tell him." Several seconds passed, with Beaucroix drilling Hogan with those terrible eyes. "Kutu, this is Beaucroix. We have a small problem at Bopolu. It seems the soldiers here have all died in a drunken accident, and all the generators are down. I want more soldiers here tonight and those generators running by midnight."

Suddenly it sank in, and M'butu knew his duty. The lieutenant moved up slowly behind Beaucroix and drew his pistol as the conversation continued. "Yes, General. We very much appreciate that. Oh, and is it OK if the lieutenant dies in a drunken accident as well?"

Waydner quickly looked at Beaucroix, who held the phone tightly, his eyes still locked on Hogan. But somehow, fantastically, Waydner felt Beaucroix's eyes on himself and M'butu as well. *How can he see behind him?* It was impossible!

Meanwhile, M'butu had holstered his gun in fear and retreated to a spot against the wall between the sofa and the door.

"Is that so? He's your second wife's favorite brother? Well, maybe he hasn't drunk as much as I thought. Thank you, General. Good-bye."

Beaucroix softly hung up the phone and walked over to Hogan, stopping less than a foot away. "I'm late to an appointment, and I need your jeep. My driver crashed mine when I slit his throat." The Monster extended his right hand with his palm upward.

As Hogan held out the keys, a look of fury passed over Beaucroix's face. He had been hoping Hogan would fight him. But Hogan only answered that evil stare with defiance. Beaucroix glared for a few seconds more, then furiously grabbed the keys from his hand and headed for the door.

"Have a nice day, Emily." Hogan smiled his farewell as Beaucroix froze in his tracks.

The Monster just stood there, not moving, not turning, with a simmering rage bubbling within him. Suddenly, only three feet from the door, he swung around and, stepping to the side, grabbed a surprised M'butu by the epaulets and slammed his knee into the gasping lieutenant's groin.

Waydner looked on in terror as the Monster tossed the soldier against the wall and then hammered a crushing, ham-size fist into M'butu's face three times, each blow sending a fresh shower of blood onto the wall of the hut. Only when the lieutenant's face was completely broken did Beaucroix let go. M'butu left a trail of blood against the wall as he slumped to the floor.

Beaucroix took two steps toward Hogan as he shook his finger at him. "You're dead!" Then he spun around and headed for the door.

January 23, 1963
St. Paul, Minnesota

Jon Terry looked nervously around at the casual flow of parents and prams that drifted through the green arteries of the Como Park Zoo. As he approached the monkey cage at the appointed hour, he quickly made his way to the bench to answer the secret summons and collect on certain cash promises that had been made.

Suspiciously he eyed the sundry lumps of humanity beneath the crisp, tan Stetson that sat upon the largest man he'd ever seen.

"Have a seat," the huge man offered, indicating the stone bench.

Terry looked down at bench, but the big man's thighs flowed over it and practically concealed it from view. He could find no empty purchase for even a slender man such as him.

"No, thanks," Terry replied with confusion, wondering why such an impossible offer had even been made. He looked around the bench and, finding no briefcase, turned to leave.

"It would be unfriendly not to introduce myself." The big man offered his right hand as he deftly swung his left into his vest and produced a bulging manila envelope, obviously filled with the graffiti of former presidents. "My name is Robert Lee Parker. Most people call me Bob," he continued in a too-casual manner, frowning that the little man hadn't joined him by taking a seat. "If you don't want to sit, I'll go right to business. You said you know something about the killing of Benjamin Waydner. If you have anything worth selling, let's start dealing."

Terry looked down at the envelope, wondering about its contents.

"I hate bookkeepers. If your information isn't worth ten thousand dollars, I'll have to return some money and void my last voucher. That means I'll have to fill out two more vouchers, and I really don't want to be bothered. Sometimes my boss says I overpay for every bit of information. Then again, he's a Greek. He's so tight with money his butt crack squeaks when he walks." The big man laughed heartily as he egged the smaller man on.

Terry was in shock; no amount had been mentioned. He'd been hoping for eight hundred dollars so he could repair his tired Ford Ranchero truck. For the first time, he was worried about whom he was dealing with.

"Are you with the FBI?" Terry asked.

"Nope," the fat man curtly replied.

"The CIA?"

"No, not exactly."

"Then you must be a reporter," Terry offered.

"Do I really look like a reporter?" The big man grinned.

"You're with the Mafia, then?" Terry asked with more than a little fear and almost in a whisper.

"Do I look like a hood?" the fat man asked with another grin.

"I don't know," Terry quietly and very nervously replied.

"Well, set yourself at ease." The big man was a little hurt to be seen as a criminal because he had sworn an oath. He had chosen his side a long time ago, and it was a decision he never would regret. It was better to be a poor man in heaven than the wealthiest king in hell.

"I'm one of the good guys!" He smiled as he tried to set the nervous little man at ease.

"Then you're some kind of cop?" Terry concluded with satisfaction.

After a somewhat pregnant pause, the fat man addressed the question. "Well, not exactly. I don't think you could call me that," he vaguely replied.

"I've got to go!" Getting really scared, Terry turned to walk away.

The huge man bolted up and anchored the man's arm. "You wouldn't want to leave without this." He jammed the envelope into Terry's gut and tossed both the envelope and Terry onto the bench, and then he somehow found room to join them on the warm granite. "There's more than one kind of crime and more than one kind of cop. Think of me as a cop who can't arrest anyone and who has no need of jails. Nevertheless, I fight crime—but not the kind you're familiar with."

"Will I get in trouble talking to you?" Terry asked from deep within a cloud of confusion and uncertainty.

"No one can arrest you for talking to me, and I can't be arrested for anything." The big man smiled again and patted the little guy on the back.

"Then you have some kind of diplomatic immunity. You're with Interpol!" Terry surprised himself with his own cleverness.

The big guy laughed. "I like you. You're very funny. A very funny man indeed! Interpol doesn't have any sort of immunity, so no, I'm not with Interpol. But I am hungry, and you're making me late for lunch. I think I've lost five pounds just sitting here talking to you. I'm also keeping you from counting your money, so let's both cut to the mustard and get down to business. OK?"

"How do I earn this?" Terry was gripping the envelope to his flat belly, his fingers probing the bulges, trying to verify its contents. He couldn't believe he had fallen into so much cash.

"Tell me every detail, everything you can remember about the murder of Dr. Benjamin Waydner. Then there will be a few questions."

The little guy was still nervous. "How will you know if I'm telling the truth?"

The big man pressed the envelope harder against the thin man's belly. "The Shadow knows."

CHAPTER FOUR
Toward a More Military Direction

February 12, 1963
Bopolu, Liberia

Every list Waydner had given to Hogan had been the same: fresh note-paper, writing tablets, more test tubes, sundry chemicals, and some Coke, always some Coke. The doctor had become a Coca-Cola addict. On Sundays, Hogan showed up to check on his progress and approve the supply list. But it was just a formality because Waydner always got everything Waydner wanted. Hogan obviously knew the good doctor was developing a passion for soda pop, and he obviously didn't care.

If Waydner wanted heroin, Hogan would've supplied it, provided it didn't interfere with his progress. Coke was completely harmless. Heck, the caffeine probably increased the doctor's productivity. So every Sunday, the list said, "some Coke," and Hogan knew "some Coke" meant five cases; so he always scrawled "five cases" next to the "some Coke" before handing the list to the military driver, who would then fetch the supplies from town.

Waydner tossed the empty soda bottle into the bin. With a loud clink, it bounced off the full container and rolled across the laboratory floor. He bent over, with his right hand stretched down as he walked, tracking the rolling bottle in a semicircle across the floor. He captured the offender and walked it back to the bin, and his left boot made a crater for it in the trash can among seven of its drained brethren and four empty test-tube cartons.

He popped open a fresh Coke as he seated himself on the lab stool, then pulled the latest rack of test tubes closer. After removing the cork stopper from one, he carefully spread a drop of the contents onto a glass slide. He replaced the cork and then slid the glass under the microscope. He paused, leaning back on the stool, and took a deep breath, followed by another, as he gathered the courage to test his gamble.

Finally settling over the eyepiece, he fiddled with the double knobs and the mirror, anxious to get an answer. As this miraculous miniature world came into focus, his world fell apart. Through the Bausch and Lomb eyepiece, Dr. Waydner confronted the very same Rotifera-A, happily swimming along, he had started with seven weeks before. It was completely unchanged; the gene alterations had failed. He slammed his fist on the lab bench in a fury, but his anger quickly morphed into a self-pitying state of frustration.

The last seven weeks of work had been a total waste of time. All that work and all those experiments would have to be trashed. Waydner was moving toward a genetic dead end and would have to find a new direction. He sighed in disappointment and scratched his right side. He was the first, the smartest, and the best genetic engineer who ever had lived—he certainly deserved better results than this. His ego was larger than the sum of his critics, and it wouldn't permit him to fail.

Waydner laid his head on the table, and, lacing his fingers behind his head, he moaned to himself because he'd been the victim of a false hunch. Stupidly, he had blindly followed a trail blazed by nothing more substantial than an unproven hypothesis and a hope for the assistance of dumb luck.

These mistakes could well cost him his job and possibly his life; the CIA demanded results. He knew these were no Boy Scouts he was working for. From now on, he promised himself, if he was to survive this captive nightmare, he would be more methodical, more scientific. He would go only where the evidence led and nowhere else. In his despair, he even imagined the stupid rotiferans to be gloating and laughing at him, staring up the eyepiece at the moronic scientist who had wasted seven weeks and a lot of expensive lab equipment to do what the rotiferans could do by themselves in twenty minutes—make more identical rotiferans!

What could he do now? At the university, he had felt so superior, knowing his theories were sound and his hypothesis correct. His colleagues and critics had laughed and banded together to ridicule his words on genetic engineering, yet he knew that someday, his theories would be the gateway to a better world. With genetic engineering, there would be no more birth defects, no more starvation, and no more disease. The earth would become a true paradise, the new Eden. Waydner was positive he had the key to open the door. He would be the first in a long line of genetic pioneers. He would be respected and admired, with a gleaming Nobel Prize gracing his mantel. But then came change, and then came Africa.

Beaucroix scared him—the Monster was quite a few dozen zip codes beyond unstable—and the CIA really terrified him, with its stern, demanding intolerance of failure.

Now Waydner found himself separated from both the critics and the theories; he found himself away from the podium and the classroom. He had been tossed into the terror of the real world, where talking theory was never enough; one had to perform. A wave of anxiety passed over him as he cursed the egotism that had caused him to speak out time and again before he had achieved any concrete results.

"God help me!" he cried as he sobbed and wished he were back at the university, teaching invertebrate zoology to his captive, anemic audience of bored English and boring science students.

He sat slowly upright on the stool and rubbed his eyes. Was that little swimming bastard still taunting him? He leaned over the microscope and fiddled with the eyepiece. As the slide came into focus, he located the rotiferan in the lower-left quarter, just leaving his field of vision. It was still gleefully swimming along, with not a care in the world or concern for the doctor's dilemma.

Waydner momentarily leaned away from the eyepiece, but a subconscious reflex suddenly sent his head forward, smashing into the eyepiece and blackening his eye. Had what he'd seen been an illusion? He rubbed his eye and then twirled the microscope's knobs wildly, trying to get it to focus, but to no avail. Quickly he closed his injured eye and refocused the eyepiece. The slide was empty. Slowly he moved the slide around as he fiddled with the eyepiece, searching for the rotiferan.

Several seconds passed, and then, heart racing, he had a new organism centered below the eyepiece. There, rapidly swimming, was a rotiferan that had characteristics of both Rotifera-A and Rotifera-B in one organism. Waydner was ecstatic; he was a genius, and now he had the proof of it stupidly swimming beneath his eyes!

Hurriedly he removed the slide and made a fresh one from another tube. He took a huge guzzle of Coke, the foam spraying the bench as he removed the bottle quickly from his lips. Wildly turning the microscope adjustments, he brought a batch of fuzzy spots into focus. His pulse quickened as he found himself staring at fifteen perfect A/B rotiferans. They were identical. The doctor smiled as he considered his stupendous accomplishment. The world must be told; his genius would be declared.

"I am no quack!" He slammed his fist upon the lab bench again. "Just try to deny my genius now. I dare you, you insipid, STUPID proselytes! You are less than nothing, and I am a stupendous success, a *SUCCESS!*" he shouted to the empty room. The brilliant Dr. Waydner had done it. Dr. Benjamin Waydner had done what sorcerers, wizards, magicians, and sundry scientists before him had been unable to do. He had engineered new life.

"I've done it you, bastards! Progress, you idiots! Your hypocritical academic university prejudices can't stop true scientific progress. *I have succeeded! Succeeded!"* he shouted boldly to the world, to the universe!

"Having an orgasm, Doctor? I can return after you climax, if you like," Beaucroix offered.

The Monster had managed to silently enter the laboratory and was leaning against the storage racks across from the freezer, casually puffing a Camel cigarette. His cold eyes quashed Waydner's joy and brought a chill that crawled across the surface of the doctor's rigid spine and drove an iron vampire's spike into his celebrations.

Beaucroix's voice seemed to have a wry humor in it—that is, as long as you didn't look into his cold steel-blue eyes. Those eyes told only one story—only one message—and they told it only one way. There were no confusing undertones, and that message was incorporate to itself. The message was death—a ghastly, completely uncompromising, painful death.

If it had been anyone else, Waydner would have been terribly embarrassed, but since it was Beaucroix, he was terrified. He looked toward the door. It would be easy to find an excuse to walk across the compound toward the supply shed and therefore the barracks, where he might find at least the protection witnesses might offer.

That bastard Beaucroix caught the direction of his eyes. He headed across the room and planted himself squarely in the doorway. "I am not the AMA, Doctor. If you walk out on one of my speeches, I won't censure you—I'll kill you!"

In the space of a couple of minutes, Waydner had gone from pure elation to mortal fear. How could the CIA put such an unstable psychotic in charge of anything and expect something useful to come of it, or anyone to survive?

"Let's start with new business," Beaucroix continued sarcastically. "Tell me about your little orgasm. Were you just making it through puberty when I came through the door?" It was obvious Beaucroix was on about something, and the Monster was pissed.

With the good comes the bad, thought Waydner. It was just his luck to get an insane man on an off day. Beaucroix advanced toward Waydner, who backed up and bumped into a bench.

"If you want to know about progress," the doctor said, "you can talk to Hogan. I no longer want to deal with you. You frighten me. I'm not a brave man—I'm a scientist, and I can't work under such pressure." Beaucroix suddenly looked surprised and less threatening. Waydner continued, "Hogan and the Liberian army keep me very safe here at Bopolu. I think we'll send a message to Washington that you are no longer needed here. Besides, a great spy like you must be in high demand in many other, more exciting places."

Waydner didn't have time to gauge a response; Beaucroix was moving too rapidly across the floor. Grabbing Waydner by the jacket, he slammed his other fist into the doctor's face, breaking his nose. He then tossed him, gasping for air, across the lab floor to a sliding stop in front of the desk. The Monster whipped out his pistol and shook it angrily at the doctor, his left fist still clenched in fury.

"Don't ever mess with me!" shouted Beaucroix, waving his bloodied fist in the air as the pistol in his right hand shook. "Don't you ever even dream that on your best day you can even think to dick me around!" With this, he headed past the desk and dragged Waydner off the floor and then deposited him roughly onto the lab stool. He raised his arm to strike the doctor's face with the weapon's icy-cold steel when a sudden movement behind him startled him. Beaucroix cocked his nine-millimeter pistol and turned to face it.

"Little late in the day for sex, isn't it, Emily?" Max George stood in the doorway, grinning. Poised and with perfect balance, he stood ready. Without a shadow of fear, he jumped into the face of the Monster's game. Max hoped that by going heels with this devil, Beaucroix the Monster would slip and would give him the chance, the opportunity that he had long lusted, prayed, and hoped for: an excuse to kill the Monster.

Turning swiftly, Beaucroix lifted Waydner by the jacket and hurled him across the room, and then he prepared to face the only man who had the nerve and ability to kill him.

"Don't ever call me that, asshole," Beaucroix growled. "The next time you do, I'll blow your brains out! Get out of here, George. This is my operation and my affair. Besides, shouldn't you be behind the Iron Curtain, murdering fat communist politicians?"

Max George smiled broadly. "Been there, done that." Max rubbed his knuckles across his breast pocket and then blew on them. "Besides, Beaucroix, you know I only terminate men who deserve to die." And then, as an afterthought, he continued, "Say, you belong on that list. You don't know how much I look forward to opening that little slip of paper and seeing your name on it someday, maybe tomorrow. Heck, maybe today. I haven't opened the morning mail yet. It might be good news!"

The doctor hadn't tried to escape—why should he? This was fascinating. Many times he had heard Hogan speak of Max George, the legend. He was a man—maybe the only man—who showed absolutely no fear of Emile Beaucroix. Waydner forgot about his pain and his injury. He wanted to see Beaucroix die.

"You don't have the balls to kill me!" Beaucroix taunted. Furious, he pointed his shaking pistol at Max. He was as much agitated by his confusion as he was by the amalgam of rage and fear.

"You'd like to see my big, furry balls, wouldn't you, Emily?" Max taunted, baiting the Monster's inner demons.

Waydner couldn't understand the "Emily" bit; he hadn't seen the earlier play.

"Faggot, I should kill you!" Beaucroix roared.

"Please do," Max invited.

"I should!"

Max dropped his hand and slid it across his belt, opening his jacket. Beaucroix jerked his hand twice. He jerked once to squeeze the trigger and a second time to stop. He had heard Max was fast; maybe he would be too fast.

Max George scratched his side as he laughed. "Got the twitches, Emily? Maybe you caught syphilis from that last ostrich you corn holed. Male ostrich, wasn't it?"

"You don't scare me, George," Beaucroix replied, boiling mad with five flavors of fury.

"Beaucroix, I saw an ape on the trail outside of camp, a really big one," Max offered.

"What are you talking about, you idiot?" The Monster was confused.

"Well, it was a male ape, and he was masturbating. I thought maybe you'd want to check it out. Maybe ask Cheetah if he wants to play hide the sausage with you." Max knew the secret of the Monster's rage and made another play to tickle the inner demons within him.

"Just tell me what you want, and then get the fuck out of my face, queer..." Beaucroix's eyes narrowed, and his lips sneered. "...or I might retire you."

"Retire me? That's impossible." Max raised his eyebrows quizzically.

Meanness and fury welled inside Beaucroix. "You bastard, you know I'm the toughest player in the history of the CIA. All I have to do is squeeze this trigger." He shakily lifted the cocked pistol and aimed it at Max's temple. "Tell me what makes you so bad that I can't cash in your chips here and now. Come on, asshole. I demand an answer, you fairy. Tell me why I can't kill you here and now."

"My back isn't turned," Max coolly replied.

The tips of Beaucroix's fingers involuntarily had worked themselves over the trigger and pressed it within an ounce of its release. His eyes bulged, and his temples visibly throbbed. His neck shook with fury as his face flushed fiery red. "This is my operation," he said. "Leave immediately, or I *will* kill you."

"Doctor…" Max addressed the gaping mouth that graced the laboratory floor. "Do you play spades? It seems I've got some free time," he inquired as he strolled across the floor, never quite taking his eyes off Beaucroix, who might soon explode.

"Die, you arrogant bastard!" Beaucroix roared. As he swung his pistol to track George, the room spun around. He found himself facing General Kutu, who was beaming and firmly gripping the Monster's lapels.

"Gentlemen, gentlemen, please!" The general was radiant and expansive. Few men are more gregarious than a Third World general who's rapidly becoming a very rich man. "We must all be friends. You see, you are my retirement, all of you. Your country pays me a lot of money to keep you healthy and happy. Yes, healthy and happy."

He ceremoniously straightened and brushed off Beaucroix's lapels. Then he patted him on the shoulder as he continued.

"Mr. Emile Beaucroix, I am hosting an elegant banquet at my house this evening for some very special foreign guests. They expressed a most sincere desire to meet you. My wives would also enjoy your wonderful company."

Beaucroix glared knives at Max George. The bastard hadn't even drawn his gun.

Max smiled broadly because he had heard the jeeps drive up and seen the general approach Beaucroix from behind. Besides, even if the agency wouldn't let him kill Beaucroix, he wouldn't miss an opportunity to torment him; he hated and despised the Monster.

"Mr. Beaucroix, please…" With his hand, General Kutu tried to guide Beaucroix toward the door. "Do me the favor of riding in my jeep." The general placed a little more pressure on the Monster's arm. At first, Beaucroix resisted, but then he complied, scowling one last time at Max as he headed out the door.

As Beaucroix cleared the doorway, Kutu paused and then turned. "Ta-ta, my good friends. I hope to see you very soon." He waved and grinned broadly as he turned and exited.

"Too bad," said the closet.

"Yeah, well, it was still kind of fun." Max offered a hand to the doctor, who was staring at the closet. "Is something wrong, Doctor?" he inquired.

Waydner could only gape and point at the laboratory closet.

"Still, it was great to see him sweat. It made my day, I can tell you that," the closet said.

"It always has been," Max replied, grabbing the doctor's hand and ceremoniously pumping it. "Let me introduce myself, Dr. Waydner. I'm Max George. Hogan has told me so much about you. He says that you are the smartest man he ever met, and he has met a lot of men." The doctor pointed dumbly at the closet, his mouth still agape.

"You probably wouldn't guess it from my odd occupation, but science fascinates me. It certainly does."

"Max has quite a collection of ancient instruments," the closet offered.

Max smiled. "Yes, in my home in Tunis, I've been lucky enough to acquire some fine astrolabes and telescopes from tenth-century Alexandria. Back then, the city was the Muslim light and center of the scientific world!"

Waydner, who was still in a state of confusion, could only stand dumb, his blank face painted with the brush of the village idiot and pointing to the closet door, which now opened.

"Good to see you, Max," Hogan greeted him as he emerged and brought the double-barreled 600 Nitro Express rifle to order beside him. "What a missed opportunity!" he mused, wishing General Kutu hadn't arrived and Beaucroix hadn't left.

Max looked at the twin-barreled elephant whacker beside Hogan. "Did you expect him to trumpet before he charged?" he asked.

"They always do!" Hogan replied.

Max laughed as he slapped Hogan on the back. The best thing about having a job with great danger was that you made great friends.

August 11, 1949
New Orleans, Louisiana

Now, before we can proceed with the story, you need to understand that New Orleans wasn't just another Southern city; neither was it a black or white city.

The Big Easy was so much more than that. It was the flavorful scent of cayenne pepper and garlic—it was a savory stew of Cajun and Creole, delicately seasoned with the wafting aroma of a little French elegance and topped with the traditional heaping helpings of Southern hospitality. It was the city that made the blues bluer, gave jazz a heart, and put the soul in rock 'n' roll.

It was the Big Easy that gave jazz that fat, full, elegant flavor that soaked right into a man's soul and soothed his sorrow and gave him hope. It wasn't a perfect city, no city is, but it was a fantastic city. And it was in this fat, fantastic city, on February 2, 1932—Groundhog Day— that Robert Lee Hogan was born.

A lot of things can affect a man, build him, and shape him, and it was a childhood memory and a few pain-flavored words recalled to Hogan in his formative years by a wrinkled old man that he would carry as a defining force to his character and into the great adventure that was Africa.

The old man now smiled a bit and scratched the stubble on his chin as he watched the football game with interest from the bone-dry cedar porch, and he rocked a little in the creaky maple rocking chair as he swatted away a horse fly damn near the size of its namesake. The once-read newspaper had been abandoned upon the brittle floorboard, and, with his shaking right hand, the old man clutched the knob of his carved wooden cane as he watched these young men toss a football across the dirt lane in front of his time-weathered vine-and-moss-covered Louisiana home.

Now, most days, he generally enjoyed watching these boys drive the football back and forth, back and forth, under the hot August sun. But today he didn't like what he was seeing—or, more specifically, he didn't like what he was hearing.

That evil word passed into his ear and jammed into his craw like two pitted grindstones grating together. It tore deeply into the old man's heart; and, with all the length of his soul-trying days, he had long hoped that two hundred years of suffering and pain would have taught the South there was a better way, a way to a better world than the one he saw before him.

Bobby Lee Hogan now bolted to the left side of the dusty street and, dropping his right shoulder, plastered the safety, opening up the makeshift football field for Toby Jackson, who had just broken free of the cornerback and was now clear in the open. Continuing his run, Toby raised his right hand as he shouted at the quarterback, "Toss me the ball, nigger! Toss it, nigger!"

Big Jim Stubblefield shot to the left to fake and then bolted to the right as the great quarterback stretched the pocket. His eyes had just nailed Toby as he pushed the rushing blitzer to the ground. He dropped a bit farther back to let Toby gain more ground and then shot the football across the field. Toby snatched it out of the sky and ran for the third touchdown under the blazing-hot sun.

"You're one worthless stupid redneck, Billy Ray!" the nose tackle shouted at the cornerback.

"Why didn't you tackle Toby before the nigger caught the football?"

That did it! The old man couldn't take any more. "Boys, you all come over here, please, and you come over right quick! 'Cause I got something to say to all of you," he shouted.

Toby tossed the pill to the ground, and the rest of the boys followed him to the porch.

"Hello, boys. You all sit down and get comfortable, because this may take a while." The old man had calmed down a bit, and the young men found their seats—some on the porch and some on the warm Louisiana grass.

"Now, I intend to give you all a bit of history, my history.

"The best I can recall, this all happened about fifty-six years ago, when I was a brassy young kid like you boys, just maybe a tad shorter.

I was around fifteen years old and lived on the north side of the parish with my mama, two sisters, and three brothers. We lived only two blocks from the fine, painted school. But it was a whites-only school, and I had to walk five miles every morning to get to the nearest school that would take blacks."

These young men loved to hear a bit of local history, and the old man noted with satisfaction that he had their full attention.

"One day I left school a tad late. I'd gotten detention for some silly thing I did. I don't remember what foolishness it was. I only got half a mile when I had to take the devil's own crap, but I still had four and a half miles to go to get home. I begged Mr. Jones to let me use the bathroom in the Standard Oil gas station, but he wouldn't let me because their toilet was for whites only. As I walked tight assed and trying to hold it in, I made it to Earl's Diner on Buford Street.

"The waitress, Miss Beverly Ann, wouldn't let me use the can either. She said it wasn't like she minded, but the white customers wouldn't want a black behind on their fine white porcelain toilet. I can tell you it was the devil's own crap, and I couldn't hold it tight assed no longer. So I squatted behind the Dumpster in back of Earl's Diner and laid a log big enough to rebuild the pyramids of Egypt!" The old man paused. He had the boys' rapt attention and more than a few snickers as well.

"As I was pulling up my britches, I saw Joe Bob Clemens just getting out of his patrol car. He's a sorry, sad drunk today, but at that time, he was the deputy sheriff. Do you boys know what happened then?" The old man traveled the group with his index finger, looking for a volunteer.

"The asshole gave you a ticket for taking a crap?" Bobby Lee Hogan shouted.

"Now, that isn't precisely or exactly what happened." The old man scratched his head, not that he would ever forget that day. "He took me to the jail, where Sheriff Jimmy Joe Taylor Press joined us in the patrol car, he called me a filthy nigger with no respect for decent white society. And then he punched me repeatedly in the face, knocking loose a tooth. I lost that tooth. Looksee here!" The old man stretched his lip as he leaned forward, revealing the gap where that tooth had been. Scooter

Ray pushed Bobby Lee aside so he could lean closer to a get a better look. It looked cool.

"After the sheriff finished working over my face, they took me to the old cotton mill outside of town." The old man's eyes now wandered far, far away.

"They made you pick cotton because you needed to take a crap?" Toby was incredulous.

"I wished they only wanted cotton," the man said. "They chose the cotton mill because it was deserted and far from town. They chained me to a rusty bailer, and they whipped me. They whipped me with a horse-whip seventy or eighty times. They whipped me until I bled clean past my ankles. Then they took off the chains and told me to get home and never crap in a white part of town again.

"It was a ten-to-twelve-mile walk to get home. To make matters worse, I had to crap again. So I walked all those miles with my butt cheeks squeezed together. I didn't dare even to try the trees at the side of the road, because I knew with my luck, it would be a white-owned tree and I'd never see mama again.

"What you young men need to understand is that the Civil War changed things, but it didn't solve things. What the Civil War did was change the physical slavery of the African American into the economic slavery of the African American. The Civil War gave us the right to live free but left us enslaved to an unequal economic poverty. As a people, we were whole but had a hole within us. That hole is what I want to talk about today.

"Now, all you young fellows are out here spending your time playing football in this dusty street together, and that's fine. Because a good mind isn't worth squat without a sound body, and you got what I never got. Look at each other. I mean it—look around."

The young men looked at one another and smiled—except for Bobby Lee; he stuck his tongue out at Toby. Just because he could and because he liked being silly.

"You see what I mean? Here you are—white boys and Negroes— and you're all playing together. We never had such joys when I was a young man. You couldn't mix without getting a beating and into a whole lot of trouble with five passels of grief on the side.

"With education and hard work, we can escape economic slavery. But the thing the African American hasn't been able to escape is the slavery within his own mind, the slavery that has become a part of him, and that slavery is embodied in the word *nigger*. If you understood the word *nigger*—if you truly knew what that word means to a black man's soul—none of you young fellows would utter it again.

"Now, when you call a fat person lard ass, you're insulting him. When you call a Mexican a wetback, you're insulting him. And when you call a fool a fool, you're just bringing the obvious to light."

The boys chuckled.

"I want you all to listen up, and listen up right sharp. This is what I want you to understand, and this is what I hope you teach your children so they can understand. When you call a man or woman a nigger, you're stealing from them. You're raping and defiling them. By calling them a nigger, you're calling them a slave, and you're causing the hole within them to grow much bigger.

"When you call anyone a nigger, you're a thief, because you're morphing them. You're changing a human being from person to property. You're stealing, because when you call a person a nigger, you're taking from them the very ownership of their own body, mind, and soul. You're robbing them of the very essence of their being. You're a low-down, dirty thief—and in my book, you are the very lowest flavor of a thief there is. Robbing a man or woman of the ownership of their own body isn't right in my book, and it isn't right in God's book. I hope that after today, it's not right in your book either. *Nigger* is a word I let no man or boy utter in my presence."

The old man planted the ball of his cane on the weathered cedar planks of the porch as he leaned forward and wagged his index finger.

"The word *nigger* is painted with twelve coats of suffering into the souls of all African Americans, and every time we hear that word, it gets a fresh coat of paint. We need to come together as a nation to erase this word not only from our soul but also from our memory as well.

"Now, I will tell you boys something else, and this is what really burns my black ass. It's when a black man uses the word *nigger*, because it's *much, much worse*, and they should really know better. Because when a black person uses that hateful word, they are causing the restive ghosts of thousands of their ancestors to relive the burning, blood-splattered bite of the whip with its degrading lashes across their naked backs.

"Using the word *nigger* is unforgivable and disrespectful, and it's downright insulting.

"Let me tell me tell you about this old black man's dream. It's the very same dream shared—and unfulfilled—by the descendants of millions of freed slaves. I dream that someday we will be truly free, both spiritually and economically.

"But we as a people need more than just freedom, because we need to be much more than free. We need to be equal, and we need to be seen as equal as well, by men and woman of all colors.

"I truly believe that day of freedom will come. I surely do, and it'll probably happen long after I'm gone, dead, and buried. But I hope you young men live to see this day of freedom, and if you do, please remember me and what I told you today. Because on that day of freedom, our day of freedom, the word *nigger* will finally be spoken by the very last bigot and for the very last time. Because only after the word *nigger* is spoken for the very last time—and only on that day and not before—will the African American finally, truly be free!'"

CHAPTER FIVE
Satan's Little Helper

June 7, 1963
Chatsworth, California

The taxi drove slowly into the upper reaches of the Sepulveda Pass, leaving behind the cool Pacific air and the lively, carefree beaches of Santa Monica. A very bored Dr. Oliver Tindal glanced out of the open window as he pondered the burned, barren, dirty sides of the pass, wondering how anyone could want to live in this hot, smoggy, congested hellhole.

The taxi crawled along through the crammed mass of cars at fifteen miles an hour as it shuffled within the occluded artery that was the San Fernando Valley's gateway to the greater world. As the taxi descended the pass, the San Fernando Valley spread out below, barely visible through the orange sulfuric haze. Tindal frowned as he surveyed the vast, hot, dusty, and smog-capped basin that sprawled defiantly before him. God, he regretted this trip. Surely if he didn't suffocate in the thick, yellow-brown ooze, he would succumb to the heat and oppressive humidity.

What could Professor Harwood have been thinking when he had recommended him for a position here, and where the heck was *here*? He was familiar with hundreds of good hospitals, none of which, to his knowledge, were located in the San Fernando Valley.

Traffic had fairly halted now as passing drivers gawked at the four captive young and prostrate Hispanic men. Handcuffed and prone, they lay aside their stolen Camaro, now gently smoking behind them and resting upon its battered side. Five bored and stoic highway patrolmen stood warily, posted left and right, as they waited for the airwaves to decide the young men's fate.

Turning his gaze to the west, Dr. Tindal regarded the concrete edifice and tentacle that was the Sepulveda Dam and its broad channel to the Los Angeles River. He never had liked Los Angeles, and he hated California, mainly because he hated Californians. They were nothing more than pretentious hypocrites and fools.

Thankfully, they finally passed the police stop, and things began to open up. The cabby was shooting the holes and making a solid fifty miles an hour. Tindal couldn't believe the congestion, the raw amount of humanity that clogged and impacted the slim freeways of Los Angeles in 1963. He smiled; it was obvious even to a dullard that these freeways never could support more than the three million unfortunate souls who lived there today. It was doubtful that Los Angeles ever would grow larger than this; it just was not possible.

For the next ten minutes, his thoughts drifted as the cab reached the Devonshire Street off-ramp and began its journey west across the ranch- and orange-grove-pocked northern San Fernando Valley. Turning north on Topanga Canyon, the cab had but a short journey to the entrance of Chatsworth Park. Soon Tindal would arrive at the site of his interview.

A park was certainly a very funny, odd, and inappropriate place to interview a doctor, but Professor Harwood had assured him it was the opportunity of a lifetime—the kind of opportunity most research physicians could only dream of, beg for, lie for, steal for, and falsify data for to reach the level of fame and competence to which such an offer might be tendered.

As Tindal paid the driver, he looked around the deserted parking lot. He noted with dismay that his appointment was nowhere to be seen. He hated people who weren't prompt, people who missed appointments. Clearly, such fools had no respect for a busy man such as Dr. Oliver Tindal.

The park seemed to be empty, save for a scruffy outcast wearing a red bandanna and sitting alone at one of many concrete picnic tables. As the young doctor walked over to the unkempt transient, the man seemed to ignore him, preferring to concentrate on what appeared to be a ham sandwich.

"Excuse me," Tindal said as he approached him.

"Too late. You're too late! I don't have any more sandwiches!" the bum protested as he munched greedily.

"Hey, err, no. I just wanted to know if you've seen someone else around here." This was without exception the most ragged individual he'd ever seen. Tindal's mind drifted; he wondered if people really knew why doctors washed their hands after every patient. It was because they wanted to!

"Nope. I seen nobody else, only you!" Scruffy produced an apple and assaulted it with such intensity that Tindal felt silly and superfluous. He turned and walked over to the climbing rock to wait out his tardy appointment.

Chatsworth Park was a very popular hiking and picnicking site in the northwest corner of the San Fernando Valley. But on a hot June day at 2:00 p.m. and 113 degrees, it was almost barren, peopled only by the bum, who had no place to go; Dr. Tindal, who had no way to get anywhere; and a hundred gray squirrels that couldn't care less where they were.

He lit up a cigarette and sat on the small boulder a little to the left of the climbing rock. He was sweating profusely through his gray wool Brooks Brothers suit as he sat smoking and quietly surveying the empty parking lot. He wished he were somewhere else, anywhere but Los Angeles.

After twenty long, sweaty, frustrating minutes, he gave up. He would try the bum one last time.

"Excuse me," he offered. As he once again approached Scruffy, Tindal twitched his nose; the bum didn't really stink, but he certainly looked like he did.

"No more sandwiches, fool. I et my food already," the bum declared.

"I don't want your sandwich," Tindal protested. "I just want you to tell whoever comes by that Dr. Tindal couldn't wait. They can contact me back in Seattle if they so choose." The doctor turned to leave.

"Who's Tindal?" the bum inquired. "Whoops!" Scruffy jumped up as his hand emerged from his pants pocket. He offered a massive dill pickle for inspection, then plopped back down on the bench, and, tearing into it with his teeth, Scruffy munched noisily away.

This is crazy, thought Tindal. He wondered why he'd even worn a suit to such a ridiculous place. As he looked at the bum before him, it wasn't hard to imagine that the man belonged here. He deserved Los Angeles.

"Look, just tell anyone you see that the doctor has left. OK?"

"Are you leaving?" the bum asked.

"Yes."

"OK. Let's go!" the bum stood up. Having finished his pickle, he carefully folded his paper lunch sack and placed it in his back pocket.

Tindal was getting nervous. "No, *you* stay here," he said. "I've got an appointment to go to...*alone!*"

"Let's go. Let's go," the bum repeated with a burp. He now had a hold on Tindal's arm and was guiding him along. With a jerk, Tindal freed himself and ran toward the parking lot. After a few dozen feet, he realized he wasn't being pursued. He slowed to a jog and turned to view the bum behind him.

The bum hadn't moved. Scruffy just stood there, his right arm fully raised, his fingers snapping like mad.

Am I a dog? thought Tindal. *Does he expect me to come at the snap of his fingers?* As he turned and walked back toward the parking lot, he almost stepped right into the cream-colored Ford Fairlane that barreled out of the parking lot and onto the dry, close-cut grass.

Dust and shaved Bermuda grass clippings flew into the doctor's eyes as the car skidded to a sideways halt not four feet in front of him. And it was still sliding when three tough-looking men jumped out and blocked every avenue of escape. Turning away, Tindal blinked his eyes as he rubbed away the dust, suddenly wishing he had brought more money; if he offered these hoods enough cash, they might settle for that and let him live.

"Hey! Hey! What are you doing to ma buddy, you dirty *bums*?" The bum was back and now totally grinning. As Scruffy came closer, the three tough guys broke out laughing. The bum walked up to Tindal and flashed a green ID card—CIA, it proclaimed with green ink and certainty.

Tindal had no time to react as the bum roughly grabbed him and deposited him into the rear seat between two of the tough guys, who slid in close to seal him in.

The bum, who was now sitting in the front, was clearly in charge.

The Ford sped past the pony rides and through the east gate. After turning north on Topanga Canyon, it snaked west onto a twisted Santa Susanna Road. As the landscape grew bleaker and bleaker, Tindal was certain he was going to die.

The car swung a hard left onto the short dirt driveway that led to the Spahn Movie Ranch. It suddenly rolled to a halt next to one of the trailers, and the four men disembarked. The man next to Tindal roughly pulled him out of the car.

Dr. Tindal stood shaken, confused, and almost alone. Only the bum remained; the other three had fantastically disappeared.

Then, without warning, the silver trailer door swung open to the right of them, and a tall man stepped out. Cool and in control, he strolled into the hot summer air.

"Hello, Emile. Still fightin' the good fight?" John Wayne asked.

"You bet. Just making the world a little safer for democracy!" Emile Beaucroix warmly shook the Duke's hand. The Duke looked over Beaucroix's ragged costume.

"Looks like you could do with a new set of duds. How 'bout I have wardrobe set you up like Doc Holliday, vest and all? You can keep the clothes. I bet your wife and kids would get a kick out of it."

Beaucroix, of course, wasn't married; men who got their thrills in the perverse fashion of Emile Beaucroix rarely were.

"Follow me to wardrobe, and I'll see you get fixed up," John Wayne drawled.

Beaucroix grinned and released the Duke's hand. The Duke admired genuinely tough men—men like Emile Darwin Beaucroix. The Duke was a terrific actor, but in his own way, Beaucroix was better. People who looked into his eyes frequently mistook cruelty for strength; William Hampstead, like the Duke, repeatedly made the same mistake.

John Wayne noticed Tindal in his Brooks Brothers suit and assumed he was also high up in the CIA. "I'd like to introduce myself, mister," he said. "They tell me I'm John Wayne." He extended his hand, and Tindal took it by reflex, shocked to have been tossed into a situation for which there was no possible explanation or understanding.

"What are you doing here?" Tindal asked the Duke. Why would John Wayne want to kidnap an immunologist? And to what possible end? Because any doctor would happily, rapidly come running at the summons of such an excellent actor and fine human being.

"Well, mister, I'm doing my damnedest to make a movie." He waved at the two writers standing outside one of the sand corrals angrily discussing an entry in the script—one furious and the other defending his work.

"Some wet-nosed pilgrims seem to think they know more about a gunfight than the Duke. I don't know if I should spank them or fire them. Say, mister, do you have a name?" John Wayne was getting tired of shaking Tindal's hand. People often were dazed in his presence, but the Duke didn't mind. It was an old hat, but a good hat.

"Tindal, Dr. Robert Oliver Tindal," he responded as the Duke released his hand.

"Well, Mister Dr. Robert Oliver Tindal, it's been a pleasure to meet you. Now if you'll excuse me, I've got a movie to make. See ya later, Emile!"

Beaucroix nodded as the Duke strode away and up to the two arguing writers. He slapped the angry one playfully on the ass then walked off to face the camera; the two writers followed in happy tow. Everybody loved the Duke!

"Good morning, sir." The new man smiled.

Beaucroix grunted as William Hampstead's errand boy walked up. Turning his back in disgust, the Monster walked away. It was time to find new recreation and new fun.

Tindal hadn't noticed the man approaching him. He tried to size him up. This new man looked sort of like a bodyguard or a rent-a-cop—tough and strong but not overly aggressive. A cautiously defensive kind of man, alert to everything around him. He stood sharply dressed in a blue homegrown suit with a Yale tie secured with a diamond pin. He extended his hand toward the doctor. Tindal was surprised by his two-second flabby handshake, a far sight different from the long, warm, firm shake of John Wayne.

"I see you met the Duke! Now there is one great American!" He pointed toward John Wayne, who was shouting at the director, his two writers now firm allies. The Duke argued with the man because he knew whom he worked for—he worked for the public; he worked for his fans. When he did a movie, he always wanted to do it right. Because if he disappointed his public, all the money in the universe could never make it right.

"Do you have a name?" Tindal didn't like dealing with the nameless; it was gauche. It was bad manners.

"Of course I do," the suit smiled.

"Well?" Tindal cut an irritated stance.

"Doctor, we'd better get started." The man in the suit brusquely returned Tindal's mind to the matters at hand. Tindal was no longer afraid; he was going to go with the punches. This nameless man, Tindal was certain, was going to clear things up. The man grasped the doctor by the elbow and escorted him across the hectic ranch.

Passing through the hustle and bustle that defines the production of a Hollywood Western, they passed shiny new studio vans and trailers. They walked by the east corral as Shorty Shea, a ranch hand and Hollywood wannabe, practiced his two-pistol quick draws, hoping the Duke—or anyone—would spot him and give a chance.

Why shouldn't they? Shorty looked real good in his work-worn Western duds—damn good—and he looked authentic, not out of place like so many bush-league actors in those 1960s Western flicks. Besides, Shorty was a terrific actor and deserved a break; he deserved to be famous. The poor guy eventually would get his wish; he was unfortunately on the road to becoming a minor celebrity. But it wouldn't be in Hollywood. Years later, he would find fame in death as a minor footnote to a creature called Charlie Manson.

"Who was that man who brought me here?" Tindal stopped walking. It was kind of curious how the bum didn't even acknowledge the appearance of this man and had just walked away.

"Who?" the blue-suit man asked, still smiling.

"The man who brought me here, the one who walked away as soon as you arrived." Tindal pointed at the direction Beaucroix had taken.

"Yeah, him." Blue Suit frowned as he considered the matter. He took Tindal by the right arm and pulled. "You have an important meeting with a very important man, and he mustn't be kept waiting."

Walking east, Tindal and the man in the blue suit eventually reached a dusty, shabby, old trailer that was definitely out of place for the Hollywood of the 1960s, or a ranch from any era. Two Indians galloped by as Tindal and his companion reached the trailer door. The taller of the two braves turned in the saddle and gave the two men an empty stare. *Shit*, Tindal thought. *Indians really are dour, dull, and emotionless beings.* He had thought it was just an act they put on for the camera—just a little bit of Hollywood hoopla.

But then again, perhaps Tindal would smile a whole lot less if he were to endure a little touch of genocide and two hundred years of rotten bad luck.

The man in the blue suit opened the flimsy door and motioned for the doctor to go in first. Tindal entered the crowded living quarters alone; the suit abruptly closed the door, remaining outside.

"Come in, Dr. Robert Tindal," said a voice from the depths of the aluminum abode.

Tindal hated trailers and the class of people who called them home. They rarely worked, often stole, and seldom paid their bills on time. Tindal had been born in a trailer and was one of them; his own mother had been trailer trash as well. His father had left them, like a smelly pair of socks, in a trailer park in Tallahassee, and his mother had done a lot of things to get by—things the doctor wished he could forget. Tindal always had hated trailer trash because no one knew he was a part of that world, and it was a hidden part of him. He had to hate trailer people, and he had to hate them all in order to defend himself and hide the fact that he was one of them.

Like a burst dam, those rusty, forgotten memories—those bitter, rancid, long-repressed memories—flowed over him, engulfing him. Suddenly, the dark interior of the trailer caused something to move deep inside him. The shock of meeting John Wayne had come and gone, and from within his tortured soul, a tidal wave of forgotten memories roared and crested, amplifying the fury and indignation at the way he had been deceived, abused, and forced to come here. He found the man seated in the kitchen, but before the man could offer him a seat, Tindal charged into the matters at hand.

"Why did you kidnap me, you dirty bastard? What do you want? Your ass is in deep trouble, because my family has connections, and I'll sue you for everything you've got! Damn your crooked, slimy, cloak-and-dagger bullshit!" Tindal ranted with uncontrollable fury, a fury that surprised even him.

"Relax, Doctor Robert Tindal," the man said calmly.

"That's *Dr. Oliver Tindal* you pathetic asshole!"

"Sorry, my mistake." Hampstead looked down at his notes on the trailer's fold-down Formica table. "It says Robert Tindal here." He smiled.

"Robert was my father. I was named after him. He is a useless drunk; I go by my middle name, the one my mother gave me. Oliver."

"I see." Hampstead made a quick note.

"I hope what you are writing there is your bank account number, asshole, because I plan to sue you for every penny you own, or will ever own!" Tindal offered his erect middle finger for surety.

"Relax, Doctor. You have read me all wrong. I am the best friend that you will ever have. Because I plan to make you rich! You'll be admired by your peers and famous beyond your wildest dreams. I'm sending you to the most exciting place on earth, and I'll provide *unlimited funds* to finance the research of your dreams, research that is certain to add the name of Dr. Oliver Tindal to the elegant and exclusive club of Nobel Prize recipients. I'm sending you to Africa, and I am authorized to pay you whatever it takes to make you happy. I'm sending you to a brand-new research facility, equipped with everything you could imagine. You'll find yourself working with the greatest immunologist who ever lived, Dr. Benjamin Waydner, the founder and father of genetic engineering. But after examining your credentials, I have no doubt you'll quickly become as famous in your own right. You, Doctor, are going to be a very rich and famous man!"

Hampstead smiled as he spread his arms for emphasis. Tindal positively glowed.

William Hampstead was an agile liar and a master manipulator of the weakness in any man. The director of European operations executed a flawless performance because he was good; he was damn good. He was a magnificent bastard.

June 21, 1963
Monrovia, Liberia

Tindal had left the little airport at Monrovia and begun to wander the city. The agent who was supposed to meet him at the airport had never showed. Damn those cloak-and-dagger idiots. They hadn't even given Tindal a name, so he didn't know for whom to inquire. When he'd asked Hampstead about it last week, he was simply told, "He will find you."

If the medical profession were run no better than the CIA, he was certain aspirin never would've been invented.

As he walked down the busy street, he spotted a man lurking in the shadows; he recognized the look: old, shabby tourist clothes, a faded pith helmet dimmed with the yellow passing of time. As the man stood silently in the shadows, his eyes flashed left to right, auditing the world around him. Dr. Oliver Tindal had seen a lot of spy movies—in fact, he'd seen practically every spy movie ever made—but he couldn't believe they actually went to such silly extremes in real life. The man caught Tindal's eye and cautiously motioned for the doctor to come closer.

"Elephants!" the stranger declared. "Round, tight-assed and luscious elephants, deliciously packed in gravy on a bed of raspberry Jell-O."

Acting crazy was always a good cover, Tindal noted, because people never took you seriously, and they avoided you as well. The man smiled and winked as he absorbed the advancing image of Oliver Tindal.

"Are you the man?" Tindal whispered, surprised he had found the agent so easily. But then, after being exposed to the disguise of Emile Beaucroix, he had learned to recognize the look.

Shocked, the man glanced around. He placed his finger to his lips, indicating they must be cautious. Then he looked up and down the street. When he was certain they were quite alone, he quietly answered this query with the utmost gravity.

"Yes, I *am* the man. But we must be careful," he whispered as he cast the world a furtive glance. "Around here, no one knows who I *really* am, so we must exercise caution. We must go to the director. Follow me quickly, because the spies are everywhere!"

He grabbed Tindal's arm and steered him out of the alley and across the avenue.

"Where are we going?" Tindal asked as they turned left and snaked through the back streets of Monrovia. The man stopped and looked around again. A woman had stepped into the street to dump her wash water into the gutter; the man watched and waited for her to return inside.

"Spies are everywhere. We must use caution, or we'll surely be killed!" He again put his finger to his lips, indicating he wanted silence. Tindal nodded as the man guided him cautiously through another alley and stopped in a dark corner.

As a sharply dressed gentleman in a safari hat approached from the street, the man quickly grabbed Tindal by the arm, pushed down him to a crouching position behind some empty crates, and motioned for him to remain silent.

Cautiously the man lifted his eyes over the top of the crates. Recognizing Robert Hogan, he grabbed Tindal by the sleeve and pulled him to his feet.

"Hogan?" the man whispered as his eyes surveyed the alley. "I'm glad you came to relieve me. We were almost killed!"

"Hello, Timothy," Hogan said with a smile. "Dr. Tindal, I was detained. I'm sorry. I'm Robert Hogan. Emile Beaucroix was called away on urgent business and will be gone a long time, so I will attend to all your needs." Hogan turned to the other man. "Oh, by the way, Timothy, the president needs to see you immediately. He's waiting for you at the Red Lion Tavern. Here are your orders." Hogan slipped something into the man's shirt pocket.

"I knew these were deep matters!" The man pointed at Hogan. "Take care of him. He's our most valuable spy!" he ordered Tindal.

"Yes, I know," Tindal replied with gravity.

The man surveyed Tindal. Satisfied, he nodded and set off down the alley to meet the president.

"What the hell were you doing wandering the streets with Crazy Timothy? You could have gotten lost, or worse," Hogan inquired.

"Wasn't he the agent you sent to fetch me?" Tindal asked. Didn't the CIA know what its left hand was doing?

"*Agent?*" Hogan grinned broadly. "That man is crazy! He lives here in the streets of Monrovia. He's a sorry sot who lives on handouts. I just gave him ten dollars to get drunk. Ten bucks to dream his way through another day. He thinks everyone is a spy!"

Tindal looked down the alley. The crazy man had stopped about seventy yards away and was watching them.

"I like round, plump, luscious elephants, Hogan!" he shouted at the top of his lungs. "I'm going to meet the president! We're going to fuck elephants together—round, *luscious*, tight-assed elephants—and we're going to screw them right on the White House lawn. Lovely, round, plump, luscious elephants, and the president and I will fuck them together! Be careful, gentlemen. Spies are everywhere!" Timothy gazed cunningly around and then crept off in search of a bottle of redemption. Tindal looked at Hogan, who read the confusion in the doctor's eyes.

"That poor guy is a paperback," Hogan explained. "We call them paperbacks because they read too many dime novels. They come to Africa expecting adventure and grand romance. But Africa is a hard, hard mistress. Most of these paperback adventurers are broken, crushed, crippled, and shattered by the harsh reality of Africa. Willingly she offers unforgiving hardship, disease, mad animals, and madder men.

"That poor slob was one of them. He was a successful banker from San Diego, I think. He came here on safari in 1959 with his wife and young son. They went to Rhodesia to hunt elephants. When a bull elephant charged, his tracker ran off in terror as Timothy lost it—he couldn't fire his gun. He froze in his tracks. He didn't even hear the screams of his wife and only son as the bull charged past him and devoted the next thirty minutes to stomping his wife and child into two bloody pulps.

"The wife was the first to get it, and his son—the poor, brave kid—tried to help his mom by beating on the giant's belly. His fists were the only weapons he had. There aren't even any rocks in that part of Rhodesia—nothing but grass and sand. It took only twenty seconds for the bull to impale him and spray his guts across the Kopje. Timothy was found three days later, crying and beating the ground with his fists, surrounded by circling hyenas that were hoping to make it a family dinner, having already consumed his wife and son.

"It was Jack Blacklaws who found him, the famous Rhodesian white hunter. He was out on safari for *m'bogo*, Cape buffalo. He had come out of Kenya with the American writer and sportsman Charles O'Connor. They're as fine a pair of sportsmen and gentlemen as any man could hope to meet. Jack took Timothy to the hospital at Gaborone, but there was nothing they could do because the fellow's mind had snapped. In pity, Jack gave him the cash for a ticket home, but the poor guy couldn't leave Africa. He couldn't face his friends or his wife's family. Africa had eaten his soul, the poor devil!"

Hogan looked across the city at the Africa he loved, the Africa that returned the love to so precious few. He shook his head sadly.

"We had better get going, Doctor. Your buddy Dr. Waydner is stressing out under the pressure. I promised him some help today. We've got a little drive ahead of us, but I think you'll enjoy it. This part of Africa is beautiful this time of year."

Two patrolling Liberian soldiers noticed the Americans talking and quickly caught up with them. The corporal demanded to see some kind of identification. Hogan passed him one of his several passports. The corporal stuck it into his pocket, completely uninterested in what it might have to say.

"This is not sufficient. You will come with me." The corporal loved pushing Europeans around and harassing them. It was a happy fringe benefit he delighted in. It was why he had joined the army in the first place.

"I have important work to do. I'm here at your country's invitation. Check with your damn superiors." Hogan reached out his hand, indicating he wanted his passport back. The soldier glanced up and down at the two Americans. They didn't appear to be armed; this was promising to be fun.

"You are under arrest!" the corporal barked. "Since you white pigs like to tour our country, you should tour our jails. Since you *claim* to be here at my government's invitation, the least my government can do is to provide you with first-class room and board. I know imperialist white garbage like you prefer penthouse suites, but this is Liberia, and we Liberians are a poor people. A fine, dark cell in the basement of our jail will cater best to your needs. If you get hungry, you can eat the crap off the floor, just like you accuse us Africans of doing."

"You should be careful," Hogan warned as he brushed aside the racist baiting. "I'm here under the protection of General Kutu. Check with him if you have any questions. Now give me back my passport." Hogan extended his hand. He didn't deal with enlisted men like these; he dealt with generals and kings.

"I don't know any General Kutu," the corporal said coolly. "Is he a dumb Nigerian pig that has crawled across our border, or just another thieving white invader who came here to rape my people?"

The roaring blast of the Springfield rifle echoed through the street, and the corporal was knocked down by the thirty-caliber slug and driven sideways to the ground and into the dust, his shattered skull slowly trying to paint a circle of red upon the street, but the hungry and dry African dust greedily sucked in the blood. General Kutu and his men had arrived.

"Pity—he was such an ignorant man. Such a naughty, naughty, and naughty fellow. There is no excuse for a soldier to be ignorant of his chain of command." Kutu smiled as he sat in his jeep and rubbed his expansive belly.

The horrified surviving private immediately saluted and stood at attention, freezing in terror. Nineteen years old and just out of training, he'd never expected the army to be so real. Since its founding in 1821, Liberia never had been to war; there was no reason for such despotic acts.

Kutu jumped lightly out of his jeep. His favorite sharpshooter and assassin followed him closely with the still-warm rifle gently smoking in his hands. The man grinned broadly; he was General Kutu's nephew and a man who lived and loved to kill. The other two jeeps had stopped also, but the soldiers hadn't dismounted.

General Kutu walked to within five feet of the petrified young man. As he stopped, he clicked his heels and gave the private an exaggerated Hollywood-style salute. "General Kutu present, sir. He returns your salute." The general stood at silly cadet attention, still saluting as the private stood in terror.

Protocol dictated that the ranking man must drop his salute first, but Kutu didn't move.

Confused, the private cautiously lowered his hand. The general snapped his own right hand back down to his side in best cavalry fashion and stood stiffly at cadet attention. The private was dumbfounded; why was a general acting like this? The men in the jeeps snickered. This was going to be good; this was going to be a lot of fun.

"Do you know who I am, sir?" Kutu barked, still at attention, eyes posted straight ahead.

"Sir, you are General Kutu, sir!" The private still stood at attention. Surely, he thought, this must be some kind of test.

"And who is your superior, sir?" Kutu was doing a marvelous job playing against the private. The general's men grinned and poked one another in the ribs. Kutu had a very clever sense of humor and often treated his men to a very special sort of fun.

"Sergeant Tully, sir!" the private replied.

"And who is his superior, sir?" Kutu stood rigid, a wonderfully comical figure of a plebe cadet.

"His superior is Captain Mobu, sir!" The poor man tried to be as serious as Kutu but was placing a very poor second. This exchange brought another round of chuckles from Kutu's men.

"And who is his superior, sir?" the general continued, still standing rigidly snapped to cadet attention.

"Colonel Tutu, sir!"

"And who is his superior, sir?" the general asked.

"You are, sir!" the private responded, grateful that he had run out of superiors.

"And who am I, sir?" Kutu snapped his right hand to his eyebrow in a crisp cavalry salute.

The private returned the salute and stiffened. "You are General Kutu, sir!" Glad the inquisition was over, the private waited for the general to drop his hand.

"Am I a dumb Nigerian pig, sir?" Kutu tossed a comical expression at his men, who snickered.

"No, sir!" The young man started shaking. He was rapidly becoming even more frightened.

"Am I a dirty, white, stinking imperialist pig?" Kutu raised his eyebrows and cast a wink at his men, who were in hysterics. Sergeant Goodluck laughed so hard that he leaned a bit too far back and fell backward off the rear of the second jeep and onto the dusty street with a thud.

"No, sir!"

"Good! You do know who I am, and you do know your chain of command!" Kutu snapped his right arm down to his side. Then he grabbed his Smith & Wesson revolver from its holster and fired, blowing the private's brains out. He watched, grinning, as the dying man fell to the dust. Then, with a shrug, he turned to his men.

"He should have told his friend this information!" Kutu shook with laughter while his men roared in hysterics.

Tindal was terrified as he stood transfixed by the drama. Nervously he looked around the street as civilians walked by, ignoring the show lest they become a part of it. As he had watched it unfold bit by bit, no part of it had been more real or less confusing than the bit before it. Even now, as he stared at the two corpses lying a scant twelve feet in front of him, it was hard to believe it really had happened.

Hogan caught the doctor's eyes and whispered, "Africa is a hard place, Doctor. But don't worry—I'll protect you. Don't ever go anywhere without my permission or my company." He then turned to Kutu. "General, how the heck are you?" he inquired as he extended his hand, seemingly unaware of the human mess before him.

"Wonderful. I am just wonderful!" the general declared as he accepted Hogan's hand, shook it, and released it. Then, accusingly, he dared Hogan to challenge his authority. "What do you think of this mess?"

Hogan looked at the two dead men and shook his head. He cast a glance at the soldiers in the jeep. They had begun to quiet down; like hungry wolves, their noses twitched, trying to catch the scent of blood. "I'm really pissed, General. I certainly intend to report this. This incident should never have happened!" he said with conviction.

Kutu's eyes flashed hard and cold; the soldiers' eyes filled with fury as they raised their weapons.

"They should have known their chain of command!" Hogan replied firmly.

Kutu exploded in laughter, his ample belly bouncing like a basketball being dribbled toward the hoop. His men were beside themselves as the sharpshooter dropped his rifle, which fell to the ground and discharged with a large crack, announcing the conclusion of yet another a chapter of the game.

The act had ended, but the play had just begun.

CHAPTER SIX
The Bug No Man Can Kill

November 5, 1963
Bopolu, Liberia

What could be more useless than this stupid experiment? Big-daddy redundant! Bore me with a drill, Tindal thought as he repeated test after test, marking all the results in the logbook Dr. Waydner had given him. Even a high school student could see this was just the same test repeated hundreds of times with only minor variations. It was as if Waydner were giving him busywork to keep him from being underfoot.

Yet he had seen the notes and the genetic logs and even read the lab journal. That was the curious thing, the lab journal. The entries from last November to January were enlightening, often brilliant. They showed Waydner's stupendous intellect agilely breaking new ground and surpassing all previous genetic research. Those notes showed a clear, progressive, linear direction, and that had been the case until February; then, without explanation, the brilliance ended, and the journal became dry and academic. It was as if Waydner were killing time, looking for a way out. *A way out of what?* Tindal wondered.

Still, why complain? Here he was: Dr. Oliver Tindal, only twenty-six years old but already with a PhD in biochemistry from Southern Methodist University and a medical degree summa cum laude from Harvard Medical School. Tindal was working as the sole assistant to the man who was quite likely the true father of genetic engineering.

He would work hard and learn all he could. Then, when they parted ways, he would build upon the work of Dr. Benjamin Waydner and become famous in his own right.

Seven cultures prepared and three more to go before he dared take a break. It was so silly, so ridiculous the way Waydner gave him all these useless tests to perform while constantly pressing him to work faster, faster, and faster.

This was especially true on Sundays when Hogan was visiting. On these weekly visits, Dr. Waydner could be relied upon to make a real spectacle of himself as he prodded Tindal to "Work faster, faster! We have so much work to do!"

He might be fooling Hogan, Tindal thought. *But I know how to read a lab journal, and for eight months, he's just been killing time.*

"Well, Doctor, kill time if you must, but give me something real to do, or this boredom is going to kill *me*," Tindal spoke softly to the room.

"Do I sense some insubordination?" growled a deep voice behind him.

Startled, Tindal sent the whole tray crashing to the floor as he whirled in fright; his worst fears had become reality. Beaucroix was sitting at the next lab bench, drilling him with that cold, deep stare. The doctor quickly shot a glance at the creaky lab door; it was shut! Nothing human could have entered this room without making a sound.

"G-good afternoon," Tindal stammered, trying not to appear surprised or afraid. "Look—let's forget the past. Let bygones be bygones, as they say." With a warm smile, the doctor stepped toward the Monster and extended his hand, only to be coolly ignored.

He hadn't talked to Beaucroix since the man had delivered him into the hands of William Hampstead on that miserable, hot June day in Chatsworth, California. Tindal was a little confused because no one ever had told him exactly who Beaucroix was and why he came to camp so often. It appeared Robert Hogan did all the work, and Beaucroix's visits seemed menacing but superfluous. Although Tindal had seen Beaucroix in camp many times, the Monster always had ignored the doctor, never tossing him so much as a glance. He acted as if Tindal weren't even there, like a wisp of smoke so fine and delicate it couldn't be seen unless one were searching for it.

Several times Beaucroix had come in a jeep with his six Liberian soldiers. On these occasions he'd silently sit in the jeep while the lieutenant fetched Dr. Waydner. Then the doctor would disappear into the supply hut, followed by a table and one chair. A soldier would then position himself on each of the four sides of the hut. After carefully marking twenty paces from the walls, they'd stand with their M1 rifles at the ready. Then, with everything in place, Beaucroix would toss his cigarette to the ground and stroll to the hut. Striding purposely in his forest-green cargo pants, tan British safari jacket, and worn Australian bush hat, he'd then disappear into the supply hut, oblivious to everything around him.

One hour later—sometimes less—the Monster would emerge from the hut and climb back into the jeep. Then, in silence, the soldiers—and sometimes the lieutenant—would join him and, without as much as a word to anyone, slowly drive off down the road.

One especially humid Sunday afternoon, Tindal had asked Dr. Waydner why Beaucroix came to the compound so often. "Pray you never learn," the doctor had quietly replied. The fear in his voice had convinced Tindal not to press the issue.

In the laboratory, Emile Beaucroix slowly drew upon his Camel cigarette, sending wisps of smoke in Tindal's direction, along with that incredibly cold stare. The longer Tindal looked, the more menacing the Monster became.

"It's a beautiful day outside. Thankfully, it's not too hot or humid today. The heat bothers the hell out of me. I have trouble sleeping when it's both hot and humid, don't you?" Tindal tossed a lifted eyebrow at Beaucroix.

This was creepy, and even though he thought he hid it well, Tindal was terrified. Why didn't Beaucroix reply? Was he going to kill him?

"You must be from Washington. I bet you're a very important man," Tindal offered in a lost attempt to solicit some form of response. Ignored, he shrugged and quickly turned back to his bench with his back crawling, somehow sensing the evil presence behind him.

He reached for a fresh tray and a box of test tubes, preparing to redo the experiment. Listening, he hoped he'd hear the slightest noise behind him, indicating Beaucroix had left.

But the room was dead silent. Tindal worked slowly and deliberately, pretending to be absorbed in his work.

It took him fifteen or twenty minutes to prepare the base mixtures and stack the tubes. His spine still crawled, but his traitorous ears heard nothing. His back and shoulders involuntarily tensed as he turned slowly to face the lab bench behind him. His breathing was loud and labored; he feared Beaucroix might strike him down at any moment. Then, suddenly, his muscles eased, and his arms fell limp at his side as he faced the empty bench behind him.

He sighed deeply and rubbed his forehead as his fingers paused; he marveled at the blood still pumping madly through his temples. He sighed, yawned, and then scratched his back as he picked up the second tray to carry to the specimen cooler. He took a cautious step before a lightning bolt of shock struck the base of his spine and sent the second tray crashing to the floor.

Beaucroix was leaning against the cooler with another Camel Cigarette pursed in his lips below that same cold, deep, and demonic stare.

"What do you want? Who the hell do think you are?" Dr. Tindal demanded.

Beaucroix slowly pulled on his Camel and then produced two perfect smoke rings and sent them lazily floating in the air.

"Look…" Tindal implored; irritation had replaced fear. "I was talking to myself before. It meant nothing, OK? And I'm sorry, OK?"

Beaucroix continued to pull on his Camel, his face devoid of emotion, save for that cold, hypnotic stare.

"What is this? Are you an imbecile? Can't you talk?" *This'll get him*, thought Tindal. "Are your cheap Hollywood-hoodlum dramatics supposed to scare me? Well, they don't. Grow up and get out. I'm a scientist, and I've got work to do!" Suddenly, Tindal was surprised he'd ever been frightened at all.

Beaucroix smiled ever so slightly as he leaned away from the cooler and tossed his cigarette butt to the floor. The cold eyes narrowed as his hand produced a Walther nine-millimeter pistol from the flap of his jacket. Tindal's terror returned as his mouth fell open and his fear ordered his legs to break for the door, but those dark eyes of death froze his boots to the floor. As Beaucroix's smile grew imperceptibly wider, he flashed Tindal a leering wink as his other hand produced a long silencer from his left coat pocket.

Tindal tried to scream, but his chest couldn't produce much more than a hoarse whisper as a grinning Beaucroix slowly turned the silencer onto the barrel. The doctor's hips twitched as he tried to free his feet from the floor. The cold eyes grew deeper and narrower as Beaucroix raised the Walther's barrel and aimed it directly at Tindal's nose. Tindal tried to speak, beg for his life, but neither his lips nor tongue could move.

Then, impossibly and in a wink of an eye, Emile Beaucroix had pocketed his pistol and returned to his position against the cooler. His face morphed toward boredom as he withdrew and lit another cigarette in a single fluid motion. After a lung-deep draw, the Monster slowly exhaled and sent another perfect smoke ring floating lazily toward the doctor.

"So, Dr. Livingston, Hogan is a fool, and Dr. Waydner has been dicking me around?" The Monster raised an eyebrow, his eyes still cold but now questioning. "Talk to me!" Beaucroix demanded.

Tindal's legs collapsed, and he barely caught himself against the table as he plopped onto the lab bench. He was gasping like a marathon runner, his heart trying to tear itself out through his chest. This idiot was a sadist, a fricking master psycho sadist.

"Simba got your tongue?" Beaucroix inquired haughtily.

This guy really is an ass, thought Tindal. He not only scared Tindal to death but also wanted to ridicule him. "Look, I don't know who you are," he panted, leaning unsteadily against the lab bench. "I'm sorry. I talk too much, OK? I just got here. This is my first real job, and I was mumbling about things I really don't know anything about."

Beaucroix just stood there, stared, and blew another perfect smoke ring in his direction. *Oh, God, not again.* Tindal was as exasperated as he was frightened. He wanted this day to end.

"So let's talk about that mealy-mouthed professor who thinks he can dick me around and fuck the US of A," Beaucroix continued with a broad smile. But no matter how much his smile beamed, his eyes never seemed to lose an iota of their demonic chill.

"I'm sorry. I really don't know anything for sure," Tindal protested.

"Relax. I won't kill you—if you tell me what you know." The Monster grinned.

This last part sent a chill racing through Tindal's spine. The young doctor gulped. "It's just that after reading Waydner's notes and journals, something seems fishy." Tindal paused as the Monster's eyes narrowed and his hand slid into his right cargo pocket.

Who is this animal? Tindal wondered. *Is he a serial killer? A mob hit man? A lunatic? Or just a career psychotic? This is it—talk or die.* If he told all his suspicions, the Monster might kill him anyway. But if he lied or held anything back, the Monster would kill him for sure. He decided to take a chance with the truth and his suspicions.

"After looking at the lab journal since last year, I noticed something very interesting and disturbing." Gratefully he noticed the Monster's hand emerge from the cargo pocket with nothing more menacing than a fresh Camel cigarette. "In the first few months of the journal, things move in a very linear direction, but starting around February, everything seems to regress to a redundant rehashing of previous experiments that accomplish nothing."

Beaucroix raised an eyebrow and glared. It was obvious that he was catching little of this and getting irritated. *I'd better keep it simple*, Tindal thought.

"Look," the doctor continued, "if you say a scientist's research is moving in a linear direction, that means planned progress is being made. It's like building a bridge out of ideas—each experiment, or girder, builds upon the previous experiment. Around February, Dr. Waydner started repeating experiments or doing the same experiment several different ways, thus guaranteeing the same result and ensuring no progress would be made."

"So you think Waydner is incompetent or perhaps has reached the peak of his usefulness. Maybe his brain is out of gas?" Clearly Beaucroix was looking for something specific, but what?

"No," Tindal replied. "I don't think he's shown the bulk of his potential. I read his notes, and he's head and shoulders above any genetic theorist or bioengineer on this planet. Quite simply, he's the best. The problem is that it appears he's procrastinating—delaying or playing for time while he performs useless experiments. He's always careful not to progress in his work. Stagnation—that's it. He's purposely allowed his work to stagnate, and I can't understand why."

"You're supposed to be helping him. Are you also stalling for time?" Beaucroix growled as he slowly moved his hand toward the pocket and the loaded pistol that rested within.

"I work for Dr. Waydner, and he assigns the work to me. He gives me only useless tasks—tasks that waste my time and accomplish nothing," Tindal said, defending himself and thus defending his competence.

"Do you know what the doctor has been paid to do?" As Beaucroix's hand paused on its journey to his pocket, he scratched his right side and wondered how much the stupid pup had been told.

"I think so…maybe." Suddenly becoming more frightened, he had corrected himself.

"If something happened to the doctor, an accident, perhaps…" Beaucroix seemed to be searching for words. "…your existence would pose an unacceptable inconvenience to me."

Staring into the cold, hungry smile of the Monster, Tindal was sure he saw the face of the devil.

"I don't think you'll harm me." Tindal suddenly had determined that the only way he could think to save his own life was to offer his soul to the other side of heaven.

"Why, pray tell, wouldn't I kill you? And this had better amuse me!" the Monster growled as cold waves of pure, distilled evil rippled across the room as they emanated from the Monster's face, which telegraphed a soon-to-explode fury.

"I can give you something better than my death." Tindal smiled, fully committed now to joining this devil's camp. "I can give you success. I'll deliver a better weapon to you—a weapon for which there is no defense. You see, whoever you are, I know you're trying to develop some kind of biological weapon." Tindal was getting braver.

"That guess is a very good one, and that guess will cost you your life." Beaucroix grinned as fun replaced fury. He once again produced the pistol and cocked the hammer with a loud, satisfying click. "I congratulate you, though, as it was certainly a very perceptive guess." He extended the pistol to mark a spot between the doctor's terrified eyes.

"If I die, you lose! Go ahead. Kill me." Now Tindal was certain he had found an ace. He was still nervous but no longer quite so afraid because his massive ego, arrogance, and ambition had now swatted away his fear.

"This had better make me laugh." The Monster pocketed the pistol and fished in his back pocket for the straight razor. He would kill this pup slowly and with a lot of blood. He smiled and hummed "Dixie" as his hand touched Italian steel.

"I know I can complete Waydner's experiments, but I won't." Tindal tossed the dice; this was perhaps his last gamble. The doctor saw the razor flash, and, once again, terror gripped his breast as the blade swung open. "I...I've got a better offer." His ego was again fighting a close battle to brush aside the fear. "I can give you a much better bug than Waydner can—a bug no man can kill!" The doctor tightened his lips and nodded to add gravity to his offer.

With this new information to process, Beaucroix raised his eyebrows, detecting a coup he hadn't anticipated falling into his lap. He considered the matter briefly. A victim was a hard thing to lose, but perhaps *someone else* could die. Suddenly, the big picture was drawn. Beaucroix froze, his thoughts wandering far away as he speculated as to how this coup could expand his power. He then smiled broadly, nodded with satisfaction, tossed his half-burned Camel with contempt at Tindal's feet, pocketed the razor, and headed toward the door.

"Wait!" Tindal shouted.

Beaucroix stopped in the doorway, unmoving and with his back to Tindal.

"I don't even know who you are," the doctor protested.

Beaucroix continued to stand in the doorway, facing Hogan's hut across the clearing. He thought for a few moments. "You will continue to assist the professor," he curtly ordered. "You will not mention any of your own ideas to Waydner. You will forget them for now. I'll tell you when you have my permission to remember them. *You will not tell anyone* about this meeting or do any experiments on your own." He put a cold chill into a measured pause. "Should you violate my orders or any other order I give you, you have my permission to tell the devil"—again he paused—"that you were killed by the toughest man who ever lived. Tell Lucifer with pride that you are just another joyful little demonic gift from Emile Darwin Beaucroix!"

Slowly Beaucroix pulled out another Camel and, casually lighting it, remained in the doorway silently smoking, seemingly unconcerned with the world around him. Then, completely out of character, Emile Beaucroix walked quietly and bloodlessly away.

November 9, 1963
Havana, Cuba

"Since we removed the missiles and sent our nuclear submarines back to port, I've added more than thirty agents to this hemisphere. I assure you, Prime Minister Castro, that there is no buildup of an invasion force or active plans for the United States to invade Cuba. The Soviet Union regards Cuba and the Cuban people as its closest friends." Slava Kurnov shook his finger at Fidel Castro.

"But we have evidence they plan to invade Cuba. I can show you the plans we captured," Castro replied.

"Yes, I know. I have copies of those same plans and newer ones as well. Those plans are merely a contingency. The United States has dreams of invading Cuba, but that doesn't mean it will happen." Kurnov slowly inhaled the smoke through the excellent Cuban cigar and exhaled, savoring the fine tobacco. "The Soviet Union certainly will not allow this to happen. In the Soviet Union, the supreme command also has contingency plans. Surely, Fidel, you understand this. Cuba will be defended. The Soviet Union and the Soviet people will not allow Cuba to fall." Seeking affirmation, Kurnov looked at Castro.

"What if the United States did, in fact, invade Cuba?" Castro pressed for an answer as he took a deep draw from his own cigar. "There are several people in the Cuban government who question the extent to which the Soviet Union would be willing to go to ensure Cuba's survival, and they need reassurances. You did remove the defensive missiles, remember? So there are voices that say if the Soviet Union backed down once, they surely could back down again." Castro pointed the smoking cigar at Kurnov as he continued. "How do I answer these voices that ask me why the Soviet Union backed down and removed the missiles? And how do I answer those in Cuba who question the commitment of the Soviet Union to Cuban independence? How far are you willing to go to defend us?" Castro bobbed the cigar at the spymaster again.

"We have no intention of allowing the United States or anyone to invade the free and independent people's republic of Cuba," Kurnov assured him.

"I have generals who would question how far the Soviet Union would be willing to go in the event of war, if Cuba were invaded. I must have something to put their fears to rest." Castro replaced the cigar to his lips and puffed religiously.

"Surely, we would not allow that to happen."

"Then how far are you willing to go? How far are you willing to go to defend the people of Cuba?"

"We would certainly have a response," Kurnov replied.

"Yes, but what would that response be?"

"We would respond to the threat," answered Kurnov, always the cautious KGB man.

"The United States possesses an enormous nuclear arsenal. They have proved in the past that they are willing to use it," Castro pressed on.

"So?" Kurnov replied. Apples had nothing to do with oranges.

"Would the Soviet Union be willing to respond to a nuclear attack on Cuba with a nuclear response?"

"It is the position of the Soviet Union—and the position of all our allies—that we will not be the first to launch a nuclear strike," Kurnov firmly replied.

"How would you respond to a nuclear strike to Cuba?"

"We would not be the first to strike!" Kurnov repeated.

"But how you would respond? Would you call them dirty names on the United Nations' assembly floor and refuse to sell them any more caviar, and, if they continued to attack, withhold selling vodka as well?" Castro asked, one eyebrow cocked.

"I don't think that would be the Soviet Union's response to a nuclear strike anywhere, against anyone." Kurnov smiled; he liked Castro because Fidel was a real communist. He wasn't like other Soviet allies, who claimed to be communists but were plastic, hypocritical socialists whose leaders lived like kings.

Castro insisted on an answer. "How would you respond?"

"We would have a response," Kurnov repeated.

"Comrade Kurnov, I insist on an answer. If the United States launched a nuclear strike on Cuba, would the Soviet Union be willing to provide a nuclear response?" Castro locked onto Kurnov's eyes.

"Our response would be immediate and measured," the cautious spymaster assured him. Kurnov was meticulous in his answer because he always edited his thoughts.

"Would you respond with a nuclear strike? I require an answer, Kurnov."

"There is no way we would tolerate a nuclear strike anywhere, especially on the Cuban people. The Soviet Union will protect all her allies, no matter the cost." Kurnov not only liked Castro but also respected him; he was an honest man, and even if the Kremlin didn't keep him in power, Kurnov certainly had people who would.

"My good friend, you do not have to play politics with me, but I have to play politics with the men around me and a few fools also." Castro spread his arms and laughed. Then, smiling, he removed his cigar and pointed it at Kurnov. "Please humor me, Slava. I am a politician, not a spy, and we are good friends. Give me a one-word answer to take to the Cuban people. If the United States used a nuclear weapon on the Cuban people, would the Soviet Union provide an immediate nuclear response?" Castro scratched the left side of his beard as he puffed his cigar.

The great spymaster regarded the red linen curtains at the far side of the room as he pondered the possible repercussions an answer might bring.

"Yes," Kurnov said, curtly closing the topic.

"Thank you, comrade, and we accept your assurances. There's another reason I invited you here today." Castro's expression became dead serious. "We have learned that the United States is working on a new weapon, one that it is more devastating than anything in the world today."

Kurnov smiled. "My friend, the Cuban people have nothing to fear. Besides, I have just assured you we will defend Cuba."

"Cuba is not the target. You are the target for this new weapon, because it is designed to destroy the Soviet Union!"

"Fidel, I have a lot of agents in this hemisphere—everywhere in it. There are no new weapons facilities in North America and no new plans," Kurnov assured him.

"No, this is not being created in America. It is hidden from you." Castro glanced across the room to be certain the beautiful hardwood door was bolted securely.

"There is no new weapon being created anywhere. The KGB is everywhere, and we watch everything. There is no new weapon." Kurnov smiled again; his allies were always trying to get him to chase two-headed horses, to chase fairy tales and rumors.

"This thing is deadly. It does exist. And it is almost ready to use."

"Where exactly is this wonderful weapon I know nothing about? Is it hidden in Buckingham Palace? Perhaps it is concealed in Queen Elizabeth's ass?"

"Cuba, Comrade Kurnov, is dedicated to helping all workers of the world. Cuba is dedicated to improving the quality of life of people everywhere. As you well know, Cuba produces the highest-quality medical personnel in this hemisphere. We provide doctors and nurses to developing countries around the world. We provide doctors to countries that can't afford the immoral fees charged by Western doctors. We provide doctors to dying children whose parents can't even afford to feed them."

Kurnov shrugged. "Fidel, these are facts known and appreciated throughout the world. What does this have to do with weapons?"

"We provide doctors to many countries in Africa," Castro replied, leading him on.

Kurnov didn't see the point or the connection. "So?"

"Our doctors have ears, and patients talk. Outside of Bopolu in Liberia, the CIA has built a medical research facility where they are working on a biological weapon they intend to use to destroy the Soviet Union. We've had reports from our agent in Sierra Leone that they're very close to having a viable weapon." Castro knew all too well that the defeat of the Soviet Union would lead to the fall of Cuba.

"This information you are giving me…is it reliable?" Kurnov was now intensely interested. Cuban intelligence operatives were excellent; they had been trained by the KGB!

"Completely," Castro replied.

"I will need names." The meeting had ended, and Slava Kurnov had much to do.

CHAPTER SEVEN
The Office of the President

November 10, 1963
Washington, DC

"Who authorized this?" President Kennedy demanded in a low, shocked voice.

Hampstead measured the president's tone carefully. "Mr. President, Wildfire was implemented by the CIA as a part of our overall Cold War strategy. It was simply one of the many—"

"Mr. Hampstead…" The president weighted his words carefully. "I asked *who* authorized this operation. The CIA is a *what*, it's not a *who*!"

"Sir…" Hampstead sharpened his response. He was unaccustomed to having his authority challenged by someone he considered an intelligence amateur. "In light of the very serious global and postwar situation, as well as the Soviets' *stated* intention to take over the world, the agency—"

"*Who* gave the OK? Was it the president?" JFK coolly interrupted.

Hampstead was silent.

"Then was it the Senate? Did they authorize this?" The president believed all men in power needed to account for their actions. Those who held public trust must dodge neither responsibility nor consequence.

Fidgeting in his chair, Hampstead shot a glance around the room. LBJ returned his glance, a revelation Hampstead quickly filed for later use.

"Mr. Hampstead, you will answer me," President Kennedy continued. "Perhaps it was your left toe that authorized you to engage in an *illegal* operation that not only threatens our great nation but also spits on the principles upon which our great democracy is based. The president of the United States of America *demands* to know who gave the authority." JFK was beyond furious, and if it weren't for the president's deep respect for his office, Hampstead surely would be sitting in the middle of Pennsylvania Avenue, writing his resignation, as well as nursing a black eye and a size-ten Boston shoe print on his ass.

"Mr. President, as a matter of security, neither the office of the president nor the Senate was informed of—or had any knowledge of—this operation. Given the high security and need for absolute secrecy—" Hampstead stopped as the president abruptly raised his hand.

"That will do." President Kennedy had both heard and swallowed enough. "I think we all know upon whose authority you acted." He turned to the vice president. "Lyndon, contact Director Gaines and tell him his vacation is over. I want a full report as to how this happened. I want him in my office the *minute* I return from Dallas, and I want answers. Set up a meeting for November twenty-third."

He turned to Hampstead, whose mind was working like a gristmill, plotting how he and the agency would save America from this incompetent man.

"Mr. Hampstead..." JFK raised his voice and traveled the room's collective faces, in turn locking each pair of eyes with his own. "The *president of the United States* is ordering you to *immediately* close this base and destroy Wildfire and all documents relating to Wildfire. I want everyone associated with this unfortunate operation to be debriefed and directed that they are under *presidential order* to maintain their silence and are never to acknowledge or discuss this misguided, illegal, regrettable affair." Again he turned to the vice president. "Lyndon, I want you to handle the FBI. I want everyone involved with this operation placed under full surveillance to ensure their silence for the rest of their natural lives."

Vice President Johnson nodded.

"Gentlemen..." Kennedy stood, thus prompting Hampstead, the vice president, and then all present to rise. He then locked eyes with

Hampstead and burned into his plotting gaze. For several moments, the president continued to challenge Hampstead's glare. He wanted him to be 100 percent sure that when the director fired him, he would know it had been under presidential orders. "This meeting is *over!*" Kennedy bluntly declared. Then, against all protocol, he stormed out the door. But Hampstead smiled inwardly. A career had certainly been destroyed by today's events. Happily, he knew that career wasn't his own. Soon the pope could count one less altar boy, and William Hampstead would pick the new king.

November 10, 1963
South of Bopolu, Liberia

"So you don't like niggers?" General Kutu matter-of-factly asked the man who stood naked, his hands and feet bound, submerged to the neck in an old metal cattle tank. The man begged and pleaded for his life, but Kutu ignored the tourist's shouts and pleas. "You should know a general's uniform when you see it," Kutu explained.

The man had been passing through the countryside, taking nature photographs, when he had come upon General Kutu, sitting alone in his jeep, which blocked the road while his men collected his fees inside a small hotel. The man, late and in a hurry, had honked his horn and given a healthy "Move it, nigger." The rest you can gather for yourself.

"I myself hate all niggers, the dumb and stupid ignorant monkey men who give all of us Africans a bad name. But your mistake was to call an educated, erudite, sophisticated man such as myself a nigger." Kutu swatted the huge galvanized tank with his swagger stick, eliciting a dull clang. The man watched in terror as Kutu's men brought armload after armload of wood, stacking it neatly around the base of the metal tank.

"You see, I am a very educated man," the general continued. "I have been to college in Paris, Dublin, and London. But since you wish to consider me a savage and a nigger, I will not disappoint you." The general grinned. Then he reached into the tub, and, squeezing the terrified man's arm, he licked and then smacked his lips and then declared, "Relax. We are friends, and I am having you for dinner. I am sure you will be delicious!"

The young boy had just poured the last bucket of well water into the giant makeshift dinner pot. Grinning, he walked over to General Kutu with his hand outstretched and facing palm up.

"Now I must give you your shiny new penny." Kutu smiled and patted the lad on the head. He reached into his pocket, forcing his fat hand past the huge wad of paper money, searching the depths for a small coin. Finding one, he retracted his hand and tossed the boy the promised copper and then slapped him on the ass to send him on his way. The boy bolted off, excited by his new fortune and eager to brag about his newfound wealth.

Sergeant Goodluck struck a match, then leaned over and lit the fire. Taking a seat in the flimsy wicker chair a captain had brought, General Kutu rested, blissfully humming to the tempo of the man's screams as he awaited the smells of roasting flesh and the satisfying bliss of a full belly. As his good friend Emile Beaucroix always said, one could never have too much fun!

November 10, 1963
Tunis, Tunisia

"Why haven't you ever gotten married, Max?" She ran her fingers across his hairy forearm, testing its muscles and hungry for its embrace.

"For men in my position, marriage doesn't work out. In my line of business, it's more of an illusion than a reality. Men like me have no time for marriage. I can easily afford the first installment, but I could never keep up the payments."

She looked down at the bulge that punished his tailored khakis. "I don't think a powerful man like you would ever miss a payment."

Max grinned; he was proud of his manhood. "That's not what I mean. What a marriage needs—and the investment I was referring to—is time. Marriage takes time together, and lots and lots of time together. For a marriage to work, it must be an equal partnership, and in my line of business, there simply isn't enough free time to get to know anyone that well."

"You're not really a spy!" she teased. All men were liars, ready to fabricate at the drop of a hat any tale they felt would get them to that special place. She didn't care that Max had lied to her—lied about being a spy—because she wanted him in that special place, and she wanted him bad.

"Yup, I'm a spook." He smiled as he pulled a cocked pistol from under the sofa cushion and expertly tossed it across the room, the gun softly coming to rest in the exact center of the cushy leather of the Victorian chair.

"You're a liar," she teased playfully.

"Yup, all spies are liars," he affirmed as he played with her.

"Now you're making fun of me," she lamented, hurt and turning away.

Max grabbed her delicate face between his large hands. Turning it toward his, he dove deep into her eyes. "If I've lied to you, it was only because I love you so very much. I'd do anything to swallow you deep into my soul." He smiled and dove into her deepest depths as she shook and then melted in his powerful arms.

She had to change the subject, or she'd have to have him this very instant, and she wanted the evening to last forever. "How can you say you have no time for a wife? You have time for your friends. You hunt with and travel with Robert Hogan." She used a woman's logic.

"A lot of the time I spend with Robert is business. The rest is relaxation. Having a best friend is much different from having a wife. Men are different because we understand each other."

"So it's different with men," she observed, trying to figure this out.

"Totally!" Max declared.

She smiled coyly and rubbed his crotch as she again teased him. "So it's better with men."

"Don't be disgusting!" Max pushed her hand away as his betrayed manhood began its retreat into his belly. "You sound like Beaucroix!" Being compared to the Monster was insulting and did nothing to enhance his romantic mood.

"Who is this Beaucroix person? He sounds like a wealthy gentleman. Is he your friend also? Can I meet him?" She wanted to know Max; she wanted to find out everything about him.

"Beaucroix is not a who—he's an *it*. He's no friend of mine, and if he came within nine zip codes of you, my darling, I'd kill him!" Max smiled; he would defend her. Besides, he loved insulting the Monster.

"Then tell me why you can't marry me." She pleaded for an answer, hungry for his reasons and certain her woman's logic could tear them apart.

"Would you like me to show you what marriage would be like for a man like me?" He smiled as he drove the question deep into her eyes.

"Sure, but I'll need a few days to send out invitations and find a dress." She was only half kidding. For the most part, she was wishfully serious.

"Oops!" He had stumbled into that one. "Then I will *tell* you what it *could* be like." He cleared his throat and authored a silly tale.

"'Where are you going, Max?' wife says in a whining fashion.

"'I'm going to save the world, baby. I'll be back for dinner,' the spy says.

"'You don't love me!' Wife wails and sobs.

"'But, baby, the world—all life—will end,' the spy pleads.

"'If you loved me, there wouldn't be a world. You don't love me,' the wife wails.

"'Baby, I do love you. But if I don't meet with some Russians today, there'll be a nuclear war. Millions will die, and there would be famines. Radioactive fallout,' the spy answers.

"'If you loved me, there wouldn't be nuclear fallout. You don't love me.' Wife turns the other knob and doubles the torrent of tears.

"'Darling, the Russians…'

"'You don't love me! If you did, you wouldn't care about Russians. You don't love me!' The wife sobs even harder.

"'But, sweetness, the Russians…' the spy pleads.

"'If you truly loved me, there wouldn't be any Russians. You don't love me.' Wife is now wailing at gale force nine.

"'Honey, if I don't save the world, I don't get paid. We won't be able to pay the bills.'

"'If you loved me, we wouldn't have any bills. You don't love me!' wife declares.

"If I don't do my job, I don't get paid. How could we survive?"

"'You can survive off my love. That should be tons more than enough for you.' Wife dries her eyes in conviction. 'You don't love me.'

"'What?' Spy is not sure he is standing on the same planet as this dingbat.

"'See? I knew you didn't love me.' She wails like a jet reversing its engines as it taxis to a stop, and she opens both taps further, sending torrential rivers of tears down across the floor and ruining the spy's favorite Persian rug."

She laughed because he was hilarious, especially his wailing, falsetto rendering of the sobbing wife. Then again, his injured, pleading male voice wasn't half bad either.

"Now," Max declared, becoming serious, "let me illustrate how it is between two friends.

"'Robert, I can't go bowling with you tonight. I've got to save the free would.'

"'Not a problem. Give me a call when you get back. We'll hunt buffalo.'

"See how easy that was?" Max spread his arms to emphasize his point. She took the opportunity to melt and snuggle into his armpit as she painted herself upon his right side.

She laughed because no relationship could be that simple. It was impossible; she really couldn't understand. Women never did.

November 10, 1963
Seattle, Washington

"What is this? This is a lot of money." Slava Kurnov pointed to an entry in the ledger Ross and Marinovich moved in closer and followed his index finger to the entry. "Here it is again. What is this?" He pointed to another entry. "And this and this!" His finger moved too fast down the sheet for the men's eyes to follow. Kurnov pointed to another entry in the same column. "See this number? It's a code, and it means the money has been allocated by Robert Hogan."

Ross nodded solemnly, but he didn't have a clue.

"Look down here. This code indicates Emile Beaucroix." Kurnov had dropped his finger down the column.

The men simply nodded. They were spies, not accountants, and they were still lost in this numeric haze.

"Now we move over to this column." Kurnov snapped his finger to the right. "Their authorizations come together under a single code. This important project, whatever it is—along with a lot of money—is dominated by two of the Americans' most bloodthirsty players. I need you to find out about this project. If I read the code correctly, the project is called Monkey-Man General. You need to find where all this money is going, what it is being spent on. I need to know what the Americans are up to. I need that information. It doesn't do me any good to see stolen CIA budgets if I don't know what the entries are for. Get me that information, OK?"

CIA agent Michael Orman had altered the documents' project code from Wildfire to Monkey-Man General in reference to General Kutu to have a little fun with the paper-pushing lackeys back home. Besides, Orman despised the fat, arrogant blowhard.

With this directive, the meeting ended, and Kurnov headed out the door. The other two men stayed in the room. Staring at the copy Kurnov had left on the table before them, Ross scratched his chin and then gestured to the documents; the other man shrugged in response. Kurnov's agile mind had outsprinted both of them. He possessed a well-known talent for leaving lesser minds in the dust. The two spies stared blankly at the CIA budget; they honestly didn't have a clue.

November 11, 1963
The Bar None Bar; East of Dallas, Texas

"You can't park there, son. It's a loading zone." The sheriff walked up to the man who was exiting the driver's door. Leo Pagetti had just climbed out of the passenger side; he grinned broadly because this was going to be good.

The driver smiled. "It's OK, sir. We're only going to be here a few minutes."

"Boy, you didn't hear me. I said move it now!" The sheriff hated city types, especially dandies in suits. But only to Sheriff Bob Roy Tulles would Leo Pagetti and his companion look like anything less than hot-blooded killers.

"What's the rush? We won't be here long." The driver looked briefly at his Cartier wristwatch.

"Look, assholes—now I'm going to run you in." The sheriff advanced as his hand slipped down to comfort his Colt M&P pistol.

"Hey, just how long will it take…" the driver deftly advanced and grabbed the sheriff's jewels in a crushing left-hand grip while his right hand snapped open a stiletto and held its gleaming blade to the left side of sheriff's throat. "…to cut off your balls?"

Terrified, the sheriff eased his hand away from the pistol as sweat poured down his sunburned cheeks.

"Are you sure you're a man?" Beaucroix queried. "Because these are awfully tiny balls!" The Monster crushed them harder as the sheriff grimaced in pain and shook in terror. Pagetti smiled; he loved tough guys.

"Maybe I'll cut off these tiny balls and plant them in the ground to grow these stupid hicks two more tiny little sheriffs." Beaucroix drew the blade lightly across the folds of the sheriff's neck, drawing tiny rivulets of blood as he smiled at the terror that had been only moments ago a sheriff's cool eyes.

Beaucroix nodded to Leo, who was also grinning. The Monster then slowly turned and moved his face to within inches of the sheriff's. With his cruel eyes less than two inches from the sheriff's, he smiled, winked, and in a flash released the sheriff's jewels, causing him to promptly collapse with relief onto the road. Turning away, the Monster pocketed the stiletto and walked casually into the bar. Pagetti followed and then cast a glance backward and laughed at the idiot as he followed Beaucroix through the Bar None Bar's open door.

Sheriff Tulles tried to stand but fell back and stood leaning against the car, still terrified but even more confused as he watched the two men calmly enter the bar. He touched the Colt, then snapped back his hand in fear. He couldn't believe the two thugs had let him keep the pistol. He wished to God they hadn't, because he knew fate was summoning him to his demise. Duty and mortal terror welled inside him and tore him apart, because whatever happened next, he knew he never would return home. He wanted to run to his car, mash metal, and get the hell out of there. To hell with duty—he had a wife and a two-year-old son.

Part of him wanted to walk into the bar and arrest them—teach them to respect the law and respect him. But another jolt of pain in his groin reminded him who the badass really was, and the blood wetting his shirt lapels told him the cost.

Shaking and exhausted, he collapsed on the curb and stared at his Plymouth cruiser, wishing he had the strength to reach it. Weeping, he buried his face in his hands and cried for his fatherless son.

"Hello, faggots," Beaucroix offered as he and Pagetti reached the two men at the table. Across the room and about twenty feet away, two grizzled cowboys seated at the bar turned to look around; faggots weren't welcome here.

"Hello, wimp," Oswald tossed back.

Beaucroix quickly flashed red. Nobody called him that; nobody was allowed to insult him.

"Boss, you did some great work last week, and that was one smooth operation. You're the man!" Jack Ruby noticed things had gotten hot. He knew Beaucroix, and he knew someone needed to ease back on the trigger. "Did you get any booty?" Ruby steered Beaucroix away from a confrontation with Oswald.

"Yeah, I made some Romanian bitch suck my cock!" Beaucroix boasted.

"Was she any good?" he knew the Monster loved to tout his manhood; he needed to.

"You'll never know." Beaucroix looked over to Oswald and ran his finger across his neck and winked to illustrate the tale. "I killed her after I fucked her the first time. The second fuck was better than the first." He grinned at Ruby.

"Did the bitch kick a lot?" Ruby smiled and leaned back on the stool. He loved a good piece of ass.

"Only the first time. The second and third time, she barely whimpered," the Monster said with a laugh.

"This is sick!" Oswald wanted none of this. It was time to get to the business at hand, because he was a man in search of his destiny, and Ruby had promised him a contract to end all contracts: the opportunity to kill a president.

Beaucroix wasn't ready to leave the subject. Oswald had pushed his Queer button. "Don't you fuck women? Or do you prefer plump sheep? Or is it pubescent little boys you like, *faggot*?" A defensive rage rose within the Monster as it projected his inner thoughts, inner demons into the world around him.

"Hey, hey, Beaucroix…Oswald is taking on a very complicated job for us. He's got a lot of work and planning to do. Isn't that right, Oswald?"

"Yeah, but only if we can agree on the money thing and the immunity thing. I'll need a place to live, somewhere I can't be arrested." He knew he could easily escape the police, but he could never escape the CIA.

Beaucroix wasn't convinced Oswald was normal. This faggot thing needed to be looked into; faggots should never be tolerated. "Do you need a little cash on the deal? Maybe a little for your boyfriend?" he baited with a cold, accusing stare and a raised eyebrow.

"Now hold it, Beaucroix. Oswald likes pussy just like the rest of us. He's just in a hurry to get the contract started. Maybe after we finish here, we'll all go up to Fort Worth and slap some sluts around." Ruby looked to Pagetti for support. Pagetti was an important errand boy for Hampstead and certainly knew the plan.

"You'll get twenty thousand after the job is done." Pagetti tossed a bulging envelope in front of Oswald. "Here's five grand for expenses. You'll get twenty thousand a year for life for every year you remain silent. Slip, and the money dries up like a wilted pansy, and you with it!"

"Fat chance, Jack. Why should I let you watch me fuck some bitches?" Beaucroix growled. He wasn't listening to the offer. He was still on about the faggot thing, but now his suspicions had expanded to include Ruby.

"You really think I'll let some little fairy homo see *me* naked? I should kill you for even suggesting it, Jack." Beaucroix was rapidly heating up.

The Monster leaned forward and reached inside his jacket, but Pagetti was faster. He grabbed Beaucroix's neck and placed his long Sicilian nose above the Monster's ear as he whispered, "Boss, Hampstead already told me we're going to ice the shooter. He said we can't risk having any witnesses. But he must've meant we could ice the other fairy too, because nobody talks like a bitch in heat."

Pagetti knew Jack Ruby was a horn dog; the man wasn't anywhere near gay. He was a slut-bar daddy, for Christ's sake; he practically lived in a sleazy topless bar he owned called Heads 'n' Tails when he wasn't wanted for a job. But Pagetti also knew Beaucroix and knew the Monster's sickness and delusions. The Monster was the only thing Pagetti had ever seen that he was truly afraid of. But the Monster had a lot of power, a great deal of power, and Leo Pagetti needed power.

Pagetti didn't have any need for principles and cared even less for the principles in the world around him. This made his alliance with the Monster both useful and easy. But to be allowed into the Monster's world, one must share his delusions and worship his power.

"We'll kill both these bitches," Pagetti whispered coarsely into Beaucroix's ear. "But first, smile and have some fun and pretend everything's OK. Once they kill the altar boy, we'll kill both of them…but not before we have some fun."

Pagetti let go and sat down, smiling at Ruby and Oswald. But Oswald was caught between two exits. He was usually a man with tunnel vision, and he was trying to focus on the job, the money, and the escape. He was a macho kind of guy and was confused by whatever the homo thing was. Oswald sort of thought Beaucroix was accusing Jack Ruby of being queer, but he couldn't see how that had anything to do with the matter at hand. Hell, like most macho guys, he couldn't care less if some guy was gay. It just meant more pussy for the guys who knew what to do with it. Then again, his little voice told him the Monster was somehow insulting him also, and when a man was insulted, he kicked ass. That was yet another macho thing.

Ruby now looked at Beaucroix and scowled. The Monster glared back and bolted from the chair. Pagetti was again faster and jumped in front of him. He grabbed Beaucroix's neck and buried his nose in the Monster's ear again. "We have to obey orders, boss; there's no two ways about that. It's why we're here talking to these two fairies; we need both these pussies in order for Hampstead's plan to ice the altar boy to work," Pagetti reminded him in a whisper. "But if you play along with us, we have a little bonus for you. After we use the two fruits to do the job, I'll cut the balls off this little fairy, and you can watch Jack Ruby eat them. How does that sound?"

Beaucroix's eyes shot from furiously narrow to a glorious, sick epiphany.

"Now smile and pretend it was all a joke." Pagetti released him and returned to his seat.

Beaucroix laughed as he sat down and leaned back in his seat. He reached over and slapped Oswald on the shoulder. Ruby only glared, fuming. "I fooled you!" Beaucroix said with a hearty laugh. "Wasn't my little joke funny? I bet you two thought I was serious. My sister always said I was a natural actor."

Oswald laughed nervously, something that was not lost on Beaucroix, who was taking mental notes. Ruby tried to smile and ease up, but he had been insulted, and he was sure of it, and he would strike back; he knew he would. But he would have to bide his time. Revenge was fantastic, but money was better. Today was about the money.

"Yeah, that was funny. You're a funny bitch!" Ruby fired back.

Pagetti quickly grabbed Beaucroix's arm to restrain him before things turned deadly. But it was unnecessary; amazingly, Beaucroix was calm and totally in control. Ruby frowned, wondering why Pagetti had grabbed Beaucroix.

"Let's return to matters at hand and then to making you men rich!" Beaucroix smiled and spread his arms *à* la Hampstead for emphasis.

That was more like it; Ruby cooled down one hundred degrees. He wanted to hear the offer. Hampstead had given him this job, but he didn't know all the details, although he could guess most of them. Hampstead only had said he must control a risk (he realized this meant Oswald), and Leo Pagetti would give him the specifics. Pagetti had promised him that everything he promised Oswald eventually would go to Jack Ruby. Oswald would kill President Kennedy, and then Ruby would kill Oswald.

"What about the immunity thing?" Oswald asked, because money bought very little when you had to run from place to place.

"You'll be given Israeli citizenship. Mossad will guarantee that no one will look too closely at your past. We'll say you're a nonpracticing Jewish immigrant from New York City; your family hasn't practiced the religion for three generations. With this package, you'll get a fifty-thousand-dollar home on the beach in Tel Aviv. In Israel, fifty thousand dollars buys a really nice home." Pagetti detailed the vaporous plan, something he knew Hampstead never planned to deliver. To Pagetti's memory, this was the third person to whom Hampstead had promised the Tel Aviv home. He had begun to wonder if the house existed at all.

"What about the FBI?" Oswald asked.

"They won't find you. The CIA will ensure that. We will build walls." Pagetti was very convincing.

"Are you planning to buy any pussy with that money, or will you share it with your boyfriend?" Beaucroix indicated the envelope as the monster within the Monster stirred.

"This is how it goes down," Pagetti quickly interjected. Everyone in the CIA knew about Beaucroix's homosexual fixation and how dangerous it was—that is, everyone except William Hampstead. Pagetti had to divert the conversation before Oswald could react to the bait. "We finally got a man in the Secret Service. There are a lot of streets in Dallas, but our man will pick a route right beneath the depository window. Your escape will be uncomplicated, and it'll be a piece of cake. We'll pack the street with so many spectators that it'll be impossible for the police to move freely. The Dallas police have been paid off, and, as arranged, most will be elsewhere and slow to respond. You can crawl back home, and you'll never get caught. You'll have a full day to pack and hit the airport."

Pagetti pointed south and grinned. "You'll fly first to Mexico City." This was a favorite exit/entry point for the CIA and the KGB—America's semisecret back door. "You'll travel under the name of George Harris, a clothing manufacturer."

Jack Ruby now brought in his part of Hampstead's bogus deal. It was an old CIA trick. If two agents detailed separate parts of a deal, it made the deal look real, genuine. The subject always felt that if it took more than one person to put a deal together, it couldn't be a sham. The agency wouldn't waste the time or so much talent.

"Once you're in Mexico, you'll become Joseph Maritz, a widowed Jew. You'll be placed on a flight to Tel Aviv then driven to your new home. Joseph, by the way, is Yoséf in Israel." Ruby played his part perfectly.

Of course, Ruby knew the whole deal was phony. He certainly had been well coached in his performance. Sure, Oswald would kill Kennedy, and sure, it would be easy. Also, as advertised, Oswald would easily escape. But that was it; beyond that, there was no deal. The CIA couldn't risk a slip or a loose end. There would be multiple high-profile funerals in Dallas that week: the president *and* his killer.

Beaucroix was Hampstead's big cannon, and Pagetti also was a big deal. He was liked and needed by both Beaucroix and Hampstead. But Jack Ruby was different because he was replaceable. Jack Ruby was like so many men who are ordered to do evil; they never consider that some-day evil will get around to doing them.

Beaucroix and Pagetti knew everyone was expendable, but they knew they themselves were safe today because they were still needed. Ruby had made the stupid assumption that since he was loyal and competent, he was safe. But he too would be killed, but it would have to take longer, and his death couldn't appear suspicious. There must be no doubt that his was a natural death.

There was little chance that after the end game, Jack Ruby would talk. His prison access would be carefully monitored. There were a great many less pleasant ways to go than a natural death, and, after the arrest of Jack Ruby, he would be secretly interviewed by the Agency and reminded of every one.

"When do I get the rest of the money?" Oswald needed to see more green. Once he did the hit, he knew the CIA would have no incentive to pay him a red cent. He also knew he wouldn't be able to do a thing about it. He was smart enough to realize that no one had ever blackmailed the CIA. What wasn't paid up front might never be paid at all. After the deed was done, it would be a tad too late to negotiate, and it was already too late for JFK.

CHAPTER EIGHT
Hampstead Finds a King

November 14, 1963; 5:00 p.m.
The White House

Agent Big Bob Baker jabbed his left elbow into Tom Kroger's ribs as he motioned with his chin toward the gate. Agent Kroger folded the paper and placed it on the seat between them. Then he turned the key, bringing all eight cylinders to life in the Ford sedan.

By this time, the long nose of the black Cadillac was fully out of the White House gate and on its way down the tree-lined street.

"Ha! Gotcha!" Baker remarked. "Look through the rear window, Kroger. See how his head seems to go through the roof? That's the vice president for sure. Remember, when he doesn't want to be followed, he never wears his Stetson. That's the real clue. If you see the Stetson, you hang close and let him know we're there. No Stetson: Hang well back, and keep a low profile. We want to protect the VP, not decorate his bumper."

Baker knew that most of the time protecting vice presidents was a cakewalk for the Secret Service. That was because vice presidents were mostly the flotsam and jetsam of high politics—good enough to invite to the party but never quite good enough to dance with the hostess. They were the political eunuchs of American politics. They mostly tended to be lapdogs and gofers who were usually grateful for the extra attention and protection afforded by the Secret Service.

This tall, independent Texan, however, was nobody's lapdog. It was a real job to protect this man, thought Baker, especially since they got so little cooperation from him. But LBJ didn't need any man to cover his ass—he was a Texan!

The Ford sailed quietly along the leaf-scattered road with the beautiful fall scenery flashing past as they drove farther from the city. Baker glanced out the windshield, noticing with satisfaction the black Cadillac just rounding a bend. Kroger was a good man and a good driver. Baker stole another glance at the agent, noting that Kroger's eyes were focused through his gold-rimmed glasses at a point three hundred yards ahead. He was lucky to have been assigned with him because Kroger was a good man in a scuffle. He didn't need to see Kroger fight with his hands to tell he had considerable physical prowess. If Kroger's huge, square face and rocklike jaw didn't give him a clue, perhaps his frying-pan-size hands did.

Baker noticed the Cadillac's speed suddenly had increased; he nervously glanced ahead, afraid they may lose the vice president. As the Ford swung around the bend, he spotted the Cadillac a couple of hundred yards ahead. *Good*, thought Baker. The VP had sped up, and Kroger was just compensating.

This was one of the key things about protecting the vice president: To do it well, you had to be a thinker. When you served in the Secret Service, anonymity and invisibility were your greatest assets because you served silently and without fanfare deep within the bowels of a Washington few Americans knew existed. Consequently, you rarely talked to other agents, and when you did, the dialogue was invariably brief and professional. It was said the agents who lasted the longest were the ones no one knew anything about, and that was true.

Political opinions were something you simply didn't have. You observed and protected, but you never commented. If a new man was liked and enormously lucky, one of the old-timers might confide in him the secret for survival in the Secret Service: "Remember, anything you say to an agent will get repeated, and everything that's repeated sooner or later gets written down. Once it's been written down, it becomes a record that someday, somehow, will return to haunt you." When an agent considered the full potential consequence of this to himself, his career, and his family, he learned to say very little and carefully censor even what little he said.

Baker glanced at the odometer. They had traveled sixty-one miles since they'd left the White House gates. This was going to be another long one. In another twenty minutes, he would pick up the phone and update the White House with their status and location. He also would have a message relayed to his wife not to expect him home for dinner. Yawning, Baker leaned back in the seat and searched his pockets for a matchbook. As he reached for the window crank, he was just in time to see the taxicab barreling down the narrow alley that intersected with the oak-lined street.

"Nail it!" agent Baker screamed.

Without asking why, Kroger hammered the gas, sending a trail of white smoke as the V-8 engine roared and spun the tires, which furiously dug for a foothold on the hard, flat street. When Kroger was sure of the path ahead, he rapidly glanced around, searching for the danger. As he looked to the right, a yellow Checker cab manned by an ash-white driver nailed them in the right rear passenger door and sent all 220 pounds of Kroger into Baker's lap. The impact made the Ford spin both forward and sideways until it went tail first over the curb, slamming the driver's door into a massive oak and stopping the now-battered Ford in a cloud of steam and burning transmission fluid.

The cab kept spinning clockwise until it came to a backward stop forty feet behind them with its front passenger wheel severed at the hub and its front end grotesquely twisted. Baker's forehead, just above his right eye, was cut and bleeding badly as he forced open the door and stepped clear of the vehicle. Kroger was unhurt as he crawled across the front seat and emerged through the passenger door. He had been cushioned mainly by his impact into Baker.

"Buddy, are you boys all right?" The slovenly cab driver waddled in an uneven, bowlegged dance toward the Ford. "It was those brakes— dirty, damn, sorry, pitiful, cursed brakes. I keep telling the dispatcher this car's no damn good! I told him to give me a different car, but he doesn't like me much. He says one car is just like another and to take this one or go home. I took this car 'cause I need the money. My old lady goes through cash quicker than a spastic tourist in Mexico goes through toilet paper. Are you boys OK?" the man asked again as he waddled closer to the two agents.

Baker eyed him carefully as Kroger intercepted him and cut off his progress with a badge and an attitude that said, "Stay back," in no uncertain terms.

"Shit!" They had lost the vice president. They were at least seventy miles from the White House, and there was no hope of getting another car for an interception. Still, Baker was the man in charge, and he'd have to be the one to make the call.

As the cabby surveyed the badge, his pudgy eyes widened, and he grinned and stepped forward. "Wow, whoopee!" He lit up all over. "Are you guy's spies? Real James Bond–type secret agents?"

Kroger held up his hand. "Stay back, sir. We're Secret Service." He glanced back to Baker to see if he was still OK, but he was already back in the car and radioing in a report. "Step over to the curb, sir. Are you armed?"

"Gosh, are you guys looking for KGB mice? Can I help? I used to act in high school. I did lots of plays and such. I did some tough-guy rolls; played Humphrey Bogart's role in *Casablanca*." He began his waddle in the direction indicated by Kroger toward an open area on the curb. Then Waddles placed his hand inside his grubby brown leather jacket.

Swiftly Kroger drew his Beretta. "Sir, don't put your hands in your pockets. Are you armed? If you are, it'll be a whole lot better for you to admit it now. If I find a gun when I search you, I promise you'll be sorry."

"I don't own a gun. They scare me. My old lady won't let me even buy one because she says I have a temper. I asked her once what would happen if criminals broke into our house and I didn't have a gun to protect her. She said if criminals broke into the house, then I should lose my temper. She said that would scare them worse than any gun. I got this frightful temper. Sometimes I even scare myself!"

The cabby took a step toward Kroger but changed his mind and timed his halt to the clicking of the Beretta's hammer.

"Say, you guys are CIA and looking for one of them rats."

"They're called moles, not rats, and we don't do that, sir. We're Secret Service, and we protect diplomats, important men. Now, no more questions. Please remove your wallet and drop it to the ground. Then step back two paces, and make sure you do it slowly."

By this time, Baker had finished radioing the report and walked up just as Kroger was checking the cabby's wallet. He looked at the license in Kroger's hand. "What we got, Kroger?"

Kroger handed him the wallet. "Just a cabby who thinks this is Los Angeles, a crazy, dumb-fuck driver. I don't think there's any more to it than that." He looked Baker in the eye. "What did they say?"

Baker gingerly touched the gash on his forehead. "They're sending a car for us. They've got somebody in the area already. They said maybe fifteen minutes."

"What about him?" Kroger motioned over toward Waddles, now grinning on the curb, as he holstered his gun.

"The White House said to use our judgment. We can bring him in for questioning, or if his story checks out, we just turn him over to the cops."

"Wow, the White House!" the voice behind them exclaimed.

Baker jumped as he turned. Waddles was grinning and standing just two steps away. Baker cast an irritated frown at Kroger, who looked embarrassed.

"Sir, I told you to stay on the curb. Go there *now!*" Kroger motioned toward the curb then looked at the man's license. "Mr. Boyle, you don't realize the kind of trouble you're in. This is your last warning."

Kroger turned back to Baker as Mr. Boyle obediently waddled back to the curb, looking downcast and dejected.

"What about an ambulance?" Kroger asked. By now, the trickle of blood down Baker's cheek was fairly a river.

"No reason for them to send one. I didn't tell them anyone was injured," Baker replied.

Just then the police pulled up. As the cops stepped out of the Dodge cruiser, Kroger walked over to present his identification and give them the story. Baker was starting in the same direction when a black Ford furiously skidded to a stop, and both front doors flew open.

"Baker, what's up?" Agent Harris demanded, his hand already inside his overcoat, searching for his revolver as he moved briskly toward Baker.

"It's over. Just some clumsy-fuck cabby," replied Baker as he waved a hand, indicating the revolver wouldn't be needed.

Agent "Denver Dave" Dibble had just left the passenger door and taken a position ten yards behind Harris. "Is that the goof?" Dibble motioned toward the cabby, who now had been joined by a policeman with pen and pad.

"Yeah, that's our big KGB assassin." Baker grinned as they all smiled at the thought of that bowlegged, shuffling moron as a KGB player.

"Hey dick lips!" Dibble shouted at the cabby. "These cops are going to take your license and shove it right up your ass, and they won't be using any Vaseline, either!"

"Shut up, Dave." Harris cautioned. How had this idiot ever gotten into the Secret Service? Good agents never commented; they just did their job quietly and as low key as possible.

Baker grinned as he scratched his chin. "Let's get out of here."

Kroger had finished debriefing the cops and was getting into the front passenger seat at virtually the same moment that Harris entered the driver's-side door and pulled it shut. Just as Baker climbed into the rear seat next to Dibble, he happened, quite by chance, to glance toward the curb where the cabby stood. As their eyes met, a lightning bolt of shock and terror shot through Baker's spine.

Before his eyes, the stupid, slovenly cabby transformed into a cunning vision of pure evil. Baker's lungs dropped past his gut as he found himself staring deep into the deepest, coldest, and cruelest eyes he'd ever seen—a spook's eyes, one of the CIA's so-called deep operatives. This was no cabby. Baker had been fooled, and it hadn't been any accident; it had been CIA all the way, and this man was no small player. He was one of the big guns of the CIA, and, incredibly, Baker feared they planned to kill the vice president.

"Are you OK, Baker? Is something wrong?" Kroger inquired as he noticed his partner suddenly flush white.

Baker knew that whatever game the CIA was up to was certainly completed already. There was no use for him to tell Kroger or the others what really had happened. Baker had failed in his duty to protect the vice president; he only hoped to God that LBJ survived.

"I'm OK," replied Baker as the Ford sped away. But he never looked at Kroger. Evil had stolen his eyes, and it would have his soul. His terrified eyes had been locked onto the gloating eyes of the Monster, and he couldn't pull them away. Long after the Ford had rounded the corner and the cabby was far from sight, he continued to see those hideous eyes.

November 15, 1963; 1:00 a.m.
Aiken, South Carolina

The tall Texan took his seat at the table. He winked as he picked up the wine list from the red-and-white-checkered tablecloth and handed it to the ash-blond waitress who stood beside him. "I'll just have a cold beer, sweetie." He tossed her a generous, easy smile, and she blushed as she looked into those quiet, kind eyes.

"Be right back, handsome." She placed the order pad in her apron pocket as she turned and left to bring LBJ a glass and a bottle.

Lyndon Baines Johnson had been a politician for a long time, and, having served a lot of that time in Washington, he had long been part and privy to the real workings of the US government. Several days earlier, he had seen the mistake the president had made. It certainly had been made plain enough for the autocratic eyes of Hampstead to see. LBJ never could make such a mistake. He knew from experience how cruel politics could be.

The president was a good man—too good a man, LBJ thought—to realize the coldness of politics and the unsavory sacrifices a man sometimes had to make.

The president had taken great pains to choose a leadership for the CIA that was both competent and visionary, but he was unwilling to believe in the true source of power. He had too much faith in America.

The CIA, just like the machine in Washington, wasn't something you could appoint or elect. It was just there, an indecipherable thing that had created and fed itself over a period of many, many years. Often an elected president found out the uselessness of fighting the political machine in Washington; it often was an incredible accomplishment just to obtain a compromise. Far, far fewer presidents had threatened the machine that was the CIA.

President Kennedy had appointed Hanson Gaines as director of the CIA. But the director wasn't the true power; he was only the figure-head—just as the president isn't the absolute ruler of the US government; he's just its public leader. The president can say, "I will end corruption in American politics" and fully intend to do so, but if the machine says, "No," that will necessarily be the end of it. Ultimately, this is why great presidents don't always accomplish great things.

Technically, Hampstead, as director of European operations, was three or four rungs down on the official CIA ladder. But it made sense that he was the real head of the agency. The center of American intelligence was the Cold War, and the center of the Cold War was Europe. The director of the CIA could come and go according to the wit and whim of politics. But the Cold War and Hampstead would be there for many years. Hampstead and his KGB counterpart, Slava Kurnov, kept the Cold War cold, and the status quo prevented the devastating heat of war.

The waitress brought the beer and placed it next to the thin, top-heavy glass. *A Miller beer*, LBJ mused. If this had been Texas, it would've been a Lone Star beer poured into a mug so heavy that, even empty, it would've constituted a lethal weapon.

Another smile and a wink from the vice president made the waitress blush and smile shyly as she stepped lightly over to greet two more men who had entered the little diner.

"Good evening, sir." Without an invitation or offering their hands in greeting, Hampstead and the other man rudely ignored the waitress. Brushing past her, they helped themselves to seats at the vice president's table.

Hampstead surveyed the room cautiously, marking the position of the two men he'd planted earlier at a table by the door. He didn't like the look of the heavyset man drinking alone near the kitchen entrance. He pulled his earlobe and inclined his chin slightly. One of the men at the front table nodded. The big man would be checked out.

"Good evening, gentlemen," the Texan drawled. "My friends call me LBJ. Could I order you a beer?"

It was a little late to offer a beer to the other man. He already had arrogantly helped himself to LBJ's. This bit of arrogance didn't bother the vice president in the least. As a Texan, he was used to people who boldly strutted their stuff, trying to impress him by showing him who the top dog was. Johnson was a top-notch Texas politician, and part and parcel of being a good politician in Texas was getting the most out of any deal. If you were any good, you forgot your feelings and just looked at the bottom line. Besides, there was a whole lot of beer in America.

"Darling…" LBJ snagged the passing waitress with his easy smile. "Could you kindly bring us all some fresh beers?" She smiled and blushed. "Oh, and you'd better bring two for me. My thirst seems to be about double today."

Bingo—the VP nailed him, thought Hampstead. He looked as the man scowled after LBJ's more-than-successful attempt at humor.

"Mr. Vice President…" Hampstead got down to business, and he was fishing for a king. "What did you think of our meeting with the president?" He carefully gauged LBJ; it was vital that he read him fully.

"I think, Mr. Hampstead that decisions might have been made without fully weighing the facts or consequences. I also feel insufficient weight was given to the opinions of those who probably know more about the matter than anyone else." LBJ laid on the rich Southern but-ter—smooth, thick, and heavy.

Hampstead smiled. If his intelligence was correct, this could be his candidate. He glanced at the bar and noticed with irritation that the huge man had left—disappeared—and not through any door either. Hampstead caught the eye of the man he'd sent to check him out and motioned toward the bar. Confused, the agent looked around the room and shrugged. Hampstead would have to move on, but this was something he didn't like to see—an agent who couldn't follow instructions and, much worse, an agent who didn't watch everything around him.

With a jolt, Hampstead noticed something unusual about the counter: the big man had placed nine dimes upon it. Arranged into a perfect arrow, they pointed directly at William Hampstead. He frowned at the implied threat, but the interview would proceed; it was just too damn important.

LBJ ignored the man who had swiped his beer. By now it was obvious Hampstead never meant to introduce them. The vice president knew Kennedy had made a terrible mistake, but he also knew Kennedy had too much faith in his convictions to turn back. Whatever Hampstead planned to do, nothing could stop it. LBJ could only try to do what was best for the American people; the president could not be saved.

LBJ started to reach for his bottle of beer. Then he stopped and indicated the beer to Hampstead's thirsty companion, who narrowed his eyes and growled under his breath. With a shrug, the Texan lifted the bottle and took a deep, foamy swallow.

The agent behind Hampstead covered his face to hide a snicker. He knew the man's aim was to scare Johnson, but LBJ was a Texan and, as such, was a hard man to scare. The agent admired how LBJ was putting this ass in his place. He admired the vice president and hated the asshole Hampstead had brought to this meeting, especially because he knew who and what the asshole was and why he had been invited here tonight.

"Then you see my concerns, Mr. Vice President." The director of European operations leaned back in his chair, taking his beer with him. He took a frothy swallow as he surveyed the man, reading every muscle in his face and weighing every nuance in his answer.

LBJ continued, "Mr. Hampstead, personally I feel we should've delayed any action on the matter until after the next election. Then, in a calmer light, we could have weighed the various attributes of all the affected issues." Yup, there was a lot of horseshit in Texas, and Lyndon Baines Johnson felt free to dump a hefty pile of it right here.

Hampstead beamed. This was a politician's way of brushing something under the carpet.

"You OK, son? Can I order you another beer?" The Texan turned to Hampstead's companion, who scowled and looked away.

Hampstead cast his line as he continued to fish. "Communism is the greatest single threat to our way of life, because communism has sworn it will destroy every noncommunist government on earth."

Hampstead paused as he searched LBJ's face for some sort of reaction, but he read only earnest attention. He glanced at the other man, who continued to scowl at what he thought was LBJ's phony compliance. LBJ caught his grimace and passed him his half-consumed Miller to supplement his own.

Hampstead almost laughed at LBJ's ability to capture the stage and outwit the irritated man. He also wondered whether LBJ would be so brave if he knew who this man was and what his purpose really was.

"I don't think any price—any price at all, be it blood or dollars—would be too high a price to pay to once and for all eliminate communism as a threat to our way of life. Now what I need to know, Mr. Vice President, is your opinion on this situation, and it is a very serious situation. I need you on the same page." Hampstead paused as he waited for the reply; LBJ wouldn't disappoint him.

"Well, I would be in agreement except for one matter." As LBJ said this, Hampstead's eyes narrowed; LBJ knew history hinged on how he worded this. "Could we properly manage and control the political repercussions and consequences that might follow, and could you guarantee me that no leaks would occur or that any leaks that did occur would be mitigated before they got to the national press?" This was a perfectly politically correct answer that pleased Hampstead greatly; it expressed both faith and confidence in the CIA.

Jack Ruby scowled because he had hoped this conversation would put LBJ deep in the ground. But LBJ wasn't ready for the undertaker. No matter what happened today, he still had things to do—things for America.

Everything had gone OK so far, thought Hampstead. Now everything that followed depended on how the final question was answered, the question that necessitated Hampstead's companion. If the question were answered to Hampstead's satisfaction, the night's work would be over, and it would be time to contact Lee Harvey Oswald.

If the vice president didn't provide the correct answer, Jack Ruby would have one more job to do—a job he both enjoyed and excelled at.

"Mr. Vice President?" Hampstead became very serious and formal. "Which is more important, the president or the office of the president?" He leaned back as he waited for the answer.

"The office," Johnson fired back without a hint of pause.

Hampstead slapped both knees with his hands and rose to leave; he was fully satisfied.

Jack Ruby, on the other hand, was disappointed. Hampstead had promised him the scent of blood, and all he'd gotten from Johnson was contempt and a touch of good ol' Texas humility. Jack Ruby wasn't a humble man, and tonight he wasn't a happy man.

Hampstead, however, was ecstatic as he advanced toward the door, because he had his man, and the United States would have a new president. William Hampstead had found a king.

November 17, 1963
Moscow, USSR

"There he is." Agent Georgi Gregor motioned to the huge man energetically shoveling stroganoff into his cavernous mouth. The five KGB agents deftly strolled across the dining room of the Metropol Hotel toward their target while the surprised foreigners looked on. The locals wisely buried their faces in their noontime repast, fully knowing anything they might see could jeopardize their future freedom. It was better to see nothing and remember even less.

"You will come with us!" demanded KGB Captain Sergei Makinov, the first to reach the fat man's food-laden art deco table. The fat man looked up, smiled, and returned to his noisy chewing.

"Sir, you are going to have to come with me!" Makinov slammed his fist on the table, sending red wine splashing from the finely cut crystal glass.

The big man put down his fork and, casually unfolding his napkin, dabbed a bit of sauce off the side of his face. Then he smiled politely at the man.

"No!" the Shadow curtly replied as he picked up his spoon and attacked with gusto his sugary, teasing dessert. He chose to ignore the Russian as he diverted his full attention to far tastier matters.

Frustrated and beaten back by a roomful of surprised, covert Russian glances, Captain Makinov retreated to the lobby to use the bell captain's phone.

Slava Kurnov always took joy in reading between the lines, and he had a special talent for it. Sitting in his office, the spymaster poured another cup of tea from a sterling silver samovar as he read the stolen French letters before him. The Belgian prime minister certainly had eloquence and an appealing way with words. Kurnov grinned; the prime minister's words had probably been wasted on the fourteen-year-old girl he was trying to seduce in these purloined letters.

It absolutely astounded Kurnov how many famous or powerful men were perverts or child molesters. His sharp mind went into mental calisthenics. Perhaps these aberrations were latent in all of us. Did wealth and power simply make these things bubble to the surface?

Nonsense! Kurnov answered his own internal dialogue. He had no such aberrations, and neither did his father, who also was a powerful man.

The ringing phone ended his internal session in abnormal psychology. He placed the letter back in the stack as he answered the phone's ringing summons.

"Yes?" he inquired into the disinterested receiver.

"Sir, this is Captain Makinov. I have found him in a hotel, having lunch."

Kurnov frowned; it always aggravated him when junior men couldn't follow instructions.

"Thank you, comrade, for humoring me. I must be getting old and senile because I seem remember telling you to bring him here, when obviously I merely indicated I wanted you to watch him have lunch. Did he enjoy the aperitif?"

Silence greeted him on the other end of the phone.

"Well?"

Still silence.

"Well?" Kurnov impatiently inquired again.

"Sir, I don't know what you want me to say." Captain Makinov was nervous and a little afraid because he never had dealt directly with a legend like Slava Kurnov before.

"What I don't expect from you, a professional of the KGB, is a stupid soliloquy," Kurnov barked. "I expect you to bring the American here. I want him sitting in my office, answering my questions. What I certainly don't expect is for a professional in the KGB to call me and waste my time by telling me he is watching someone have lunch. I am familiar with lunch. However, I am not familiar with what that man knows and why he is in Moscow. That, comrade, is precisely the reason I sent you to fetch him to me."

After Kurnov hung up, Makinov returned to the dining room. He found the fat man had finished dessert and had ordered anew and was happily attacking a fresh plate of beef.

"Sir, I need to see your passport immediately." Makinov extended his hand to indicate he was ready to accept it.

"No," the fat man replied calmly as he assaulted the pan-browned beef with a ladle of rich, savory gravy.

Makinov returned to the lobby and again picked up the phone. This man just would not be arrested.

Kurnov answered the phone. "Yes?"

"Makinov here."

"This must be a bad connection, as I must have misunderstood what you just said. I distinctly thought I heard you say, 'Makinov here,' when obviously the problem is Makinov is *there*. You see, I want you here, not there. I want to you in my office, with the American answering my questions, within fifteen minutes. Is that clear?"

Kurnov waited but was greeted by an irritating silence.

"Has this phone gone dead, or am I speaking to an idiot?"

"This is Makinov here." That was all the poor man could think to say.

"Good, I had forgotten to whom I was speaking. Thank you for reminding me," Kurnov offered. "Comrade Makinov, if the American isn't sitting in front of me in fifteen minutes, I shall have you on a train to Siberia in forty-five. Is that quite clear enough, Captain? Am I getting through to you, you insipid, lead-brained idiot?" Kurnov delivered his arctic ultimatum with precision.

"Then I should save you the cost of a train ticket. It must be very expensive to send someone to Siberia this time of year, and besides, the weather is so lovely right here!"

Kurnov fairly bolted. Sitting in front of his desk was one of the largest men he'd ever seen.

"Hold it a moment, Captain." Kurnov covered the receiver with his hand. It was impossible that this could be the same man Makinov had cornered in the Metropolitan Hotel two kilometers away. It also was impossible for him to have gotten into KGB headquarters without a personal pass from Kurnov himself.

Kurnov glanced at his door; it was shut securely. His door always squeaked badly when it opened, and he liked it that way, but today, he had heard nothing. Even so, he was the best the Soviets ever had; he would show no surprise.

"Welcome to the KGB. I am Slava Kurnov. But you knew that, or else you wouldn't be here." The spymaster smiled and leaned back in his chair. "I take it you're the man they call the Shadow. How did you get in here?"

"Through the door," replied the big man. "I've always found them useful in some small fashion. I take it you would like my passport?"

The spymaster lifted an eyebrow. "Why? Surely it has someone else's name on it."

"Slava Kurnov, you wound me deeply. I assure you the name on the passport is mine, or at least one of them."

"Nevertheless, I will call you the Shadow, and you may call me your host."

"Truly a gracious host you are." The Shadow helped himself to a few crackers from a fine ceramic jar and opened the tin of caviar on the spymaster's desk. "Do you have any vodka?" Caviar always made the big man thirsty. Kurnov indicated the sideboard, and the Shadow heaved himself up, walked over to it, and picked up the bottle and two large glasses.

"Make yourself comfortable, as you may be here for some time. Will you excuse me for a moment?" Kurnov smiled and indicated the receiver in his hand.

"Certainly, but I promise you, Kurnov, I will be your guest no longer than I choose." The Shadow grinned as he brought the vodka bottle, the glasses, and a fresh tin of caviar back from the sideboard and returned to the chair in front of Kurnov's desk.

"Spoken like a true spy. I take it that's what you are?" Kurnov looked beneath the man's fleshy brows and into his eyes. He read a deep intelligence and an even deeper secret. "I see you enjoy my caviar. I have it sent fresh from Odessa every Monday, and you are most welcome to all of it." Kurnov reached for the bottle of vodka and poured himself a brimming glass.

The Shadow smiled. "I consider caviar an integral part of my diet."

"Diet?" Kurnov tossed back his drink and reached for the bottle and a refill.

"Yes, my see-food diet. I see food, and I eat it." The big man grinned and rubbed his massive belly.

"Very funny. I like that. I will have to use that on my wife the next time she accuses me of making a pig of myself when we have a guest for dinner. You are indeed a clever spy!"

"I am not a spy, Kurnov. Call me a spy hunter." The caviar was fantastic; he smacked his lips as he finished the second tin.

"Then you have hit the jackpot, my friend. This is the headquarters of the KGB." Kurnov lowered his voice, leaned forward, winked, and whispered in a conspiratorial fashion, "This place is crawling with spies!"

The big man grinned.

"Will you give me a moment?" Kurnov requested.

"Of course. After all, I did show up uninvited."

"Oh, you most certainly were not uninvited. Today you are my most honored guest!" Kurnov was a master of his profession. Even though his perimeter had been breached, he knew how to take back the leading role in the play. He placed the receiver back to his ear. "Makinov, you spastic idiot, are you still there?" he asked casually.

"Makinov here," the captain replied.

"Thank you for reminding me. I seem to have forgotten your name again. I have just received more information about the man you have cornered in the hotel. He is very dangerous. He is the greatest threat to the security of the Soviet Union, and he is to be arrested immediately." Kurnov smiled across his desk at the fat man, who was beaming broadly. He loved a good joke and knew he was going to like doing business with this man.

"Makinov, I want that man sitting in this chair in front of my desk in fifteen minutes. It is that important. If you fail, I will have you shot first thing in the morning. Is that clear?"

"Makinov here. Damn!" The poor man was so intimidated by Kurnov that he couldn't command his wits.

"Makinov, you insipid idiot! Are you paying attention to this conversation, or am I wasting my time by trying to teach a pregnant pig to fly?" Kurnov grinned and winked at the fat man; Kurnov was having fun!

"Makinov here. Damn!" the poor captain repeated.

"Oh, good. Thank you for not leaving there and coming here like I ordered you." Kurnov expertly placed a rising anger into his request. "Are you going to bring that American to me immediately, or will I have to assemble a firing squad?"

"Yes, sir. My men have just now taken him into custody. We will be there shortly. You can rely on me!" Makinov replied with gravity, bluffing. He had no way of knowing the fat man was sitting in Kurnov's office, listening to the whole conversation.

Kurnov no longer ordered assassinations. Those days had died out with Stalin—mostly. But he knew the young man had heard rumors, just as Kurnov had when he was a young spy.

"Good!" Kurnov fought a back a chuckle and a grin. "If you don't show up here within fifteen minutes with a body, I will send someone to get yours!"

"Sir, you can rely on me. You will have your body. I guarantee it!"

"Good. I know I will!" Kurnov winked at the fat man again. He gently placed the phone in its cradle and smiled at the big man, who also was grinning broadly. Kurnov had grabbed the stage—he was truly top dog, and the big man knew it—but he didn't care because it didn't matter. The only thing that mattered was the mission—the mission and the game.

Kurnov leaned back in his chair and folded his hands together. "I know of a restaurant not far from here that serves superb French cuisine, and the wine list is out of this world. You will be my guest for an excellent dinner! But first, let's get down to business. What can I do for you?"

CHAPTER NINE
The King Is Dead, Long Live the King

November 23, 1963
Cartagena, Spain

Founded by Hasdrubal Barca, an uncle of the great Carthaginian General Hannibal Barca, more than twenty centuries ago, Cartagena was truly the most beautiful of the little-known jewels of the Mediterranean. The city was one of the treasures of Europe, with its tile-capped homes known for their classic, grand Spanish elegance. Its mild climate and spotless beaches drew vacationers from around the world. Today its peace and tranquility would stand in dark contrast to the ruthless murder Emile Beaucroix had meticulously and flawlessly planned.

The true beauty of genius lay in appreciating the brilliant machinations of a carefully wrought plan. In this Emile Beaucroix stood alone, unimpeachable. Fully he was the man he felt he must be to appreciate his own genius. He must constantly exceed himself in order to equal himself. Surely history has taught you this about all evil men: evil as we know it is never truly satisfied unless it can delight in the realized perfections of its plan.

With the blood still fresh in Dallas, Beaucroix had very little time to act. Although Hampstead was a loyal soldier, the killing of the president lay heavily on his mind. Beaucroix knew that with the director faltering, he needed to position himself quickly to succeed Hampstead as director of European operations.

If Max George were dead, Beaucroix would have the best chance for the job. Hogan was a real possibility, but Beaucroix knew Hogan could be made to quietly disappear. Max George was different. If he were made European director, Beaucroix never could get to him. Max George was too damn good.

After pulling a chair to the window, Beaucroix popped the cork in the tall bottle of Polish vodka as he positioned himself front row center to today's planned misadventure. Today his fat lady would sing.

He uncased his Canon binoculars and trained them on the café veranda three hundred meters down the hill and only sixty meters from the seductive blue Mediterranean waters. Briefly scanning the noonday crowd, he saw that Max George wasn't early, but he wasn't expected to be. After swinging his binoculars across the street and up four floors, he fixed them on the roof of the merchant building. A slow, careful scan revealed the muzzle and wooden forestock of an English Mark III Enfield rifle. Smiling, Beaucroix grunted his satisfaction. Behind that rifle lay a four-hundred-dollar investment he had made concerning the future of one Max George. Impatiently, Beaucroix glanced at his watch. In eighteen minutes, he would meet Max George in the café below.

The happy noonday light danced playfully across the busy shoreline, gently kissing the waterfront and parboiling the pale British tourists lying prone on the warm sand. The Monster watched with interest as Max George strolled casually onto the flagstone patio from the blind beach side of Café Carthaginian. This would give Max the longest, clearest approach possible to the table where Emile Beaucroix now sat. When one was approaching a dangerous man, it was best to give oneself the longest possible reaction time as well as the clearest field of fire.

Leering at Max, Beaucroix twisted his evil grin and softly laughed him to the table. "Sit, George. That's what chairs are for." Beaucroix indicated the chair across from him, knowing full well that Max would take one of the others.

Max, however, sat in the chair indicated, pushing it well back to give himself the most mobility. Clearly he didn't trust the Monster. Beaucroix smirked because George thought himself so clever. *We'll soon see who the clever one is*, he thought.

Max noticed the three shots of vodka standing in formation before his host. "More games, Emily?" he queried, indicating the three brimming glasses.

Beaucroix snarled; under any other circumstances, he would have drawn his pistol and fired instantly, blew the top of the bastard's head off. But Max George was no piker; he was a dangerous man, one whom even the best assassins in the world had found too difficult to kill. Beaucroix smiled, and instead of getting furious, he slapped the insult quickly aside. There would be a lot of time for this very clever cat to play with his mouse.

"Now, George," his host began, "this is a business meeting, and we have no time for frivolity. Have a drink, and we'll get started."

"Pardon me, Emily. I should be better behaved in the presence of a lady!" Max never liked to see Beaucroix at ease; he needed him off balance.

Beaucroix glared at him with suppressed rage. "Watch it! You'd better be careful, George. Mind your p's and q's if you want to live through this meeting."

"What do you mean by p's and q's?" Max parroted. "You mean as in perverts and queers? I thought we were discussing me, and not you." Max winked and mouthed a kiss.

"Watch it, sissy. I could have you killed!" Beaucroix was dangerously close to boiling, which was precisely where Max needed him to be.

"That's impossible," Max replied, fully serious.

"What do you mean, asshole? It's impossible to kill you?" Beaucroix growled.

"You're awake!" Max stated the simple truth because he was too smart to ever give the Monster an advantage.

"What does that have to do with anything, shit face?" The furious Beaucroix added a scowl to his growl.

"Because the only way a psychotic hack like you could kill a man like me is in his dreams." Grinning broadly, Max reached for the third vodka glass in front of Beaucroix, only to stay his reach as the Monster's forearm came crashing down, walling in all three glasses.

"Not these," the angry host protested. "These drinks are *mine*. Order your own, shithead!"

With this pronouncement, Max captured the eyes of a waiter and snapped his fingers. The slender server instantly appeared before him. Max was fast; even before the Spaniard could begin, Max interrupted his protocol.

"I'll have three of those," he firmly declared, indicating the platoon of potato spirits arrayed before his host.

The waiter looked surprised. He glanced first at Beaucroix and then at Max. Puzzled, he suddenly realized these silly fools must both be Americans. When it came to Americans in Europe, all waiters knew that weird behavior and bizarre requests were more the norm than the exception. He floated quickly away to fulfill Max's order.

Beaucroix and Max sat quietly, neither one offering nor soliciting conversation. After two minutes, the slender Spaniard returned, smiling broadly. The Americans might be a whole lot weirder that the English, but they tipped a whole lot better.

"That will be all," Beaucroix curtly informed the waiter as he unloaded Max's three spirit glasses from the tray to the round table. As the waiter opened his mouth to speak, Max waved him off, expertly tossing two large gold coins onto the moving tray.

Astoundingly well tipped but dejected, the waiter skulked off. He might as well be dumb, he thought. He had just greeted the men, taken an order, and filled that order—all without saying one word.

Beaucroix smiled. "Now we come down to business, asshole."

Max sat nonchalantly, his expression vague and unconcerned. He would give the Monster no pleasure.

Beaucroix positively beamed as he began. "You are to stay away from Bopolu. I will be handling all security there from today forward. You can check with Hampstead if you like."

Ho-hum, thought Max, who had expected this. Why else would Hampstead want them to meet? He looked at Beaucroix's untouched drinks and then carefully lined up his own three tipsy soldiers, making certain they were arrayed for battle.

Beaucroix was clearly a madman, and, like all madmen, he had a monstrous ego. Max guessed correctly that those three glasses were part of some twisted game. What Beaucroix didn't know was that Max intended to break the house.

"Furthermore, you are prohibited from having any contact with Robert Hogan, by any means or for any reason. Hampstead agrees with me on this. We can't afford to lose two great operators in one fell swoop. For security reasons, you two are forbidden to meet anytime or anyplace. Again, you may check with Hampstead on this." Beaucroix paused for effect.

Max visibly paled, which wasn't lost on Beaucroix. If the Monster had smiled any wider, the top of his head would've fallen off.

"Now we begin. Here are your new orders from Hampstead. Contact with anyone from Bopolu by nonessential persons provides an unacceptable security risk. All violators will be terminated. Again, you may check with Hampstead if you like. I don't think he likes you much, though. It's too bad. I know you and Hogan are close. But this is strictly a security issue." Beaucroix paused, fighting hard to restrain a smile and a chuckle at his own forthcoming wit.

"To show you I'm not a bad fellow and there are no hard feelings, I've bought you a gift." Beaucroix raised his right hand and snapped his fingers. A young boy entered the patio with a plump sheep decorated with a pink ribbon. "I named her Hogan." Beaucroix shook as he restrained his laughter. "Perhaps you could teach her to bleat, 'Fuck me harder, harder, Maxie!'" As the Monster finished, he lost it, holding his belly with both hands and bursting into uncontrollable laughter.

Max stood to leave. "Thanks for the update, Emily!" Max had recovered his cool, and he *would* check with Hampstead.

"Sit down!" Beaucroix roared, and slammed his fist on the table, causing all six glasses to splash a few vodka puddles upon the white tablecloth. "This meeting is far from over!" the Monster briskly waved the boy and the sheep away.

Max yawned, sat down, and propped his boots on the table. He scratched his ear as he waited for the cat to pounce.

"And now for the good news you've been waiting for!" Beaucroix was in rare form. "Your commie-kissing faggot president is dead! Hampstead ordered his brains blown out." The Monster grinned as he stared into Max's steady, deep gaze.

Max was frozen. Could the CIA really have whacked its own president? Max knew Hampstead could order such a thing. But how could he expect to get away with it? If this was true, Hampstead must have had considerable help from some very high places.

"Why would Hampstead have the president killed?" Max was weighing whether there was any advantage Beaucroix could gain from authoring such a fable.

"I'll humor you this time, George, and I'll take this bit of time to educate you, since pussies like you know little of the workings of real men. There's no room in this world for communism, not even half a square centimeter! Hampstead knows this, and I know this, and before the Cuban missile crisis, we believed JFK knew this also. But after the missile crisis, JFK went soft. Secretly he contacted the leadership of the Soviet Union on several occasions to discuss a world in which communism and capitalism could coexist. He held several covert meetings with his advisors and a small, select group of senators to discuss this unacceptable plan. Fortunately, Hampstead had the White House bugged."

"Beaucroix, if any part of this is true, you and Hampstead will hang for it!" Max pointed his finger at the Monster's forehead and lifted his thumb to mimic pulling back a pistol hammer.

"I don't think so," Beaucroix replied smoothly. "You see, Hampstead and I had a meeting with an even larger group of senators. They were all in agreement that something had to be done. They approved the termination and even agreed on a replacement."

"Beaucroix, you're an idiot. Killing President Kennedy will guarantee an investigation, and neither you nor Hampstead will escape its wrath."

"That is correct, George! Well, at least the investigation part." Beaucroix raised a finger for emphasis. "That investigation already has begun and is chaired and seated by the very senators who approved this necessary, and expedient, political adjustment." He grinned widely.

"It also appears Hampstead isn't tough enough for his job. He unfortunately seems to have a conscience—a problem I certainly don't share."

No kidding, thought Max. In Emile Beaucroix there was truly no conscience, or integrity, or humanity. With so much ego and evil in him, there was little room for anything else.

"With Hampstead leaving, I'll be the logical choice to replace him, which will make me your boss. And when that happens, you'll be finished. Here are your first orders from your future boss." Beaucroix grinned again as he reached for the first glass.

"One: As mentioned, you are forbidden from having any further contact with Bopolu or Robert Hogan." Beaucroix downed the first shot of spirits, slammed the empty glass hard on the table, and reached for the second glass.

"Two: Your commie-kissing president is dead, and I'll soon be your superior." Beaucroix downed the second glass, turned it upside down, slammed it on the table, and then reached for the final glass, the glass that would end this meeting and the life of Maxwell George.

"Are you finished?" Max said, pretending he wasn't at all concerned.

"Yes, almost." The Monster lifted his third glass high in a salute to his own perfected genius.

"Three: Say good-bye, George!" Beaucroix grinned again as he downed the third glass of vodka and slammed the empty glass on the table.

Max hadn't risen; he hadn't even moved. He just sat there grinning. "Curious?" he observed. "What's that man doing on that roof? It's an odd place to pull down one's pants. He has to be British. No, I guess he isn't British. I don't see any whips or paddles."

Beaucroix didn't turn; he didn't care that Max had seen the shooter. He didn't know what silliness Max was up to, and he didn't really care.

"God, Beaucroix. That's disgusting. I thought California had all the perverts. Is that his wanker he's pulling out? Is he really going to take a piss up there? Damn, why doesn't someone call a cop and have him arrested?"

Beaucroix, half wondering why his shooter hadn't fired and half wondering what Max was talking about, turned just in time to see his shooter tossed screaming from the roof by two very large men.

"Damn, that was a really nasty fall," Max coolly replied as he raised his first glass to salute, then downed the contents and slammed his glass hard upon one of Beaucroix's glasses, shattering it but leaving his intact.

"If any *accidents* happen to Robert Hogan, I'll send your smelly ass to hell, Beaucroix, because it would give me great pleasure!" Max's glare had gained such a cold intensity that for the first time in his life, Emile Beaucroix, the world's most vicious killer, felt a twinge of terror traverse his spine.

Max gave the Monster a moment to soak that in and then tossed back the second glass and sent it crashing down, shattering Beaucroix's second glass while remaining unbroken itself.

"Steer a wide path around me, Beaucroix. I don't like you much. The fact that you live and breathe is really starting to bother me, piss me off. Avoid me, Beaucroix. Avoid me like the plague, and there will be a microscopic possibility you may stay alive!" Max drove daggers of ice deep into the spine of the Monster.

Beaucroix was rapidly losing his advantage and needed to quickly regain his domination, because evil always must dominate. "You don't scare me, fairy," he began.

Max stood up. "Beaucroix, everyone is a fairy to you. Let me tell you a secret about people who are always worried about fairies: These kinds of people are cursed. They're forever hounded by a secret order of fags. These fags follow them wherever they go, interfere with every thought and action, and defeat their every plan. But if you're very cunning and clever, you can catch them. All you have to do is carefully, quietly, and with great stealth sneak up on a mirror, and then you'll catch the real queer! The one you're really trying to escape. Because the one you see in the mirror is really the one you need to kill.

"Real men—unlike you, Beaucroix—aren't bothered by homosexuals. It just means more pussy for the rest of us. Closeted homosexuals like you, on the other hand—"

Beaucroix flushed red with rage. "Fuck you, faggot!"

"I have just one more thing to say to you, Beaucroix." The coldness emanated in waves from Max. "I don't mean to scare your closet-hiding ass—I mean to kill you!"

With this, Max raised his left hand. Uncertain from which direction the danger would come, Beaucroix was instantly alert to all his surroundings. He turned partly toward the street as frantic honking grabbed his attention.

The driver of a dirty, much-abused 1948 Studebaker tow truck waved happily at his generous new friend, Max George. He continued to honk wildly as he rattled his tired, dented truck past the Carthaginian Café. He was honking because he was towing Beaucroix's rental car—a car he had adorned with that man's baggage on various points around its now bullet-riddled corpse. The car was completely covered with the slogan "Liquid Lips Beaucroix, the Cockateer" as well as a very boldly written "Free Oral Sex for the Homeless!" in English and Spanish upon every spot the phrases would fit.

Tourists and townspeople alike were laughing hysterically at the bullet-pocked but interestingly annotated car traveling behind the tow truck, nudging one another and pointing as it rattled noisily through town on its circular way back to Beaucroix's hotel.

Max smiled with delight. "You'll never replace Hampstead. You're just not tough enough." With this, Max raised his third glass of vodka, tossed it down his throat, and placed it softly on the table. "Have a nice walk home, Emily!" Max smiled as he stood and casually strolled back to the beach.

Beaucroix would be killed; at least after today, he would know for certain that Max would try. But Max would wait; he'd toy with the Monster and make him guess where and when the final hammer would fall. With today's business now concluded, Max George, the toughest man in the CIA, quietly walked away.

November 27, 1963
Tunis, Tunisia

"Maxie, what do you enjoy most about making love?" she asked as she rested in his strong arms.

"Not being called Maxie afterward." He gently petted her silken hair.

"OK, Maxwell George, what do you enjoy most about sex?" Her hand journeyed across his flat abdomen.

"Sex? What is that?" He scratched his head and regarded the ceiling in dumbfounded amazement.

"Now you're being mean. You're making fun of me." She looked hurt.

"What do I like best about it?" He pondered the question. "What I enjoy best comes later."

"What!" Certain she was being set up for a joke, she made a fist and playfully sent a blow to his belly.

"Ouch! Please don't hurt the baby!" Max doubled over and feigned agony.

"Now you're being mean again." She snuggled closer into his right side.

"What I like most isn't the making of love," he began. "It's the perfection of love. The day before you make love, you have only lust. The day you're making love, you have only pleasure. The day after making love, you have only gratitude. But a few days after you make love, the lust has passed; the pleasure is only a memory; and gratitude becomes a debt already paid. That means gratitude, lust, and pleasure are gone. What remains can only be love, and that is the perfection of love.

"That's what makes any relationship real. It makes what could have been simple lust an experience worth having. That's why I look forward to the future—because I look forward to the perfection of love!" He gathered her tighter in his arms, pulling her closer.

"Do you love me?" She searched his eyes, hoping to breach them and enter his soul.

He grabbed her firm breasts and, like Magellan, circumnavigated the dual globes as the khaki of his trousers strained against his passion.

"Did you hear me?" she asked him, grabbing his hands and forcing them deeper into her breasts.

"Give me some time. You're very beautiful, and I have a lot of ground to cover here." He grabbed her love handles, and, leaning down, stuck his tongue into her navel.

"Do you love me?" she pressed.

"I love your breasts. I love kissing your hungry, full lips; and I'm crazy about your tight, luscious ass."

"Are you ignoring my question? Do you love *me*?" She slapped the side of his head.

"Ouch! My tongue was busy. I couldn't talk just then." Max held his head and pretended to wince in pain.

"Do you love me?" she repeated.

"Check with my secretary in about two days," Max countered, prompting her to push herself away.

"How dare you? Do you tell *everyone* about us?" she jokingly protested.

"I don't tell Mrs. Max George anything. She reads it in the *London Times*. That's where I publish all my sordid affairs. 'Publish or perish,' I always say. You wouldn't want my sex life to perish, would you?" Max grinned.

"Are you really married, Max? Are you hiding a wife in, say, Lisbon? I don't trust you because you're too good to be true," she said playfully as she tugged his earlobe.

"I'm not hiding a wife anywhere! She sits on the front veranda in Lisbon and waves at everyone who passes by. She even waves at my other wives when they pass by and invites them in for tea."

"You're making fun of me again. You're being so mean to me!" she said with a touch of hurt and then playfully socked him in the belly again.

"Ouch! Be careful! You might hurt the baby!" he teased.

"Now you're definitely making fun of me again!" she replied, pushing him away and climbing out of bed.

"I never could make fun of you. I find it more pleasant to make fun *with* you." He grabbed her arm, swung her around, and gave her a firm slap on the buttocks. "Now turn off the light and bring your luscious ass back into this bed!"

"I think I have a headache!" she said, toying with him.

"Now you're just being naughty. You need it, and you want it every bit as bad as I do." Max grinned. He caught her eyes looking down at the massive bulge straining against his khakis, begging to be set free.

"Whoops. What's going on down there?" Max feigned surprise at the bulge in his pants.

She couldn't take her eyes off that bulge. "What would you do if I were naughty, really naughty?" she addressed the bulge.

"I would spank you twice!" Max smiled and raised the flat of his hand to punctuate his point.

"Twice?" she asked as she directed her eyes to his.

"If you were naughty," he said with a smile, "I would spank you until you were good!"

"You said twice." She felt she had missed something here.

Max wagged his finger. "You didn't let me finish! I would spank you until you were good—and then I would spank you until you were grateful!"

"That could be fun! Will you paddle me to paradise, or take me half-way across the pond and toss me into the water?" She returned her gaze to the bulge in the tortured khakis.

He grinned. "If you're naughty enough, you'll have your answer."

Tonight he would rock her world. She would be his—totally—and he needed no other. It would be a night she never would forget.

November 28, 1963
Seattle, Washington

Hampstead absolutely loved apple pie, but it wasn't a weakness. He never would admit to that, because he had no weaknesses. As the CIA's director of European operations, he felt he had to be invincible, untouchable, and always in control. But he did love apple pie, and when he visited Seattle, he always, *always* stopped in at Larry's Green Apple Pie.

But today wasn't like most other days. It was somewhat different because something strange was in the wind. He played with the crumb crust with his fork and adjusted the slices of apple on his plate. Looking out the restaurant window, he saw nothing amiss. Outside there was a soft, soft rain that was typical of this time of year—or any time of year—in Seattle.

He scanned the restaurant, but it was barren. He was the sole inhabitant, save for the waitress and the two cooks practicing quietly deep within.

Suddenly the door to the street opened, and a man in a trench coat and hat entered. He had his back to the door as he removed his coat and hat and placed them on the nearby wall hooks. Deftly the man turned and moved quickly across the room. Before Hampstead could react, the man was sitting in the chair across from him as he launched his accusation.

"We know you did it, so don't even try to deny it. We need to know what your intentions are." Slava Kurnov had entered the United States through Vancouver with one of his many forged passports; he knew Hampstead was far too arrogant to try to have him arrested here in Seattle. The KGB's passport forgeries were so good that many preferred them to the legitimate ones; they looked more genuine.

Hampstead turned his gaze to his plate and, with his fork, slowly spread the vanilla ice cream across the apple pie. Kurnov had surprised him, and he needed a little time to prepare his frame of mind to deal with this clever man.

"Of course I did it. I always order the apple pie here. It's delicious. That's why I come to Seattle." Hampstead had ignored the bait. He knew Kurnov hadn't followed him to Seattle to kill him. He was just doing a little harmless fishing, hoping to get lucky. He wasn't surprised that Kurnov had guessed he had been involved in the murder of JFK. Kurnov was a bright man, and the KGB had many ears in and around Washington.

"Very funny, Hampstead. We know it was you who planned the murder of your own president. We just need to know why, and what your plans are." Kurnov looked from Hampstead down to the apple pie. He couldn't understand why the pie seemed to fascinate Hampstead enough for him to ignore the rare opportunity of speaking to the most powerful man in the KGB.

"Kurnov, this is America. What do you care who sleeps in the White House? Are you a Republican or a Democrat? Are you registered to vote?" Hampstead wished he'd known about this meeting in advance.

He would've liked to gather his own questions. If he had been prepared, there was some useful fishing he might have done also.

"No man can be as big a fool as you pretend to be," Kurnov said. "It is just not possible. Now humor me and tell me why you murdered him so that when I return to Moscow, I can lay some rumors to rest. We will both sleep easier—that I can promise you." For emphasis he wagged his finger under Hampstead's nose.

"You read the American papers more judiciously than I do; is that not correct?" Hampstead asked. "Surely you know a lunatic murdered JFK. Can I order you some pie? It is delicious. Apparently you knew I come here often."

"Perhaps later I will try the pie." Kurnov smiled, changing the pace of the conversation. "So you are telling me the press was correct? You allowed a lunatic to kill your president?"

"Kurnov, I'm not with the Secret Service. It wasn't my job to protect the president. But in answer to your question, yes, it was a madman." Hampstead smiled.

"You know something? You're not the first person to tell me that it was a madman who murdered your president. The consensus in the Kremlin is that Kennedy was in fact murdered by a madman." Kurnov looked away as he said this, pondering its possibilities.

"There you are. You see, Kurnov, you should listen to your own people, because they seem to have more sense than you. The killer was a madman, just as the press reported." It was now a grinning Hampstead's turn to wag a finger.

"That was not the only consensus reached in the Kremlin regarding this matter." Kurnov dangled the bait.

"Really?" Hampstead was curious.

"Yes," Kurnov added. "The other consensus they reached was that the madman was you."

"Now how about that pie? It will be my treat," Hampstead offered, closing the subject.

"Thank you, Mr. Hampstead." Kurnov motioned for the waitress to approach. "I think I will try some of the some of this very tasty-looking pie." Kurnov had learned all he needed to know.

CHAPTER TEN
Removing Excess Baggage

December 4, 1963
Washington, DC

"**D**id any of these letters get out?" Hampstead was extremely worried.

"No, sir, not one. I caught the messenger, a Liberian army private, on the same day. He decided to cooperate with us rather than face a firing squad. My interview was most enlightening." Beaucroix grinned as he recalled the man's screams.

"This is hard to believe." Hampstead shook his head as he reread one of the forged letters. "How much do we pay the bastard?" The spy was wondering what the price was of a man's honor.

"Absolutely nothing," Beaucroix replied truthfully.

"No, I mean how much did we *agree* to pay him?"

"Fifty grand a year. He thinks we're holding it for him at the Bank of New York."

Hampstead smiled; the CIA was the bank's biggest depositor, even though they didn't have a penny in that institution. "What did the communists offer him?" Hampstead wanted to weigh the numbers for future reference.

"As far as I can tell, we were never compromised. He never made contact with them." Beaucroix carefully led Hampstead down his clever path to murder.

"Then what was he asking from the Russians?" Hampstead bought the lie as willingly as Beaucroix sold it.

"He was asking for one hundred thousand dollars a year and his own deal in Moscow." Beaucroix raised his eyebrows to feign surprise at this fictitious but paltry deal.

"Greedy bastard. Didn't he know the Soviets never could pay that kind of money? I would have given him three times that!"

"It has been my experience that some men put a small price on patriotism. Mr. Hampstead, I'm thoroughly convinced Dr. Tindal is qualified and with minor assistance is capable of finishing this project on his own. After all, most of the work has been completed. I expect we're very close to having a workable weapon and no longer need this man. I suggest we cut our losses and reduce our risks." Beaucroix wanted vengeance; he wanted some fun.

"Beaucroix, take whatever assets you need and deal with this dirty traitor. I don't want to hear or read about how you dealt with this, or what became of Dr. Benjamin Waydner. This matter is now closed."

The Monster grinned as his inner demons danced with joy; his forgery had worked. It was true, the demon shouted from the depths of the Monsters rancid soul, one could never have too much fun!

December 15, 1963
Monrovia, Liberia

"Is he still inside?" the captain asked as he stepped briskly out of the lorry onto the soft mud and into the hammering tropical rain.

"Yes, he is still here. He is the fattest American pig to ever come to Liberia. I would like to take him to my wife's village because he would feed her family for ten years." The corporal licked his lips and rubbed his stomach, having sport with the rumors that his tribe still practiced cannibalism.

The captain stepped onto the hotel veranda and, with a thud, dropped into one of the tattered wicker chairs. "Then what are you waiting for? Bring him here to me. I might want the first bite myself—that is, if he is as juicy as you say." He pulled out a cigarette butt and lit it as he took in the storm from the protection of the covered veranda.

The corporal grinned and headed into the hotel's dining room to fetch the American.

"You, stupid pig, come with me!" He pointed at the American comfortably reading the *London Times* as he happily dove into his noontime meal.

The fat man grinned as he shoveled another massive spoonful of curry and drove it into his mouth. The corporal waited as the fat man stood, adjusted the position of his chair, sat, and returned to the culinary job at hand.

"I said, come with me, you big fat pig!" The corporal was getting mad. He drew his Colt pistol, cocked the hammer, and pointed it at the fat man. The big man carefully wiped his face with the blue linen napkin. He smiled at the corporal, burped, and continued with his meal. Frustrated and confused, the corporal went to find the captain.

The corporal smartly saluted as he returned to the veranda and reported back to the captain. He raised his voice in order to be heard above the hammering rain. "The pig is eating. He will not come."

"Did you say please?" the captain asked sarcastically, raising an eyebrow.

Confused, the corporal opened his mouth to speak.

"Idiot!" the captain shouted, then jumped out of the chair and stood and faced the corporal a scant few inches from his face. "Bring him here now!" he demanded, indicating with his right hand the spot the soldier now occupied.

Frightened, the young man turned and reentered the hotel.

"Follow me, pig!" he ordered, his gun drawn and pointed to the fat man's right side.

"I'm not a pig. I'm a Democrat," the big man informed him with a smile as he returned to his assault on the delightful curry. The young solder stood frozen, his face marked with the brush of confusion. He had never been defied before, and a response escaped him faster than the wild mountain hare outruns a pampered housecat.

The captain was now relaxed, enjoying the storm, which had now reduced itself to the delightful ping and patter of rain on the tin veranda roof. He was certain his corporal would do his duty. It was a hot, wet, and humid African storm that had raged its fury just beyond the veranda, and he was grateful to be doing security duty in town instead of being in the field on this rotten tropical day. He smiled as the corporal ran up, then frowned when he perceived he was alone.

"Where is the American?" In his experience, those cowardly white dogs often ran out the back door.

"He wouldn't come," the young man replied.

"Was he inside?"

"Sure. He is eating his lunch. Perhaps you could go to him," the young man suggested.

"What did you say to me, soldier? Go to *him*? You are acting like a little girl! This is my country, and I am your commanding officer. I ordered you to bring him here, so you will bring him to me now!" the captain demanded.

"But what if he won't come?" the corporal asked, confused and hoping for helpful advice.

"Then drag him out here. You are a soldier. Behave like a man and show some balls!" The captain glanced toward his open Jeep and frowned. The rain was once again a torrent, and the water had now filled the Jeep and was flowing like a river over the doorsills and turning the muck below into a slippery, unwalkable slime.

"Yes, sir." The young man turned and retreated to the dark-paneled dining room once again to fetch the fat man.

The captain motioned to the private who stood guard in the driving rain across from the veranda. "You, guard the back door of the hotel and see that no one leaves."

"Do you have any pudding?" the big man asked the waiter, ignoring the young corporal who was rushing up, his gun drawn, to his table.

"Get up," the soldier demanded, the heavy pistol shaking in his hand.

"I'm very comfortable, and I'm eating lunch," declared the Shadow. Smiling and pointing at the shaking pistol, he winked as he added, "But you don't look too comfortable. Why don't you move me?"

Confused, the young man started toward the door and then started back again, and then headed to the door again. The big man chuckled at the soldier's dilemma as he began a siege upon a huge slab of cream-smothered melon pie the waiter had placed before him.

"I will kill you if you do not obey." The young man returned to the table and dug deep inside himself; delving into honor and duty, he would find the strength to obey his orders.

"Then please be quick about it. Kill me before I finish this delicious melon pie. Surely I would be a better man without these two thousand calories." The fat man winked as he rubbed his astounding belly. "I weighed myself this morning at the ten-cent scale in the airport lobby. To my surprise, it said three hundred ninety-five pounds. I've weighed three hundred ninety-four since college, and I think I might be getting a tad fat."

Completely frustrated, the corporal returned to his captain, who still sat smoking in the tattered wicker chair.

"I can't budge him. He won't move, and he is too heavy to drag," the corporal explained.

"You have a gun. Force him to come, you useless fool! Oh, and Corporal, the end with the hole in it is the end where the bullet comes out."

Completely embarrassed, the corporal once more returned inside to fetch the fat American.

"Move it!" the corporal demanded, having returned to the table.

"Why don't you just shoot me?" the big man suggested, drawing an X with his finger and marking a spot on his left chest.

The corporal just stood there, mouth open, and, having lost the script, was unsure of his role in the play. If God ever painted the picture of a perfect idiot, now was the time to get the camera. This young man presented the picture-perfect display.

"He won't come," explained the young man as he returned to the veranda. Removing his helmet, he scratched his ill-used cranium.

"Listen, boy!" the captain growled, tossing the cigarette butt to the ground and pointing for emphasis. "You have three choices here. One: you can bring the fat pig to me, and I will forget your disobedience. Two: you can shoot him where he sits and drag his big fat body to me, and I will send you to patrol the stinking border for a year. Or three: you can come back out here alone, and I will shoot you myself. Now please do one of the three. I am getting bored here, and there are young ladies in town needing to get pregnant, and, as an officer of the Liberian army and as a gentleman, I feel an obligation to offer my assistance." The captain grinned and with a stern expression pointed the way back into the hotel.

That was it! There was nothing more to it. He would kill the fat man in cold blood and return to his wife and family in the small, backward village. At least the people back home respected his authority and treated him as a man, as someone who mattered.

The corporal checked his pistol, making certain the hammer was cocked and the safety released. He entered the dining room with his pistol raised and his index finger tight upon the trigger. As he crept up to the table, he possessed for the first time this afternoon the guts, the will, and the purpose to fulfill the captain's orders.

But there was a slight problem. The young man froze in his steps, and his eyes, in shock, polled the empty room. The food-barren table was now deserted, and the rear door to the dining room that served as a fire exit was closed as well.

Cautiously he advanced, with his shaking pistol raised, and, with a brisk jerk, he opened the rear door. Surprised, the wet and bored private guarding the rear entrance looked around the room through the open doorway.

"Didn't you arrest him? Where is he?" the guard inquired.

"Fuck you!" the corporal tossed back as he slammed the door and returned to the veranda to meet his fate.

The fat man was gone, incredibly, impossibly, and, as usual, the Shadow had vanished back into the game.

December 24, 1963; 7:00 a.m.
Bopolu, Liberia

Major Chafa M'butu sucked in his gut as he buckled his belt. Protecting American secrets not only paid more than any other duty but also fed him better. M'butu was profoundly grateful for the Westerners' picky palate. He turned right as he left the latrine and slowed his pace as the old jeep rolled slowly into camp, several days early and minus Beaucroix's private army. The Monster was in it, accompanied by an intense, brooding-looking younger man. He was a dark-eyed and slimmer but wilder version of the demon beside him.

Curious, thought M'butu. It had just struck him. He never had seen Emile Beaucroix drive. Perhaps he didn't know how. Or perhaps being chauffeured massaged his astronomical ego. *Yes, that's it*, he thought. *Pure ego.*

M'butu slid behind the barracks, where he could watch unobserved. Then some unknown inner thing told him that he should quietly walk away, that he would be better off not to be a party to this, whatever *this* was.

The jeep rolled to a stop as Beaucroix left the passenger side with a catlike jump and then dusted off his britches with his worn hat. The driver showed no reaction whatsoever, staring straight ahead over the much-worn wheel of the old American jeep. Like an automaton, he seemed cognizant of neither his passenger nor the world around him.

Quickly and clearly in a hurry, Beaucroix rushed to the lab building, entered, and then rapidly burst out through the dented lab doors, dragging Waydner by his white lapels across the veranda and toward the jeep; all the while, the doctor was loudly protesting and trying to pull free.

"Hogan! Hogan! Help me!" Waydner shouted at the top of his lungs.

Upon reaching the jeep, Beaucroix released Waydner as he moved leopard-like, and, circling to the right, he planted his right buffalo-skin Wellington boot square into Waydner's private package. Waydner folded like an old letter and fell to the African dust as he immediately passed out from the pain. Beaucroix grabbed the doctor's belt with his right hand and his lab coat with his left, hefted him into the air like a sack of yams, and roughly tossed him into the hard, dirty back of the running jeep.

Looking to his left, Beaucroix fixed a stare at a young Liberian private who had been watching the whole affair. "Get over here!" he demanded.

The private came running over with the unquestioning obedience that is the son of mortal fear. As the young man came within reach, the Monster grabbed him, turned him, and, as a violent encore, kicked him so hard in the buttocks that it drove him into the back of the jeep.

"Hold him down!" Beaucroix ordered as he indicated the moaning ball that once had been the world's foremost genetic engineer.

With the terrified private restraining the doctor, Beaucroix took his seat, and the jeep roared noisily out of the clearing and out of Bopolu, leaving a blowing trail of dust to mark its escape.

"What the hell is going on?" Hogan tucked in his shirt as he entered the clearing and watched the cloud of dust snaking into the morning sun.

Corporal Tomes ran up to Hogan; hidden behind the barracks, he had watched the whole thing. "They took the doctor. The general's friend took him!" He was panting, as he was fairly out of breath from rushing up to Hogan.

"Beaucroix?" Now what was the Monster up to?

"Yes, Mr. Beaucroix and a thin, dark man—maybe Italian. He was new."

Damn, thought Hogan. The bastard had linked up with Leo Pagetti, a young ex-Mafia assassin who had decided to join the CIA because he found killing was a lot more fun when you got a steady paycheck. Hogan looked down at the deep, fresh ruts the frantic tires had slashed into the flat clearing.

"Bring me a jeep and my chopper—it's next to my bed," Hogan demanded as he turned back to the corporal. The soldier regarded him blankly, and Hogan caught on to the confusion. "Chopper—that's my machine gun, you idiot!" he explained. Time was quickly running short, as the guilty were flying away across a rapidly widening gap.

A look of relief spread across the man's face; for a moment, he'd thought Hogan wanted some false teeth.

Hogan looked at the man, incredulous that he was still standing there. "Well, are you going to bring me a jeep?" he demanded.

"I can't, sir. Before first light, General Kutu came and took all the jeeps and trucks. He even took the busted motorcycle."

"Did he say anything?"

"No. Mostly he was joking with Mr. Beaucroix and pointing at your hut. I didn't hear what Mr. Beaucroix said. But the general just laughed."

With this new information to process, Hogan fell silent, his eyes cast down and regarding the dust of Bopolu. He stood there, his mind compiling the plot from what he knew of the actors. As he raised his gaze, he spotted an orphan beer bottle twenty feet away, resting beneath an acacia tree on the African duff. Quickly Hogan drew his Colt officer's model and blasted away at this mortal enemy, rapidly emptying the seven rounds in unrestrained fury at this pseudo Beaucroix.

Satisfied, Hogan produced one of the spare magazines from his shirt pocket, deftly popped the empty magazine free, and slapped the new one home. With his thumb, he sent the slide slamming forward, preparing his Colt for another day. Quietly he holstered the pistol and, without a word, walked slowly and quietly back to his quarters.

The corporal followed the retreating back of Hogan, pushing him with his eyes until he disappeared into his private hut. Slowly he walked up to the remnants of the beer bottle. He smiled, his grin growing wider and wider as he chuckled. The bottle was uninjured and whole. *These Americans are not invincible,* he happily concluded. He had done his little job; the general would indeed be very well pleased.

December 24, 1963
Coastal Jungle, Liberia

Turning away from the river, Leo Pagetti bullied the jeep across a game trail and deeper into the jungle. After crawling along for about a quarter of an hour, they emerged into a small clearing. Beaucroix motioned toward a rotting stump, and Pagetti turned the wheel and then rolled the jeep to a squeaky stop.

Beaucroix jumped off the jeep. "Bring him here!" he barked, indicating the spot in the clearing where he wanted the Liberian private to bring Dr. Waydner.

The Liberian complied, escorting the weak, stooped-over doctor to the area Beaucroix indicated.

"Thank you," Beaucroix said graciously as he deftly drew his pistol and blew the private's brains into the jungle, causing him to slowly collapse into the warm African mud.

Waydner, overcome by shock, fell to the ground and wept profusely, begging for his life. Leo Pagetti smiled and chuckled; this was going to be truly great entertainment—even the Mafia back home in New York City didn't have this much fun.

"So, Dr. Asshole, where are your rich friends now? What has your selfish, piggish wealth gained you? And what of your social privilege and snootiness now? Where are your silver Rolls-Royces and your rich, faggot, country club friends now? And what has any of it gained you?" the Monster screamed in fury. "All my life I've had to work and scrape, suffer, and do without. I had a miserable childhood, constantly tormented and bullied by a vengeful older brother while worthless pieces of privileged shit like you have everything passed to them on a silver platter. Now, for the first time in your life, you're going to have to earn it!"

Beaucroix was struck with a fresh epiphany as he flashed instantly from fury to glee. "Here, Doctor." The Monster walked closer as he unzipped his trousers. "I have a job for you." He pulled out his organ as he moved closer to the kneeling doctor's face.

"Hey, what's this? What's going on here?" Leo Pagetti protested.

"Shut up, Pagetti!" an irritated Beaucroix ordered; he had business to do that required no interruption.

"Suck it, Doctor. Suck it good!" Beaucroix demanded as he brought his swollen member closer to Waydner's sobbing face.

"Hey, Beaucroix. What is this? Don't do this weird stuff. Kill the son of a bitch. Blow his brains out and cut out the shit!" Pagetti was getting totally weirded out by all this.

"Shut up, or I'll make you suck it too!" Beaucroix was furious that his will was being questioned, his fun interrupted.

"Beaucroix, I wasn't kidding when I said end this thing!" Pagetti demanded as his dark eyes narrowed.

The Monster was beyond angry; he was so furious that his organ had now gone flaccid. He turned his anger toward Leo Pagetti. "You're not tough enough or man enough to stop me. Just what the fuck do you think you can do about it?"

Pagetti drew his Colt pistol and, in a single fluid motion, fired and sent the .45-caliber slug into the head of Benjamin Waydner, shattering his skull and causing the doctor to slump motionless into the slurping mud. He then pointed the pistol at Beaucroix and waited to see what action the Monster would take.

Beaucroix looked without emotion at the smoking pistol in Pagetti's hand. With silence and purpose, he quietly tucked his organ back into his pants and zipped his khakis. He looked again at the smoking pistol; then he looked down at the dead body of Benjamin Waydner.

Pagetti sweated and watched Beaucroix like a hawk, unsure what the Monster would do next. Beaucroix pointed at the dead doctor as he tightened his lips and looked Pagetti directly in the eyes; then he winked and broke into hysterical laughter.

As the Monster laughed, Pagetti lowered the pistol, holstered it, and joined him. Murder was all right; it was what he had done for the Mafia, for God's sake. It was only the weirdness that had bugged him.

The sudden sound of a snapping twig instantly broke the spies' carefree mood and caused Beaucroix to dive behind the old jeep and draw his pistol. Pagetti turned, also drawing and swinging his pistol toward the sound. He abruptly halted his swing when he noticed the two cocked hammers on the Holland & Holland Express rifle.

Max George casually strode out of the jungle, seeming to have appeared from nowhere.

"Looks like a good day to die." Max recited what the young Sioux Indian braves had said two hundred years ago before they went into battle. Cradling the two-barreled elephant whacker in his arms, he seemed to be concentrating on Beaucroix, a fact that promised an interesting opportunity for the blood-hungry Leo Pagetti.

"C'mon, Beaucroix, don't be a fraidy-cat. Come out and play. It's only the boogeyman," Max taunted him.

Beaucroix stood and turned to face Max. He knew a rifle was no match for a pistol at close range, as it was faster to swing a pistol. Besides, he had his loaded pistol, and he had an ace, Leo Pagetti, a man who loved to kill.

"Get out of my face, George. I'm acting under directive." Beaucroix wisely holstered his pistol. Something wasn't quite right here because Max had walked into a situation where he was outnumbered two to one. Max clearly wasn't that stupid; so something was extremely fishy. There were two things you could always count on Emile Beaucroix to be: psychotic and cautious. Today he chose cautious.

"What are you doing creeping through the jungle? Hoping to corn hole a hippo? I can't help you there, but I noticed a plump pig a kilo or so back down the road. I could give you directions," the Monster sneered.

"Nope, no pigs or hippos today, but I just may kill an ass!" Max replied distractedly.

Already Pagetti had begun to circle, creeping quietly to the left. Max didn't seem to notice.

Suddenly Pagetti achieved his position. He swung the pistol, and, as he brought it level to Max's eyes, Beaucroix went for his own Beretta. An instant before Pagetti could fire, however, he was driven backward fifteen feet and thrown motionless to the ground. A widening circle of red marked his left shirt pocket.

Beaucroix quickly dropped the Beretta. There had been no sound, not even the muffled *pfffft* of a silencer. Max and the express rifle hadn't even been in play.

Max walked over to Waydner, bent over, and checked his pulse at the neck. Then he looked at the dead Liberian. With three-quarters of the man's brain missing, there was no need to check his pulse. Frowning, he turned to Beaucroix, who was listening intensely to the jungle, wondering what the killer was and where its master was hiding.

Max motioned toward the dead soldier. "Is it your directive to kill the whole Liberian army or just this part of it?"

"I'm following orders, and you're interfering. I intend to report this to Hampstead. You killed a man who was vital to my operation. If you're smart, you'll crawl back into your fucking jungle." Fear was something killers like Beaucroix simply didn't have; he could, however, be practical.

"Yup, I might just do that. But I haven't killed anyone today—not yet, anyway. Still, the day is yet young, and who knows what pleasures it may bring? Now, toss your pistol into the jeep, Emily," Max ordered as he looked around absent-mindedly.

Beaucroix toyed briefly with the idea of pulling out his second pistol and killing Max. But Max acted as if he didn't have a care in the world. Of course there was that still unseen accomplice—or accomplices—hidden by the blanketing jungle. He picked up the Beretta and tossed it into the boot of the old jeep.

"Pimp pistol too, Missy." Max pointed at the Monster's crotch.

Growling under his breath, the monster reached into his crotch and removed the .25-caliber Beretta he kept concealed in a crotch holster and flicked the little gun into the jeep.

"Pagetti's also." Max indicated the pistol resting on the muddy ground.

The Monster walked over to the Italian, bent over, retrieved Pagetti's pistol, and tossed it into the back of the jeep.

Max climbed into the jeep and started the engine. "I'll return this jeep that you borrowed to Bopolu. No, no, there's no need to thank me. It's no problem," he taunted Beaucroix. He had merely planned to strand Beaucroix in the jungle, but then, as a clever afterthought, he said, grinning, "Put all your clothes in the jeep."

Beaucroix shot daggers of hate at Max George, who sat matter-of-factly in Beaucroix's former jeep. Suddenly a sensation drifted out of the jungle, like a finger slowly tightening a trigger. Rapidly the Monster removed his boots, shirt, and pants and tossed them into the back of the running jeep.

Max looked down at the furious killer and was gifted with a delightfully humiliating afterthought. "Shorts and socks too, Emily. I wouldn't want them to get dirty on your walk home."

The Monster glared satanic waves of payback promise. Furious and enraged, Beaucroix quickly removed his boxers and knee-high socks and tossed them with fury into the jeep. If looks could kill, Max would have been blasted clean past heaven.

"You ought to work out more, Emily. Because you've got one flabby ass!" Max pointed at the pale, pimply ass flesh.

Beaucroix could only glare pure hate because he was helpless as long as he couldn't make out the location of the threat from the jungle. Max was sorry but not surprised that Beaucroix hadn't forced a play.

Max put the jeep in gear and rolled forward, following the curve of the clearing and using it to turn the jeep around. As he approached Beaucroix on his way out of the clearing, he rolled the jeep to a stop.

"Just one other thing, Emily…" Max swept his arm around and over the three dead bodies on the ground. "Clean up this mess."

Max George popped the jeep into gear and waved a grinning good-bye as he roared out of the clearing and back to the place that is Bopolu.

December 26, 1963
Washington, DC

"Gentlemen, this bickering isn't taking us anywhere useful." Senator Mack Murphy energetically banged his gavel.

"My brother was murdered, and there are people who know who did it and why. I want those men brought to justice!" Bobby Kennedy looked around the room for a consensus.

"The Warren Commission produced thousands of documents saying there was no conspiracy," Senator Hastings interjected.

"How dare you insult me or the memory of my dead brother, President John F. Kennedy, with that idiotic statement!" Bobby Kennedy's face flushed an angry crimson red.

"Hold it now. Just hold it." Senator Murphy again slammed his gavel against the mahogany desk. "None of us would be here today in this meeting if we believed the Warren Commission. Senator Hastings, would you please clarify to Mr. Kennedy what you just said?"

"What I'm saying, Robert, is that none of us can call the Warren Commission a pack of liars without some measure of proof." Hastings regretted that he hadn't said this in the first place. Robert F. Kennedy wasn't the right man to rile.

"I think the thing to do here is for the Senate to create its own commission—a special investigation commission to follow where the Warren Commission left off. I would be happy to chair such a commission," Senator Herschel offered.

"I just bet you'd just love to chair that commission, you power-greedy Jew!" Texas Senator Earl Dudley Duncan drawled.

"Gentlemen, there's no need for profanity here." Senator Matt Murphy wagged a finger at Senator Duncan. "And there's no call for rudeness either, Earl. We're here on a common mission. Now let's act like senators, not schoolyard brats!"

"Did I hear you right?" Senator Herschel was indignant. "Did I hear right? Did you call Jews profane?"

"You're all just pissing me off! Bobby is the only man here who has a right to be upset, and he's the only man here acting like a senator. You gentlemen even have got me acting like a silly fool banging this stupid gavel." Senator Murphy banged it again to emphasize the point. "The president of the United States—Bobby's brother and our good friend—was murdered, and all you fools can do is to argue about profanity and bigotry. I'm sick of the lot of you!"

"Jews are not profane," Senator Herschel insisted, scratching his nose.

"Gentlemen, I would like to suggest that anyone who does not want to make progress on this issue to please leave the room!" Yet again Senator Murphy banged his gavel energetically upon the unyielding mahogany desk.

"Jews are not profane!" Senator Herschel repeated.

"Listen up, all of you! I would like to make it a matter of record that Jews are not profane!" The senator again struck his gavel.

"Thank you." Senator Herschel sneered at Senator Duncan.

"I would like it to be further made a matter of record that if a certain Jewish senator doesn't keep his mind to the task at hand, I am going to punch him squarely in the nose!" Senator Murphy pointed his gavel directly at Senator Herschel's nose.

"Thank you, Senator." Senator Duncan sneered back at Herschel.

"All of you, cut this out. We're not here to discuss bigotry, gentlemen. We're here to punish the dastardly, murdering swine who killed our president! We're here to castrate and hang the men who planned it and who hired those murderers who carried it out."

"Let's get back to the commission," Senator Duncan suggested. "How are we going to form it, and who will be the chair?" He would just love to chair it himself.

"Gentlemen…" It was time for Robert Kennedy to step up and say his piece. "The Warren Commission was supported by the majority of the Senate, specifically the most powerful men in the Senate. Now, we know there was a conspiracy, and we know it had to come from some very high places. The chances of our putting a commission together—a fair commission—are something around nil. Whatever solution we take, gentlemen, must be formed within this room."

"I am a powerful senator, and I wasn't there. I have power too," Senator Herschel insisted indignantly as he rubbed his itchy nose.

"Shut up!" Senator Murphy again pointed his gavel at Herschel's nose.

"Fellow senators, there is no question Mr. Kennedy has something here. Since we don't know who in the government—and possibly even the Senate and the White House—was involved in this murder, it would be foolish for us to trust anyone outside this room." Senator Barbara Horton swept her hand around the room, encompassing those present.

"Good morning, Barbara," Senator Murphy said with a smile. "It's nice of you to jump in and contribute."

"Well, Mack, being the only lady present, I thought I'd leave the cat fighting to you gentlemen!"

Senator Duncan laughed, Senator Herschel fumed, and Senator Murphy covered his mouth to hide a chuckle.

Bobby Kennedy, however, was dead serious. "How can we do an investigation without the Senate's approval? Can anyone tell me that?" Kennedy wanted this ship back on course; he wanted to find these killers.

"Now that you mention it, Robert, more than anyone in this room, you know who we need to get this job done." Senator Murphy lifted an eyebrow for emphasis.

"What are you talking about, Mack? If I knew how to get this done, I wouldn't be sitting in this room with you gentlemen…and lady! Sorry, Barbara."

"What I mean, Mr. Kennedy," Murphy clarified, "is that the office of the attorney general has the power and the means to launch its own investigation. Robert, you once held that office and that power. You know what that office can do."

A collective jolt circled the room as one of the largest men Robert Kennedy had ever seen was sitting at the table. The Shadow had moved even deeper into the game. Kennedy turned toward Mack Murphy, pointed at the big man, and began to mouth a question.

"Someone call security! Who the hell said you could attend this meeting, and how the hell did you get in here?" Senator Earl Duncan was livid.

"I was invited to join you all." The fat man leaned back in his chair and with his arms indicated the expanse of the room. "As to how I got here, I used the door. I've always found them useful in some small way. Besides, I'm too fat to make it through the mail slot! Mr. Kennedy, I'm truly sorry about your brother. He was a very fine man and a great American—though I only knew him slightly."

The Shadow in fact had known President Kennedy quite well. He felt guilty and regretted that he had been so wrapped up in tracking the Bopolu nonsense that the plot to kill the president had slid right by him, even though most of the players in both games were the same. The Shadow had given Hampstead notice with the nine dimes that he was on his trail, but that was over Bopolu. He stupidly hadn't stayed long enough to overhear the offer to LBJ.

"Senators," Mack Murphy said, grinning expansively, "I would like to present the Shadow, the greatest intelligence officer the US Army has ever seen."

"Retired from the army, actually. I now work directly for Mack and his agency."

"Thank you, Shadow." Senator Murphy banged his gavel to cut off the fat man before he revealed what most men in the government didn't need to know.

"Exactly what agency is that, Mack?" Kennedy wasn't a fan of secret government operations, especially the ones the government knew nothing about.

"I meant to say I'm now working for you gentlemen, and it was Mack who asked me to get involved." The Shadow had deftly saved the senator's secret. He wished he had known the senator hadn't confided more with the people in this room.

"Good," Kennedy said. "That clears that up. Now what was this business about the attorney general?"

"If you tried to launch another government investigation into the murder of your brother, you wouldn't know whom to trust. I can guarantee someone—possibly several people—would be salted on that commission to reach the same conclusion the Warren Commission reached before.

"But by using the office of the attorney general, you would put all the power in the hands of one man, and, as such, you need only one honest man." The Shadow folded his hands on the table and smiled. His point was generally well taken around the room.

"But how do I know the attorney general will be able to find my brother's killers? With so many allies in this conspiracy, their tracks probably have been well covered."

"There's no need to find your brother's killers. This is not what we need the attorney general for." The Shadow leaned back and scratched his belly; it helped him think.

"How dare you! How can you say there's no need to find the murderers of the president of the United States of America?" Kennedy was livid.

"I already know who killed your brother. I know who planned the murder of the president. I know who ordered the murder of the president, and I know why." The Shadow continued to scratch his belly.

Kennedy tore off the top sheet of his notepad to make way for a fresh sheet. "Who are they? What are their names?" he demanded. He was ready to write their eulogies on the paper before him.

"Robert, the Shadow and I have discussed this already. These men are too well insulated to name." Senator Murphy knew this wasn't going to be easy for Robert Kennedy. But he had discussed this matter with the Shadow, and they were in agreement that naming names without the means to punish would only make the situation worse.

"Then we're just going to let them get away with it?" Kennedy's face was red as a beet as he glared incredulously.

"Naming names would do no good. We first must have the means to prosecute these murderers and their coconspirators. That's why we need the attorney general." Senator Murphy shook his finger for emphasis.

"The president of the United States controls the attorney general," Kennedy pointed out.

The Shadow raised his index finger. "Exactly!"

"Only the president orders the attorney general." Kennedy couldn't understand why they were missing his point.

"Exactly!" The Shadow again raised his index finger higher, lowered it, and pointed it directly at Kennedy. "We want to you to run for the Senate first, then later for the presidency of the United States of America. We need to lay some groundwork. Justice will not be swift. These criminals and their coconspirators are too well insulated, and justice will take time. To succeed, we must be clever." The Shadow snapped his fingers and pointed again toward Bobby Kennedy as Senator Earl Duncan rose and began to applaud.

"You can win, Bobby. You can win. I know you can!" Senator Horton came to her feet and joined in the applause.

"Thank you. Thank you. But I don't think I could win. I'm probably not your man. I don't have Jack's charisma." Bobby Kennedy really did believe this. He'd never really been the public man that his older brother had played so well.

"Robert F. Kennedy, you can win in the Senate and win the presidency. Take my word for it." The big man rose and energetically joined in the thundering applause.

"How can you be so certain?" Bobby was still unconvinced.

The big man stated the obvious and the inevitable. "The Shadow knows!"

December 28, 1963
Free Methodist Hospital; Monrovia, Liberia

"This is going to revolutionize diagnostic medicine!" Dr. Theodore Mason proudly pointed at the ten newly painted cartoons on the faded ivory-colored wall. The two African nurses looked on proudly, amazed that such good fortune had blessed them not only with a new doctor fresh from America but also one who was destined to rewrite medical history.

"One of the greatest challenges facing a diagnostician always has been in determining precisely the amount of pain a patient is in. Over the centuries, this has resulted in countless cases of overmedicating and a few cases of seriously under medicating patients, often with life-threatening results."

Harvard ego and pride, pride and ego continued as the doctor lectured to his audience of two very proud, smiling nurses.

"Since the days of the legendary Greek physician Hypocrites, doctors have grappled with drugs, treatments, and dosages, hampered by never being certain exactly how much discomfort their patients were in. I have solved that!" Grinning, Dr. Mason walked over to the first cartoon.

"In my junior year of medical school, I realized there was no way a doctor could ever tell what a patient was feeling without suffering the malady himself. I knew there had to be a better way, and here it is!" He waved his hand across the cartoons.

"I hired a professional cartoonist in Madrid to paint ten pictures showing Warner Bros. character Elmer Fudd in varying degrees of pain, from the first cartoon, which shows Elmer with a tiny tear, to the last, which shows him in absolutely unbearable agony. They are numbered one to ten. I call them Dr. Theodore Mason's Scale of Patient Discomfort." Dr. Mason picked up a yardstick to point with, then moved it right to left across the scale.

"All a patient has to do is to point to a picture, and any physician instantly will know exactly how much pain his patient is in. I am going to revolutionize diagnostic medicine."

"Doctor, that is absolutely brilliant. We're so proud to be working with a gifted doctor like you." Nurse Betty clasped her hands and gave the good doctor an approving smile.

"Good. Now send in the first patient!" He placed the yardstick back on the sideboard.

The first patient, an elderly native woman of undetermined age, wobbled into the room.

"Good morning. I'm Dr. Mason. What seems to be the problem?" he inquired.

"It is my knees, Doctor. They hurt me. They hurt me all the time, and it makes it difficult for me to walk. Some days I hurt so badly I can't make it to the market to buy my food." She rubbed her knee and winced in pain to demonstrate her suffering.

The doctor quickly examined her, even though there was no need. Given her age and symptoms, simple arthritis wasn't hard to diagnose. But this was what the doctor was looking for, a chance to put his new methods to the test.

"Now, Mother, I'm going to give you something powerful to ease the pain, but I need your help. I need you to look at these pictures on the wall and point to the one that best describes your suffering, how much pain you are in." The doctor barely could contain his pride. All his theories would now be put to the acid test.

The doctor frowned as the woman immediately pointed to number ten, the agony picture.

"No, Mother, you don't understand. These pictures indicate the degree of your pain. Picture number one indicates just a little pain, like you have when you stub your toe. Number two is a picture that indicates a little more pain, like when you stub your toe and cut it at the same time. The next picture represents a bit more pain, and the one after that indicates even more pain—severe pain. The picture you indicated, number ten, represents the worst kind of pain, absolute agony. That's the kind of pain that would make most people want to die rather than endure. Now, Mother, do we understand?"

"Yes, thank you. Now I understand what you're saying." She nodded and then winced as she crossed her legs.

"Good. Please point to the picture that best represents your suffering." The doctor smiled. Now he finally would vindicate his test, but his smile instantly crashed into a frown as she again pointed to picture number ten.

"Thank you, Mother. Give this to the nurse at the front desk, and she'll give you a bottle of powerful medicine for your pain." On a slip of paper, he scrawled out a prescription for common aspirin.

So went the first patient—so much for the first test. But in retrospect, Dr. Mason wasn't surprised. One had to make allowances for the elderly, and the old woman's senile inability to understand the cartoons in no way invalidated his revolutionary test.

The next patient was son of a local missionary, an eight-year-old English boy who had skinned his knee.

"I see we have a little boo-boo here. What's your name, big guy?" the doctor said to the boy as he examined his knee.

The boy nodded as he wiped a tear from his eye. "My name is Jimmy, and she pushed me down and made me hurt!" he told the doctor as he pointed to his skinned knee. "She hurt me! She made me hurt," he cried and wiped his eyes.

"Who pushed you down?" asked the doctor as he washed the scratch and applied a shiny, new two-cent bandage.

"Stinky Mary Ellen. Stinky Mary Ellen pushed me down, and she hurt me!" He began to cry louder, hoping the doctor might spank his mean older sister, stinky Mary Ellen.

"Can you guess what I'm thinking?" The doctor patted the child on the head.

"No?" The boy wiped another tear from his eye.

"I think if I gave you a piece of candy, it would take care of mean Mary Ellen. Don't you think?" The doctor smiled; working with children was the best part of the job.

"*Stinky* Mary Ellen!" the boy quickly corrected.

"OK, if I gave you a piece of candy, do you think that would take care of mean, stinky Mary Ellen?"

"Yeah!" The boy lit up like a blazing bonfire.

"Well, you go right out the door, and you tell Nurse O'Grady I said to give you two pieces of candy!"

"Yeah!"

"Oh, Jimmy," the doctor added, almost as an afterthought. "Do you remember how bad it hurt when stinky Mary Ellen pushed you down?"

"Yes, stinky Mary Ellen pushed me down. She made me hurt lots!"

"Do you see my cartoons?" the doctor pointed to the ten Elmer Fudds on the wall behind him.

"Yeah, neat!"

"Can you show me which cartoon shows how badly mean, stinky Mary Ellen hurt you?" Many times children were a lot more honest than adults. Dr. Mason felt certain he was on the right track.

"Yeah!" Jimmy jumped off the exam table, slapped cartoon number ten, and ran from the room in search of the promised candy.

The doctor shook his head. He knew he was on to something, and that something was brilliant. His pain scale would be a breakthrough in diagnostic medicine. He just needed to find reliable subjects for the tests. He stuck his head out the door and called for the next patient.

"Good afternoon," Dr. Mason said to a pretty, young, blond settlement woman as the nurse escorted her onto the exam table. "How are we today?" the doctor asked with a smile.

"You look fine doctor, but I hurt all over," the pretty girl moaned.

"Which of these cartoons represents the level of pain you're in? The first cartoon represents very little pain. The next represents a bit more, until we come to cartoon number ten, which is a person in absolute agony. Are we clear on this?" He watched with satisfaction as the pretty blonde tracked her eyes across all ten cartoons, carefully considering all the options.

"The last one, number ten. Is there a number eleven?" The woman winced in pain.

"No, just ten," the doctor replied in considerable frustration, flavored with a halo of disappointment.

"Let's start the examination with your telling me just where you hurt." The doctor would forget his cartoons for now and concentrate on the patient.

"Everywhere, Doctor. It's just horrible because I hurt everywhere!" The young woman winced again in pain.

"Could you tell me a specific location where you hurt? Perhaps you could give me an example."

Nobody but nobody hurt everywhere, except perhaps a doctor during a tax audit.

"Well, if I touch my knee, it hurts. If I touch my wrist, it hurts. If I touch my neck, it hurts, and if I'd touch my leg, that hurts too. I hurt everywhere, Doctor."

Dr. Mason thought about this for a moment as he looked at her beautiful, blond, silken hair. They had joked about a patient like this in medical school, but the doctor hardly believed he'd ever see a case like this. "Hold out your right hand, please." Dr. Mason examined it carefully, but he didn't have to look for long.

"Am I going to die, Doctor?" she pleaded.

"Miss, you're going to be just fine!" The doctor reached for a splint and some bandages.

"What's wrong with me, Dr. Mason? Why do I hurt everywhere I touch?"

"Miss, you hurt everywhere you touch because you have a broken finger on your right hand. I'll have you fixed in no time."

"Doctor, you're miracle worker!" The young woman sighed in relief.

It took only another ten minutes before the doctor had her finished and out the door. He'd had enough for one day. He headed down the hallway toward his office.

"Doctor, we have an emergency, a gunshot wound. A hunter was shot in the chest. Can you take him now?" Nurse O'Grady was frantic.

"Of course. Take him to room number four." He was grateful to get away from those damn cartoons. He had done his internship in East Texas and had patched up more than one hunter's wound.

"Dr. Cohen has a cardiac patient in room number four. Number seven is the only room available," the nurse replied.

"Fine. Take him into number seven." *Damn, that's where the cartoons are,* he thought.

"When did you get shot?" Dr. Mason asked the man, who was breathing heavily and gripping the side of the exam table to cut his pain.

"A few days ago, I think. I passed out and don't really remember." The man dug his fingernails deeper into the exam table as the doctor cut away the blood-matted shirt.

"You're very lucky. The bullet headed straight for your heart, and then it hit this and was knocked to the side. It's still in your right chest cavity," Dr. Mason said as he continued to work. He removed a flat, bullet-twisted piece of metal on a chain that hung around the hunter's neck.

"What is this thing? It certainly saved your life." He held it up to the light and turned it as he tried to divine its nature.

"It's my Saint Christopher medal." Still breathing deeply, the man winced in pain.

"What's that?" The doctor, who was not much into jewelry, never had heard of such a thing.

"It's what we Catholics wear. It protects us when we travel. Am I going to make it, Doctor?" the man asked.

"You're going to be just fine, young man. The bullet is resting comfortably in your right chest and hasn't severed anything important. As soon as I get you cleaned up, we'll take you to surgery. When you wake up tomorrow, you're going to feel a whole lot better," Dr. Mason said with a smile. "Did you say you were Catholic?" The doctor hadn't been really paying attention to what the young man had said, as he had been occupied in examining the wound.

"Yes, Doctor. That's why I was wearing the medal." Already the man felt much better knowing he would live.

"Oh, that's OK. We treat anybody here." The doctor was now occupied cleaning the wound.

"What's that supposed to mean?" The young man started to lift himself off the table, but the doctor gently restrained him.

"Oh, nothing, nothing. I was just making idle conversation while I worked on this wound. There, we're finished. Now we can get you to surgery. What did you say your name was, young man?" The doctor helped him off the table and into the wheelchair Nurse O'Grady had just brought into the room.

"Oh, and one last thing, young man. I need to finish your chart, so I have to ask one final question. Do you see these ten cartoons on the wall?" The doctor gestured to the ten Elmer Fudd cartoons gracing his wall.

"Sure, Doc. I like them. It gives your office a lot of character!" The young man winced as he lifted himself into the wheelchair.

"Thank you. Which of these cartoons represents the level of pain you were in when you entered my office?" The doctor was certain he finally would get valid data for his test.

"Number ten is the highest, the most pain?" The wounded man carefully surveyed the cartoons. "Is there a number eleven?" he queried.

"No, just ten. Ten is the highest." The doctor frowned; he was struck with a disappointing premonition.

"Number two, definitely number two." The young man winced again in pain as he settled into the wheelchair.

The doctor scratched his head as he leaned over and picked up the chart. He turned his back in order to hide the confused dichotomy of his disappointment. "What's your name, young man?" Dr. Mason turned back to the man as he suddenly remembered the question had been left unanswered. He needed it for the chart and for the police accident report.

"My name is Pagetti, Leo Pagetti," he answered across his shoulder as Nurse O'Grady pushed the wheelchair out of the room.

CHAPTER ELEVEN
Rats!

December 28, 1963
Bopolu, Liberia

"I want him dead!" Dr. Tindal scanned the compound, making sure his little wish hadn't been overheard.

"We all want him dead," Private Gartee said, describing the general consensus of everyone who'd ever met Emile Beaucroix.

"I know for a fact he murdered Dr. Waydner." Tindal had turned against Beaucroix, at least until Beaucroix returned.

"You saw him do it?" Gartee nervously searched the horizon for Emile Beaucroix.

"No, but I know he did it," Tindal murmured, almost to himself.

"Do you know someone? A witness?" Gartee asked, more than a bit hopeful. "If you have a witness, we could go to General Kutu. He would help."

Tindal had often been amazed that Kutu's men had been so successfully neutered. Tindal considered Kutu to be the petty version of Emile Beaucroix. While Kutu was simply a monster, Beaucroix was a monster on steroids.

"I don't need a witness," Tindal addressed the horizon. "I know he did it. I know he did it because I can see it in his eyes. He killed Waydner in cold blood and enjoyed it, and he's probably going to kill more of us."

Subconsciously, Tindal knew the Monster's true plan; deep inside he knew, but it hadn't yet sunk in.

"Then why don't you kill him?" Gartee inquired.

"What? I'm no James Bond. I'm not even an Alice Bond. I'm a doctor, for Christ's sake. Do you know what waiters are? Do you know what they're for?"

The private looked on in confusion. What did waiters have to do with murder?

"Waiters exist because of doctors. We need their strength to pull the cork out of the bottle. Think about it: we can't even uncork a wine bottle without help. If a waiter could kick my ass, what hope could I possibly have against a psychotic professional killer like Emile Beaucroix?" Tindal looked down at his feet as his left toe adjusted the dust of Bopolu.

"Not much, under ordinary circumstances," the private admitted. "But you are a doctor, and you have access to ways—like how to kill so as not to cause suspicion. I have read a lot of European books, and there are secret ways, such as poisons that cannot be detected." The private mulled this over as his eyes regarded the monkeys in the trees.

"I'm a doctor, and I've taken an oath—a sacred oath—to preserve life, not destroy it!" Tindal stated, offended that someone would even consider that doctors could have such thoughts.

"As a doctor, you must be very smart and well educated. I ask you this as a reasonable man: Wouldn't the accidental death of Emile Beaucroix certainly preserve more life than the miserable one that was ended?"

"I won't even honor such an ethically odorous question with a response." Tindal, however, couldn't impugn the logic behind it.

"Then show me how, and *I* will do it. I am a poor man in a poor country. Ethics are for the wealthy. A poor man cannot afford ethics. He has only honor," Private Gartee offered.

Dr. Tindal wanted none of this. "Kutu would have you killed."

"Then my uncle would kill *him*. General Kutu's brother would then kill my uncle, and so on and so forth. What's your point?" Feuds were a fact of life in Africa; family honor was paramount and was valued more than life itself.

"If I were Kutu's brother, I bet I still wouldn't mind seeing him dead." Tindal switched toes as he readjusted the small pile of African dust.

"You are probably right. Kutu's brother is a general also. He probably would give a medal to the man who killed his brother, and then he would kill him. It would still be a matter of family honor," explained the private.

"Man, you Africans have one crazy stupid set of values," Tindal observed.

"My society is *not the one that produced Emile Beaucroix!*"

"I see your point."

This conversation was going nowhere fast, and Private Gartee was no closer to gaining an ally for the murder of Emile Beaucroix than he been before their discussion had started. He would have to try a different tactic.

"Where do you think you'll be and what will you be doing three years from now?" Gartee asked nonchalantly.

"I'll likely have a position teaching in some ivy-walled detention facility, probably at Harvard Medical School." That sounded about right.

"Will you be married?" Gartee was leading and luring him into his trap.

"I don't know…maybe, probably." Tindal pondered as he played with his pile of dust.

"Do you think you'll have children, and how many?" The crafty private was luring him in deeper, opening the trap wider.

"I don't mind children—maybe a boy and a girl." Tindal's mind floated lazily into the future.

"What about your home? Where will you live?" Gartee was gathering up the string; soon he would spring the trap.

"Oh, I'll probably have two homes—one near the campus and a weekend retreat on the cape." Tindal smiled as he drifted into his dreams and pushed the dust pile to the right.

"Your country must be very different from mine," Gartee casually observed. "In my country, dead people don't have any of the things you described, as they are simply buried with little more than the clothes on their back."

The trap snapped shut. Tindal's toe jerked involuntarily and decapitated the perfectly shaped pile of dust as he found himself torn away from fantasy by a reality he had refused to allow himself to admit. Deep inside, he knew Emile Beaucroix planned to kill him, but he was now rudely aware that he had been suppressing the extent of the danger, even to himself.

"He plans to kill you." Gartee almost had him turned. "He plans to kill all of us because he is *N'devli*, the devil. He kills because it is the only thing that keeps him alive. Like a devil, he feeds off blood, and he will drink your blood too, Doctor, unless you drink his first. In your Western culture, you would call him a vampire."

Tindal's mind once again returned to his medical school training in psychiatry and to scientific reason. It was amazing how primitive cultures considered men like Beaucroix to be merely a tool of some unseen malignant force. Tindal was a doctor, and as such, he was a highly educated man. Even though he was terrified of Beaucroix, he knew the Monster was a quite ordinary man afflicted by a terrible disease.

It was true that he hated Beaucroix, but he pitied him also; as a doctor, he felt sorry for him. Beaucroix knew what Tindal thought of him because he had known other doctors before; he had been analyzed and pitied before. Emile Beaucroix, however, didn't mind a little pity because he considered it an amusing, pleasant diversion. Being a psychotic was not only very satisfying, but it was also a heck of a lot of fun!

"I don't really think he'd actually kill me." Tindal veered off the subject and away from the obvious reality, his thoughts wandering back into the mind of a clinical physician. "Schizoid personalities mainly get their kicks from scaring and manipulating people. They're mostly gas and hot air unless you push them against the wall, which could be dangerous," Tindal cautioned.

"I promise you he plans to kill you." Gartee wasn't convincing the doctor, and he knew it.

"How can you be so sure?" asked Tindal, who already had forgotten his own certainty.

"Because General Kutu told all of us to protect you, to see that nothing happens to you. The general warned all of us that if anything happened to you—even an accident—there would be the devil to pay."

"So that's your job. It's why you're here," Tindal replied, getting irritated.

"You don't understand. Beaucroix told the general to order everyone to leave you alone because he wants you for himself—he wants to kill you."

Tindal jumped, and his throat fell to his colon. Reality had charged in with the fury of a runaway train. He dove deep inside himself and then far outside, but as far as he searched, both within and without, there was but one option. Gartee had been right—clever and cunning—but still right.

"If I were to give you *something*, like an aspirin, could you trick the cook into putting it into his food?" Tindal chose his wording carefully.

"Attending to Mr. Beaucroix's innards would give the cook great pleasure. The cook this week is a great friend of mine and hates Beaucroix because he hates all white European imperialist pigs. No offense, Doctor," Gartee apologized for his honesty.

"None taken." Tindal was smiling for only the second time since he'd arrived in Bopolu. "Tonight you'll meet me behind the barracks around eight, and we'll finalize the plan."

They jumped as a sharp blast of a pistol echoed through the compound, scattering a medley of birds. The two men swung to meet their fates.

Standing a scant six paces behind them was the leering presence of Emile Beaucroix, holding the still-warm Beretta as it emanated a playful wisp of smoke. The Monster stood grinning, playing his favorite game. The terrified men shook as Beaucroix casually shrugged and swung his pistol slightly to the right. He gestured toward the woodpile and the fat, dead rodent that lay before it.

"Rats!" explained Beaucroix, but he wasn't referring to the rodent he'd just shot. He wanted these dirty little rats to know their plan was now a bust. They'd been caught. Never mind the devil; it would be Beaucroix they'd have to pay.

Beaucroix was happy, delighted, and thoroughly energized. Things had been too boring lately—boring and insipid. He had considered killing Tindal tonight because the rich little twit's attitude really irritated him. He wasn't happy with the progress the doctor had been making lately either, and he really needed a bit of fun.

But now he would wait, perhaps even being a little more solicitous and polite to the good doctor. Now that Gartee and Tindal both knew he would kill them, he could wait. Making a victim wait while you played and toyed with him and extended the torment was a heck of a lot more fun. It was the sort of clever game Beaucroix loved and lived for.

Emile Beaucroix was a man who firmly believed that one could never have too much fun. You may quote him; he is big that way. He considers himself a demon for the ages.

December 30, 1963
Washington, DC

"I don't trust him farther than I can throw the great state of Texas. We need to protect our asses by getting him out of the way." Senator Jorgensen turned to Hampstead for support.

"You handpicked the man, all of you. Now you want me to kill him too?" Hampstead surveyed the room. "What has he done?"

"It's what he's planning to do—that's what worries me," Senator Thurston said, "and it should worry even you. He's in this as deep as the rest of us, yet he's doing some very disturbing things. President Johnson can no longer be trusted. He needs to go."

"You still haven't answered my question, Thurston. I work for the CIA, not Murder Incorporated. Tell me what the man has done, please!" Hampstead had nothing against murder, but he couldn't see the upside for him in all this.

"Lyndon Johnson plans to support Robert F. Kennedy in his run for a Senate seat. Now that we just put the Warren Commission to rest, we don't need an angry, vengeful senator screaming for a new commission." He looked around the table and received several nods of affirmation.

Hampstead shrugged. "Who cares if the man goes into politics? What's your point?"

Senator Fred Haney slapped the heavily varnished walnut table. Apparently Hampstead didn't realize who was in charge here. "The point is this, Mr. CIA: Lyndon Johnson was the mortal enemy of Bobby

Kennedy when Kennedy was attorney general, and he tried everything—and I mean everything—this side of hell to get JFK to remove him from that office. The only reason he could be supporting Bobby Kennedy now is guilt, and if he moves that guilt a step further, all of us in this room will hang like bulbs on a Christmas tree. Hampstead, I don't intend to hang like a bulb on a Christmas tree! I'll see your balls dangling from the Statue of Liberty before I let them hang me."

"Senator, are you threatening me? I wouldn't recommend that. It wouldn't be wise." Hampstead leaned forward; he had begun to boil.

"And if I said I was, what would you do about it, Hampstead? Order me killed?" It was Senator Haney's turn to pass simmer and head to boil.

"Stranger things have happened," Hampstead calmly replied as he leaned back, lacing his fingers together and placing his folded hands upon the beech wood table as he tilted the right side of his head toward the senator and winked, grinning.

"Hold it, Hampstead," Senator Thurston ordered. "I'm going to pretend none of this was said by either one of you. Now, let's move on. It seems to me we made a mistake with Johnson. His conscience could prove an inconvenience to us. What's particularly disturbing to me is the stand he's taken on civil rights. He damn well knows how we feel about that. When Johnson was a young senator, he was one of us. He hated niggers too!

"I think LBJ is pushing his civil rights agenda as a vendetta. It's revenge against the lot of us for killing the president. Johnson is totally unstable and can't be trusted. He needs to go. Who agrees with me?" Senator Thurston looked around the room; a few nods greeted his question, while other dour faces looked down at the shiny, waxed conference table before them.

Murders had been committed before in the name of protecting America's democracy, but for a few of these senators, it was still a nasty pill to swallow.

"Gentlemen, killing a president is one thing. Killing two in a row would be a tad suspicious, probably even to someone like you, Senator Thurston," Hampstead observed.

"I still say he has to go!" Thurston insisted.

"So you want me to murder the president of the United States because you're afraid your pretty blond daughter will date a black man, and maybe enjoy it?" Hampstead looked around the room.

"Hell, yes! I mean no." Senator Thurston's red neck was showing.

"Damn you, Hampstead, you're not in charge here. What we decide, you will damn well do. Is that clear?" Senator Haney had gotten a hold of a bone and wasn't done chewing.

"Do you have life insurance, Senator? I wouldn't want your wife to suffer," Hampstead offered with a faint grin.

"What!" Haney bolted out of his chair.

"Sit your ass down, Fred, and Hampstead, you shut the fuck up!" roared Thurston. "We really should concentrate on covering each other's asses. We're all guilty here. What we did was right for America, but if the American people find out what we did to JFK, we'll all fry like shrimp in Louisiana. I don't intend to fry like a shrimp in Louisiana!" Thurston slapped the table and leaned back. That was his opinion, and it wasn't going to change.

"Senators, I work for the CIA. I killed the president for you because you convinced me it was in America's best interests. I don't intend to make a habit of bumping off presidents because you can't make up your mind who you want in the White House, or what color fellow comes knocking to see your pretty, blond, virgin daughter." Hampstead was getting tired of these idiots. He had a war to fight elsewhere—the Cold War—and he intended to win it.

"I don't see how it affects America's security for me to worry about what color ass sat on the toilet seat before me," he continued. "I hope you're not wasting my time by calling me here just to pander to your narrow-minded, redneck bigotry." Hampstead didn't like politicians much; in fact, he wouldn't much mind terminating this entire room.

"This meeting has nothing to do with civil rights. We're concerned about the future of America and the values we all hold dear. I think we can all agree on that." Thurston cast his eyes around the room. All nodded, except Hampstead, who didn't seem happy with any of this.

"Cut the bull, Senator. Your only concern is saving your own ass." Hampstead looked the senator right in the eyes. He was rapidly starting to hate this man.

"You're damn right, Hampstead, I'm trying to save my ass! And his ass, his ass, his ass, and all your asses." Senator Thurston pointed to each and every man in the room.

"Senators…" Hampstead was getting exasperated. Politics had nothing to do with him, but he knew a way out. "Let's look at this supposed situation logically and stop wasting my time. President Johnson isn't the problem. He isn't what you're worried about. You're afraid Bobby Kennedy is going to get elected to the Senate and press for a new commission. Is that right?"

Hampstead surveyed the room and was rewarded with several nods. "Senators, I understand that junior senators don't sit on any committees. All committees are put together by seniority. You gentlemen have that seniority. The people in this room control who sits on which senatorial committees.

"Let Robert Kennedy run for the Senate, let him win. He won't be able to do anything for at least two terms, and if he does, call me again. Now, is this meeting finished?"

Half the room nodded, and that was enough; Hampstead rose and left the room. Unknown to him, four years later, they would take him up on his offer and call him back.

December 30, 1963
Bopolu, Liberia

"I am by nature a lovable man, and you know this—you all know this," Kutu said, smiling broadly. "Thanks to my many great, wonderful, brave American friends, I am also a very rich man." He motioned toward Emile Beaucroix, who rendered a friendly salute.

As Kutu raised his arms, the assembled bunch of Liberians applauded robustly, filling the compound with echoes of their enthusiasm. The Liberian soldiers were well accustomed to singing praises to his kindness, generosity, and love for his men. To imply that the general was less than wonderful always had been a guarantee of disaster.

"Brave soldiers, fellow Liberians, the Americans have been good to me, and they have been good to you. You eat the best food in Africa, you have the best medicine, and you get to work with these wonderful people." He motioned toward the four Americans.

Hogan nodded; Tindal smiled; and Michael Orman clapped politely, but Beaucroix positively beamed as he tossed Kutu another friendly salute.

"But what kind of man am I? Could I really keep such riches and good fortune for myself?" The general paused, waiting for the effect, but the soldiers were slow to respond. Disappointed, Kutu thought, *These stupid monkeys. They should have had better coaching lest they embarrass me.*

"Come on. Come on," Kutu continued. "You know me, you know my great heart. Could I really keep all this good fortune and all these riches to myself?"

"No!" shouted a tall Liberian sergeant as the others finally figured out the play and guessed their roles. As a group, they joined and blasted at the top of their lungs a resounding "*No!*"

With this, General Kutu rose from his chair on the veranda and raised his hands above his head, which prompted the soldiers to enter a resounding chorus of "*No! No! No!*" This scene played out for a full three minutes before Kutu lowered his arms.

"Wonderful! Wonderful!" Kutu smiled broadly as he turned toward Michael Orman, the new kid on the block. "Can you see how they love me? Soon they will love you too! I have such wonderful men. They adore me, but you cannot blame them." The general raised his arms, which prompted more loud applause until he lowered them fully two minutes later.

Orman was willing to bet that if he offered to shoot the fat blowhard right now, these Liberians would really get to cheering.

"Now, my wonderful, brave, brave soldiers…" He raised his arms again, prompting more cheers. But he lowered them with a snap after only three seconds, instantly killing the applause.

Orman wondered, *What the heck was that about?* He glanced at Beaucroix, but the Monster simply smiled.

"The American government is very grateful for the safety and security you have provided this medical research facility. On this very spot, hardworking American doctors and medical research technicians are working on the cures of tomorrow. They plan to make evils such as cancer and malaria nothing more than memories, and you, gentlemen, and I are privileged to be a part of this great but secret endeavor.

"But there are evil men on this continent and corrupt nations all over this world who would like to get their hands on this good research for evil purposes. Thus, for the benefit of all mankind and for the glory of Liberia, we must maintain the utmost secrecy surrounding Bopolu.

"As an expression of its gratitude, the American government has approved, at my robust urging and suggestion, a five-dollar monthly supplement to your already-ample Liberian military pay."

With this totally unexpected fiat, the soldiers applauded, shouted, cheered, and sent the birds in the jungle, departing as one to find a quieter abode.

Hogan smiled. He was giving the general twenty dollars a week for every man and five thousand a month to general Kutu. But this hadn't started last week. He had been faithfully paying it since the base at Bopolu had opened thirteen months ago.

Kutu angrily waved his arms, finally quieting the assembly. He was upset the idiots had applauded before he had a chance to prompt them, and these asses had applauded louder than before. Showmanship—that's what good leadership is all about.

It was impossible to put on a good show with bad actors. *Stupid monkey actors*, thought Kutu. Recovering his composure, he took a deep breath as he remembered the script and returned to the play.

"Mr. M'butu, please come forward." He motioned the lieutenant forward and brought him to within arm's length. "The Americans have insisted on certain changes." Kutu paused for effect. "And I fully concur." With this, he snapped his fingers, prompting a sergeant and three privates to run forward, stopping six feet from him as they leveled their rifles at Lieutenant M'butu, who stood with the frozen posture of sheer terror.

"We are very, very dissatisfied with you, Lieutenant M'butu," the general growled and raised his right hand.

The lieutenant was too shocked to move. Fear chased terror through his mind as he tried to remember what terrible thing he had done.

"This is a situation that cannot be tolerated, and, as your commanding officer and a representative of the Liberian government, I intend to resolve it now!" He dropped his hand to his side, and the shocked silence was shattered by the blast of three Mauser rifles.

Jumping forward, Kutu grabbed a slumping M'butu by the shoulders, forcing him to shakily stand. He deftly ripped off M'butu's lieutenant's epaulets and then stepped back and raised his right hand in a snappy salute.

"Relax. We didn't shoot you. Relax and stand, Major M'butu." The general was laughing at his brilliant showmanship, his clever little joke.

M'butu, suddenly aware of a sharp pain in his right shoulder, quickly identified its source. Kutu cleverly had pinned major's insignias on his uniform as he had helped him rise. One was sloppily pinned to khaki and the other firmly in flesh.

"I just promoted you to the rank of major!" General Kutu, ever the prankster, adjusted his khaki-torturing belly, which responded with a bounce and a few quaking ripples. "Yes, Major M'butu, you are now making forty dollars more a month, and you are officially my second-in-command, at least here in Bopolu."

Kutu glanced at the crowd. A private had begun to bring his hands together in applause, but a quick, cold stare from the general froze them before the twain could meet. Slowly Kutu began to raise his arms, but as a cheer threatened, he immediately dropped his arms to his side, quieting the crowd with an angry stare. Slowly he raised them to shoulder level; as a corporal applauded, however, he immediately dropped his arms, prompting silence. Two more times Kutu slowly raised his arms, dropping them at the slightest sign of applause. Finally he was able to fully extend them above his head in total silence.

"Well?" the general, beaming broadly, asked with a silly, questioning expression. The soldiers went wild, and he was beside himself with joy. As he held his arms up, the applause echoed unabated for a full five minutes.

B. F. Skinner was right, thought Kutu. *Stupid monkeys can learn, but only if they have the right kind of teacher.*

Michael Orman was silently taking notes. He would like to kill this man—this spastic, ass-blasting, blowhard general—and he would find the time and place to do so. That was a little promise he made to himself. Yet another player was setting his own rules to the game.

But the Monster also was deep in the game; nothing got past the eyes and ears of Emile Beaucroix. The genius of the Monster—his incredibly brilliant, psychotic genius—lay in his ability to work all the rules of the game into his own rules. Beaucroix glanced at Orman, reading his mind. It reminded him of his favorite credo: One could never have too much fun.

January 3, 1964
Washington, DC

"Senator, the forces behind the Wildfire project are exactly the same forces within the US government that ordered the murder of our own president!" Senator Murphy banged his gavel on the mahogany table.

A number of senators had covertly contacted Mack Murphy and asked him to set up a secret meeting with all concerned parties to deal with the rumors that had been floating around the dark corners of Washington. Murphy had decided not to inform these senators of the earlier meetings with RFK and the other senators, just in case.

"I object to that statement, Senator Murphy. It's never been proven that there was any kind of conspiracy. After exhaustive inquiries, the commission ruled there was no conspiracy," Senator Charlton Brook declared.

"Now, gentlemen," Senator Murphy said, "if the Internal Revenue Service informs you that it has found irregularities in your tax return, does the IRS charge you with investigating these irregularities and accept your own conclusion as to whether additional taxes are owed?" This logic brought muffled laughter from more than person seated at the table.

"Senator Brook, the Warren Commission was commissioned by the US government to determine whether, in fact, there was a government conspiracy. The conclusion of the Warren Commission, a *government-appointed* commission, was that there was no government conspiracy." Senator Murphy raised a sarcastic eyebrow. "Senator Brook," he continued, "what you actually object to—and what we all object to—is learning that forces within our government murdered the president. If this knowledge became public, it would harm America and usurp American ideals. But by crushing the Wildfire project and punishing those responsible, we'll also be punishing the assassins of America's leader and American ideals.

"Senators, I intend to go after these madmen and renegade scientists and shut down this evil project for good, but let us not kid ourselves—we're very much up against the best of the CIA, and they're the best there is.

"Clearly they've found powerful, evil allies within our own government and possibly even within this room. If that's the case, gentlemen, then by inviting that person here, we're all surely dead. I've chosen very carefully whom I invited here today, and I hope for all our sakes—and the sakes of our wives and children—that I have not chosen in error.

"Gentlemen, we'll need the very best agent there is because the CIA is the best there is, and I fear they've employed the best of the best they could muster to protect Wildfire. To counter this threat, I've hired the best intelligence officer the US Army ever had or ever will have. Without a doubt, he's the only man who can best the best of the CIA. It's been my pleasure to work with him in Japan, China, and Korea. Gentlemen, I present to you the Shadow." Murphy gestured toward the closed, elegantly carved, oak double doors.

With this announcement, all eyes turned toward the doors. A second passed, then two, then three, but the doors didn't move. Senator Beau Duran looked toward Senator Murphy, who could only shrug. Irritated, Duran glanced at his watch and then turned to confirm its results with the large wall clock. But his glance was halted with a jolt as he spotted a large object directly to his right.

"Good afternoon, gentlemen," the Shadow greeted, and all present turned with a collective jolt to the far end of the oval table, where the huge man sat, casually smoking a Corona.

The big man had appeared out of nowhere and already had helped himself to a comfortable chair.

"How did you get in here?" Senator Schumer demanded.

"I tried the window, but it was locked. Then I tried to slip under the door, but I got stuck." He removed his cigar and grinned. "So I walked in the open door with the rest of you. How are you doing, Mack? How are the wife and kids?"

"Just how the hell did you get in here, smartass? You didn't walk in with us," Senator Sam Toole demanded in a winding Southern drawl.

"I told you he was good. That's why we call him the Shadow!" Senator Murphy stated with satisfaction.

"Why are you called the Shadow?" General J. G. Holder inquired, offering his first and only contribution to the meeting.

"His shadow would blot out Montana," Senator Tim Booker whispered into the ear of the senator next to him

"And it could surely darken parts of Wyoming as well!" the big man boomed out to a general round of laughter, which wilted the young senator. Caught and embarrassed, Booker cast his eyes at the table.

"Don't be embarrassed, Senator. I'm a big man who's often asked to do big jobs. My hearing is legendary, so there's no offense taken. Now let's move the wood closer to the fire and get down to business."

January 4, 1963
United States Embassy; Freetown, Liberia

"A virus, gentlemen," Dr. Tindal began, "has a coating of proteins that makes it susceptible to attack by any immune system that recognizes a pattern it identifies as a foreign body. Once the human body recognizes an invader, it will marshal the entire immune system to destroy it. Therefore, an invader gets only one chance to destroy its host. Thereafter, if the host fully survives the first attack, it not only becomes immune, but also, its descendants can inherit that trait.

"Eventually, a virus will mutate enough so it can re-infest the descendant of a previously immune host. Normally, this mutative process takes many years and thousands of generations. Simply by virtue of change, this host no longer can identify it. This is true of all bacteria and viruses, but bacteria can be killed with antibiotics, while a virus cannot."

Even Beaucroix, who couldn't follow a word of what the doctor was saying, was fascinated by this: the birth and genesis of a killer deadlier and more cunning than he was.

"What I propose, gentlemen," Tindal continued, "is to engineer a unique virus that cannot be destroyed except by its creator. An auto mutating virus that has never existed in nature—a virus that doesn't mutate every ten thousand generations but rather mutates from host to host.

"I want to give America a weapon for which there is no defense. Gentlemen, I can offer you a bug that is bigger than the H-bomb. Think of it. The H-bomb costs millions to destroy a city and then billions to rebuild it. With this new weapon I created, you can take a city for pennies and have it intact. Dropped on a military installation, it will spread like wildfire, killing soldiers but leaving the buildings and munitions undamaged." Tindal smiled as he reached for the peak of his power.

"Dr. Tindal..." Senator Thurston had removed his pipe and was pointing it at the doctor. "Wouldn't such a virus kill our own troops also?"

"Senator Thurgood, what I—"

"That's Senator Thurston, not Thurgood, Doctor."

"Sorry. I offer my apologies, Senator Thurston. Actually, Senator, I'm engineering the virus to work specifically with human hosts only. This virus, I am confident, can be engineered to 100 percent effectiveness."

"Then it will kill our own boys too," the senator pointed accusingly with his pipe.

"Not at all, Senator. What I said was that the virus being created can live only inside a human host. Once you attack a city, a military base, or a population center with this virus, you need wait only a week or so until the last human has died. Lacking anywhere to go or the means to reproduce, the virus simply dies out—it disappears.

"This city, military base, or factory is now free for the taking. The virus no longer will exist in that location. Lacking a living human host, it will no longer exist anywhere but within the test tubes of our secure armory. That, gentlemen, is the genius of this weapon. If a nation dares to challenge America's righteous might, this virus will quickly knock them to their knees. This will end the bloody cost of war by causing the aggressor to pay the entire cost of America's true and righteous rage."

Now Tindal paused, considering what he had said earlier about the virus spreading like wildfire. He already had spilled the beans, so he might as well tell them. Hogan had approved the code name some time ago.

"That's what we've decided to call this virus, our supreme weapon. We named it Wildfire. It's a weapon for which there is no defense, a weapon that will make America greater by tenfold than the sum of her enemies. It is truly a bug too big to kill. Wildfire, gentlemen, is the future of war!" He struck the podium with his palm to drive home the point.

Beaucroix slammed his fist on the table and bolted upright.

In terror, Tindal wondered what he had done to offend the Monster. But the Monster just stood, holding captive the gazes of everyone present, who looked with amazement as a grin passed across those evil lips. The Monster raised his right arm and, with his finger, indicated he was speaking to the entire room.

"Wildfire!" shouted Beaucroix, and the group collectively jumped. He surveyed them with his psychotic leer, which appeared more demonic than ever. "Wildfire!" the Monster shouted again. The Liberian ambassador and assembled senators were taken by surprise by Beaucroix's outburst and were too shocked to speak.

"I like it!" he shouted as he rushed forward and grabbed Tindal. He tore the doctor from behind the podium and roughly shook his hand like a tire pump in congratulations. "You've got the job!" Beaucroix bellowed as he tossed Tindal across the room and back toward the podium, smashing the young doctor's knee against the hard mahogany base. Then the Monster slapped the podium, turned, and strutted out the door, clearly delighted. It was true, one could never have too much fun.

CHAPTER TWELVE
The Candidates

May 31, 1976
Damascus, Syria

Casually the old woman snuck a few sheets of flatbread into her burka. She pretended to be testing the onions with her right hand as her left deftly slipped three more into her cloak.

"Pardonnez-moi, monsieur," Baron Le Boeuf quietly addressed the man at the counter. He could not tolerate thievery. "Are you the grocer?"

"Yes, how may I help you? You are a Frenchman. *Comment allez-vous?*"

"Très bien. Merci. But that woman is stealing from you, the old one over there." The baron motioned toward her as she popped a package of salt into her bulging burka.

"Yes, I know she is stealing." The grocer smiled and winked at the old woman, who noticed the two men looking in her direction.

"Don't you care?"

The tall Arab smiled. "Not really. The third week of the month, she always comes in and steals from me. Then, on the first day of the next month, which is when she gets her husband's small pension, she comes to me and invents a story and then pays me. Every month she gives me a different story. Last month was the best! She told me she came in the week before, picked out all her food, and suddenly remembered she forgot to water the flowers in front of her home. So she rushed home and simply forgot to pay me. If she didn't rush home immediately, the flowers would surely die, and the women on her street would start a rumor that she kept a poor house!"

"What if she doesn't pay you when her check comes in?" the baron asked. "She could just go to another grocer and do to him what you let her do to you."

"No matter. The Koran requires me to be charitable, and the Koran requires her to be honest. Muslims trust all such things to Allah. She either pays me or not. If she does not, she has lost far more than I."

"Your beliefs, monsieur, give safe haven to thieves, so I do not agree." The baron despised the poor. They were beneath contempt and certainly beneath him.

"You do not have to agree with Allah, nor do I. We simply must obey him. A good friend of mine is a Christian, born in Jerusalem. He once said something about Christians that might interest you. He said when a Christian steals, he will not be lonely in hell, because his preacher will be there to comfort him. He was, I think, a cynical Christian." The tall Arab bobbed a finger for emphasis.

"Then we Christians are all thieves as well?" Baron Le Boeuf was irritated that he had forgotten his breeding and had engaged a mere tradesman in conversation, an unforgivable faux pas for the upper classes.

"No, monsieur, the saying applies to everyone. It simply means that when a person does evil things, it is because they learned to do so from people around them. When we cheat, harm, or treat another person with disrespect, it is because we learned to do so from others."

"Well, I must go," the baron replied in a huff. He'd had enough of this plastic philosophy. "If you do not mind being stolen from by this thief, it is your affair. You have your God, and I have mine. Your religion is a closed religion, and it is not open to the views of others!"

"You have misread my religion, like most Europeans do. Christians and Jews are both mentioned in the Koran. They also are people of the book, children of Allah; and the revelations of the holy prophet Mohammed—blessings be upon him—require all Moslems to accept this. I agree with you, Christian—tolerance should be a part of all religions, because tolerance comes from Allah; it comes from God. Allah alone is perfect, and he desires all of us to strive toward perfection.

But he does not require us to be perfect; the Prophet Mohammed has told us we are imperfect flesh-and-blood men. But speaking of tolerance, my friend, were the Crusades, the Spanish Inquisition, or the genocides created by or carried out by Muslims? Was Hitler a Sunni or a Shi'ite?"

"You're speaking of past history, long dead, and buried, monsieur. That is long past and irreverent today." Baron Le Boeuf would end this conversation with this ignorant commoner.

"Ah, you speak of history, my friend. History is the world's worst teacher, because mankind seems unable to learn from it!" the grocer said with a smile.

"Monsieur, you are simply a dull grocer. You know nothing of history, religion, or philosophy. I am a man of letters, and you're wasting my time. I must go."

"Monsieur, your God is my God, and my God is yours. There is no God but God. I repeat this five times a day and will do so with pleasure until the day I die. It doesn't matter what you call him; he is still Allah, and he is still there. No, Christian, God does not care what you call yourself as long as you obey him and treat others well. If you told me you were a Buddhist, a Jew, or a Hindu, I would neither like nor dislike you. I would like or dislike you because of what is in here." The Arab placed his fist over his heart. "All wisdom is with Allah. I am fortunate to be a Muslim. But if I were not, I would still wish to be a good man!"

"Only a Christian can gain access to the gates of heaven. The Bible says so." Baron Le Boeuf closed the discussion.

"Muslims and North Africans are too well educated to insult strangers and ridicule their beliefs. Western media glosses over a simple truth, that true Muslims recognize both Jews and Christians as people of the Book and believe that they also are children of Allah. The Koran requires this. We are required both by the Prophet and the Koran to respect them. In the most holy Koran, in 29:46 AYA, the book speaks of and to Christians and Jews. It says, 'We believe in the Revelation which has come down to us and in that which came down to you; our Allah and your Allah are one.'

"But I was educated in an excellent French school in Lebanon, so I can give you a little insight. I will tell you what no other Muslim would." The grocer grinned as he said this.

The baron grinned also.

"You are an ass!" the grocer returned to counting his cabbages.

The smile left France, but it glowed even brighter on the man who understood God.

July 4, 1976
Billings, Montana

The big man exited his Cadillac with a thud and dusted off his new, ill-fitting Levi's. He stepped onto the porch of the hot, dusty, summer-baked Montana farmhouse. "Who do we have here, and where is my big, giant, huge, monster hug?" The Shadow scratched his head as the young boy swung the door wide open.

"The kid! I'm the kid!" the boy shouted, and flew into the big man's waiting arms.

"Jason! Welcome back to Montana. Bring your backside into the kitchen. You got here just in time. Martha is just putting the food on the table. I expect you still have a taste for good Montana beef." Carl warmly shook his favorite brother's hand and, with his other hand on the big man's shoulder, guided him through the rooms and into the kitchen.

"Uncle, Uncle, do you know what day it is?" the boy shouted, more excited than he'd been in weeks.

"Calm down, Derek. Your uncle just traveled one hundred miles of Montana dust to get here. Let him catch his breath. He's going to be with us quite a spell." They had reached the kitchen, and Martha ran forward to embrace their guest.

"Jason, come give us a big Montana hug—that is, if you can remember how we hug 'round these parts. I surely missed you. Billings is a whole lot less interesting with you out of town. The most excitement we've had since you left was when Billy Two Moons got drunk and woke up Sunday morning, naked as a jaybird, on the bench in front of Gardner's store. You should have seen the reverend's face when he walked past him on his way up to the church, escorting Widow Hawkins. I do believe Widow

Hawkins plumb forgot what a man's business looked like, given the odd expression she tossed toward his naked joy. Welcome home. I hope you plan to stay for a while."

The big man advanced, gathering her in his arms as he embraced her, reaching into her soul as his fingers affectionately caressed her tight back, firmed by the demanding but soul-fulfilling life of a farmer.

"Uncle, Uncle, what day is it? What day is it?" The boy couldn't hold it in any longer.

"It's the Fourth of July, the day our great nation was founded!" The Shadow smiled, but, as he saw the hurt in the child's face, he quickly added, "That's not all it is. It's also the fifth birthday of my favorite person in the entire world! Let me see…Now, whose birthday is it?" The Shadow examined the ceiling, seemingly deep in contemplation and searching for the answer.

"The kid, the kid! It's my birthday. I'm five, and it's my fifth birthday!" Barely able to contain his excitement, the boy stomped his foot.

"Are you sure?" The Shadow glanced at the ceiling as he pondered the information.

"I'm five…*five*! And it's my birthday!" Derek stomped his foot again.

"Do you know what I know?" The big man asked in a conspiratorial whisper, putting his index finger to his lips to emphasize the need for secrecy.

"No! Tell me! Spies never reveal secrets!" the boy promised with conviction.

"I know that my most favorite person in the world is the only boy in Billings, Montana, who owns two genuine African ivory elephant tusks!"

"I want them! I want them. Where are they? I want them!"

"Now what do we tell Uncle Jason, Derek?" Martha smiled, grateful to have the finest brother-in-law in all of Montana.

"Thank you, Uncle. Where are they? Where are they? I want them! I want them!" the boy exclaimed, jumping up and down.

"Derek!" Carl wanted his son to calm down. Jason had only just arrived, and he needed a chance to get comfortable and clean himself up for dinner.

"A good spy always follows the evidence." The Shadow wagged the Cadillac's keys at the eager boy. "My car has only two locked compartments, the glove box and the trunk. Where do you think you should look first?" The big man shook the keys again and smiled at the restless boy before him.

"The trunk—they're in the trunk!" The boy grabbed the keys and bolted out the front door.

"Jason, you're going to spoil him!" Martha scolded.

"Yes, I know. That was my intention," the Shadow replied as he watched his nephew through the window struggle happily to pull a massive tusk from the Cadillac's trunk.

"How long can you stay this time?" Carl asked him. He could use his help on their ranch for a few days. Jason was a damn good man with a tractor.

"Only a couple of days. They need me overseas. There's some pretty nasty business afoot, and our country needs me. I miss my nephew, and I miss both of you. I wish to God I could stay longer, but duty calls, and we live in a world with so much evil and so few giants."

The Shadow was still watching his nephew, recording every movement in his mind. It might be a long time until he got to see him again.

"You be careful, Jason…real careful. Derek thinks the world of you. You damn well better be careful," Martha cautioned.

July 7, 1976
Tunis, Tunisia

Max George always knew what he wanted, and this French-Spanish beauty definitely fit the bill. She was young, lively, and capable of good conversation and happy diversion. He often had seen her at the Hannibal Club in the company of other men, and he wondered when they might finally meet.

Today she was there alone, bored and picking daintily at a Caesar salad. Suddenly she looked up and noticed his stare. It was too late to cover his rudeness; he could do no more than post a silly grin. Smiling back, she glanced at her table's empty chair. Max dropped his silverware onto his table and went to join her.

"Hello," he said, smiling as he helped himself to a seat. "Tell me, is it legal in Tunisia for a woman to be so beautiful?" Max raised an eyebrow as he admired the way her halter top fought to restrain her huge breasts.

She blushed deeply. She had heard he was charming.

"My name is Maxwell George. Friends call me Max. I hope we can become friends."

"Yes, I know," she replied, blushing again.

"What do you know, my goddess, my Cleopatra? Tell me lest I melt in front of you."

"I know you're a drug dealer, a Casanova, and a flirt. You're a man who should be avoided like the bubonic plague."

Drug dealer was good. He hadn't blown his local cover; besides, it didn't seem to matter much to her.

"Am I a drug dealer? Not so, my lady. Consider me rather a person in search of drugs. I am a man in search of the sweet opium of your lips!"

The beauty blushed at this compliment. Out of the corner of his eye, Max caught a quick thumbs-up and grin from the table of Robert Hogan.

"To further the insult, you call me a Casanova? A Casanova, my lady, is a man who has vaulted through a thousand bedroom windows. I could be no Casanova because once I vaulted through your window, I could go no farther." He smiled as her cheeks flushed a deeper red.

"Now I could be called a Don Quixote perhaps, and you would be my sugar-sweet Dulcinea," Max added. "And shame on the day you call me a flirt, my goddess. Consider me instead a slave to your beauty and an overseer to your every desire." Max tipped his faded, floppy legionnaire hat. "I would have crawled naked through the Gobi to meet you. I would sleep on a cactus a hundred lifetimes just to hold your hand."

"That could be fun," she said playfully.

"What? Sleeping on a cactus would be fun? Would you help me pull the needles from my naked butt?" Max quizzed as his eyes passed up and down her dress and paused twice at the fabric fighting to restrain her firm, sassy, luscious breasts.

"No, the fun part would be watching you crawl naked to my bed. That could be fun," she replied.

"Then, my goddess and my lady, so you shall!" Max gallantly stated as they both rose and headed out of the Hannibal Club and into the warm morning air.

From his table, Hogan offered a salute with his whiskey glass to their retreating backs as the two lovers departed.

In the dim light of the bedroom, he grinned in anticipation. He couldn't believe how those fresh, creamy, white thighs seemed to go on forever. He planted his tongue just above a shapely knee and began to circle, working up slowly an inch at a time. He teased by circling his tongue and licking his way up and then down back to the knee, often bringing furtive giggles as he gave the inside of each thigh a silly, little, snaky lick.

The moaning and the parted full lips told him he was doing something right. He advanced his skilled tongue to the other thigh and began torturing the kneecap, assaulting it with pleasure. Again he teased and taunted, bringing his skilled tongue farther and farther up that fantastic, creamy, white thigh, but then he'd pause, never making it all the way up—up to that special place. A place where he was the master and his flickering tongue a legend.

"Take me again. Please, you've got to take me again!" The pleasure was almost too much to bear.

Moving up to the full, shaking lips, his smooth tongue wetting them as it sailed across them, was too much for *him* to bear. Jumping up off his knees, he dove deep into those lips as his tongue flickered, exploring rapidly and hungrily, seeking new spots of ecstasy upon the road to sexual fulfillment.

"You wanted it, bitch, and now you are going to get it. I'm going to ram you in the ass so hard and blast so much cum into your big, meaty butt that it will shoot out your ears and spray onto both walls!"

Suddenly the door crashed open, announcing a roaring pistol blast that shattered the vase beside the bed and sent clay fragments flying through the air. Three more rapid rounds hammered the headboard above them as they both dove deeper into the mussed covers.

Michael Orman rolled off the side of the bed, and Major M'butu dove under the covers.

"Faggots!" screamed Beaucroix as he grabbed Orman from the bed and pistol-whipped him in an uncontrollable rage. He smashed the pistol repeatedly into Orman's face until he fell from the bed and was nothing more than a bloody pile on the floor. Satisfied with his work, he groin-kicked the groaning agent and turned his fury to the other bitch.

Now it was Chafa M'butu's turn. He tried to retreat and defend himself, but Beaucroix was too fast. The Monster leaped across the bed and, powered by rage, grabbed the major and gave him the same bloody pounding Orman had enjoyed. In a psychotic rage tainted by his inner demons, Beaucroix hammered M'butu until his knuckles were bloodied and swollen.

"Damn faggots!" the Monster shouted as he continued beating M'butu's face into an oozing, bloody pulp. Major M'butu screamed and begged for mercy as he tried in vain to deflect the blows, but Beaucroix was too fast, too furious, and too practiced. M'butu soon passed out from the pain.

When the bleeding pile no longer reacted, Beaucroix slowed his anger and surveyed his work. He needed to make certain they were both in agony. Fully satisfied, he stuck his head out the door.

"Guards!" the Monster bellowed into the compound as three of M'butu's men swiftly ran onto the veranda. "If anyone tries to leave this hut, kill them—and I mean anyone—or you'll wish you hadn't disobeyed me!" Beaucroix stormed off, urgently in need of the doctor's vile potion. God must be satisfied; the faggots needed to be punished.

The jungle reacted noisily as the monkeys chattered in the trees. The gods of Bopolu were indeed angry—furious, in fact—and not at the two bleeding young men.

Tunis, Tunisia

"How do you like my digs?" Max asked her.

"They suit you." She smiled as she moved her eyes around the room, taking in the antiques and ancient treasures. "Please tell me about this place. I want to know." She needed to know because he was a deeper man than any other she'd ever met. She wanted to know everything about him.

"Legend has it that the great Arabic General Abu Bekr spent the night here. This is the reputed site of the home of the Barca's of the Barcid Dynasty."

"Abu what?" she asked as she looked around the room, soaking in its history and power.

"Well, this house at one time was actually a small palace. It was built by Ben Wadi Abu Rashid in about one thousand AD as a monument to the Carthaginians, the only force that ever dared challenge the might of Rome and almost win.

"That legacy means a lot to North Africans. You see, the site is famous to all North African people. This house was originally much larger than it is today. It was destroyed and rebuilt several times over the centuries and always on exactly the same spot. Abu Bekr was the Prophet Mohammed's greatest general and best friend. Around 630 AD, he brought the Muslim army through here on their way to conquer Spain."

Max was amazed; never before had he met a woman who was as fascinated by history as he was. Never before had he met a woman with sex on her mind who could be diverted to anything else.

"This spot was the very site destroyed by Rome in about 180 BC, when it was the home of the Barca family. They were patricians of Carthage. It was Hamilcar and Hasdrubal Barca who conquered Spain for Carthage years earlier. When a rebel killed Hamilcar, his brother Hasdrubal continued the expansion for Carthage. He who founded Cartagena in Spain—New Carthage, he called it."

"Wow! How do you know so much?" She was fascinated by all the facets of this man.

"History is like a conscience. She reaches into a man's soul and teaches us about our follies and makes us—if we listen to her—better men and women." He was inspired by her interest.

"When the great Hasdrubal died in Spain, his nephew took over. He was the son of Hamilcar, Hannibal Barca. I think maybe you've heard of him?" He smiled into her love-hungry eyes.

"I think he was a lot like you," she flattered him sincerely. She could tell this man was a hero and destined for great things. "Hannibal was the king who rode elephants, wasn't he?"

"He wasn't a king," Max said. "He was a general and one of the best the world had ever seen. He had around forty-seven elephants, and but all but one died before he could reach Roman soil. Mostly he had packhorses and donkeys." Max was afraid he was boring her; besides, he needed some nooky.

Smiling playfully, she looked down at his crotch. "Are you part donkey?" She paused. "I think a man as romantic as you must have the means to turn a girl into a lady."

"And are you a girl or a lady?" Max ran his hands around her full breasts, cupping and caressing them as the fabric of his crotch fought valiantly to restrain the rapidly expanding stable within.

She brushed aside his hands. "I'm a very disappointed young girl."

Max knelt in front of her and dove into those deep-brown eyes. "Disappointed? At what, my lady? What part of me has disappointed you? Pray tell, and I will cut off the offender and cast it off! Tell me, my lady, and send me on a quest to slay the dirty dragon that has dared displease you!"

"You promised I could see you crawl naked across the floor." She playfully pushed him, laughing.

"Is that all, my lady? Is that all that has displeased you? My promise to let you see me crawl naked, gone unfulfilled?" Max thought for a moment then smiled. "And so you shall, my darling, and so you shall!"

Bopolu, Liberia

Like an angry buffalo, Beaucroix charged through the laboratory doors, shattering them and blowing wooden door fragments from the veranda all the way to Tindal's desk. His eyes were inflamed, red, and swollen with rage. He grabbed Tindal by the collar and lifted him off the lab stool high into the air. He shook the doctor violently as he screamed into his eyes.

"Where's the virus? Where's Wildfire!" he demanded.

Tindal was once again terrified, but, incredibly, he was more confused than scared. He could only stammer, "It's...it's in monkeys and rats," he gasped. "I'm working as hard as I can, as fast as I can. The research takes time!"

The confusion must have been contagious, because now it passed across the Monster's face. Grunting, he tossed Tindal to the floor as he moved to face the storage cabinet. Quietly, Beaucroix addressed the heap on the floor behind him. "Get me a syringe, Doctor."

"What for? Are you hurt?" Tindal asked.

"Get me a syringe, asshole," the Monster angrily demanded. "Two syringes with needles. Any questions, and I'll kill you!" His anger seemed to double every second—an exponential fury that swirled around him and filled the room in a fog of evil, immoral rage.

Tindal quickly jumped up from the floor and pulled two 30 cc syringes from a cardboard box and deftly popped two stainless-steel needles onto the nipples. "Here you are." He extended them toward his tormentor.

"Thank you." Beaucroix's rage was painfully measured. "Now fill them with the Wildfire virus."

Tindal was shocked beyond any response, and he had ceased to breathe as he saw the evil within the Monster's rage. Besides that, he never had heard the Monster say thank you before.

Beaucroix stepped forward and, in one fell swoop, unsheathed his razor-edged hunting knife and held it to the doctor's throat.

Tindal took the less immediate of evils. "I'll do it," he declared quietly.

After Beaucroix lowered the knife, Tindal carefully filled both syringes with the Wildfire virus. As he turned to offer them to Beaucroix, the Monster grabbed them from his hands and shoved him to the floor. Beaucroix then quickly headed to the door, then stopped, frozen in his tracks.

Standing halfway in the lab and halfway on the veranda, he spoke quietly and purposefully to the frightened doctor behind him. "If anyone finds out I was here, or what I took with me, I'll kill you, and I'll use the slowest, most painful method known to mankind. Is that clear, Doctor?"

"Very clear," replied Tindal as he watched Beaucroix cross the clearing and turn toward the barracks.

Somehow, Tindal was less afraid. He had spent much of his time in Bopolu in fear for his life, in fear of an evil that went beyond even

Beaucroix. Now something told him that he, like Beaucroix, had become a part of it.

Beaucroix turned sharply right and, as he stormed across the clearing, he noticed a small boy who had entered the compound, marshaling his pet goat via its leash of frayed twine. Without breaking stride, Beaucroix pulled out his pistol and fired across the compound, hitting the goat squarely beneath the horns and killing it instantly. The boy dropped the twine and fell to the ground, hugging the dead goat and bawling uncontrollably.

In the barracks, the guards had just been paid. They were fairly drunk and playing cards when the Monster flew in with eyes bulging. His heart was jumping, his pulse hammering, his blood pressure climbing higher as every molecule of his being cried out for revenge, punishment for crimes beyond description, crimes against God.

"Get your fucking asses outside and follow me *now!*" he ordered, storming out of the barracks and back to Michael Orman's quarters. The soldiers quickly retrieved their rifles and were running to catch up with Beaucroix and take their places in tow as he reentered Orman's quarters.

Inside, Orman was using a damp towel to help clean the blood off Major M'butu's face.

When Beaucroix saw this, he frowned; God, he hated fags. When the two men saw Beaucroix and the four soldiers standing with rifles ready, they were terrified.

"Beaucroix," Orman began.

"Shut up, faggot!" the Monster screamed. He turned to his men. "Grab him."

The soldiers grabbed Orman and headed to the door, but Beaucroix barred the way.

"What are you doing, you fuckheads and idiots? Where do you think you're going?" the Monster screamed at them. "Did I tell you to take him outside?"

The guards milled about, confused.

"Lay him on the bed and hold him down." Beaucroix readied a needle. "Since I'm in charge of this camp and in charge of security, it's my job to investigate any security leaks that might have occurred. A little sodium thiopental will give me the truth."

Orman relaxed as Beaucroix injected him and then pocketed the needle—evidence he later would destroy. He then tore Orman from the bed and out of the soldiers' firm grasp. He lifted the man off his feet and roughly tossed him across the room, sending him crashing into the dresser, shattering the mirror, and falling to the floor.

"Grab the nigger queer! It's his turn now. Hold him down on the bed!"

This was an odd way to word an order to four well-confused black men. But the soldiers complied because they knew from sad experience that it was better to be a tool of Beaucroix than become one of his victims.

Quickly the soldiers grabbed M'butu and restrained him on the disheveled bedcovers. Beaucroix injected him with the second needle and placed it, now empty, to join its conspirator in his right chest pocket.

"Let him up." Beaucroix, a bit calmer now, pointed to the door. "You soldiers may go. Return to your drunken orgy." Happily, and much relieved, they hurriedly left the room.

Beaucroix turned to Orman. "I'll be back in twenty minutes, after the drug has had some time to take effect. Then you'll tell me everything you know," he said with a grin. "Faggots!" he tossed over his shoulder as he headed toward the door.

Orman helped M'butu back to his feet and returned to dressing the Liberian's wounds.

"What are they going to do to you?" M'butu asked. In the more educated circles in Liberia, homosexuality usually was no big thing, but he was worried about Orman's fate.

"Nothing. After a few minutes, we'll both get very talkative. We won't be able to help ourselves. When it wears off, we'll probably have the biggest hangover—the biggest headache—of our lives."

"I mean, will he kill you? Jail you?" M'butu asked, concerned for his friend's safety.

"No, Beaucroix will come back when the drug's effect is the strongest. Then he'll ask a lot of questions, get all the details. He'll want *all* the details." Orman grinned; Max had told him the secret of the Monster's inner demons.

"Will they fire you?"

"I doubt it. The asshole will send a report to Washington. Maybe I'll be reassigned or maybe just warned and then watched closer. It's going to be OK!" Orman smiled.

As Beaucroix left, he turned to the two guards on the veranda. "Watch this hut for thirty minutes. Let no one enter or leave, and then you may go." Beaucroix turned to leave.

"What do we do about our major, Chafa M'butu?" the senior man questioned.

"The major…" Beaucroix stopped in his tracks and grinned. "He's still your commander. Nothing is wrong! We're just playing a little joke on him and Michael Orman. The situation is well in hand."

Beaucroix paused to light a Camel cigarette. After inhaling deeply, he exhaled three absolutely perfect smoke rings into the warm afternoon air. Then, placing his hands in his pockets, he strode off into the jungle as he merrily hummed "Dixie." It was a happy ode to the genius of his revenge.

In the trees, the five ancient monkeys watched sadly. The gods of Bopolu were not pleased. Wildfire was loose upon the earth. Wildfire had been set free.

CHAPTER THIRTEEN
The Shadow Knows

July 30, 1976
Washington, DC

Clearly Hampstead felt dirty; he had to fight the impulse to flee to find gloves before he could face this meeting. Beaucroix, for his part, wanted Orman dead, but then Beaucroix wanted everyone dead. Hampstead was very uncomfortable dealing with homosexuals, and the CIA hated them. They considered them the most easily compromised players.

But Hampstead had a problem. With the deaths of two key agents, Phil Reed and Ed Paris, he was treading too lightly in the Cold War and needed all his cannons. What Orman had done was revolting and unforgivable. But in no way had he violated national security, nor had he ever been disloyal to his country.

Hampstead, after considerable hair pulling, had come up with the perfect solution: he would move Orman to Haiti, a Third World cesspool that had been vacated due to the death of Ed Paris. Its proximity to Cuba made it important, but its size and other attributes warranted only one major player.

Haiti, Hampstead felt, was where Orman's vast though perverted talents would be best utilized, and the quaint local custom of hanging homosexuals would tend to keep him on the straight and narrow—literally. Hampstead only hoped Orman wouldn't want to shake hands with him. The very thought of touching a homo gave him the willies.

Orman was ushered into the room by one of Hampstead's stone-faced minions, who promptly left the room and sealed the soundproof door. As Orman advanced across the faded brown Berber carpet, Hampstead quickly divined that the man planned to shake his hand.

"Have a seat, Mike," Hampstead said, and quickly buried his attention in sundry papers, shuffling folders and pretending to be consumed by some urgent detail. After a full three minutes, he felt safe to raise his attention. Gratefully he noticed Orman had both hands in his lap and showed no intention of rising to shake hands.

"Well, you probably wonder why I've called you here, Mike." Hampstead smiled.

"Why was I taken out of Africa?" Orman covered his face to hide a sneeze. He wanted an answer, and he was going to force the matter.

"Ed Paris has been killed, and you're the logical choice to replace him in Haiti."

Hampstead didn't dare tell him Beaucroix wanted him out, wanted him dead. He couldn't tell him he was going to Haiti merely because Beaucroix wouldn't tolerate fags.

"What did Beaucroix tell you about Bopolu? I want to know exactly what you were told," Orman demanded. He drove his stare forward as he tried to capture Hampstead's eyes.

Hampstead again looked down at the papers on his desk, shuffling and pretending to search for something of importance. Orman waited patiently, but Hampstead showed no inclination to pursue the agent's steering of the conversation.

"I want to know what was said. You owe me that!" Orman struck his fist on the desk as he suppressed a cough.

"I'm your superior. I owe you nothing," Hampstead fired back.

"Damn it. You owe me an explanation!" Orman again slammed his fist on Hampstead's desk and sneezed once more.

"You need to see a doctor. Why don't you take some time off? Take two weeks with pay, and then report to Haiti."

"I have no intention of going to Haiti. I intend to take the next plane back to Monro…" Mike bent over Hampstead's desk as he hacked uncontrollably for several seconds.

"You are ill?" Hampstead leaned back in his chair as he tried to read the story.

"Fuck you!" Orman shouted, having regained control over his aching chest.

Hampstead flashed fury and then instantly replaced it with his mask, the inscrutable mask all great spymasters wear. "You are here because Beaucroix said you couldn't get along with people. He said you were making things difficult. Hogan and Tindal came to him and asked that you be removed and reassigned." Hampstead addressed this to the wall behind Michael Orman; he had no desire to meet those eyes.

"That's a lie! And a total, fucked-up fabrication! It was that jackass Beaucroix who wanted me out of there. Not Hogan, not Tindal, not Elvis Presley, and not the Tooth Fairy—it was Beaucroix!" He covered his face as he coughed again.

"Beaucroix was your superior," Hampstead cautioned him.

"Beaucroix isn't a turd's superior!" Orman said, voicing what everyone in the world knew about Emile Beaucroix—that is, everyone except William Hampstead.

"Insubordination is something I never view lightly, Agent Orman. If you can't take discipline, there's no place for you in the CIA." Hampstead returned to shuffling the papers on his desk.

"Bopolu is the most important operation we have. Haiti is a sideshow, so you can damn well send someone junior. I intend to go back to Africa!" Orman was final, and all this shouting was driving his aching fever to new levels of pain.

"That won't be possible. I'm assigning you where I feel American interests will best be served. You'll go to Haiti because I'm your superior and because it's your duty to go where I assign you. That is all."

The meeting ended as Hampstead dropped his eyes to the pile of folders and shuffled through them yet again. He did this for several minutes before he raised his eyes. Startled, he saw Orman standing, his right hand stretched halfway across the desk.

Hampstead stood and took the outstretched hand. In a masterful act, he even shook it warmly. "Thank you, Mike. That will be all." He looked into Orman's eyes.

"Please get better. Take care of that cough and take that paid holiday I offered you." Hampstead painted his face with a look of kind concern.

Orman continued to grip Hampstead's hand and fiercely challenged his eyes. But those eyes were painted blinds and would reveal no secrets. Finally, Orman relaxed his grip and, losing the fight, left the office coughing, depressed, suicidal, and very much alone.

Hampstead watched the door quietly close. Satisfied, he rushed into the bathroom. But no matter how long or hard he scrubbed, he never could get all the filth off his hands.

August 27, 1976
Paris, France

The Left Bank in Paris was a haven for artists, writers, and dilettantes. It also was an extraordinary place to recruit spies and informants. But today, Slava Kurnov had no intention of recruiting anyone. Today would be about old business. The spymaster scratched his chin, deep in private thought as he sat alone at the checkered table nearest the banks of the River Seine.

He rolled the delightful deep-red 1962 Rothschild wine around in the crystal glass, contemplating the depth of its color as his mind wandered back to the purpose of this mission. Lost in thought, he forgot Paris; he forgot the café; and, with a mistake not usual to this cautious character, he spoke aloud.

"I wonder what Hogan is really doing in Africa?" Kurnov offered to his inner doppelganger as his voice tossed the question into the warm Paris air.

"The Shadow knows, and so should you."

Kurnov fairly bolted before his seasoned skills gained the upper hand. Coolly he turned and snapped his fingers at the wine waiter for another bottle of this excellent French wine.

Cleverly he acted as if the fat man had been sitting across from him the entire time; there was no way the big man could have seated himself without Kurnov noticing, but he had.

"It seems to me"—Kurnov smiled as he displayed his well-known humor—"that what you know best, my friend, is quality food. Perhaps you would be good enough to join me for lunch and help me order."

"We have bigger fish to fry than salmon. Larger issues than my belly are at stake here, Kurnov." The big man was all business, but Kurnov would have none of it.

"Tell me, my friend, just what does my shadow know?" Kurnov grinned. He regretted having made the comment about food. It was obvious the big man liked to poke fun at his own size. But it wasn't the socialist way—or Kurnov's way—to find cheap humor in regard to a man's obesity, so the Russian ignored the dangling bait.

"I know your country is in a lot of trouble." The Shadow leaned back and scratched his belly.

"I think my country can take care of itself. We have beaten war, revolution, famine, and purges. We can probably handle our own affairs." Kurnov was amused that so many people always seemed to have things for sale that they felt the KGB never could survive without.

"Yeah, you murdered Leon Trotsky with an ax in front of his own son. You made lovely borscht out of Joseph Stalin, and you taught the Germans that it's impossible to goose-step on ice. But those were visible enemies, Kurnov. How would you defeat an invading army that you couldn't see?"

The Shadow had found out a lot—a whole lot more than he wished he knew—and he badly needed a powerful ally. Kurnov was the man who had the most power in this part of the world—more power than Robert Hogan, Baron Le Boeuf, and William Hampstead combined.

"I would deal with them in the Russian way." Kurnov smiled as he leaned forward and raised his index finger. "I would get some sleep and drink a lot less vodka until the hallucinations went away."

"You're a very funny man." And now it was the Shadow's turn to wag a finger. "I suppose you find considerable humor in the fact that in two years' time, the Lithuanian soccer team will be able to field more able-bodied men than the entire Soviet army. Since you find this humorous, let's have a good-natured drink to this fact."

The fat man raised his glass as the wine waiter poured a sample from the freshly uncorked bottle. Kurnov, however, brusquely waved off the sommelier before he could fill the glasses and indicated with his finger a spot on the table where he should leave the bottle.

"Are you threatening the Soviet Union with nuclear war, or do you just plan to give us all an unbearable case of fleas?" Kurnov knew the Shadow was good, but what he didn't know was exactly who the Shadow was and which powers he commanded or advised. This item was a matter of grave concern to Kurnov, as the high art of the spymaster lay in always being the one man who knew the unknown and the unknowable.

"You stupid Russki, he plans to eat you, and he plans to eat you all. He'll make sausages from your stinky Cossack asses, and he'll swallow them with beer," a drunken German at a table across the patio interjected. He grinned as he dropped a forkful of soufflé upon the impeccably clean cobblestone patio.

"Do you mind?" Kurnov was irritated at this interruption; he hated drunks and considered drunkenness to be the greatest moral weakness. Bad manners were one thing; a public drunk was far worse.

"They can't be trusted, you know—the Americans. They always want more than God puts upon their plate. They are greedy scum!" the German declared from his unsteady perch two tables away.

"Democracy—it is the public tolerance of idiots!" Kurnov rolled his eyes toward the heavens.

"Look what they did to us Germans—twice! Poor, poor Hitler. He was such a nice man; he had such beautiful eyes. Pimped and betrayed to the devil by that filthy weasel Stalin." The German shook his finger at the Russian to drive home the point.

Kurnov ignored the fool. He indeed knew the Germans had been screwed twice—first by European squabbles and second by a dictator named Adolf. The Americans were just flotsam that had been sucked into the storm by Hitler and tossed energetically into the whirlpool by the pompous Winston Churchill.

"You know what I think, you stinky Slav?" The German answered his own question with a loud, punctual, and fragrant sausage-flavored fart. "I think Stalin was a girl. If he had been a man, he would have loved Hitler!"

"If Stalin had in fact been a girl, Hitler would have dropped down on one knee, kissed Stalin's boobs, and proposed marriage, madly in love," the Shadow noted as he raised his wineglass and toasted the drunken fool.

"Waiter, I will speak to the maître d' immediately!" Slava Kurnov snapped his fingers as he shouted across the patio to the startled waiter.

The waiter quickly discharged the contents of his platter to the table of a young couple, apologizing and assuring them he would be right back. But there was no need; the maître d', like all great headwaiters, had been standing in the shadows, gauging the situation. He crisply snapped his fingers and advanced with two very large chefs in tow.

The drunken fool cursed in English, French, and German as the two chefs tossed him, kicking, into the warm, sun-kissed street.

"Excellent. We were blessed with a trilingual idiot! In East Germany, they have the good sense to arrest such fools!" Kurnov smiled as he toasted the bruised, rejected idiot, who was still cursing as he retreated down the street.

The Shadow leaned toward the Russian and indicated for him to move closer. "My country has perfected a biological weapon. It's like nothing you've seen before." The Shadow leaned back and took a sip of wine to allow Kurnov time to soak it in.

"That's illegal!" Kurnov growled.

"So is assassinating Ukrainian mayors, even if they deserved it," the Shadow said, referring to a little payback Kurnov had orchestrated some years back.

"I see your point. But if what you say is true, my response would be war—nuclear war. But why would you give me this information and guarantee a nuclear strike on your country? If what you say is true, I guarantee you it will be the Kremlin's only and immediate response!" Kurnov leaned his face closer to the Shadow's.

"Kurnov, I'm giving you this information not to start a war but to prevent one." The Shadow leaned back, picked up the bottle, and refilled the Russian's wineglass. "This weapon—this biological nightmare—was created by a renegade group within the US government and a small group of criminals within the CIA. Our justice department fully intends to prosecute these individuals in power, but under American law, we must develop a case before we can remove elected officials.

"The CIA renegades, on the other hand—we don't intend to use American law on them. We intend to deal with them the only way they deserve—the same way you would—and I need your help." The fat man leaned back and emptied his glass as he waited for a response.

"What will happen to this weapon, the existence of which you still have not proven to me?" Kurnov asked the obvious.

"The weapon will be destroyed. All information about it will be destroyed, and all individuals who have anything to do with this crime against world peace will be destroyed. We will give you a full verification of this. You have my word."

"I want the scientist, the evil man who created this monster, terminated."

For practical reasons, Kurnov would—for the time being—believe the Shadow's story, but it would be verified before any cooperation was given, of that you can be sure.

"That's already been taken care of. The men we are after already ordered his termination. They did this to try to save their own asses." The Shadow was grateful the meeting had gone well so far.

"We will want copies of all the data and all the documentation that led to the development of this weapon." Kurnov stated the usual and the necessary; he felt he could negotiate with this man.

"No, this thing is too dangerous and too evil. All the information, all the research will be destroyed. This is a weapon we don't need, you don't need, and mankind doesn't need. The weapon will die along with all the men responsible for its creation. We won't have it; you won't have it. That's fair, isn't it?"

Kurnov raised an eyebrow. "Surely no weapon is that powerful."

"It is not only that powerful, Kurnov—it is that evil. Now this is what I need you and the KGB to do." The fat man leaned forward and whispered the plan into the Russian's inclining ear.

August 30, 1976
Rabat, Morocco

Le Boeuf shook his finger at Hogan. "He isn't even human. The man is a monster. We're not the British, after all. We need to get along with these people."

"We will forward your concerns to Hampstead," Hogan assured him.

Max grinned; he was rapidly getting drunk. The Monster was his and Hogan's secret name for Beaucroix, so it always amazed him how many men used that word to describe Emile Beaucroix.

"Baron Le Boeuf, I can assure you this incident will not be repeated." Hogan didn't like frogs much, and Max always liked to say that the French believed the sun rose and set somewhere up their asses.

"That French traitor never should have been tortured," the baron said. "He had valuable information relating to official French interests in Africa, and after seeing what remained of his body, my people seriously doubt Beaucroix's story that he revealed nothing. Any man—perhaps even a Frenchman—would talk under such circumstances!"

"Our own agents have died under interrogation without talking. Perhaps even some Frenchmen are capable of similar loyalty," Hogan shot back. He was offended by the baron's poke at cultural superiority. Baron Le Boeuf was furious, and his fine Marseille tan flushed red.

"How dare you imply such things to my face?" The baron swelled with rage as his aristocratic chest expanded with indignation; one never allowed oneself to be insulted by the lesser classes.

"Better to say it to your face than your ass—your ass is too stinky," Max muttered in alcoholic contemplation. Still drinking, he had no interest in this meeting.

"What was that?" Le Boeuf shouted. He had caught only "ass" and guessed the rest.

"Ignore him, sir. He's drunk." Hogan shot Max a disapproving stare.

Max grinned sheepishly, but he wasn't finished with the frog. "Is it true that Frenchmen use only one bar of soap a year, and is it true that the French always keep their windows open in the summer?" He smiled and added, "So they can pass that bar around France?"

"I demand an apology. France demands an apology!" Le Boeuf was indignant beyond measure.

"Every Frenchman wants an apology?" Max questioned and then burped. "That could take some time. I think I'll start with the Mademoiselles. I'll apologize to the cute ones first, perhaps apply my tongue to their boobs for forgiveness," he said thoughtfully, smiling and pleased with the general idea.

"Shut the fuck up, Max!" Hogan cautioned. The Frenchman was swelling, ready to explode. "Ignore him, sir. He's an idiot." Hogan was sorry he had gotten Max started; he knew from experience how quick he was to join a fight. The difference was that Hogan knew when he had to be political; Max didn't.

Max poured another shot. "I don't think you need to worry, Froggy-puss. I have personally have seen frogs croak without saying a word. Sometimes they say, 'Ribbit, croak, croak, ribbit,' but they never talk. I think your country's secrets are safe." Max nodded as he considered the matter through his bloodshot eyes.

"*Max!*" Hogan warned.

"I will of course protest your indignation and your lack of coopera-tion!" The aristocrat was in little danger of cooling down.

"That is your prerogative, sir. This man will be disciplined for his insubordination." Hogan pointed to Max.

"Beat me, whip me, force me to write bad checks, and make me fall in love!" Max was now five exits past sober without a traffic cop in sight. Besides, he had no respect for French intelligence. "Good-bye, mon-sieur!" he bellowed as the frog hopped up and bounded out the door, leaving behind a grinning Max George and a very angry Robert Hogan.

"Robert, that just leaves one question." Max looked serious, thoughtful.

"What's that?" Hogan asked, instantly no longer angry but curious. He searched his mind, trying to puzzle out what he had missed.

"Where's the *boeuf*?" Max grinned, winking.

"Good God, Max, that's an idiotic joke. Nobody would ever use a line that silly."

"Yup, I guess you're right."

September 15, 1976
Rhodesia

    Max cautiously moved to the right, keeping low, dodging beneath the tall brown grass as he stalked the monster slowly and with great care to remain hidden, fearful of the bastard's temper. He knew how deadly that temper was. If he or Hogan was detected too soon, the monster would unleash all his fury, and they wouldn't stand a chance. It was fortunate the monster was in the process of stupidly relieving himself in the bush, making such an approach possible.

    They had spent the last two weeks planning this, carefully working out every flawless detail. Today, at long last, the monster would die.

    Hogan watched Max and adjusted his own path forward, sliding somewhat to the right to achieve a flanking position to counter and support Max's planned frontal assault. Hogan marked his flanking position carefully; he didn't want to be hit in a deadly crossfire.

    "Move in quietly. Don't let the asshole see you," Hogan whispered.

    "We've finally got him, Max. This is his last mistake. I'm going to kill that son of a bitch!"

    "Look out, Bob. He's seen you!" shouted Max as the monster raised his weapon and bolted forward from the grass, quickly moving to the left to engage Hogan first. But it was too late; the grass swayed away evenly as the shockwaves of Hogan's Nitro Express rifle drove their stems outward toward the broad plain. The powerful shoulder cannon spat its six-hundred-grain bullet into the monster, driving him backward and into the African dust. The asshole died instantly, center shot through the skull.

    "Damn good shot, man!" Max walked up, surveying the neat but huge hole between the monster's ears. "This asshole will never kill again," Max declared. The monster had just murdered two young settlement boys, strictly for pleasure.

    "Thanks. It was good of Humphries to tell us exactly where to ambush him." Hogan grinned. He was pleased, especially since he'd been nervous lately. The monster had a killing reputation, and Hogan was relieved this kill had been so easy.

"You know, Bob, a lot of people think lions or elephants are the most dangerous things in South Africa. But next to the hippo, the Cape buffalo kills more men each year than both of those animals combined." Max looked down at the dead buffalo and wondered whether this one would prove to be good eating. "I'm not surprised. Humphries told me what happened when one of his rangers tried to stop this one last season. Humphries says a buffalo is two tons of bad temper, can turn on a dime, outrun a horse, see you a mile away, hide behind two blades of grass, and smell the aftershave you wore last week."

Hogan surveyed the massive horns that curved down and then up again. The buffalo's evil helmet was a masterpiece of offensive engineering, starting wide at a massive bone skullcap and narrowing and terminating into two sharp, upward-curving spikes stained dark with the blood of its last victims. Hogan grinned; these horns would look hot mounted above his mantelpiece in the Congo. He would leave the dried blood intact; it would make for a healthy story.

"I'm not surprised Humphries fears them so much." Max pointed northwest, toward Bopolu. "He's never met Emile Beaucroix."

Hogan laughed and then remembered something Humphries had told him. It was a dangerous game white hunters sometimes played with one another, a game of manhood as well as a game of balls and a true test of friendship.

"Ever heard of buffalo chicken?" Hogan asked.

"Nope. Does it taste like rattlesnake?" Max joked. People invariably described any unusual meat as tasting like chicken, especially rattlesnake.

"It's a game, Max. We find a real mean bull, a big one. Then we walk toward him, exactly ten meters apart from each other. When he charges, the first man to fire loses—he's the buffalo chicken."

Max grinned. Max was the toughest man Max had ever known, and Hogan was his best friend. Hogan was only man he'd ever completely trusted, and he'd do whatever it took to keep that friendship. He was amused that Hogan wanted to prove his own toughness. It was OK, though; Hogan was his pal, and Max would be the buffalo chicken because he knew he would fire first to protect his friend.

"Sounds like fun. Do you really think you even have a prayer of beating me? We both know who the king of the hill is here," Max said, pointing to himself.

"You can't kill *m'bogo* with ego. Let's make it interesting." Hogan reached into his pocket and produced two raw diamonds. "I'll bet you these two rocks."

"I haven't got any diamonds. How about money? How about a thousand bucks?"

"No deal," replied Hogan. "Money is so boring; you've got to put in something more interesting if you want to play. In other words, shit or get off the pot!"

Max thought for a minute. Then he had an inspiration. "How about Beaucroix's ears? I wager Emile Beaucroix's ears."

"Nope, that's no way good enough," Hogan said. "I want his ears *and* his tail; I want the tail too!"

"No way, Bob." A laughing Max was adamant. "I promised his tail to my girl Dulcinea. You'll get the ears. I wager Emile Beaucroix's ears."

Hogan was now fighting laughter as well, with his shaking sides about to explode. "Done!" he declared, accepting the bet as he and Max mounted the Land Rover and set off grinning in search of their new quarry.

The sun had hit its zenith when the two men located a suitable target: an ancient, grizzled, and surly bull standing alone as it grazed intently beneath a withered tree. Max and Hogan stopped the Land Rover two hundred meters away.

The bull, seeing the motion, snorted and flashed its angry red eyes. Then it continued to munch the dry grass of the floodplain, certain these unwelcome guests would heed its warning and wander away.

Max and Hogan dismounted, then checked their guns as they took positions ten meters apart. Hogan motioned Max back a bit and cautioned him to stay even. Max had taken a two-meter lead, and Hogan wasn't going to give him any grace. He wanted the bull to charge him. He was the one who felt he had something to prove. Hogan then glanced over at Max's position.

"Stay even. If you get ahead, you forfeit the bet," he warned him.

"Hey, I'm even." Max indicated his position.

"Let's go."

Moving together, they approached the grazing animal. The bull angrily watched but was too intent on eating to charge. It had been a long, hot journey from the salt flats to the dry plain. The beast was two thousand pounds of appetite and was famished. The grass, though dry, was sweet and delicious. The animal continued to munch greedily as it watched the two intruders creep forward.

"It should break soon," Max whispered as they advanced. They had just passed to within fifty meters. In Max's experience, bulls usually charged at forty because that was their danger zone. It was a distance Max and Hogan would soon pass.

"There it is!" Hogan shouted as he mounted the huge elephant gun to his tensed, rigid shoulder. The buffalo came forward two steps, snorted, turned, and trotted away. It stopped eleven meters farther away to explore another tuft of grass. The bull, having already forgotten Max and Hogan, had returned to chomping the luscious grass.

Hogan was disappointed. Shrugging, he looked at Max, who nodded. They would try again. Hogan pointed at Max's feet. "I said stay even. Let's keep this a fair contest," he warned him.

Max moved back a bit. Satisfied, Hogan nodded, and they began their advance toward the beast, which was happily devouring every blade of grass it could. As they passed to within thirty meters, the animal raised its eyes, which were suddenly red with fury. It snorted, pawed the ground, and charged. Turning instantly, it trotted off to explore a temptingly rich tuft of grass sixteen meters away. Max lowered his Rigby and frowned. Hogan frowned too as he considered the matter. Should they look for a better bull?

Hell no!

"Look, Max…" Hogan had this figured out. "The next time it starts its charge, we'll both shout and wave. That'll make the contrary bastard try to kill us."

"That'll make it mad as hell! They hate noise, and sudden movement infuriates them." Max didn't want to get Hogan killed. Suddenly he wanted out, to end this game. He would let Hogan redeem himself at darts. Darts would have to do.

"Good. I want the son of a bitch to try to kill me," replied Hogan, who was mad at the beast.

After hearing Hogan say this, Max frowned. Why were friends so difficult?

Again they began their slow, cautious advance. Max's knuckles were white from his crushing grip on the heavy Rigby. Hogan was nervous but alert as they crossed to within twenty meters; suddenly, the buffalo snorted and began its charge.

"Come on, asshole!" Hogan yelled, jumping back and forth and wildly waving his free arm.

"Fuck you! Charge me, you ugly-ass shit!" Max shouted at the top of his lungs.

Again the buffalo turned after three steps and trotted coolly away, happy to settle at a fresh patch of grass fifteen meters away.

"Ah, this game's no good," lamented Max, glad to have found a way out of this ugly game. "Let's get back to camp."

Hogan surveyed the animal, now oblivious to the world, occupied only with the succulent grass. But Hogan had his mind set. Once he decided to do something, nothing could sway him. He had to prove himself worthy. He had to prove himself a man, and he would prove it to the only real man, the only genuine man he ever had known.

"No, we'll go again. I can make him charge. Just leave it to me," he declared, then pointed at Max and cautioned, "You just stay even. Stay even with me. We'll advance together, and don't you try to sneak ahead."

Once again, they began their stalking advance. When one played buffalo chicken, it was always desirable to get as close as possible before the bull began its charge; it made things awesomely exciting because life could then be weighed in the briefest half ticks of a clock, and, as such, life became worth living.

This time the pair came to within twenty meters of the beast when it turned to face them. Snorting, the once-again-furious beast trotted forward. Hogan snapped up his Nitro Express rifle and sent a massive bullet flying through the air, exploding the dust in front of the angry, advancing bull.

Max, now getting the script, shouldered his Rigby and sent a round crashing into the dirt, six inches to the left of the advancing animal. The bull stopped, snorted, and then stared at the two smoking guns. Having no time for this silliness, it turned and trotted away. Stopping again after twenty-five meters, it returned its attentions to the vitamin-rich grass.

"That's it. We're out of here!" declared Max with finality as he turned and headed back to the truck.

"Hey, wait!" Hogan pleaded to Max, who stopped and turned to face his friend.

"Look, Bob, we've wasted enough time on this. The bull wants to eat. It doesn't want to fight—just look at it." Max indicated the animal happily gorging itself. Hogan looked at the contrary beast and frowned. Hogan still needed redemption.

"Once more, Max. One more try and we quit!" Hogan promised.

"No way. I'm hungry. I'm going back to camp."

"Look…" pleaded Hogan. "Just one more try—just one more try, and we quit! If I can't make him charge, we'll quit. We'll quit this game, and you'll never have to play it again. If I can't make him charge, I'll forfeit, and we'll never play this again." Hogan couldn't believe he'd said this, offering to give up his chance for redemption.

"All right. Let's go." Max had resumed his place in the two-man front. This time Hogan advanced at a quicker pace, with Max matching him step for step, careful to keep his place. He didn't want Hogan to cry foul. He wanted this silly, deadly game to end.

This time they were able to approach within sixteen yards, an unheard-of distance to approach a buffalo without a deadly charge. This time the animal ran away and then spun and trotted toward Max. Hogan, who had reloaded, fired and shattered the dirt to the right of the buffalo. The beast stopped, shook its horns in warning, and trotted off across the plain.

"What kind of bloody cheek is this?" The park ranger had been able to drive up unnoticed because Max and Hogan were completely wrapped up in their game.

"We're just doing a little hunting," replied Max as he walked toward the ranger.

"We've got a permit," Hogan added as he fished for it in his shirt pocket.

"I ought to stick my Wellington boot up your arses. You weren't hunting. You were bothering the animals. Now you can bloody well get in your lorry and follow me to the slammer!"

"Honest, we just needed a little meat for the boys back in camp," Hogan explained.

"Right…just needed meat?" the ranger scoffed. "How about that bloody big pile of meat you left for the hyenas back on the plateau?" He pointed in the direction of their other buffalo kill. "I followed your trail from your last little event. You're a right proper pair of geezers! You not only bother and kill the game, but you also don't even have the courtesy to pick your mess up off the plateau. It's a capital crime in Rhodesia to waste game." The ranger motioned toward their Land Rover, indicating the court was waiting.

"Wait a minute," Max protested. "We're Americans, strangers in your country, and we've been abandoned by our boys." Max cleverly authored a race-tainted tale. "Our boys split last night because we hid the whiskey. You know how Negroes are. We hoped if there was a mess of fresh meat in camp, the boys would come back. We planned to drag both carcasses back after we finished hunting." Max knew an appeal to the Boer's pretentious racial superiority probably would rescue them from this mess.

"Very well," the ranger said after briefly considering the matter. "But if I see any such funniness from you two geezers in the future, you'll both bloody well go to jail for five years—the whole, bloody, twisted-screw lot of you. Is that bloody well clear?" He set his jaw as he spoke severely.

"Yes, sir. We're very sorry. We're ashamed of what we did. We'll head back to camp and then go to fetch our buffalo," Max said with his eyes cast downward.

"In the future, show some sense and hire a boss man, a white chap who knows how to keep your niggers in line. Next time, ask one of the other Boer chaps in town to fix you up. It's really the only way to go."

The ranger looked first at Max, and then, after briefly scrutinizing Hogan, he grunted, turned, and mounted his idling lorry before heading dustily across the hot, parched plain.

"Racist bastard. I hope the lions get him!" Hogan muttered as he watched with disgust the retreating trail of dust.

"To hell with that idiot. Let's try again!" Max winked at Hogan and grinned as he indicated the same buffalo.

Now satiated, the bull suddenly remembered the pair's earlier shenanigans and was livid.

"You've got to be crazy!" Hogan replied, pointing at the trail of dust flying from the ranger's lorry, still visible across the flat, dry plain.

"But I *am* crazy. Aren't you?" Max replied, spinning his hands and making loony circles about his temple.

"Let's do it!" Hogan said. God, he loved this guy.

Slowly they worked their way forward, past the withered tree. The buffalo snorted and pawed the ground as it regarded Max, then Hogan, uncertain where first to vent its fury.

Max and Hogan stopped their advance and jerked up their guns when the bull lurched forward and then retreated, still furiously pawing the dusty ground. Lowering their guns, they continued their slow, stalking advance. Hogan looked at Max and motioned at him to stay even. Then Max shouted, "Here it comes!"

The men snapped their rifles to their shoulders as the bull drove forward, charging Hogan. Before Max could fire, the bull stopped, turned, and trotted off across the plain.

"Damn it! Goddamn it!" Hogan exclaimed as he kicked at the dirt.

"We'll try again tomorrow. We'll get a meaner one." Max was disappointed. He suddenly wanted to let Hogan redeem himself. Friends did these things for each other—even dangerous things—because they sometimes had to.

"Watch out!" Max screamed as he lifted his Rigby and prepared to fire. The bull somehow had circled around and was furiously charging out of the shadow of an old tree, heading directly toward Hogan.

Swinging the Rigby, Max centered the buckhorn sight with the post centered between the bull's eyes and pulled the trigger. He was greeted by a sick bang as the cartridge case split at the base, sending gas and smoke into his eyes and jamming the action, the wobbling bullet harmlessly flying away from the beast. Desperately he looked at Hogan, wondering why he hadn't fired. Robert Hogan just stood with his double-barreled express rifle at his side as the murderous freight train roared toward him.

Max tossed aside his rifle and drew his Colt pistol and fired. Dust shot up after a round of bullets ricocheted off the killer's skull and bounced harmlessly through the air and onto the dry plain. Again and again he fired, going for the eyes, desperate to save his friend. Finally he fired his last paltry, desperate .45-caliber round, leaving the Colt impotent and disinterested in this fatal affair.

Max threw the pistol into the buffalo's path and shouted, wildly waving his arms in a valiant effort to distract the beast and somehow save Hogan. It was no use, however, as the freight train almost had reached its target.

Hogan smoothly lifted his rifle and fired in one liquid motion from five yards away. As he took a casual but quick step to the side, he watched the dead bull come sliding forward, stopping inches from Max's feet. Max was stunned and still breathing deeply.

"Hey," Hogan shouted, whining. "You cheated, broke the rules. I never agreed to pistols. It was supposed to be rifles—rifles only!"

Max was still stunned; he wasn't comfortable that his best friend almost had died and he had been completely impotent to stop it.

"Hey," Hogan repeated, trying to bring his friend back to reality and more than a bit pleased with himself that he had won. "You cheated. So I want the tail. You owe me the tail too!" He walked over to Max, who was still shaken, and patted him on the back. "We both need a drink!" Hogan said with a grin.

"You may need a drink, but I intend to finish the whole damn bottle!" Max put his arm around Hogan's shoulders as they headed back to their Land Rover.

Robert Hogan and Max George had survived wars, intrigues, assassinations, and betrayals. Today they had climbed much higher and overcome far greater. They had survived the toughest battle of all—they had survived Africa.

CHAPTER FOURTEEN
The Sacrificial Lamb

January 1, 1981
Harbel, Liberia

From every corner of Liberia they came: north, south, east, and west. The monkeys and apes of Liberia gathered in the trees surrounding the village and quietly took their seats in the high places as they waited for the trial to begin.

From the south, the five grizzled old monkeys wobbled across the duff and swung branch by branch with agile dignity to the topmost tier of the great tree commanding the town square. The court, the gods of Bopolu, finally had arrived. With all in place, a stubby bonobo bailiff screamed and shrieked the court into session.

The happy, melodic jungle sounds so typical of a warm January evening quickly faded. The delightful chorus had been silenced by the racket in the street. A man, as frustrated as he was angry, pounded with vigor on a bolted hardwood door.

"Damn you, woman. Let me in. I am the man, and this is my home!" he shouted as he pounded and screamed to the heavens above.

"You aren't a man. Why do you hate me?" the African woman sobbed from behind the bolted door.

"Damn you, bitch! I'm going to beat you if you don't open this door right now!" He pounded harder, bruising his reddening knuckles and cracking open the flesh.

"I thought I married a man," she called out, crying profusely. She hadn't left the house for two days. She couldn't bear to face the other women because she couldn't handle the small minds and accusing small-town stares.

"Bitch, I'll show you a man," he shouted, still hammering on the door. His knuckles were now broken open and bleeding freely. "Are you going to let me into *my* home?" he demanded.

"I thought I married a man," she wailed as she leaned against the bolted door.

"Look," Chafa M'butu implored. He sensed his anger was getting him nowhere. "Let me in, honey. I want to talk and explain." His pounding grew softer and less threatening.

"I will never let you in. I thought you were a man," she shouted through a veil of tears.

"Look, darling, I was drunk and confused. I didn't know what was happening, and it will never happen again. I swear!"

"Why did you do this to me?" The wailing and sobbing flowed from behind the hardwood door.

"Baby, I'll never drink again. Let me in, please. I love you!" he pleaded as he knocked softly.

"What is wrong with me? Am I really so ugly?" She collapsed to the floor, face in her hands and safe behind the bolted door.

"Ugly? Baby, you are beautiful. I love you. Let me in, please." Suddenly he sensed motion to his left, which jolted him and turned him from the door.

"Good evening, faggot. What are you doing to my sister?"

Chafa M'butu whirled around to face his brother-in-law, who stood trembling with rage in the center of the dark street. Ten feet away, Ben Kyu stood shaking but braced square and determined, because he had a job to do—defend his sister's honor.

Holding a long stick in his right hand, Kyu slapped it against his left palm as he sported an evil but nervous grin.

"I'm in no mood for you tonight fool!" Major M'butu advanced to face him and kick his ass. But suddenly he froze as two other men joined Kyu from the shadows, armed like their brother. They seemingly had appeared from nowhere, like phantoms in the warm, dim evening light.

M'butu turned and ran because he knew they meant to kill him. But he didn't get far. Three more angry black men had distilled themselves from the darkness, completely arresting his escape. The two closest men grabbed him roughly and tossed him to the ground in the exact center of the hard, heartless street.

Kyu stood above him and struck the thick hardwood stick against the back of M'butu's head, driving him into the soft, damp ground. Kyu's stick struck so hard that it dazed the major. Ben Kyu proceeded with fury as he struck M'butu's bleeding ears and face again and again, while M'butu tried to shield the blows.

"How dare you disgrace my sister and my family?" Kyu shouted, still pounding his brother-in-law, swinging harder and adding the Major's crotch to the targets of his fury. M'butu was trying again to cover his face and shield his privates as he curled up as best he could on the dusty, uncaring street.

"Dirty faggot!" the other angry men chanted as they formed a circle around the bleeding man. They joined in with clubs of their own and pounded energetically, swinging their weapons against the man's bleeding body and breaking bones. They chanted and pounded, pounded and chanted as the noise of their fag party brought the small-town women to their windows and delighted, giggling small-town boys into the street.

This was the sort of spectacle that fascinated small towns and small-minded people. To them it was entertaining, but to Major Chafa M'butu, it was nothing less than murder.

As the major drifted off into a tortured, twisted unreality of suffering, he and his pain blended into one, and together they floated off into unconsciousness.

As the bloody pulp of a man no longer responded to their blows, it ceased to provide much fun. Kyu first slowed and then stayed his swing and looked down upon the battered mess. The others, who had turned to him for affirmation, also curbed their fury.

Smiling with satisfaction and nodding to the others, Kyu tossed his stick upon the body and wandered off into the night in search of a tavern, a proper place to boast his deed, thus proudly confirming his own tested manhood. The others tossed down their clubs as well and joined him, eager to boast their own glory. With the fag party now over, all save for M'butu melted away and into Africa's forgiving darkness.

The smallest chimpanzee, who was too young to understand proper court protocol, swung up and into the high places and, with the speed of youth, swung past the bailiff. He seated himself before the gods of Bopolu and pointed at the human bleeding below.

"Why so severe? Why have you ruled with such cruelty and dealt such severity to this mortal who did nothing more than follow his mortal path?" The young always needed an explanation when elders did to others what they were told was forbidden to do by anyone else.

"We have judged no one. We have not judged this human." The oldest god smiled; he loved dealing with the young and having the opportunity to be a teacher.

"Look at him. He is dying!" The chimpanzee pointed at the curled human, who was squirming like an eel in a quivering sea of blood.

"Yet we have still not judged," the god replied.

"Then why are we here?"

The bailiff, who'd had enough of this impudence, swung forward to remove the young upstart, but the gods indicated for him to stay well back. Lack of knowledge of court etiquette by the chimpanzee did not justify rash disrespect to youth.

"We have not come to judge. We have come to witness." The god smiled.

"To witness this?" The young chimp pointed to the bleeding mess below.

"No, we find no fault with this bleeding human. He is not yet dying."

"Then what have you judged?"

"We have judged nothing. We have only witnessed. Today this village represents all humanity, and by their actions today, they have all judged and condemned themselves." With this said, the gods of Bopolu dropped to the ground. The rest of the monkeys and apes followed as they retreated silently and in single file back into the jungle.

The townswomen gossiped in their homes. Posted furtively behind their windows, they stood gloriously proud of their men and pointed, smiling, not at M'butu but at his bolted door. Behind that still-locked hardwood portal, Tina M'butu sobbed to the gods above as she beat the floor and wailed her final eulogy.

But her brothers, neighbors, friends, and family wouldn't test her bolted door. They couldn't, because she was now unclean, disgraced, and dead to those around her. Tonight, in a river of tears, she would take her life, ending a world she didn't deserve and could never possibly understand.

Tomorrow, her door would still be left untested when her family, good friends, and neighbors lit and burned her home and her memory back into the dust of Africa.

May 4, 1981
Tunis, Tunisia

Puzzled by Max's detachment, Hogan downed his whiskey as he regarded his buddy. By force of habit, he glanced around the mostly deserted café, and, finding nothing amiss, he returned to the matter at hand. "Why are you being so damn talkative?" he asked somewhat sarcastically.

"Sorry, Bob. I'm just having an off week," replied Max.

"Hey, I've had nothing but off weeks since Hampstead moved Beaucroix into our theater." Hogan grinned.

"It's a stupid Scotsman I do business with—that idiot O'Grady. Last week he challenged me to a friendly pistol match. Bottom line is, I had an off day, and he had an on one. Now the idiot won't let me live it down. Every time we're with clients, he brings it up—how I have such a reputation as a grand *pistolero* but how he's much better. I want to kill the SOB!"

"So kill him. What's the problem?" Hogan lifted his right eyebrow.

Max shrugged. "I'd love to, but he makes me money."

"Just how good is he? What does he shoot?" Hogan was thinking, plotting.

"Ninety-three or ninety-six points out of a hundred. Who cares?"

"Cool down, buddy." Hogan had a mysterious, far-off look in his eyes. Suddenly they flashed with divine revelation. "Tell him we'll shoot with him again, next week. He's a Scotsman, you say? Tell him we'll put up fifty pounds, just to make it sporting."

"No way. With you there, I could beat him easy. Then he'll claim to have had an off day. We'll be tied one-one, and we'll have to do it again another day. I hate that asshole!"

"Max, pal, I didn't say *you'd* shoot against him. I want to." Hogan winked and tossed him a fiendish grin.

"Hah! Robert, this guy was the Scottish pistol champion. You couldn't hit an elephant, unless I let you stick your pistol deep in the elephant's ass before you pulled the trigger, even then it would be only a fifty-fifty chance." Max laughed.

Robert Hogan was pretty good with a rifle, but with a pistol, he was no more than a fair shot. "I'm asking you as a friend, as your best friend. I know what I'm doing, so just set up the match. I'll be back in about six days. I've got a little something to do back home." Hogan stood and turned to leave.

"OK," Max conceded as he rose from his seat as well. "I'll make the arrangements. But don't cry to me when that Scotsman cleans your clock and laughs in your face as he parts you from your fifty pounds. I won't cover your mad bets either, so don't come up a fiver short and ask me for a loan." Max poked Hogan in the chest.

"Not a problem," Hogan said with a wink.

May 11, 1981
South of Tunis, Tunisia

Spring mornings in Tunisia were beautiful, with the air fresh and cool and the magnificent desert light sharply and playfully dancing off the rolling hills south of Tunis.

This was the region the Carthaginians had fled to when the Romans destroyed their capital city of Carthage and eliminated it to the last stone. Rome wasn't satisfied to have beaten the army of Carthage; the Roman senate wanted to wipe Carthage off the earth.

Max and the Scotsman, Sean O'Grady, had just finished tying the two cables between the green willow trees and had paced backward twenty meters. Hogan was now taping the twelve targets to the lines, with six to a row. When he was finished, he walked back to where the two men were using sticks to cut a firing line into the cool sand. They were finished by the time Hogan walked the twenty meters to join them. Max officiated.

"The first shooter will shoot the top row of targets, and the next man gets the bottom," Max began. "Firing order will be decided by a coin toss; the winner chooses to start or follow. It'll be international rules. If any part of the shooter or the gun crosses the firing line, he must reshoot a new target with a five-point penalty. Seven rounds will be fired. A perfect score will be seventy points—that's seven bull's-eyes. If a round breaks a line completely, the shooter earns the higher score. A tie will be decided by a shoot-off. In the event of another tie, the shooters will reshoot at a distance of ten meters greater. If there's still a tie, the distance will increase by ten meters until a winner has been decided."

Max knew the rules because he was the best marksman—rifle or pistol—the CIA had ever had.

"Gentlemen, Mr. O'Grady is the one who's been challenged, so he'll call the toss." Max showed the obverse, then the reverse, then tossed the flashing gold franc into the air.

"Tails," O'Grady called, and tails faced up on the cool morning sand. "Hogan." The Scotsman graciously allowed him the first shot, and why not? He knew Hogan never could beat him. Max George frequently had talked about his safaris with Hogan. He often said Robert was a great friend and a fair shot, while O'Grady was a two-time Scottish pistol champion.

"Before we begin, just to make things fair, I think we should use identical guns." Hogan opened his duffel bag and produced two perfectly matched custom Colt Commander pistols.

O'Grady eyed Hogan suspiciously as he scratched his thick black beard; he smelled a rat.

"You will of course have the first pick of weapons," Hogan offered, and O'Grady considered the matter. The two pistols appeared identical; there was only a fifty-fifty chance of hanky-panky.

"Thank you," O'Grady replied as he took the pistol that was farther from him. Hogan popped two magazines out of his pocket, and, after he offered one to the Scotsman, they loaded their weapons. Hogan stepped up to the firing line and slowly, carefully fired his seven rounds.

"I count one bull's-eye, three eights, and three fives—forty-nine points total," Max announced from behind the field glasses.

Max was disappointed for his friend. He had hoped Robert wouldn't be too embarrassed. But it was too late now, as it was the Scotsman's turn to fire. After stepping up to the line, O'Grady rapidly emptied his seven rounds into the target. Why not hurry a bit? Even a one-legged blind man on crutches could beat forty-nine points.

Max George slowly glassed the target with the field glasses. He then glassed the target again just to be sure there had been no mistake. He never had seen the Scotsman shoot like this.

"No hits. Zero points," Max declared with confused amazement.

"What! Surely you're glassing the wrong target." The Scotsman reached for the glasses and quickly confirmed what he already knew—he had been cheated!

"Nothing wrong with my eyes, O'Grady." Max shook a warning finger at the Scotsman. "And don't call me Shirley!"

"That's right. His given name is Brenda," injected Hogan.

"Did you say something, pookie?" Max addressed Hogan in a falsetto.

O'Grady scowled. He couldn't believe any man would joke about his manhood; it just wasn't right. But he had been cheated, and it was time to strike back. He was a Scotsman, and he could be clever as well as mean.

"Nice bit of shooting, lad. Are you on for double or nothing?" O'Grady was certain he could outwit this Yankee. O'Grady was, after all, a Scotsman and, as such, a more than passably clever man.

"Sure, if you really want to. You shoot first, O'Grady," Hogan offered courteously.

"Good. We have a bet!" Then, craftily, O'Grady added, "Mind if I use your gun, the one you're holding?"

Hogan hesitated. "I don't see why we need to change guns. They're identical. Let's just continue the contest with the guns we have." He motioned toward the targets.

"Is there something special about the gun I'm holding? Perhaps something I should know?" O'Grady asked accusingly.

Hogan looked surprised, and the Scotsman smiled. O'Grady had caught him...or had he?

"Sure, let's trade. One gun shoots much like the other." Hogan handed O'Grady his Colt and a fresh magazine.

The Scotsman handed Hogan his pistol, but now he was more suspicious than ever. After moving to the firing line, O'Grady carefully fired his seven rounds.

"Two bulls, three paper cuts, and two fliers—twenty points," Max observed through the glasses, amazed at the poor score.

"My turn." Hogan briskly pushed the Scotsman back from the firing line because O'Grady had been too shocked to move. Robert took his time, carefully aiming every round.

"Four bulls, one nine, one five, and one flier off the paper—fifty-four points total." Max wondered how his friend was doing it.

Hogan smiled and turned to O'Grady. "How about we go once more for double or nothing?" Hogan asked as he produced two new magazines from his tan outfitter jacket.

Sean O'Grady was now well past simmering, and Max imagined he saw steam shooting from the Scotsman's dense black beard as he headed to a boil, angry that he had been duped somehow. But O'Grady wasn't a man to lose lightly, and he wasn't the sort who would willingly part with his pound of flesh. Hogan had tricked him, but Hogan wasn't Scottish. Hogan was neither mean nor clever; the Scotsman would win it back.

"I welcome the opportunity, because it's good to test my mettle against such a right good shot!" O'Grady's lust for revenge had morphed into cheerful good manners; he was, you remember, a very clever Scotsman. "But let's make it even better sport and a tad more interesting, lad. How about we shoot for *one thousand pounds*?" The Scotsman took a magazine from Hogan and slapped it into his pistol.

"Hey, let's keep this friendly. One thousand pounds is definitely not friendly. It makes for hard feelings, no matter who wins." Max tried to inject a little sanity between the two rutting bulls.

"Are you trying to hustle me?" Hogan asked the Scotsman, completely ignoring Max.

"Not at all. I just think a bit of sporting money would improve my chances. You shoot first." The Scotsman indicated the last target in the row.

"Well, if that's the way you want it." Hogan slapped a clip into his own pistol and stepped up to the firing line.

"Hold it a moment, lad." The Scotsman knew he was being cheated, and the key had to be a combination of pistol and magazine. He walked up to Hogan and removed the loaded pistol from his hands and replaced it with his own.

"Now then, you may begin." O'Grady smiled with satisfaction as he pointed at the target.

"What's this?" Hogan looked first with confusion at the Scotsman, then at the pistol, then back at the Scotsman. He furtively winked at Max, who looked on incredulously; Max didn't have a clue.

"It's an old and honored Scottish sporting custom. In Scotland, we call it *fair play*," the Scotsman said dryly.

"Not a problem." Hogan shrugged it off and then turned his attention to the target, punching two bull's-eyes, four eights, and a flier.

"Fifty-two points," Max called out from behind the field glasses. This was close to Hogan's usual score.

O'Grady smiled. He knew full well that any good shot could beat a fifty-two. He moved up to the line, planted his feet, and carefully squeezed the trigger just once.

"Mr. Spotter?" O'Grady turned to Max George, who lifted the glasses.

"On the paper with no score," Max announced.

"Where on?" the Scotsman inquired.

"On the lower quarter, about four thirty, and one inch from the outer ring," Max announced.

The Scotsman smiled with satisfaction. He turned to Max and nodded; it was payback time. He checked his stance, took several deep breaths, and fired six perfect rounds.

Max painted the target with his field glasses; he couldn't believe his eyes.

"Is that how you like your eggs and bangers?" the Scotsman gloated to Hogan.

"What did he get?" Hogan asked anxiously. But Max was still survey-ing the target; he had to be certain.

"Well?" asked the Scotsman, who was now more than ready to push these ballsy Americans down to their proper place. "Tell Mr. Hogan who the best shot in Glasgow is." The Scotsman was expansive, well pleased that his Celtic wit had handily beaten Yankee foul play.

"No score, with six fliers, and they were all off the paper," an aston-ished Max replied.

Hogan quickly tossed Max a wink, but Max couldn't see how his friend was doing it. The Scotsman was deadly at twenty meters—*always*.

In shock, the Scotsman tore the glasses out of Max's hands. "Let me see that!" He surveyed the target, and then he surveyed all the others in case he had made a mistake and shot the wrong target.

"Right!" he said coldly as he handed the glasses back to Max.

"Hogan, I'll write you a check."

Hogan grinned. "Not a problem."

The brooding O'Grady went over to his truck, and, sitting in the pas-senger seat, he carefully drew his check, sadly parting with his thousand-plus pounds. Then he walked back to the party and handed Hogan the slip.

"We'll not do this again!" the Scotsman declared, and Hogan nod-ded. O'Grady then grunted, turned, and walked back to his truck. He would cheat Max on the next deal; he would get even. No man on God's earth—especially an American—could part a Scotsman from his pound of flesh.

Max watched the truck roll away across the sand. Only when it was completely out of sight did he turn to Hogan and explode. "*You* are an *ass* to do what you did. That man is a *business* associate, and I need his goodwill, his good graces. To cheat that man out of his money was cold—*cold and dishonest*. I thought you had more character than that!" Max scolded.

Hogan's eyes flew to the target then back to Max as he searched for an excuse, an apology for his actions.

"Yeah, you're some piece of work, you are a real *ass*, and you know what?" Max wagged his finger an inch from Hogan's nose. "You're my kind of *ass*!" He slapped Hogan on the shoulder and remembered what the great Irish writer Oscar Wilde once said: "Be clever, my lad, and let those who will, be good!"

It was great to have good friends, friends who also could be clever.

May 11, 1981
Moscow, USSR

"What is Wildfire?" Slava Kurnov was quick enough to see a brief flash of surprise in the man's eyes. He finally had found a door and an entry. Perhaps now, he would find out why Max George and Robert Hogan spent so much time in Africa accomplishing so little.

"It's when lightning strikes dry wood in the countryside, creating an inferno," the CIA agent explained, feigning ignorance. He certainly had heard of Wildfire; everyone in the agency had heard the rumors. But none of them knew what or where it really was.

"You are very brave, yet very silly. You and I both know you will talk very freely during torture in less tolerant quarters." Kurnov motioned into the room's dimly lit shadows, indicating the two grinning guards who would soon transport him to his new abode. "Why don't you save yourself the pain and save my men the inconvenience of having to clean up the mess?" Kurnov placed his hand on the man's stolid shoulder.

"I'm an American tourist. I don't have a clue what you're talking about," the agent replied. He knew the Soviets rarely tortured anyone. They merely incarcerated, interviewed, and nagged you until the end of time.

"Such a coincidence." Kurnov patted the man's shoulder. "I too have been an American tourist, many times, but only once in France. Never again—they treat you Americans like dirt. They are very unfriendly and more than somewhat rude."

"I hate the French, which should prove to you that I'm an American tourist," the man said with a grin.

"No, hating the French doesn't prove you are an American tourist. It simply proves you have manners and good sense," Kurnov answered, smiling. "What is Max George doing in Africa? And where does he go when he leaves his home in the old quarter in Tunis?" Kurnov had become serious.

"Max George? Is that a cartoon character? Is he a cat or a mouse?" the agent inquired. He knew he had little to gain by talking because he was headed to prison, and he was in a hurry to settle into his new abode, probably some cesspool in White Russia. Siberia was generally a treat Mother Russia reserved for her own.

"That was a very good answer!" Kurnov smiled. "I wish we had *Looney Tunes* cartoons here in the Soviet Union. My two children would love them. Personally, I never miss them when I have cause to visit your country. But back to the matters at hand. You are in a lot of trouble. I could kill you for being a spy, or I might simply imprison you. To make your life a little easier, you should tell me everything you know about Max George."

In the game, there were rules. Spies were captured all the time, by both sides. If you were caught, you sat and waited and waited. Sooner or later there would be a trade, and you'd be sent back home and back into the game.

"OK," replied the agent, knowing he had been beaten. His role had ended, and his part in the game had come to its just finish. "Well, first, a fellow visits George, and he's a very mysterious fellow. Someone George never had seen before."

"Is this man Hargood or perhaps Sir Kyle Morrow?" Kurnov offered.

"He's very mysterious. I don't know for certain," the agent replied.

"Yes, please go on," Kurnov whispered. Progress was always a very good thing.

"Well, then this fellow looks around. I don't know who he was. He turns to George." The agent cautiously checked the corners of the room.

"You are safe here. No one will ever know that you talked; these are my men, and they know how I deal with blabbermouths," Kurnov assured him.

"Good," the agent continued. "Then this mysterious man says, 'Which way did he go, George?' and drops a refrigerator on his ass!" The agent grinned as Kurnov turned, covering his face to hide the laughter.

Slava Kurnov knew this was all he could get from this person. It was now obvious that the man was too minor for the CIA to have trusted with the truth or anything else of real value.

"Take this joker away, and then take him to his new home," Kurnov ordered the guards. Then, still in good humor, "Don't worry," he told the agent. "Be good, and I'll send you some comics from America."

The agent was led away, and Kurnov hurriedly left to pack; he was indeed going to America.

May 21, 1981
The Alleys of Monrovia, Liberia

Society hates the homeless; it despises and ridicules them. Society berates the homeless as lazy drunkards, worthless hobos, and hopeless drug addicts. People hate the homeless because they're *visible*. They're a potent, unwelcome reminder that society isn't caring for its own. People don't want to be reminded because they don't want to be bothered. The world won't or can't admit that it has a moral responsibility. So collectively, the world wants the problem to just go away.

Spotting the lone, wandering soldier approaching, Chafa M'butu limped quickly into the shadows. He remembered all too well his trip to headquarters to inquire about his retirement and back pay. General Kutu had ordered that he should be whipped, beaten, tarred, feathered, and tossed back into the jungle.

Driven from camp in disgrace, he had fled and entered the back streets and alleys of Monrovia to join the unloved and the alone. Bits of cast-off cardboard and empty crates were now his barracks, and garbage cans were now his mess. In the spring, he wandered the docks in the evenings and feasted upon the fish heads the fishermen had cast into the surf.

Today was a good day and sort of a special day because the old butcher had died alone in his bed. Three days had passed before his body was discovered. Today, the spoiling meat from the shop had been tossed into the rusty cans behind the deserted shop. For the first time in eight months, Chafa M'butu would have beef. He dug his teeth greedily into the moldy, ripe flesh.

"You, garbage man. Get out of there!" a policeman ordered as he turned into the alley to confront the human trash. But M'butu was too hungry to care, and, ignoring the cop, he ate faster, hungrily consuming the nose-ripe meat.

"Get up, you piece of filth!" The officer retrieved his hard black club from his belt as he advanced down the alley, but M'butu just ignored him, eating even faster.

"Get out of here, you plague!" The angry cop hit the former major with his club. M'butu tried to fend off the blows with one hand while eating as fast as he could with the other. "I said get up! Get out of this alley!" He beat M'butu harder, and, with a loud clack, he gained a solid hit to the man's skull, which echoed back and forth between the buildings lining the narrow alley. The shock briefly stunned M'butu, causing him to drop his beef and crawl away.

"You get out of here now, or I'll give you the beating of your life," the angry policeman warned, shaking his club as M'butu limped away. The officer just stood there, watching until he was certain the trash had left the alley. Then, frowning with disgust, he tossed his stick into the garbage and left, badly in need of a place to wash his hands.

The injured man limped slowly down the next dirty alley, the burning rash contributing as much to his broken step as his fractured skull. He carefully marked the doorways lest someone spot him. He no longer could smell which garbage can held food and which did not. The earthy yellow-and-brown stains of his torn, unwashed khakis emanated the odors of human filth so strongly that it made it impossible for him to smell anything beyond his own ripening despair. Lying down next to the unloading dock of the closed furniture store, he slid into the pile of empty, cast-off boxes. Flattening one to make a bed and flattening two more to make a cover, he painfully lay down to sleep.

Then, completely alone, terrified, abandoned, forsaken, unloved, and forgotten, the urine-soaked, broken, once-proud body that had been Major Chafa M'butu silently died.

CHAPTER FIFTEEN
The Knights of Rabat

May 23, 1981
Rabat, Morocco

The waiter had just delivered fresh drinks and a fine corked bottle of Napoleon brandy for reinforcement. After picking up the empty glasses and bottle, he returned to his station in the kitchens of the Hotel Balima.

Max George smiled at Agent Miles Kendal. "When I was your age, I was credited with more kills than anyone in the history of the CIA. The only person who came close was Beaucroix. Once an agent suggested to Beaucroix he might have had more kills if he didn't waste so much time torturing the ones he already had. You know, Beaucroix made a whole tavern of East Germans watch at gunpoint while he forced an agent to kneel, and then he blew his brains out! He then sliced that agent's throat and cut out the man's tongue. He *ate* the tongue!"

Miles Kendal looked at Hogan in shock for some indication that Max was pulling his leg, but it was all true.

Max continued, "The dossiers at British intelligence, Interpol, and the KGB all say the same thing about me. They call me a cold-blooded killer. But, you see, men like Hogan and me don't consider that an insult. We terminate murderers, spy hunters who liquidate our own. But we also eliminate foreign politicians, scientists, and military leaders who commit actions—or who intend to commit actions—that would harm American interests and cost American lives.

"These terminations—or killings, if you will—*should* be cold-blooded killings. These people should be terminated without emotion or malice and, if possible, without pain.

"A lot of these people are not bad men. In their own minds, they are patriots. Many of them have wives and children they love very much. These terminations are just men who, if allowed to live, probably would do some very bad things that would harm American interests. Therein lies the difference between animals like Beaucroix and professionals like me. He isn't a cold-blooded killer. He's a hot-blooded, psychotic monster who takes pleasure in the torment and torture of his victims."

Max smiled softly as he took another drink of wine. "In Hogan and me, you probably have the best examples of the two sides of the CIA. Hogan is a master of infiltration and intelligence. He knows how and where to cultivate sources of information. He has the ability to play informants like a fine violin and make them dance like marionettes while he supplies bogus intelligence in just the right quantities to those who think they're stealing it from him. I've known him for many years. He's one of the few players in the club you can really trust."

"So that's what Hogan does. What's your bag of fish, George?" Kendal leaned back. He was thoroughly enjoying this. The CIA taught you nothing; its agents could teach you the world.

Max swallowed the rest of his wine and placed the glass softly on the aged gray wood of the table. "As to myself, I represent the dark side of the CIA. While Hogan deals in generalities, such as monitoring governments, obtaining information, and trying to locate documents or weapons sites, I deal in specifics. When our informants in Rumania start disappearing, I'm the one who's sent to find and stop the reason for their disappearance.

"When an American expatriate arms dealer in Israel made a deal with the North Koreans to sell advanced missiles to the Iranians, I was sent to terminate him. I killed him quickly and with no malice whatsoever, and, by doing so, I probably saved thousands of lives at some future date in the Persian Gulf. One life for thousands—it's what I do, but most people would still call it murder. But, you know, even with all the manure that goes into the construction of a politician, I agree with the official stance that such killings are expedient and not murder."

"George, how could you get a foreign agent to believe bogus intelligence? I understand some of their players are as good as ours." Kendal picked up his glass and leaned back in the ass-worn chair; this was a question he'd always wondered about and one that spy school, as it were, had failed to answer.

"MIB, Kendal. MIB," Hogan replied.

"What?"

"MIB. All players, especially interrogators, know that even under the most severe interrogation, not all the information they get will be true, and even torture has limited value. Because even under torture, most men never will give out the full picture. They'll either lie out of patriotism for their country or tell you what they think you want to hear, just so the torture will end.

"What is far worse, and a greater problem, are the many times when the idiots in the field arrest an innocent man. Under torture, that innocent man, who really knows nothing, is forced to lie, because if he doesn't pass some information to his tormentor, the torture will never end." Hogan took another swallow of beer.

"This false information wastes enormous time and talent as the agency follows down these false leads. If it were up to me, I would end enhanced interrogations, and I would treat those sadistic bastards to their own medicine. Virtually all useful intelligence is gathered in the field, not on the rack, and it is acquired not through torture but through well-practiced skill."

"But what if *I* am captured? The other side tortures too." Kendal was suddenly having his doubts on the subject of Hogan's wisdom. CIA spy school taught that enhanced interrogation was a useful and productive tool. Surely the government wouldn't lie.

"If you're captured, you use misinformation, information, and bullshit: MIB.

"Now, you know for certain they're not going to believe everything you tell them, so you mix it up a bit. You give them a little misinformation, believable stuff that may or may not be true in their mind. Then you toss in a little true information.

"If you're a good enough player, you know where you've been compromised, and you give them a little bit of information they aren't supposed to know but already do. This makes it a bit more believable. Then you toss in a little bullshit—stuff you hope they'll believe—and if they believe any part of it, you really come out ahead!"

"I was told to never, under any circumstance, reveal any information to the enemy," Kendal replied, more than a bit confused.

"That directive refers to vital information," Max corrected. "If you tell them nothing, you gain nothing. But if you tell them an ounce of truth and a pound of lies, and they believe three ounces of what you say, then the agency and America are way ahead of the game."

"It's a cold world we live in, and we're at the very heart of it," Hogan added. "Max and I are the Knights of the Cold War. He's the Avenging Angel, and I'm the Poet. We're sent to accomplish the things that threats and politics simply can't get done."

Max leaned forward in a conspiratorial manner. "One thing you need to realize, Kendal, is the fact that there are two CIAs, each very separate and independent from the other, and—"

"In fact, some say there are three or four," Hogan interrupted.

"The *official* CIA is filled with bureaucrats, pill counters, and brown-nosing civil self-servants." Max had no tolerance for lazy civil servants and paper jockeys. "These are the people who are appointed or hired, usually as payback for political favors. They're little removed from the somnolent zombies at the Department of Motor Vehicles. The only real difference is they're watched closer—not for efficiency but for but loyalty. They aren't the real CIA.

"They just print the checks and track the budget. They answer the phone and generate the thousands of meaningless reports for the elected bureaucrats who insist on having them but refuse to read them, believe them, or act on them."

Max knew the CIA's conclusions were by and large usually correct. However, Washington and its political whores usually ignored the agency's best recommendations. Max felt strongly the agency needed fewer people writing reports and more good men in the field to look after America's real interests.

"The second CIA is the *real* CIA. Men like Hampstead, Hargood, and Beaucroix are the real power. The politicians have no real control. When these elected officials try to *control* the *real* CIA, they find themselves *controlled*. Frequently they're set up with one or more of the sort of things that destroy a political career. Those whose closets are clean and challenge Hampstead's CIA are usually killed or commit suicide—sort of an assisted suicide with a little help from Hampstead's stateside players; he calls them his mechanics."

Kendal was shocked. Every American knew the agency did terminations in America's best interest, but he never knew they killed Americans, and he had never heard anyone—especially an agent—talk openly about it.

"Wait a minute!" As an American, Kendal was offended that this man was talking about *his* America as some kind of malignant Nazi cartel. "What about Director Morse and the president and the Senate Intelligence Committee?"

"The president is elected," Max told him. "He's only here for four or eight years. The CIA is forever! What would happen to America if we trusted a man who perhaps had only another year to go in office with our country's deepest secrets? What would happen if he were to let some vital information slip, perhaps during a little pillow talk to his wife or some bimbo?"

"Or perhaps to some ballerina?" Hogan offered, laughing. He was, of course, referring to the president's son, the ballet dancer.

"Right," Max continued. "Presidents come and go, but our duty to protect America and American interests never rests. There's no reason to trust the president with more information than he needs to do his job." Max leaned back and folded his arms. "The Senate Intelligence Committee has a purpose, and that purpose is to provide the illusion to the American people that their elected officials control the CIA. Of course, we three know this is neither possible nor practical."

Kendal solemnly nodded and took another drink. "Well, what about Director Morse?" Kendal named his boss—the man who had hired him, shaken his hand, and wished him luck as he'd sent him on the great adventure that was West Africa.

"The director's main purpose is"—Max paused as he leaned forward for dramatic effect—"to get every report delivered on time to the correct bureaucrat in plenty of time to be ignored—and to make sure we get paid on time!" he added, laughing. "Hampstead is the director of European operations. The Cold War is centered in Europe. That makes him the most powerful man in the CIA. When Hogan or I refer to the 'director,' we mean Hampstead. We never discuss or refer to James Morse, the director of the CIA."

"Naturally, for security reasons," Kendal offered.

"No," Hogan jumped in. "We never discuss the man because he's of no consequence to what we do. He's irrelevant."

Max nodded. "America isn't the voters. It's not the politicians, and it's certainly not you and me. America is a set of ideals. It has a goal, purpose, and direction. America is a living, breathing thing. Our country was founded by some of the greatest men who ever lived. It was founded by great men like Thomas Jefferson and James Madison, men who had unshakable principles and very high moral ideals. If the CIA ignores the ideals America was built upon in favor of the whims of politics or the unstable, quivering, and ever-changing morality of society—if we do that—I can promise you there will be *no America* for the next generation. The America we cherish will be destroyed within a decade and will cease to exist."

Hogan raised his glass in salute as Max uncorked the bottle, refilled his glass, and then offered to pour for the others.

"The best way to preserve the interests of the American people is to ignore the whims of the American people. It's the CIA, gentlemen—not the Constitution—that protects the liberty and freedom of our country."

Max and Kendal raised their glasses and toasted. This was a point they all fully, unconditionally agreed upon.

They drank quietly for a few moments, and then, filled with the spirit of wine and the brotherhood of Bacchus, Hogan rambled on. "The FBI, however, contains a lot of buffoons and jokers. The CIA isn't allowed to operate within US borders. Domestic intelligence and counterintelligence are the responsibility of the FBI. But the sad truth is that most of America's worst security leaks have originated from within the FBI." Hogan smiled. "So the CIA quietly and illegally handles security issues within America's borders and especially within the FBI."

"But the FBI always exposes the spies within its own ranks," Kendal interrupted. "Just the other day—"

"The FBI is worthless. They're idiots. They're contacted by *us*—we point out the smoke to them, and they find the fire." Now Max really grinned; he was going to talk about all the other players. "The Secret Service is different. They're some of the best and bravest guys I've ever met or worked with. As an agency, they're the toughest, most capable force America has within its borders. They are, for the most part, incorruptible and competent."

Kendal felt a swelling urge to jump in and defend the integrity and high ideals of the CIA. Then he remembered men like Emile Beaucroix and Leo Pagetti and stayed silent. "How did you decide to become a spy, Max?" he asked, changing the subject.

"I grew up in a small town in Missouri. I was a pretty laid-back guy. I was a beatnik, seriously!" Max paused, giving Kendal time to draw the picture as Hogan laughed quietly. Kendal couldn't imagine one of the world's most professional, successful killers being a peace-loving, girl-chasing, poetry-reading, coffee-drinking, goateed loafer!

Max continued, "I used to hang out with a few friends at the local diner, drinking coffee and reading poetry. Hogan likes poetry too. That's why we call him the Poet. Sometimes in our little town, my friends and I had this art show at the local store. I used to paint a little, mostly oil paintings of some of the cute girls in town.

"Our sheriff was Ricky Lee Baines Walker. He didn't care much for us, and he accused us of running around the county trying to corrupt everyone into joining sexual orgies. He called them 'ooor-gees.' He considered himself the self-appointed morals director for the whole county. Three times he beat the shit out of me and jailed me for no reason. I complained to the mayor and anyone who would listen, but the mayor just apologized and said, 'Ricky Lee runs this county his way. He don't welcome no interference from me,' and wouldn't do anything to help.

Then Ricky Lee arrested my girl; he beat her senseless and raped her. Then, as a finale, he broke her jaw. She was only sixteen!

Hogan grabbed the bottle and refilled all three glasses, Max downed his shot quickly, and Robert immediately refilled it.

"I'd finally had enough of the asshole, and I didn't turn to anyone but my own counsel for help. I decided to take care of Ricky Lee, and I vowed no one would ever beat me up or jail me again. Somehow, things were never the same with my girl and me after that. When the sheriff disappeared, she sort of drifted away from my friends and me. I think she guessed what I'd done; losing her killed me." Max looked down at the table and sadly swirled the whiskey in his glass.

"Well, for two years, the sheriff's disappearance was a mystery, and no one had a clue. At least that's what I thought, until somehow the FBI found out and came looking for me. I was out of town with some friends when some stranger left a message at my friend Paul's house that the feds were prowling around town, asking about me. It was time to split!

"Just as I was skipping town, a car swung across my path, blocking my Ford Thunderbird. Then a second car pulled up right behind me, practically nailing my bumper. It was the CIA," Max continued, never lifting his eyes from the gently swirling whiskey. "They offered me a deal. They told me they knew I had killed the man, and the FBI had all the proof they needed as well as the body. They understood why I'd done what I had, but they couldn't interfere with domestic agencies like the FBI.

"But they said if I joined them, they'd protect me, take care of me. I wouldn't want for anything, and they were right. They gave me a clean identity, and then they arranged for me to escape to Tunisia, where they set me up as an importer-exporter. They gave me the money to set up shop." Max smiled; he loved his job.

"Did you ever find out who ratted you out to the FBI?" asked Kendal.

"I was fingered by the CIA. They set me up. They told the FBI where to find me, where I buried the body, and where I dumped the gun." Max was grinning broadly.

"You're not bitter?" Kendal was amazed.

"Nope. I killed that asshole sheriff, and I'm glad I got caught. I couldn't sleep since the night I killed him. I'm glad someone found out, and I'm glad someone understood why I did it. I had turned into a useless party drunk. When I was found out, it somehow freed me.

"If I'd gotten away with that killing, I probably would've felt guilty my entire life. I probably would've ended up a homeless drunk. I knew that asshole deserved to die, but I needed someone to understand why I killed him. But there was no one I could tell, no one I could trust.

"Sheriff Walker was a piece of shit, total human garbage. He deserved to die. But I still felt like hell, and I might have killed myself. But the company has been good to me. I'm glad to be here, and I'm grateful for the wonderful friends I've made inside the company. I love the CIA because it's my family. Besides, the CIA saved me; they helped me forgive myself. I was redeemed and saved by the CIA."

"And they helped you forget what happened to your girlfriend?" Kendal asked as he turned toward the kitchen, pointed at the now-almost-empty Napoleon brandy, raised his empty glass, shook it at the waiter, and held up three fingers.

"Nope. Jessie Lorraine was the kind of girl no man could ever forget. God only lets a man find that kind of girl once in a lifetime. I guess that's why I never got married...." Max trailed off sadly.

"What do you import and export?" Kendal was curious, as he had been assigned to Max for field training. He had no cover because it wasn't necessary yet.

"Mostly munitions like rifles, light rocket launchers, military explosives, and mines, stuff like that. I do a lot of business with Hogan. I move most of the stuff on our side of the Middle East. Israel is a good and profitable customer. Hogan does all the legwork. He usually cuts the deal, and I move the shit." Max gave Hogan a thumbs-up, and Hogan grinned.

After one last drink, the three men went their separate ways. Max was headed back to Tunis via the merchant marine, and Kendal, by plane, was headed to Paris. He had a meeting with Agent Scott Parker to report on Robert Hogan. The second-most important job a spy did was to spy on and report on his fellow spies.

Hogan decided to walk to the Royal Moroccan because it was the best hotel in Rabat, and why not stay there? Big Brother was picking up the tab, and the food and liquor were excellent. He walked slowly as he turned north and strolled casually through the market. He loved to watch the locals gossip, haggle, scream, kiss, and cast accusations of profiteering as they bargained for their daily bread.

With a jolt he stopped in his tracks as his gaze was snapped to the right toward the stall of Hassan, the jeweler. He couldn't believe his eyes as he stared at her. She was working her way as easily as a gazelle past the gold merchants when he noticed her. She was an angel, a goddess, a dark-haired and tanned but fair-skinned beauty. He smiled broadly as his eyes locked upon her.

She must have been one of the results from the days when France had ruled Algeria, and tolerance and mixed marriages were taken as a matter of course. It was a very civilized attitude, and it was a pity it had to end.

Closely he eyed this incredible beauty, his eyes caressing every inch of her gorgeous body. Suddenly and without warning, she turned, and her eyes captured him, froze, and enslaved him. She had the large, dark-brown doe eyes common to that part of the world. They were the sort of eyes to kill for and eyes to die for; happily and a hundred times a hundred, he would joyfully do their bidding. He watched intently as her fabulous eyes danced and sparkled with a liveliness that defined them as the road to a heart worth having, a heart worth owning, greedily guarding, and selfishly possessing.

It was a love he could share and would share with no man, if only he could possess her. Long-suppressed feelings welled up from the depths of his soul as those eyes teased him, tempted him, and drove him to desire; he fought an overwhelming impulse to toss himself in front of her and beg to possess her.

She noticed him and sent him a smile—melting him, hurting him because he knew he dared not approach her. To have her for a night and not possess her for a lifetime would be more pain than he could bear. His eyes were still locked upon her as she returned to her bargaining.

Hogan followed her as she walked through the market. There was something to say for a woman who wore tight pants. He admired the way she moved in her starched French khakis, her tight, round bottom torturing him, punishing him, reminding him of what he never could allow himself to possess.

Her buttocks spoke to him as she walked. Her right cheek said, "Want me," and the left added, "Take me."

Her fat little ass moved as she walked away with a sassy, unlicensed glory.

"Want me, take me, want me, take me, want me, take me," her glorious buttocks shouted at him, taunting him, torturing him, daring him to follow as she walked gracefully through the bazaar.

His mind flashed back across those many foggy, faded years to a small, dark room in Korea where he sat surrounded by three dour, serious men. Robert Hogan had said yes to the recruitment officer and yes to the CIA.

"Want me, take me, want me, take me," her fantastic ass shouted and tortured him again as he fought to look away and fought to save his soul.

People think that when you join the CIA, the sacrifice you make is your safety—the possibility that you may be killed or tortured, or spend the last of your days in some medieval hellhole of a prison.

But that wasn't what you sacrificed.

Things like danger, assassination attempts, and the odd mercenary bandit or two—these weren't problems or factors to a spy. These things were your duty. Every morning you faced the possibility that this day might be your last, and you learned to accept it. So this wasn't the sacrifice you made.

What you sacrificed was a wife, a family, a home filled with the laughter of happy children. You sacrificed the smell of a home-cooked dinner drifting out from the kitchen. A dinner cooked by a woman who loved you, interrupted by the silly laughter of happy children and a rampaging English setter. This was what you sacrificed for the CIA.

Still depressed by Max's story of a love lost, he sadly turned away from the incredible-ass beauty and walked on with eyes downcast. The unbelievably glorious rump offer of "Want me, take me" would have to denied; the pain of having her for one night only and never again would kill every night of the rest of his life. Damn, he wished he were dead.

It was true that the CIA and America paid you well. But the CIA and America could never pay you back. It was a biting pain born of the knowledge that time had made many hard choices on roads past never to be retraveled. Robert Hogan sadly, painfully tore his mind away from the khaki-clad beauty and continued his journey through the bright streets of Morocco. He wanted to die; he needed a drink and a bottle to cry into, and he needed it badly.

He ignored the happy sun that caressed his shoulders with its warm affection as he walked through the busy hustle of Rabat. Today it was an affection he sadly could not return.

He had now forgotten the Royal Moroccan. As he passed the old royal palace, he coolly admired the classic Moorish beauty of its architecture. He continued down the thoroughfare until he came to the Continental Club, a popular watering hole for expatriate Europeans living in and visiting Morocco.

It was also a great place to meet spies and pick up useful gossip. But today it would be a great place to get drunk and try to drift away from the past. He pushed open the old varnish-bare teak doors salvaged from a crippled India steamer and walked inside.

The instant Hogan entered the cool, dimly lit interior, he noticed the curious gaze that weighed him, measured him as it tried to draw him into the game. As he searched the shadows, he saw the intense, stocky man sitting in the darkest corner of the Continental. Slava Kurnov had indeed been sizing him up.

Hogan ordered a bottle of Irish whiskey and two glasses from the white-wool-clad Moroccan bartender and then casually strode over to the dark mahogany table and helped himself to a seat across from Kurnov.

Hogan filled the two Irish Waterford crystal glasses and slid one across the table. Without a word to Kurnov, he lit a stogie, leaned back in the comfortable but moth-eaten leather of the tall Victorian chair, and patiently waited for the Soviet player to make his move.

"Sometimes we have to do unpleasant things. It is an unfortunate thing, but it is a fact of life." Kurnov seemed to be speaking to himself, addressing his conversation to the smoke-filled air.

"True," Hogan replied as he leaned forward and searched for the eye contact that would propel this conversation to the meat of the matter. He wondered what this meeting was about. This man was too good a spy and too tough to be defecting.

"We should not be any more unpleasant than is necessary."

"I take care not to." Hogan egged him on, still fishing for eye contact. He sensed some kind of a request for moderation, but in what? Did they know about Bopolu? Did General Kutu sell them out?

"What do you think of such people?" Firing his gaze at Hogan, Kurnov seized those eyes and challenged Hogan's will with his own.

"We would be better off without them. They're unprofessional." Hogan returned the intensity of the Russian's stare. Hogan always despised excess, and this man was clearly talking about spies who exceeded their orders, renegade players who ignored the rules of the game.

"Then why don't you control your friends? Perhaps rein them back?" the Russian both asked and accused as he hammered Hogan with his eyes, trying to beat him into submission.

Hogan released Kurnov's eyes. "I have many friends," he replied with feigned disinterest.

"Then perhaps you could help us with this one. Nip it in the bud before matters become worse." Kurnov wanted those eyes back. He wanted to challenge them and tell them he was the best. It was a macho thing; some tough men needed to do this. It reinforced their standing as a top dog, as a dominant wolf in a pack of all the best wolves.

"In my business, one must make many decisions, and subordinates must make decisions. I'm too busy to audit everyone," Hogan replied curtly. He was a superb actor, and this—whatever this was—was clearly an important matter. He pretended to be bored to trick Kurnov into overplaying his hand and giving out more information than was absolutely necessary.

"Then you refuse to moderate these things, to bring the game back within the rules?" Kurnov made another cast for those eyes.

"There's been nothing out of the ordinary." Although Hogan acted uninterested, he knew Slava Kurnov was the most powerful man in the KGB. You couldn't be one of America's best players without knowing the other team's roster. However, this was an important and unprecedented meeting. He would still have to be careful, but there was probably no personal danger. When two players met, there was almost always a truce. It was a professional courtesy they usually extended to each other. It was always the spy you didn't see who would try to kill you.

"Do you wish this matter to escalate? Do you wish to go to the other set of rules?" Kurnov questioned, threatened.

Hogan swung his eyes, slamming into Kurnov's gaze, and the Russian fought back just as hard. This was incredible; the KGB was threatening to propel Russia to war!

Hogan considered the matter carefully. This was a lot more serious than he had thought. "Which one of my friends needs to be controlled?" he inquired seriously. Spies had been killed before, sacrificed to prevent war.

"You must terminate the one you consider to be your best spy. We no longer will tolerate his behavior or crimes. What he did last week in Czechoslovakia was unforgivable; our Slavic allies are furious. Your company must dismiss him. His excesses are intolerable, and these excesses have nothing to do with bettering your situation or fulfilling your goals for world domination." Kurnov said this with a grim finality. There would be no negotiation on this issue.

Hogan was relieved; there had been some mistake. Max George had been on assignment in Africa and Central America; he hadn't been in Eastern Europe in eighteen months. Bopolu and a certain banana republic had much more urgent need of his services.

"He has been on vacation and hasn't been to Eastern Europe in some time." Hogan had released Kurnov's stare and was feigning disinterest again.

"Not him—we know where he is. You don't seem to realize the importance of this meeting. I'm threatening war. We have the power to draw your nation into a war that will drive it to its knees and destroy your capitalist world."

Hogan grabbed back those eyes. "Comrade, neither of our companies wants that to happen—it would be a war we would both lose. But you must give me a name before I can consider your request. I have superiors who must be answered to." In reality, Hogan had only one: William Hampstead.

"Beaucroix—he is the one!" Kurnov spat, surprising Hogan with the violence and hatred in his announcement.

"That one is no friend," Hogan replied, softly drilling into Kurnov's eyes. This was something he wanted and needed Kurnov to believe. It was a matter of integrity. He would not permit himself to be associated with the Monster.

"Then you agree? You will control this matter?" Kurnov inquired, trying to wrap up his mission. He had a fresh young woman in the wings, a dark-haired Arab beauty waiting for him in Cairo. He needed some recreation after this, a diversion from his hard, harsh world.

"They won't sacrifice him. He's too popular," Hogan replied. "They" referred only to Hampstead; he would never OK a termination of Emile Beaucroix. Hampstead considered him too valuable a killer. He believed Beaucroix was the best killer the CIA had ever had. In truth, he was merely the most psychotic.

"Then you will suffer the consequences. Your world has ended, fool. Imperialism shall die!" Kurnov rose to leave, furious that stupidity and stubbornness would plunge the world into war.

He had gained only two strides toward the teak doors when Hogan shouted, "Kurnov, hold it!" Kurnov froze, swung around, and advanced back one step toward the table. "You have your own personnel department, and, in my experience, some are very capable. Why don't you dismiss him yourself?" Hogan said softly, to avoid being overheard.

Kurnov returned to his seat and poured himself a fresh drink from the whiskey bottle. "Then it would not upset you?" The spymaster was amazed.

Hogan quickly audited the room with his eyes; it was largely empty. "Heck, I would help you!" Hogan would never defect; his dossier was plastered with statements to that effect. But here he was offering traitorous advice—advising foreign powers to eliminate one of his own players and kill an American citizen.

"Why should I trust you? What kind of guarantee can you give me that I will not be sending my very best into one of your traps?" Kurnov shook his finger.

"Call it honor among thieves," Hogan replied, spreading his arms in a display of generosity.

"I like that. I like that very much." Kurnov smiled. He loved clever people.

Hogan's reply satisfied him; this was acceptable. Kurnov understood that Hogan was willing to facilitate and cover up the termination of Emile Beaucroix. The KGB felt it was the best intelligence agency in the world and believed it could take out any man. Happily, the game had returned to the rules; all would soon be right. This would be a return to the stalemate that kept the Cold War cool and prevented the heat of war.

"I wonder if it's going to rain this year. One time I was here, and it didn't rain for two years." Slava Kurnov was again speaking to the smoke-filled air. He seemed to be unaware of Hogan's presence and no longer interested in controlling those eyes.

Kurnov casually lifted his glass and downed his whiskey. Placing the glass upside down on the table, he rose from the chair and headed outside into the bright beauty of the Moroccan sun.

From the darkest corner of the bar and behind the palm-filled room divider, the fat man had watched unseen; the rules to the game had been changed, and so must his part in the play. The Shadow scratched his belly and smiled as Hogan poured himself another drink.

Robert Hogan lifted his glass to God and toasted the heavens. The great poker game of life and death between good and evil would now take a surprising turn, because the next card flipped onto the table would come from the bottom of the deck.

Kurnov had slipped him an ace, and Robert Hogan had found himself a ringer.

CHAPTER SIXTEEN
The Race to Doomsday

June 3, 1981
Hogan's House in the Congo

"Are you ever going to tell me how you cheated the Scotsman?" Max asked for the twentieth time. This time, Hogan was half drunk on Martell XO cognac and would likely be more talkative.

"Hey, I beat him fair and square. I was the better shot!" Hogan defended himself.

"Robert, on your best day, you couldn't hit a barn twice—that is, unless someone held the barn real steady for you." Max laughed.

"Friendship is about trust. Why can't you believe me?" Hogan inquired with a drunken grin.

"I don't trust you because I know you better than you know yourself." Max grinned too as he poured Robert another glass, filling it a bit beyond the brim.

"Are you trying to get me drunk?"

"Of course. This is an interrogation. I'm too plastered to force you to talk, so I'm going to torture you with alcohol until you confess."

"I'll never talk. Send me to Siberia!" Hogan stated with conviction. He drained his glass and slammed it onto the table.

"Then you must be tortured some more!" Max shouted as he refilled his friend's glass, sending the cognac splashing onto the teakwood table. "Why would I send you to Siberia? That isn't punishment enough for your many crimes. I plan to exile you to Cleveland for this dastardly deed."

Max took another swallow of cognac and emptied the glass. Through a drunken haze, he groped the table as he searched for the bottle.

"Cleveland will never break me! I've seen the Cleveland Browns play and survived!" Hogan liked to poke fun at Cleveland's once-great but now-struggling NFL team.

Max had now located the bottle through the shifting fog and refilled Hogan's brimming glass. "I'll beat your liver with more cognac until you confess." He poured more cognac into the glass he had just filled, sending most of it to the floor.

"Enough! Enough!" Hogan shouted, laughing. "I'll talk—I can't take any more of this inhuman torture!"

"Good. Then I won't have to kill you with this!" Max had removed a large dill pickle from the jar and wagged it menacingly at Hogan's face.

Hogan stood, glancing about the room in a conspiratorial manor. He winked at Max and indicated he wanted to be followed. The two extremely drunken spies staggered across the floor. When they entered the hall, Hogan bumped into the wall as they navigated his narrow back hallway. Max grabbed his shoulders, centered him in the hall, and then pushed him forward. After staggering about thirty feet, they entered Hogan's hardwood-paneled gun room.

"This is the place. This is where the magic begins!" Hogan whispered.

He motioned for Max to stay put as he stuck his head back in the hallway, searching left and right; he had to be certain they weren't being followed. He was now, much like Max, six exits past drunk and still happily speeding.

"Look in here, Max." Hogan had staggered to the far side of the dimly lit gun room and opened a tall mahogany chest. "What do you see?" he said in his best and somewhat plastered conspiratorial whisper.

"I see a lot of cans. Lots and lots of pretty gunpowder cans. Here, I think I have a match." Max searched his pockets as he swayed, attempting to maintain an upright posture. He was now so drunk that he had completely forgotten about O'Grady the Scotsman.

"This is the magic!" Hogan grinned as he produced a box of clips labeled Special Medicine.

Max could only answer with a silly blank grin. "What are you staring at, you asshole?" he shouted at the stuffed hippo head gracing the far wall, just above the cool hearth.

"Hey, this is a private meeting!" Hogan staggered a bit as he pointed at the glassy-eyed hippo and indicated with a drunken circular hand motion for the hippo to turn and look away.

"Yeah, fuck you!" Max flipped his middle finger at the rude animal.

"Look here." Hogan pointed to a shelf that held three trays of .45-caliber cartridges labeled One, Two, and Three.

Max could only stand there, swaying somewhat. He was having a great time. When you were with great friends, you always had great fun!

"See this one?" Hogan pointed to the first tray. "I load these cartridges with Alliant gunpowder so they fly four inches low of aim, dead center." He winked at Max, who burped loudly in response. "Now look at this." Hogan indicated the second tray. "I load these with Hercules gunpowder, about three grains short. They fly three inches to the right and two up!" he added, laughing.

Max could only grin; he had no idea what this was about, but it sure was entertaining.

"This last one I load with Peter's gunpowder, plus six grains. They fly five inches high and three inches to the right." The excellent cognac was winning the battle for equilibrium, and, swaying to the left, Hogan grabbed the edge of the gun cabinet and dropped the tray onto the floor, sending fifty cartridges noisily rolling to all parts of the unsteady room.

"Here's the secret!" Hogan righted himself as best he could and took one of the charged clips out of another box. "I load these clips—one, two, three!" he gave Max a thumbs-up.

Staggering, Max returned the thumbs-up, though he had no idea why.

"No one except me can shoot well with these because only I know the secret." Hogan gave Max another thumbs-up. Max replied with his own thumbs-up and then surveyed his thumb with great interest. He'd never before noticed what an incredibly fascinating thumb it really was; he indicated to Hogan to check it out.

"The first round…" Hogan said, ignoring the fascinating thumb as he whispered with a burp and again glanced around the room and wondered with irritation why the hippo had neglected his request to leave the gun room. He frowned at the rude animal, but out of a sense of duty to his friend and to garner full credit, he would reveal how he had brilliantly cheated the Scotsman. "The first round I aim four inches high. The second I aim down two inches and left three, and the last I place five inches low and three inches to the left of the bulls-eye." Hogan offered Max his hand in congratulations. Max shook it, but in his deep alcoholic stupor, he had forgotten where he was and wondered if the meeting with Hampstead was over.

"And that's how I beat that stupid Frenchman O'Toole," Hogan stated, thus ending the story.

"He wasn't a fucking frog!" Max had just emerged from his drunken fog to recognition. "He was a Greek, and his name wasn't O'Cool—it was O'Connor!" Max corrected, catching himself on Hogan as he nearly lost his balance. "Do I need to kick your ass?" Staggering as he righted himself and turning to the right, Max extended his clenched fist as he again addressed the stuffed hippo head that rudely refused to look away.

"Yeah, fuck you!" Hogan flipped his finger at the nosy hippo as the two spies happily and drunkenly worked their way out of the gun room and back to the booze, which always brought them closer to redemption.

For the next twenty long years, and with neither spy remembering that drunken night, Max would beg Hogan to tell him how he had cheated the Scotsman. But Hogan never would tell; it would forever be his little secret.

June 5, 1981
The White House

The cowboy president smiled broadly as he surveyed the faces around the table. He had long since suspected John Hargood, the CIA's director of special operations, was too soft on commies and queers.

To speed things up in Bopolu, the president had insisted the director give Special Operations Director Warren Hargood the responsibility for the North African theater and for Hargood to focus the bulk of his attention on perfecting Wildfire.

With the rise of the Sandinistas in Central America, that theater became a central focus for the president, and it presented a pregnant problem he intended to deal with. With a very real danger of Communism creeping north, he needed Hampstead to concentrate on Europe so as to keep the European communists too busy to notice his blossoming and brilliant Central American plans.

But the president soon grew to mistrust the slow progress the overly cautious Hargood was making and regretted insisting the director of the CIA place him in charge. Numerous times since, he had asked the director to replace Hargood with someone more in line with his agenda. What the president didn't know was that the director feared Hargood. He was yet another Hampstead, and, as such, was too powerful to be replaced by anyone.

So when the most powerful leader in the free world looked across the conference table and into the smiling face of Emile Beaucroix, he felt sure he had effectively bullied the director into picking the right man for the job.

In point of fact, however, Hargood had disappeared several months before. Dozens of potential witnesses had been interviewed, and many others had been investigated by the FBI as to their whereabouts. But no trace—or even a hint of a trace—of evidence would ever be found.

Beaucroix was the obvious replacement. He was cunning and relentless, and he had a 100 percent efficiency rating. He liked to mix politics, social graces, and merriment with murder. He was well known in Washington and in the White House; Max George and William Hogan were not.

So on June 5, 1981, Emile Beaucroix was named in charge of the Wildfire project and inherited some of Hampstead's power. Overnight, he became the fourth-most powerful man in the most powerful intelligence agency on earth. Beaucroix knew he was the best man for the job, and he knew he deserved to be at the top. He had known that hard work, dedication, and loyalty would advance him within the CIA. But one other factor had played a minor part in his promotion. He was the only man on earth who knew what had happened to Warren Hargood.

"What do you have to report?" asked the president.

Beaucroix shuffled some papers, organizing them and opening the first of several folders. "So far, the Soviets have no idea of our progress. A KGB agent I personally interviewed in Cairo had no clue the facility in Bopolu even existed. I've been able to maintain 100 percent security and secrecy at Bopolu." Beaucroix was brief, businesslike.

Hampstead looked coldly at the president, drilling him with his eyes. He had been invited to the meeting but so far had been ignored. Hampstead was a dangerous man to slight; Beaucroix was his junior, and the president should be directing his questions to him, William Hampstead.

"Mr. Beaucroix, what about this General Kutu in Hogan's reports? Is he really a psycho?"

"Psycho?" Beaucroix was insulted and incredulous. "The man is a saint. He's my best contact with the Liberian government—he facilitates everything. Without his thorough, constant cooperation, our security in Bopolu wouldn't be what it is today. Hogan is an alarmist. He hates the general because Kutu hates communists. General Kutu treats communists how they deserve to be treated. He's hard, harsh, and unbending. Is that wrong, Mr. President?" The Monster played the B-movie president the way a Tennessee minstrel plays a fiddle.

"Certainly not. Maybe we should look a little closer at this Hogan fellow. Look into his patriotism," the president suggested.

"It will be done, sir." Beaucroix nodded as he feigned professionalism.

"Hogan's a good man; you would be wasting your time," William Hampstead offered. Controlling and allocating assets well made him the success he was today. There was nothing unpatriotic about Robert Hogan. Looking into ill-founded rumors was like looking for Bigfoot or monitoring paper tigers. It was a draining and unnecessary waste of manpower.

"What kind of progress is being made in Bopolu? When can I have the bug, and where can we test it?" The president completely ignored Hampstead as he folded his hands on the mahogany table and smiled toward Beaucroix.

Polling the table with a sharply cutting glance, Hampstead made a list. By ignoring him and withholding the respect he both had earned and deserved, these fools had stupidly tickled the belly of the sleeping dragon.

Caspar Weinberger, the secretary of defense, now butted in. "We plan to test it in Cuba, Mr. President. Mr. Beaucroix will arrange for Wildfire to be mixed in with the vaccine the Cuban medical authority dispenses throughout its state-run educational and medical facilities. Every Cuban patient who visits these facilities will become infected. The virus will then spread via sexual contact through the general population. Within six months, Cuba will be at its knees!"

"God, that's great news, gentlemen! No more *Hannibal ad portas*, no more red perverts. Just dead red commie bastards." The cowboy president leaned back in his tall chair and rubbed his chin. "Won't other countries know we were to blame? What about the Russians? They could start a nuclear war." The president loved the Cuban part, but he didn't cherish spending the next twenty-five hundred years huddled in a bomb shelter beneath the White House lawn.

"No one will know for certain what has happened," Dr. Moses Berman explained. "The world will think Cuba was struck by a natural, previously unknown disease. We'll cover our asses by airlifting tons of penicillin to our sworn enemy, the Cuban government. It'll make us look like compassionate heroes and saints on the world stage, but the penicillin will do nothing against Wildfire. It is the supreme weapon!" The doctor smiled. Greed was a great mediator of social conscience. Dr. Berman owned a lot of stock in the pharmaceutical company that would get the contract to manufacture the killer virus. He would be rich!

"But how could we use Wildfire against the Russians?" the president asked. "They're the greatest threat to the free world and our main enemies. We can't just ask them to stop shooting and roll up their sleeves, can we?"

It was time for US Air Force Major General Hallway to add his piece to the puzzle. "Mr. President, Northrop Grumman already has completed plans to modify our high-flying spy planes to drop balloons just outside all major Soviet cities. We figure we can hit four Soviet cities a night with three runs a week."

"Balloons? I want those commies dead, not given birthday presents!" The general had lost the president.

"Idiot," mumbled Hampstead under his breath. How had this wannabe cowboy hick ever gotten to be president?

"Not ordinary balloons, Mr. President—far from it." Beaucroix grinned. "They're large vegetable-fabric spheres that will split open exactly three hundred feet off the ground, releasing millions of mosquitoes, all carrying the Wildfire virus and hungry as hell. Domestic and wild animals will quickly eat what remains of the vegetable-fabric spheres on the ground so as to leave little trace."

"What if the Soviets get wise?" The president liked the plan, but it sounded too slow and too risky.

"You mean if they go to war with us, Mr. President?" The general dug into his papers as he readied his answer.

"You did say we could strike just a few cities a week. Even if I were no smarter than a Democrat and my people started dropping dead left and right, I might think something may *possibly* be going on." The president smiled.

"If the Russians do get wise and declare war, we have the first-strike ability to take out the bulk of their nuclear missiles, and our superior fighter pilots will ensure no Russian bomber reaches our shores." The general grinned with a tinge of his own hungry greed, certain this war would add another star or two to his shoulder boards. "After we destroy their offensive ability, specially equipped bombers will hit all major Soviet cities with larger mosquito balloons that will open one thousand feet above the ground and dispense billions of the hungry little bastards. They'll fall on the population centers and infect millions of Russian civilians.

"This method of war will ensure the population will be too debilitated to fight back when our brave American boys roll up in their tanks and transports. Using this method instead of traditional explosives will leave the factories and warehouses deserted but intact—to be sold to American industry after the war, thus paying all the expenses of the war." The general took a deep breath as the president broke in.

"Excellent. This brilliant plan had to be your doing, Mr. Beaucroix!" He turned and smiled at Beaucroix, who grinned back.

"Gentlemen, we'll not only free the world from the godless communist threat, but America will win the first war in its history in which it makes a profit. I'd like to see Congress complain about that!" The cowboy president slammed his fist on the table.

"Yes, sir," The general replied, having lost his place in the mound of papers before him. He shuffled his papers as he looked for his place. "After six weeks," he continued, "We'll be able to enter the Soviet Union with our ground forces, which should encounter little resistance. All infected prisoners we capture will be separated and sent to special medical camps, where they'll be quarantined until they expire."

"Kind of like Buchenwald but without the claims of torture or whines of racism," Beaucroix said with a grin. The president was glad to have this offered up. He had been thinking the same thing but hadn't dared voice it.

"It's truly a final solution for communism!" The president again slammed his fist on the table. "When can we get started with Cuba?"

"It's not that easy, Mr. President," Dr. Paxton offered. "There are problems with Wildfire. It isn't yet stable enough or reliable enough to be considered a practical weapon."

"These problems, however, will soon be worked out. They are of no consequence," declared Beaucroix, who shot a scowl at Paxton, hoping the doctor would take a clue and remain silent.

"What are the problems, Mr. Beaucroix?" The president turned to the man he trusted most, the man he thought was most like him.

"Very minor ones, sir. They will be shortly in hand." Beaucroix was determined, final.

"They aren't so minor." Dr. Paxton addressed the president, who listened intently. "The current version of the virus acts differently in different people, so it can't be predicted. We even suspect there are individuals who can carry it for years and never be seriously affected. We haven't verified this, but there's some disturbing evidence that it may be true. Mr. President, you asked for the supreme weapon. I mean to give you that, but what we have at present may prove to be more of a Pandora's Box than the supreme weapon. We need more time to refine the virus." The doctor leaned forward as he pleaded his case.

"But isn't a Typhoid Mary, or Typhoid Harry, communist even better than one dead Russian? Maybe what you consider a weakness of Wildfire, Dr. Paxton, is in fact its greatest strength!" Hampstead was adamant. Hampstead had invented Bopolu, and he had invented Wildfire. It was still very much his baby.

"The European director has a point, Doctor. Are you complaining that the knife is too sharp to cut the butter?" the president questioned.

"Well, be that as it may, the virus is still not ready. In fact, I don't consider it ready in any shape or form to be considered a weapon. We're simply not finished. We need to reengineer the DNA inside the virus, which will take some time. Genetic engineering is a new science, and we learn as we go." The doctor shrugged.

"It'll be ready in one month. I give you my word, Mr. President. You're free to learn as you go, Doctor, but I intend to go forward!" Beaucroix must have believed he could iron things out in a couple of weeks; the man rarely lied. He would kill you, torment you, rape your wife, and barbecue your children, but he probably wouldn't lie to you. The Monster did have principles—not many, but he did have a few.

"Mr. Beaucroix," Dr. Paxton said, "I'm sure you're excellent at whatever is you do, but you lack the expertise to make such a profound statement on medical matters of which you have no way of knowing all the complexities. This weapon must be made more stable, more predictable, and more reliable. End of story."

"Bullshit!" Beaucroix declared, forgetting where he was for a moment and losing his temper. "I talk to Dr. Tindal every single day. I know how fast things are progressing. I say we press our advantage and use this weapon before the Soviets invent one of their own."

"Perhaps…" Hampstead butted in, mainly to put Beaucroix in his place. "Perhaps we all would benefit by not interrupting the doctor and letting him have his full say."

The president nodded. He wanted a good bug—a great bug—to free the world from communism. In his mind, it was the greatest evil mankind had ever known.

"Thank you, sir." Dr. Paxton nodded at Hampstead, grateful for his support. "Wildfire is unpredictable. Some people, when infected, die quickly or are bedridden and die within three weeks. Others are sick in varying degrees for what may turn out to be years. It's even possible that some may be completely immune to the virus, though I admit such numbers would be few. The real danger in using Wildfire as a weapon of war is the carriers, those people who can carry the virus for years without showing any symptoms yet still infect others. After the war, every civilian and soldier would have to be tested, and those who are carriers would have to be quarantined indefinitely. Some, but maybe not all, of these victims certainly would expire."

"Mr. President, after the war, such people could simply disappear—perhaps be killed for war crimes or spying and profiteering in time of war." Beaucroix offered a simple solution.

The president rubbed his chin as he considered the matter. Hampstead and Dr. Paxton were shocked that the president would even consider such options.

"Mr. Beaucroix, may I remind you that this is the United States and not Eastern Europe?" Hampstead said. "Dr. Paxton is discussing civilian and American military lives here. Ridding the world of communism is one thing—in fact a very noble and righteous thing. But murdering innocent women and children and murdering our own soldiers who fought bravely in combat simply because they became infected in the line of duty is totally and unconditionally unacceptable. I think that maybe you forget your place, Emile. This is not your White House." He again polled the table with his eyes but found few friendly faces.

Hampstead looked at the president; the president glared back. Suddenly Hampstead hated him. He would contribute nothing else to this meeting; Hampstead would clam up while he considered darker options regarding this man.

"In communism, there are no civilians and no children," the president said. "They all are evil—totally evil—and need to be destroyed. Communism is a cancer, a disease and scourge deadlier than Wildfire. I'll accept nothing less than the total annihilation of godless communism from the face of the earth." The commander in chief's temples were throbbing, his eyes swollen with fury.

"My point being," Dr. Paxton continued, "the virus isn't fast enough, reliable enough. It needs more revisions, gene changes, and many more generations before it becomes a totally reliable weapon of war." The doctor now closed his manila folder because there was nowhere else for this meeting to go.

The president jumped in. "Doctor, I'd like to thank you for all this vital information. I'm sure we're on the right track, and you're 100 percent correct. Wildfire isn't ready yet." The president was used to manipulation and getting his own way; he would exercise both options here. "Dr. Paxton and Mr. Beaucroix, what do we need to do? How fast does Wildfire have to work before we can consider it an effective weapon of war?"

Dr. Paxton leaned back, briefly considering the paint on the ceiling. "The virus would have to begin working within three days, and it should kill or debilitate 35 percent of those infected within one week and have a greater than 80 percent fatality rate within ninety days." The doctor considered those numbers workable, ballpark.

"General, would those numbers suffice? Would they be effective?"

"Sir, with that kind of effectiveness, we would roll right past Moscow and into Peking!" the general replied.

The president grinned, wondering how the general had guessed his dream and his master plan: to completely rid the world of communism for all time. "Mr. Hampstead, how soon can you produce a virus that meets the doctor's criteria?" The president realized he had been slighting Hampstead and made an attempt to bring him back into the fold.

"Thirty days," Beaucroix butted in.

"That's impossible! It takes experimentation, trial and error, and then there's the testing." Dr. Paxton defended his stance. He believed it would take at least two years, maybe five.

"Dr. Paxton…" The president wanted to get rolling with this. History had many blank pages to fill with the name of the man who had saved the world from communism. "Doctor, I want you, Mr. Beaucroix, and Director Hampstead to meet after this and determine the maximum amount of funding, researchers, biologists, and materials that can be sent to Bopolu without creating a security situation.

"I want you to pull out all the stops here. We're onto something great, gentlemen, and I promise we're going to once and for all rid the world of communism. We must devote our full resources to this noble plan." The president stood, announcing the meeting was over. "Let's do it!"

June 5, 1981
In the attic above Bernie's News of the World newsstand

Joey Galante shook his head in disbelief as he removed the headphones from his head and flicked the off switch on the radio receiver. "Balloons? What *IDIOTS!* I never heard such a stupid plan. Look, Carlo, you kill only six key men, and you can bring down any government on earth, guaranteed! Those fools don't need the air force; they need us, the Cosa Nostra—the Mafia, like the press likes to call us."

"What was that, Joey G.?" Carlo asked. Seeing only moving lips, he had heard nothing.

"Carlo, you dull *contadina*, take off those stupid headphones so you can hear what I tell you."

"What did you say?" Carlo DiConte, the Confessor, slowly removed the headphones and placed them on the worn, varnish-bare table upon which the radio sat.

"I called you a dumb contadina, a stupid peasant girl. But don't take it to heart. I myself am only a *goomba*—a tough Italian boy—who made good." He gave Carlo an affectionate slap on the cheek.

"Balloons!" Repeated Joey G. "What idiots!"

"What are we doing here?" Carlo asked with confusion. Eavesdropping was for girls. Made men, real men, and steel-tough enforcers like Carlo the Confessor had more demanding and dangerous work to do.

"Carlo, some day Joey Junior will continue for me. I won't always be there to give him the correct Italian guidance and advice, but you are younger and a lesser target than me. You got few living enemies, I got lots. I need you to know everything about the business so you can be Joey's counselor, his trusted consigliore, after the Blessed Virgin Mary calls me home."

"Joey, you are the picture of perfect health! Don't talk like this, it disturbs me."

"Carlo, it is the way of all flesh that the purpose of all life is to pass the torch to the next generation, but I have no intention of passing that torch too soon. Joey Junior still has a lot to learn, and we must both teach him the ways."

"So, boss, what are we doing here?" Carlo was an expert on the hunting of men but knew nothing of and cared less about bigger pictures.

"Sure, Carlo. I will give the history lesson about this place. Bananas left it to me, a little parting gift to remember our friendship in the old days, the good days. Let me fill you in on a time when John Kennedy needed the Mob and Frank Sinatra sang beautiful Italian love songs to a grand Havana meeting of all the big Mafia bosses.

"It was in 1946 that the mob called a meeting of all the bosses to meet in Cuba. This Havana Conference was held on December 22, 1946 at the Hotel Nacional for the purpose of the mob staking a claim in Cuba. North America was getting smaller and wasn't as profitable as it had once been for the Mafia; they had lost a ton of money in Las Vegas. That was also the day they voted to whack Bugsy Siegel because of it.

"Lucky had just been tossed out of the USA, so it was decided by vote that Lucky Luciano would rule the Cuban underworld until it was safe for him to return to the States. Lucky even flew Frank Sinatra to the meeting to sing and provide the entertainment.

"The very next day, that New York fairy Lucky Luciano sent his Jew-boy pimp Meyer Lansky to talk with a scumbag named President Fulgencio Batista, who just happened to run Cuba.

"Meyer was one lucky boy. It was Meyer who had previously backed Bugsy Siegel and persuaded the Mob to bankroll Bugsy's plan to take over the Flamenco Hotel and Casino. Bugsy was ripping off the mob, and Meyer, his boyhood pal who sponsored him, was lucky to stay out of the heat.

"Bugsy was stealing half the mob's money and tossing the other half away. When the Mob bosses voted to whack Bugsy, Meyer Lansky was the first to vote to knock him off, and that was probably what saved his own precious ass.

"Siegel was killed in the Los Angeles home of that Hollywood whore Virginia Hill. The torpedo shot him eleven times, twice through the head, and that was the end of Bugsy Siegel.

"The very next day, half the Jewish mob walked into the Flamenco and took it over. It was Gus Greenbaum, Moe Sedway, and David Berman who showed up. They would eventually make Las Vegas the gold mine it is today. The Italian mob didn't object to the Jews taking over because they had lost so much money in Bugsy's folly and had never got one red cent out of the deal. The Italian mob considered Las Vegas a bust and a town with no future. Boy was that a prize boner!

"Meyer was smart, real smart. He knew there was real money to be made in legitimate gaming, but of the Italians, only Lucky was into that vision. Meyer was still secretly getting his piece of the pie through his connections with Moe Sedway and the Las Vegas operation. Lucky, however, had been tossed outta the country and had now partnered with Meyer Lansky with sights focused on Cuba and Batista, the finest dictator money could buy.

"Alfonse Capone of the Chicago mob had previously met with the dictator and had nixed any deals with the Mafia because Al considered the man a tyrant who abused, murdered, and raped the poor. Without the trust of the poor, there could be no Mafia. You and I know this. But big Al and Batista were definitely not copacetic on this item.

"But Meyer Lansky cared only about money, so he was able to cut an exclusive deal with Batista for all the gambling rights in Havana, including the horse racing tracks. Meyer was a pimp, but he had style. When he opened the Habana Riviera, he didn't spare any coin. He built the hotel and the casino as America's premier playground graced with the famous Copa Room, where stars from all over the planet performed. The Copa Room was opened in 1957 to the singing of Ginger Rogers—imagine that. What a babe!

"The year before Castro's revolution took over Cuba, Lansky was pulling three million dollars a month out of one Casino alone, the Habana Riviera. And let me tell you, Meyer's dirty little mitts were into a lot of Havana casinos, and most of the cash that worked its way through those grubby fingers went right into the Jewish mob. They financed Mickey Cohen's porn empire in Los Angeles, you bet.

"When Castro came to power in 1959 and the rebels entered the city, Meyer ran for the first boat off the island. It's funny, because that very night, he had hosted a packed party to celebrate the success of his newly built eighteen-million-dollar casino.

"Lucky, however, had stalled too long and almost got caught. He had to cut cross-country in his Cadillac until he caught a small plane, which he bribed to fly him to Haiti and freedom. Castro's rebels quickly trashed the opulent Yankee-only casinos, and the new Cuban government nationalized what was left.

"The Bay of Pigs invasion was not really about getting rid of Castro. The Jewish mob and Lucky had lost a hundred-million-dollar golden-goose investment in Havana and were pressing the usual buttons in Washington in an effort to get it back.

"In 1962, President Kennedy sent Bobby Kennedy to talk to Giuseppe Carlo Bonanno—we know him as Joey Bananas—and Bobby was to offer him a deal. But JFK, being a Catholic, didn't trust the Jewish Mafia, so Bobby offered Bananas this tempting deal: kill Castro, and Washington would do the rest. It would overthrow the Cuban regime and install another pro-Western puppet democracy. Then, through shadowy paper corporations that Joey controlled, plus no-interest restoration loans—which Bobby Kennedy implied could be forgiven loans—all these former casinos and hotels would be turned over to the Italian Mafia along with the gaming licenses."

"So why bug the president's office?"

"Do you know what locks are for, Carlo?"

"Yeah, to keep out crooks!"

"Carlo, you of all people know that any lock can be picked. Locks only keep honest men honest, and that is their only purpose!" Joey slapped Carlo on the side of the head.

"No locks here, boss, and the Bay of Pigs was a long time ago."

"Carlo baby, this old radio was Joey Bananas's lock. When Kennedy promised him Cuba in exchange for killing Castro, he had the Oval Office bugged just to be sure there was no double deal.

"Joey Bananas gifted this little room to me. He said some day it might save my ass. I still like to listen in from time to time, just in case some important information could come my way.

"In twenty years, this microphone has never failed, and the regular Secret Service sweeps have never found it. You see, the genius who planted it placed it directly into the side of the wall receptacle behind the president's desk. Since there is always a lamp plugged into that wall socket, it always provides a little hiss to the hand scanner the Secret Service uses to sweep the room, so it is always ignored. The microphone is located in the wall, connected to the outside of the receptacle inside the wall, where it can't be seen. And it uses the metal receptacle as a megaphone to get even better reception. Its power cable is tied into the wall two feet behind the receptacle, where it can never be seen. And the transmitter is way back against the inside of the outer White House wall.

"Let me tell you, Carlo, the guy Joey Bananas hired to bug the place was a goddamned freaking genius!"

"You hungry, boss?"

"Yeah, let's get the fuck outta here. Show's over for tonight, anyway." Joey G. adjusted his vest and flattened the front of his pinstripe suit as they both headed out the door.

June 17, 1981
Budapest, Hungary

As a spymaster, Slava Kurnov had more facets than a diamond. If you asked one hundred men who knew him what his greatest talents were, you'd get one hundred different answers. But Kurnov, being a consummate spy, was not known by that many men.

One of the many things Kurnov liked to do—and something that made him such an expert on the world around him—was his habit of taking a late-night stroll whenever he visited any of the Soviet republics. It was his way of keeping his finger on the pulse of the local authorities as well as the people and events within the entire communist world.

Kurnov slowly puffed his fine Cuban cigar and smiled as he strode down the dank, wet streets of Budapest. But at three o'clock on a Sunday morning, the streets were fairly deserted, perfect for a man who had important matters to consider. With his hands in his greatcoat's pockets, he walked for hours as he considered the two offers the Shadow and Hogan had made.

But it was his inner third eye—the thing possessed by all great spies—that warned him before his ears heard the stealthy footsteps behind him. Most crime, he knew, was rooted in one of three things: poverty, want, or greed. Although Soviet Communism lacked the abject poverty so common in the Western world, it had more than its share of want in spades; and as for greed, well, that was common in all nations and among all men. But brutal crime—violent street crime—was the sort of thing Kurnov knew had no place in a civilized world.

He could tell by the footsteps behind him that he would soon be a victim of violent crime. The urgency of those steps told him this was no spy or player but a common street thug, probably seeking both robbery and murder.

It was kind of odd, but in a way, he looked forward to being a victim—because it was better that the criminal took his chances with Kurnov than attack and possibly kill a lesser victim. Kurnov planned to bring this man's enterprise to a swift and final end. He had no sympathy for violent criminals and heartless men.

Nervously, the old gypsy woman watched the alley from the crack between the thick drapes in her darkened window. She had seen this murderer before, working deep within the evil shadows. She was afraid for the stocky man because she knew the killer was a heartless, ruthless man who would slit the throat of any man or woman for whatever coin he could find in the victim's pockets. She had seen him kill three times and was too terrified for her own safety to get involved.

She continued to watch through the window as Kurnov reached the darkest portion of the alley. The killer pounced, driving the thick Turkish steel forward. In a flash, it twisted twice as it probed deep into flesh, first seeking and then finding the racing heart within. The blade severed the mitral valve and brought almost instantaneous death as he collapsed dead onto the wet pavement.

The old woman watched in amazement at the scene that played out before her; she couldn't believe what she had seen was possible.

Faster than her eyes could grasp, Kurnov deftly had twisted the man's arm, and then, too fast again for her old brown eyes to follow, he had rewarded the criminal's crime with his own blade. That move was impressive for sure, but Slava Kurnov was more than a master spy and consummate spymaster.

Slava Kurnov held a ninth-dan black belt in the art of judo. In that great Asian art of discipline and defense, he was known as one of its greatest masters. Kurnov was indeed a very impressive man—he was the best the KGB would ever know.

June 27, 1981
Paris, France

"That man is a menace. I have complained to your superiors, yet no action has been taken." Baron Le Boeuf had come with a purpose, and that purpose was to rid the intelligence world of that idiot Max George.

"He is often drunk, granted. But he's still a spy the Soviets fear," replied Hogan, wondering what the baron's real purpose for calling this meeting had been.

"He is useless, incompetent. I don't see how you have any use for him. What does he mean to you? Is there a connection that goes beyond your loyalty to your government?" The Frenchman surveyed Hogan, searching for a telltale clue.

"Baron Le Boeuf, as an agent yourself, you must realize we all must follow orders. Frequently we have assistants who are forced upon us. Often people are assigned to us for whom we have no use and even less need. But surely you know that ultimately, we must all follow orders. Hampstead assigned him to me. I had no choice." Hogan was lying; he loved working with Max. He trusted him.

"Baron," he continued, "I can assure you I have as little need for Max George as you have for the British Empire." Hogan was lying again; he would protect his friend at all costs. But frankly, he was rapidly becoming offended at this arrogant aristocrat's vendetta.

"Then we are in agreement." The baron snapped his fingers. "The idiot is a liability and must be removed from this theater. Now let's move on to more urgent affairs."

Hogan fully agreed. There was an idiot who needed to be removed from this theater, and he was rapidly developing his plan. He needed but the smallest opening.

"The Soviets are up to no good in Afghanistan," Baron Le Boeuf began. "We must to step in and stop them. Munitions and money are a problem—a political problem in your country and mine. We need a solution!"

The baron was deadly serious and was now all business. But Hogan had been insulted at the baron's plan to remove Max, and now the Frenchman had just provided him with the opening he needed. He remembered a little place he once had run into in California, an interesting establishment he'd found quite by accident.

It was time for revenge and for a satisfying payback to this arrogant aristocratic ass. It was time to bait the trap. "I have a plan, but it is impossible for me to carry it out. I'm too closely watched." Hogan tightened the snare.

"What is the plan?" Le Boeuf whispered intently.

"I know an independent arms dealer. He's the perfect man for the job. He can move an unlimited number of arms anywhere in the world; he has connections. He has people inside Fabrique Nationale, Norinco, Grumman, Winchester Arms, and a dozen other weapons manufacturers. He can get us anything we need and through his transport connections deliver it anywhere in the world," Hogan whispered back to the baron.

"What kind of money are we talking about?" the Frenchman inquired. Among the upper class, cost was always the first consideration.

"It won't cost us a thing. I have connections in Afghanistan who would do anything to keep out the Russians. This man we'd be dealing with in California has connections in eastern Turkey. I can facilitate a deal in which we can trade raw opium for the cash to buy these weapons. It won't cost either of our governments a penny! You will need to meet with him, in secret."

"Why can't you meet him, Hogan?" The baron was suspicious. He had no reason to mistrust Hogan, but there was something fishy in the way he had never dealt with the issue of Max George.

"I can't meet him because he's in California, back in the States. I won't have any legitimate reason to return to the States until I'm recalled, which may not happen for years. Things are going too well in Africa, so there's no reason for them to recall me."

"Where can I find this man? I will go to him. You set up the opium exchange and provide me with the goodwill to show this man. I can easily cut a deal. Outside of the CIA, your country does not even know of my existence. I can pass as a tourist with little effort. I can go anywhere in America, move freely without raising suspicions."

"Good. It won't be easy, though," Hogan replied in his best conspiratorial whisper. "You'll find him in the city of Ventura, ten miles from a naval air station. He works as a handyman and janitor in a small establishment, but, in fact, he secretly owns the establishment. It's the perfect cover. He's known in the arms-dealing trade as the Dutchman, but you must be very careful," Hogan cautioned.

"I am a Frenchman—I am always careful. But why should this operation require more caution than any other?"

"The Dutchman," Hogan replied as he leaned close to the baron's ear and lowered his voice, "has been with us a very long time and is completely trustworthy. But his son is not to be trusted, and he has the same first and last name. The son is a womanizer and snorts cocaine. If you go, you must be very careful to confide only in the old man and the old man only. The son is never to be involved under any circumstances."

"How am I to know that it is the Dutchman I am speaking to and not his son?" This certainly was a logical question the baron needed to get out of the way.

"Simple," Hogan explained as he baited the trap. "Both men, the father and son, are named Harold. Their friends and family refer to the old man as Big Harry and the younger man as Harry Junior. That should make it easy for you." He scribbled the Ventura address and the contact's first and last names on a slip of paper and handed it to the baron. This, Hogan thought, was going to be really good. He didn't like arrogant aristocrats and especially disliked those who were out to harm his own friends. Revenge would be sweet.

"When do you plan to leave?" Hogan asked and then added, "I think there is some urgency in this. Oh, and another thing: If we're successful, this could be quite a feather in our cap. We could both advance in power, so I don't think either of us should mention this plan to William Hampstead. Why should we share the credit?"

"I will leave immediately. I don't see that we need to involve Hampstead or anyone else," the Frenchman replied with aristocratic greed and snapped his fingers. "I will let you know the outcome."

"Please do." Hogan grinned. This was going to be really, really good.

CHAPTER SEVENTEEN
The Creature of a Thousand Faces

June 28, 1981
Houston, Texas

Waiting, waiting, and then more waiting as the raging fever burned deeper into his temples. Michael Orman had been in the dull, white waiting room for four hours. Hospitals were for people who could pay; clinics were for people who couldn't.

Fifteen weeks earlier, Beaucroix had informed him that his services no longer would be required, effective immediately. When he asked the director about his pension, he was told the forms were being mailed to him. After three weeks, he tried to phone the agency, but no one would take his call.

Orman had made a lot of money in the CIA—everybody did—but he was almost tossed into the street when his rent checked bounced like a rubber ball. Every bank account—even three secret ones—had been reduced to one dollar and ninety-nine cents, which was coincidentally exactly what Beaucroix had said his life was worth; his fortune had disappeared.

Emile Beaucroix had ordered the man's public records destroyed. There was no record of any taxes, employment, or passports for Michael James Orman. It was as if he'd never existed.

Without an identity, he couldn't even apply for unemployment, so he had turned to burglary to survive. With the skills he had acquired from the agency, he could have made a very good living—that is, if his health hadn't given out.

Now he sat in the packed lobby of a seedy free clinic surrounded by the flotsam and jetsam of a society too wrapped up in itself to care for its own.

He surveyed the rotting humanity around him: the alone, the unloved, the abandoned, the fat, the ugly, the deformed, and the defeated. Forgetting the eye-burning fever and the lung-crushing pneumonia, he felt a rush of love and compassion for the roomful of America's exiles. He wished he could heal them, comfort them, make the wrong things right. If this cold, uncaring, self-blinkered society didn't want to love them, he would love them. He suddenly wished he were a priest or a doctor instead of a spy.

"Michael Orman?" the exhausted nurse called out. It was nearing the end of her second shift, and she had worked more than sixteen hours straight.

Orman stood up from the cracked fiberglass chair and walked toward her. He quickly took in her crumpled blue uniform, noting that the staff probably weren't so different from the patients. They were also castoffs of a hard, uncaring society in which both patients and staff must measure up, conform, or find themselves shuttered in a facility meant for everyone else.

"Follow me, Michael. I'll take you to your room." She led the way to the double doors and down the narrow, dull, white hall.

It was amazing, thought Orman. It was truly amazing. It was almost supernatural the way the walls in all free clinics all seemed to be dirty—clean but somehow still dirty. As he tried to fathom the dichotomy, the nurse opened a door and led him into the narrow rectangular room.

"Have a seat, Mike." She pointed to the ripped vinyl examination table, part of the surplus castoffs of the conscriptions of World War II. "The doctor will be with you shortly." In spite of her obvious exhaustion, she managed a droopy smile as she left, closing the door behind her.

"Shortly," of course, was forty-five minutes later, when the doctor entered the room. Removing the chart from the wall and without a word, he took Orman's wrist and measured his pulse.

"Open, please," the doctor ordered and then peered down Orman's throat and frowned. With that accomplished, he took up his pen and scribbled rapidly on the chart.

"What have I got, Doc? What's happening to me?" he asked as the doctor continued to scribble and then placed the chart on the counter.

"Open, please." Once again he peered into Orman's throat. With another frown, he picked up the chart and returned to his furious scribbling.

"Well, what do I have?" he repeated.

The doctor grabbed Orman's wrist to check his pulse for the second time. Then out popped the icy stethoscope, and the doctor placed its frigid kiss to the man's aching chest. With a frown, he reached over to the counter and grabbed Mike's chart.

"Doctor?" Orman pressed again.

"You have pneumonia, Mike." The doctor addressed the air, his eyes fixed on the chart as he scribbled rapidly. "You are lucky we caught it before it destroyed your lungs. I'm sending you to County General for a few weeks." He flipped the page in the chart and continued to scribble.

"Doctor, I don't have insurance. I don't even have any money. I can't even afford aspirin." Orman knew that without treatment, pneumonia was frequently fatal.

"Don't worry about that." The doctor looked at him for the very first time. "You're now a guest of the county. When you get to the hospital, you'll have another physician assigned to your care. The important thing is to get better." With that said, the good doctor and the chart swiftly left the room.

July 21, 1981
National Centers for Disease Control and Prevention
Atlanta, Georgia

"When were these pictures taken?" Dr. Gordon Winter looked into the eyepiece at the newly prepared sample below.

"A week ago Tuesday, with a slide prepared from the same vial you're looking at now, Doctor." The lab technician indicated the rack inside the open cabinet.

"That's impossible," the doctor declared. He picked up one of the photographs and compared its story to what he was discovering through the microscope. "Someone has messed with these test tubes. They must be from a different sample." Dr. Winter dropped the photo and returned to the eyepiece.

"No one has touched them, Doctor. You're the only one with the keys to this cabinet, and I've been here all week."

"That may be so, but someone has altered or replaced this sample!" the doctor said with conviction; there was no other possible answer.

The technician shrugged. He simply had no response to what the doctor was saying.

"Dr. Keller?" Dr. Winter stuck his head into the corridor, as he needed a fresh set of expert eyes.

Dr. Keller entered the room. "What can I do for you, Doctor?"

"I'd like you to compare the specimen in this photograph with the specimen I have in the microscope and let me know your opinion." Dr. Winter stepped back to give Keller plenty of room to work.

Dr. Keller placed his eye on the microscope's eyepiece and examined the slide. Adjusting his glasses, he picked up the photograph and surveyed it with precision. When one worked for the CDC, it was always important to get things right. Finished with the photograph, he returned to the slide, examined it thoroughly, and then removed his glasses.

Keller sat on the board of the CDC and was one of its premiere physicians. He knew more about diseases than nearly anyone alive. "Dr. Winter, what I see here are two different but very closely related strains of the same virus," he said. "Was that your conclusion?"

"Dr. Keller, both this photo and this slide came from the same sample in the same stored, refrigerated test tube. The photo was taken only a week ago. What is your conclusion, Doctor?"

"It would take years for a virus to mutate to this point. It would have to pass from host to host many times. It wouldn't be possible for the virus to deviate this far from the sample in this photograph in a shorter period of time." Clearly, Dr. Winter had mixed up his samples, Keller thought.

"Dr. Keller, I assure you they're from the same sample. These are the facts, Doctor. I would like your assessment."

"It's impossible!" Dr. Keller returned to the eyepiece to study the killer below.

July 23, 1981
The Congo

"Why do you sell guns, Robert?" she asked as she cuddled closer, safe and secure in his powerful arms.

"Because I love Africa, because Africa is my protector. She feeds me and keeps me safe. I sell arms because it affords me the means to buy the few luxuries Africa can't provide. I sell arms to give people hope. I help the downtrodden of the world fight tyranny and oppression. Men like me are the only hope for people who have no freedom, people who have no nation."

"But you sell to terrorists and murderers—and you are so kind. Help me understand you." She ran her hand over his chest, distracting herself and getting hotter as she hungered for his firm embrace.

"The American colonists were terrorists. If it weren't for three French arms dealers, there would be no America. A terrorist is only a man who hasn't yet gained a country. Yet today many Americans hate the French; it's amazing how soon we forget. Max George hates the French, and he's never been to France."

"Who is Max George, and why don't we live in Paris?" She was making a careful inventory of the powerful muscles her roving hand discovered and hungrily explored.

This "we" part grabbed him. He often had marveled at a woman's brass, like the way they usually thought they and they alone decided when a relationship started and ended and just how far it had come.

"I live in Africa because she protects me. Paris would only distract me and get me killed. Africa is my guardian. If one of my enemies approaches me from the jungle, Africa will destroy him, eat him up, and devour him without a trace. If he approaches by road, he must pass both a police station and a ranger station. First he would be arrested, and then he would disappear."

Hogan smiled into her eyes, reading the hunger and knowing that a fire well fed burned hotter. He ran his hand up her thigh and into that special place, making her squirm with almost unbearable pleasure.

"They could come up the Congo in a very fast boat." She grabbed his hand and moved it down to her knee; it had felt too good, and she almost had an accident.

"The Congo is the heart of Africa. There are fifty villages along her banks between here and the coast, and in all those places are people or relatives of people I have helped, people beholden to me. When you help a poor family, they take their debt seriously. They would die to protect me, and besides, a boat hasn't yet been built that's faster than Africa's oldest means of communication, the jungle telegraph."

His hand once again began a slow journey up her hot, hungry thighs.

"Why don't you want to get married?" Pushing his hand away, she changed the subject, wondering what it would be like to own those strong arms and spend every night in their embrace.

"Because when you get married, a woman loves you less." Hogan looked down at his misplaced hand.

She frowned. Embarrassed, she grabbed his hand and firmly planted it in that special place again. He grinned; progress was a good thing!

"Would you marry me if I promised to be good?" she coyly asked, working his hand back and forth.

"Good for a night or good for a lifetime?" he asked.

"How about one night? A night that lasts a lifetime," she tempted him, casting a glance at the flickering lamp and wishing somehow, some-way, she could find an excuse to extinguish its nosy glare.

"Are you that good or am I?" he asked as he cast a glance at the oil lamp, regretting its perch so far away.

"You are the brush. I am your canvas. Paint upon me!" she ordered him.

"Are you sure my brush is big enough?" he teased as she looked down at the massive bulge torturing the fabric of his khaki twill.

"Are you sure my canvas is tight enough?" she countered as he grinned in anticipation.

"I will test it, touch it with my brush, and begin to paint my masterpiece." He stood and quickly dropped his pants, freeing the man-pole now erected proudly before him.

Shocked at its unbelievable proportions, she whispered, "Shit!" and then got up and headed toward the door.

"Wait—what's wrong? Please come back," Hogan pleaded.

She paused near the door. Then, turning quickly, she bent over and quietly blew out the lamp. She would stay, and she would fuck him well. She would drain his manhood of every drop, every ounce. She would fuck him like he'd never been fucked before. She worked her way back to his waiting arms, shedding more clothes with every step, until she reached his hungry arms.

Finally she was his. Hungrily he had imagined pounding those tight young thighs, feeling his hard pelvis driving against that luscious ass. He would fuck her in every crevice, every hole, because she needed it— he needed it—and because he knew this was it; it would have to end. Tonight *would* have to last a lifetime.

August 21, 1981
Houston, Texas

The door to the examination room swung open, and Dr. Vernon Foster entered the room. "I've got some news for you, Michael. I've just received these reports from the Centers for Disease Control. These people have access to the very best equipment and medical personnel America has to offer."

"What do you mean, the Centers for Disease Control? You all told me I had pneumonia. You said I'd get better." Orman was clearly upset.

"Michael, you did have pneumonia—you still do. But it's what caused the pneumonia that concerns us. There's a reason you're not responding to standard treatments, and the CDC has determined the underlying cause."

"You said I was responding to treatment. You said I was getting better." Orman was getting irritated. He felt the full picture had been concealed from him; the doctor had betrayed him.

"That's not exactly true, Michael. I said you were better than when we admitted you. I said that the pneumonia had lessened, not that it had gone away," the doctor corrected him.

"Then I'm going to die. Why didn't you tell me sooner?"

Dr. Foster looked up from the chart; he wanted to word this very carefully. "You're infected by a virus. It's a new virus that's never been reported before, and there's currently no cure. This virus is why you're not responding better to treatment. Somehow this virus is preventing your body from defending itself, but we aren't sure why or how. But let me assure you, doctors at the CDC are working on it."

Orman flushed white; he had fully expected to beat what he'd thought was just a bout of pneumonia. He was a very tough man and a very tough spy. "How did I catch this thing?"

"We don't know. Nothing like it has ever been seen before in a human." Dr. Foster folded the chart, removed his glasses, and looked Orman in the eyes. "Ever been to Africa?"

The question brought a look of shock and fear from Orman, and then revelation shot across his haggard face.

The doctor raised an eyebrow. "When were you in Africa?"

Orman didn't hear that last question. These were new facts, and he needed to process them. *So that's what was at stake*, he thought, *and that's what Beaucroix was up to.* The Monster had injected him with some sort of virus, something that would kill him slowly and painfully. Orman had been in charge of security at Bopolu, but he'd never been told what the doctors were actually working on. Now he would make a list, and he would live long enough to get even.

"Michael?" This wasn't good; the patient's attention was drifting away.

"Yes?" He turned to the doctor and smiled. A man who knows he's going to die has little to fear.

"When were you in Africa?" Dr. Foster repeated.

"I've never been to Africa." Still a good spy, Michael Orman was loyal to his country. He had to protect the past.

"Have you ever been close to Africa, perhaps Gibraltar?" The doctor was fishing.

"I was born in Chicago. I've never left the country," Orman explained.

Somehow Dr. Foster didn't believe him, but why would a man with so much at stake lie?

The doctor again looked him in the eyes. "Ever been bitten by a monkey?"

"No, Doc. Once an angry whore bit my pecker when I didn't pay her, but no monkeys." Orman coughed, and his chest ached as if it had been pounded by Muhammad Ali.

"Have you ever been in contact with them? Monkeys?"

"No, Doctor. I've been with a few dogs and a couple of bitches, but no monkeys. I don't get quite that horny." Orman laughed, and the doc smiled, grateful his patient was making this easier. Doctors hated giving bad news; they had to deliver it far too often.

"How long do I have, Doctor? When am I going to die?" Orman was making a murder list in his mind: Hampstead, Beaucroix, Hogan, and Kutu. But to kill them all, he would have to know how much time there was; but he was a professional and could pace himself.

"I didn't say you're going to die from this, Michael. I said there's no cure today. When I said there's no cure, I didn't say there's no treatment. We'll take this one day at a time, because there are a lot of scientists and doctors working on this. Atlanta has the virus isolated, and they're determining its etiology—how it spreads and how we can control and kill it."

"Why would you ask if I was ever in Africa?" Orman asked.

"Then you have been to Africa!" Dr. Foster blurted out with pleasure. Doctors hated the unknown and the uncertain. They liked to have everything confirmed.

Orman shook his head. "Nope, I've never left the country, Doc!"

"Well…" Disappointment painted the doctor's face. "The only thing that remotely resembles this virus is a benign virus found in certain species of monkeys in West Africa."

Orman looked down at his feet, unsure where this revelation was taking him. If he was going to die, he needed to know when. He had a payback list and had a lot of killing to do.

"I know it's not what you'd hoped to hear, but we're all pulling for you. Oh, and another thing: The CDC is taking over responsibility for all your medical expenses. You have nothing financial to worry about."

"Then all I have to worry about is dying, right, Doc?" Orman feigned a grin.

"That's correct, Michael, just like we'll all have to do someday."

August 31, 1981
Cairo, Egypt

Through bloodshot eyes Max caught a blur that was somehow familiar. He squinted and grimaced as he tried to recognize the two swirling images making their way across the clubhouse floor toward his table. Suddenly he grinned and spilled his vodka as he reached over to jab Hogan smartly in the ribs. He had spotted a frog and wanted Hogan to share in the joke.

Damn it, Hogan thought. He thought the Russian would come alone; if he had known the arrogant French baron was planning to show, he never would've allowed Max to get so drunk.

Max quickly poured himself another drink, getting a generous two ounces in the glass and another six on the table. Then he stood to salute and render a toast to the two approaching men. "Here's the *boeuf!*" he offered.

"Shut up, Max. Welcome to Cairo, gentlemen." Hogan stood and offered his hand to the baron, who briefly took it in a professional manner.

Le Boeuf frowned as he spotted Max. He had had no idea the idiot would be here. After that last little incident, he had been certain the CIA would have banished him to some less significant theater; he had, after all, complained to higher authorities and was surprised that apparently no action had been taken.

"It is a certainly a very great pleasure to meet you again, sir. Mr. Robert Hogan, please allow me to present Mr. Feodor Fukov, the special trade liaison for the Soviet Socialist Republics. Mr. Feodor Fukov, please allow me to present Mr. Robert Hogan, president of Special Commodities, a purveyor of certain surplus military gear."

"Be seated, gentlemen." Hogan indicated the two empty chairs and snapped his fingers for the bartender as he took his own seat.

Glancing at Max, Fukov wondered why this American was so excessively drunk and why they hadn't been properly introduced. Le Boeuf, like most elitist swine, generally had flawless manners. Max was in his happy place—drunk as a preacher—and had just now fuzzily recalled the introductions.

"Excuse me?" Max grinned as he wagged his finger at the Russian and leaned closer through his alcoholic haze to get a better look. "I didn't get your name." He suddenly had forgotten everything that had transpired to this point. But what he recalled was that somehow—and in some way—Froggy had been up to something silly, and he wanted to know what it was.

"Fukov. And you?" The Russian smiled.

"I was only asking. There's no need to be rude." Max looked down into his glass. He was a little hurt; he disliked the frog, but it was a little too early to form an opinion about this Cossack, and he honestly didn't feel he had done anything to earn an insult. Ignoring the Russian, his eyes downcast, he returned to his drink.

"That's his name, Max. Feodor Fukov—Mr. Feodor Fukov," Hogan corrected.

"Fuck off!" exclaimed Max, as delight and recognition filled his bloodshot eyes.

"Yes?" the Russian politely replied.

"*Fuck off!*" Max shouted.

"Yes?"

"*Fuck off!*" Max repeated drunkenly to the world—this time with unsuppressed delight—to a shocked dining room filled with sundry locals, thieves, and spies.

"Shut the fuck up, Max," Hogan sharply admonished him.

"Excuse me, gentlemen." Hogan shot a sideways glance at Max. "When I'm tired, my manners seem to doze off."

"It's pronounced 'Foo-kov,'" offered the Russian, with unfailing good manners.

"No, please. There is no need to correct me, as I've been telling gentlemen to Fukov most of my life." Max burped, grabbed his abdomen, and grinned.

"You must have many Russians where you live in the United States if you know my family name." The Russian smiled again.

"No Russians where I'm from, just a lot of assholes who need to be told where to go and where to get off." Max burped, loudly this time.

"I apologize, gentlemen," Hogan said. "He's not usually this drunk."

"Ribbit, ribbit!" Max blurted.

"Pardon me? I didn't catch that," the Russian responded.

"You weren't expected to catch that—it's very difficult. Frogs are fast hoppers." With this, Max turned to regard Baron Le Boeuf.

"Ignore him, gentlemen. He is drunk and an idiot!" Hogan wished Max would drop it.

"Ribbit!" Max motioned to the Frenchman to hop onto the table.

"Max!" Hogan pleaded.

"Ribbit, ribbit!" Max continued to motion to the baron.

"Do you know, Mr. Hogan, what separates most Russians from all other men?" Fukov inquired.

"You take your frogs to dinner with you?" Max again motioned to Le Boeuf.

"The difference is that Russians hold their drink, while lesser men are *held by it*. I think we had best resume this meeting at a future date. Baron, I assume you're ready to leave as well?"

"Gentlemen, this has been a stupendous waste of time and will certainly be reported. My time—the time of France—will not be held cheaply!" The baron, clearly in a huff, rose to leave.

"That is your privilege, sir. I intend to report this idiot's unprofessional behavior myself," Hogan replied.

"Look at that, Robert. Look at that." Max motioned toward the baron. "Did you see how he hopped out of the chair? Way to go, Froggy. Ribbit, ribbit!"

Fukov rose, nodded to Hogan, and began his journey to the street.

"Fuck off! Fuck off!" shouted Max, who was having a stupendously drunken great time.

"Where's the *boeuf*? Ribbit! Ribbit! Bye, Froggy. Hop to it!" Max shouted to the irritated backs of the retreating men, delighted with himself and laughing hysterically.

"Max, the next time we have an important meeting, I'm going to spike your whiskey with water—dirty water!"

Max sat there, dejected and distant, staring at the empty plate before him. He pointed at the plate and gestured to the door and then addressed Hogan in a pleading voice. "Where's the *boeuf*?"

"Max, you're some kind of ass. But you're still my kind of ass." Hogan reached for the bottle and poured himself a generous jar of whiskey. He raised his glass in salute, and the two spies drank their way into the morning sun.

September 11, 1981
Ventura, California

The baron couldn't believe his eyes. The Frenchman was astounded, amazed at how well this hotel was furnished. From the tuck-and-roll red velvet on the walls to the Berber carpet beneath his feet, he couldn't believe this fabulous place was an American establishment, a California establishment.

The delightful lobby was furnished elegantly. Red-velvet settees perfectly matched the walls, and tall wing chairs and lounges with their fine silken pillows paid homage to civilization's more elegant days, which were sadly past.

In Baron Le Boeuf's experience, Yankees—specifically Californians—had exceptionally poor taste. He rang the bell at reception and awaited the response. It was but a moment until the desk clerk, a woman with astounding cleavage, answered the call.

"What's your pleasure, sir?" She winked and giggled.

The baron was flabbergasted, elated at her obvious respect, attendant poise, and admiration. This was service!

"I am the Baron Le Boeuf, here from France, and I need your help."

"Honey, I can help you with anything you need." The desk clerk giggled some more and winked at him.

"Most kind of you. I'm looking for a special man, and I need to find him quickly. He is the Dutchman!" Le Boeuf stated with the utmost gravity.

"Sorry, honey. We can give you just about anything you need here. But if it's a man you're looking for, I can give you an address in West Hollywood. Are you just looking for a handsome young blond man, or are you looking for some assless chaps and leather also?" She smiled and tried to hide her disappointment that she couldn't satisfy him here; surely this man and his money would be missed.

"Assless? What's that? Oh, never mind that, mademoiselle. I am in a hurry. I was told to ask for the Dutchman here and no place else." The baron clearly had urgent business, an item certainly not lost on the lady before him, who leaned in a bit closer, allowing a clearer view of her astonishing cleavage.

"Here? Well, what's his name, honey? He may be in back with one of the girls."

"I am looking for Harold, and I will make it worth your while," the baron replied.

"I'm sorry, darling, but I've never heard of him. I think you walked into the wrong cathouse," she replied as she leaned her breasts in a little closer again. Certainly he was lying about being a baron, but he was very good-looking and appeared to have money.

"Cathouse? What's a cathouse?" Le Boeuf was getting frustrated; he knew from Hogan's instructions and the address he was given that this was the correct place, and he was in a hurry.

"Mademoiselle, I am a very busy man, and I can pay you for the information. If you satisfy me, I can make it worth your while. I am a man who needs, and those needs must be satisfied!"

She leaned her large, round breasts in even closer and smiled. The baron sensed he had somehow reached her and would press his advantage. "I demand to see Harry, and I am not leaving this spot until you show me Harry. Is that clear?" He firmly set his jaw and awaited her response.

The desk clerk lit up and became animated. "Now I know who you want. Why didn't you say so, sweetie? No need to be shy with me. You've come to the right place! If you need it, we got it. I'll be right back."

"Wait!" the baron shouted as she started to leave the room. "You need to know exactly who I am searching for. There must be no mistake. It is that important!"

"Of course, honey. We aim to please. Tell me exactly what you're looking for." She arched her back slightly, pretending to stretch as she pushed her ample chest closer to the Frenchman.

"This is very important, mademoiselle, so please listen carefully. I have flown all the way from France to see one person and one person only: the Dutchman." The baron wagged his finger and continued. "I don't want to see or hear Junior anywhere in this room. Let's be very clear on this point—I do not trust Junior. I find his perversions disgusting, and I will not tolerate him in my presence." Le Boeuf again wagged his finger. "I demand to see *Big Harry Hooters immediately*. Bring *Big Harry Hooters* to me. Keep Junior Hooters far out of the picture. I refuse to acknowledge Junior Hooters. *Big Harry Hooters*, and nothing else—it is the only thing that will satisfy me!"

"Be right back, sweetie." The desk clerk winked in understanding and quickly disappeared behind the red-velvet curtains.

The baron waited impatiently in the lobby. He had just noticed the shabby old men in raincoats furtively entering the back rooms without even pausing to check in at the lobby. It suddenly dawned on him that he may possibly, improbably, have been taken.

"Here you are, honey!" The clerk emerged from a back room with one of the largest, tallest women Le Boeuf had ever seen. "Baron, these are the hairiest hooters and braided armpits you'll ever get." She indicated the broad-shouldered Bulgarian woman she had brought in tow. "Helga, let me introduce you to His Royal Excellency Baron Le Boeuf.

"Baron, I can again assure you that Helga has the hairiest hooters and armpits you will ever know. Do us proud, Helga, sweetie." The buxom clerk slapped Helga on the buttocks and pushed her toward the baron.

Le Boeuf paused as the Bulgarian grabbed his arm and pulled, intending to steer him to one of the back rooms.

The baron had surely been set up; that was clear. He would get back at Hogan, and he would have his revenge another day. But tonight— tonight would be for the honor of France.

Baron Le Boeuf bowed graciously and allowed the Bulgarian to escort him into one of the back rooms. It seemed it was possible to embarrass Baron Le Boeuf; unfortunately, that had been proven tonight. But it wasn't possible to embarrass the reputation of Frenchmen or the dignity of France!

CHAPTER EIGHTEEN
Just a Little Help for the Grim Reaper

September 19, 1981
Houston, Texas

The dirty bastard winked again. Inwardly, the dark-haired man was furious because he hated queers. Drawing upon all his CIA training and experience, Agent Steve Wainwright managed a smile and a coy fairy wave. Perhaps not all male nurses were gay, but Wainwright was quickly discovering his new cover was drawing homosexuals like bears to honey.

Perhaps it was the uniform. A male nurse's uniform was, after all, still a nurse's uniform, very much a feminine thing in a very feminine profession. He disliked dykes and hated queers; he couldn't understand them. God made you either a man or a woman. He had no patience for people who refused to play the hand God had given them. A man who pretended to be a woman was like a sumo wrestler riding a horse in the Kentucky Derby—not only ridiculous but also against the laws of God and nature.

He looked at his watch; twenty minutes had passed. The sedative should have taken effect by now. He patted his apron pocket, making sure the poison was still there. He grinned because it was time to murder Michael Orman, and then time to go home.

Good men, such as men of principles and humble beginnings like Joe Black, never had it easy, but hard work and honesty were a big help. Being a poor black man in a very white world was never a picnic, and that was especially so in America. But as a security guard, he had learned white people gave you respect; they were polite at least. They treated you almost as an equal, at least most of the time. But the truth was that Joe always had wanted to be a doctor. He had *needed* to be a doctor because he needed to help.

But where Joe was from, there was no easy money—no money and no free ride for a poor black kid with seven siblings and no father to turn to. So guarding the sick, injured, and infirm was as close to doctoring them as Joe could come, but it was OK; he could still be a part of the good things in the world. He couldn't heal them, but he could guard and protect them. He could still help.

Growing up in Hannibal, Mississippi, Joe had to drop out of high school to help out his family, because with Joe, family always came first. His father, however, had been of a different mind and of a different opinion. The man, like so many other little men of the Old South, had been true blue-ribbon garbage. His father had been one of those kinds of men who conned their way through life, more interested in a meal ticket than a wife. When Joe's father left seeking better pastures, his mother worked twelve hours a day to make sure her sons grew up to be better men than that.

Today wasn't really that unusual in that Joe often spent part of his off days visiting the hospital, just sort of socializing, being polite, and checking things out. He did this because it was *his* hospital, and this hospital was *his* responsibility. He needed to make sure everything was OK.

Today the CIA, FBI, and KGB would all put him to the test. He would be outgunned and outmanned, but to beat a man like Joe Black always took some doing—some considerable doing.

As Joe casually walked into the emergency waiting room, a mist of an unsettling premonition, an eerie sensation, passed over him like a shadow altering the world around him. It was as if there were something in the air. It was just sort of a general feeling he had, like the feeling of something floating around uneasily in your gut. There was nothing he could really put his finger on, but something definitely wasn't quite right with the hospital, and, by extension, something wasn't right with the world.

As with every hospital in America, ambulances rolled up to the emergency-room doors one after the other, and there were a lot of them. Joe had memorized every driver, every paramedic, and every truck. He knew each man and woman by name; he knew everyone by name. It was his job to know everyone who belonged there, everyone who was a part of *his* hospital, because it was a point of pride. He had listened well when the good Reverend Phelps had given him this advice: "Work hard, be honest, and never treat anyone worse than you would like to be treated yourself." It was good advice for Joe and good advice for all men. Joe Black took his job seriously, and he did his job well, damn well.

Joe certainly knew paramedics were hired all the time, and drivers came and went. Ambulances sometimes got old and were replaced. Looking through the sliding glass doors, he watched intently as a white-clad paramedic pulled open the rear ambulance doors and removed a wheelchair from within. The man unfolded the chair and, after setting it on the pavement, slowly and cautiously wheeled it to the entrance.

It was Joe's day off, and he was in his street clothes, which was fortunate. He alertly noticed the man was new, and his uniform was a tad too perfect. The driver who rode with him also was new, and the ambulance never had been there before, either.

These were just too many coincidences. There were too many square pegs and nothing but round holes in which to place them. Joe casually took a chair in the waiting room, and, grabbing a magazine, he did his clever best to blend in with the suffering, the impatient, and the bored.

Ross pushed the wheelchair up to the electric doors as they slid open. He continued inside, pushing the chair past the packed waiting room and heading for the central elevators beyond.

"How much do you know about Dr. Ernst Bauer, Dr. Jones?" Being the senior FBI man in the administrator's office, Agent Barry Billings addressed all the questions to the hospital's director.

"He has an excellent reputation. He's one of the finest practitioners of internal medicine ever to come out of Munich." The doctor smiled;

getting good people and keeping them kept the hospital board happy and kept Dr. Phillip Jones in power.

"Have you talked to him and discussed medical matters?" Agent Billings asked.

"No, but I met him when he was hired last week. It's part of my job to greet all incoming medical personal. Given Dr. Bauer's high standing and expertise, I didn't think it appropriate to question his credentials. We talked only of this and that," Dr. Jones replied and then added, "Why are you so interested in Dr. Bauer? Is he in some kind of trouble? Has he done something illegal?" It was Dr. Jones's job to protect the hospital's reputation, and, as such, suspect doctors must be dismissed before matters could get out of hand.

"The *real* Dr. Bauer," Agent Murphy butted in, "was found dead two weeks ago, sucking mud at the bottom of the Rhine River."

Dr. Bauer accepted Michael Orman's chart from the cute candy striper. He set the chart on the counter at the bustling third-floor nurses' station. Then he flipped it open and began writing, issuing the order that would transfer Orman to a new hospital and into the arms of the KGB. Catching the eyes of the sweet young cutie, he winked as he handed her back the chart and headed out the door. She giggled as she watched the doctor stroll down the hall and disappear around the corner. Dr. Ernst Bauer, usually known as KGB Agent Helmut Krause, quietly slipped out of the hospital—he would escape the FBI.

Reaching out his right hand, Carl Hannon grabbed the tan lip on the dashboard and pulled open the clean ashtray. He glanced up at the service entrance of the hospital in time to see a hefty nurse waddle toward her car.

Wrong target, he thought with a laugh. He had come to kill a man, not harpoon a whale. He popped his diminished butt into the ashtray, violating its virgin state. Adjusting his pistol's shoulder harness, he grabbed another Marlboro and fired it up as he leaned back into the gorgeous leather of the white Jaguar convertible.

Instinctively Carl bolted forward, gripping the wheel. His target had just exited the building and was talking to a hot little muffin. They had paused ten feet from the exit and were only two hundred feet away from him. He withdrew the Colt Commander from its holster and, cocking the hammer waited for the man to approach his car. The bastard hugged her, kissed her deeply, and then, releasing her, he began the long walk to his red Corvette.

Carl grabbed the latch to open the Jag's door. Then he froze and released it, cursing as he settled back into the lush leather. It was the wrong man; he bore a strong resemblance to the target but was still the wrong man. Did all these assholes own red Corvettes?

He had tossed his smoke when he had started for his man, so he had to search his pocket for another. He took out a package of his constant companions and cursed that he had only three left. He removed a soldier from the diminished pack and fired up again as he settled back into his game.

Suddenly another doctor emerged through the door with another cute blond muffin in tow. *Damn*, thought Carl. *Do all doctors screw their staff?* Maybe those sleazy soap operas on television weren't so far off.

A US Postal Service van pulled up as Carl puffed his smoke religiously. He wished the man would hurry; those bastards were good witnesses. Postal workers had good memories—they had to.

Casting aside his smoke, Carl again flung open the door. His target had just exited the hospital and was approaching his car. Damn that postal worker! As Carl exited the Jaguar, he took a quick step to the left as he brought his cocked steel to bear. Seeing him, the target froze in terror, confusion ruling his reaction and fear racing through his eyes.

"Freeze! FBI!" agent Burt Murphy shouted as he approached from the back.

Carl crushed the trigger; the boom and thud occurred together as Agent Brady tackled him from the right side, slamming him to the asphalt and sending wide the fat, angry round. The target collapsed to the ground, downed only by fear but otherwise untouched by his assailant.

Glancing at the target, Murphy motioned at the two other agents to check him out. By the time Murphy reached Carl, Agent Brady already had cuffed him and was busy crisply jerking him up off the ground.

"This one's got ID," Brady declared as he removed the man's wallet. KBG killers rarely carried any. He handed the wallet to Murphy.

"Well, comrade, welcome to America. I see your name is Hannon. Shouldn't that be Hannonovich?" Murphy was ecstatic; this was his first spy.

Carl was silent.

"Who's working with you?" Brady demanded.

Carl wasn't talking. Two other agents walked up with the target, who was now handcuffed and solidly restrained. The target's story of knowing nothing about this carried little water with these humorless men.

As Carl saw the target approach, he lunged forward; still handcuffed, he sent his right foot flying forward. The target's jewels headed halfway to the moon, and he crumbled all the way into the tarmac as he withered and whined in pain. Carl took his three points with satisfaction as Agents Murphy and Brady slammed him against the Jag.

"Who the fuck is this man, and why are you trying to kill him? What does he have to do with the CIA?" Brady demanded. Murphy wanted to question the target, but one quick glance at the ball of agony told him it would be some time.

"Talk now, or I promise you'll talk later, and it won't be in a public place!" Murphy threatened.

Carl glanced sideways and down at the bundle of agony and laughed. "Asshole, did that get you off?" Carl grinned; at least he had made the bastard suffer.

Murphy frowned. He'd always been taught that KGB men were professionals. The man's anger was hard to explain. *It must be frustration*, Murphy thought, grinning inwardly. This was probably the first time the agent had failed.

"This is your last chance. I mean it. What's this man's connection to the CIA?" Murphy asked Carl.

"Talk! Who else is on the inside?" Agent Murphy demanded.

"The CIA?" Carl suddenly realized he was in a lot of trouble. "This *asshole* doctor has been screwing my dingy blond wife. I didn't know he was with the CIA." Carl looked down at the miserable man who was moaning in pain and still describing a perfect ball.

Agents Murphy's and Brady's jaws dropped.

"We've got the wrong men! *Everyone, get inside fast!*" Brady shouted.

The four agents ran into the hospital, leaving the two men still handcuffed and abandoned outside. Carl looked at the downed man and grinned.

Soon a passing police cruiser would investigate the spectacle. But until then, a handcuffed Carl Hannon would spend the next twelve minutes as a cuckold with a mission, happily kicking away at the handcuffed doctor who had been caught making one house call too many.

The east entrance to the hospital wasn't guarded at all. It was the building's main entrance, and it was the portcullis for the armies of worried, concerned, happy, and relieved people come to comfort and entertain their ill friends and relations.

It was more than easy for Gunter Platz to blend in with the fleet of humanity sailing through the entrance. He wore a loud Hawaiian shirt and yellow golf pants with a green stripe. Complementing his outfit was a pair of two-toned, green-and-black, orange-laced sneakers. The epitome of sartorial travesty, he blended in perfectly with the visitors around him.

Carrying a bouquet of badly arranged flowers, three magazines, and a *TV Guide,* he worked his way to the south elevators. He was the KGB crash man. If Ross, the man with the wheelchair, got into trouble, it was Gunter's job to cover his escape.

Ross now emerged from the packed elevator onto the third floor. He turned left and pushed the wheelchair down the hall to the wing that held a dying Michael Orman. Joe Black emerged from the stairs opposite the elevator, turned right, and followed Ross down the hall. As Ross approached the yellow safety cones, he veered around them, ignorant of the blue-clad janitor lethargically mopping the floor.

As Joe passed the janitor, he glanced at the man's face. He'd never seen him before either. He quickly was jolted by confusion as the man removed a radio from his custodial cart and spoke to someone. Joe quickly returned his tunnel vision to the man with the wheelchair. He would have to return to this second problem, and he would return. This was *his* hospital.

The man with the flowers also had reached the third floor and was now working his way to Orman via the other end of the hospital. Only in a hospital could someone who dressed so outlandishly move about practically unseen.

Ross had now passed the nurses' station and was making his way down the last hallway, glancing at the room numbers as they climbed upward. Fast in tow, Joe Black jumped; he was startled as the janitor ran past him, no longer concerned with his mop or wet floor. Ross was only three doors from his destiny when two men in suits stepped out from behind the corner, blocking the hall.

"Freeze! FBI!" Agent Billings shouted, offering his badge to authenticate his demand. The man quickly abandoned the wheelchair, turned around, and ran for the stairs. He didn't get far. Halfway down the corridor, the janitor tackled him and slammed him face-first into the wall. After forcing the man's arms up, he patted him down as the two other agents, guns drawn, walked up to join them.

Joe was relieved and proud. He was always proud when the police did a good job, did the right thing. Joe was proud, but he was also good. He didn't let his euphoria interfere with his noticing that something else was out of place. It was a man who didn't look quite right. It was a man who was jolted by this for all the wrong reasons. Joe Black had noticed Gunter Platz, the man with the flowers.

Quickly realizing things had gone terribly bad, Gunter slowed his step. To appear common and ordinary, he nonchalantly checked his watch and frowned. Then he turned around and headed casually for the exit. This mission would have to wait; it would wait for a better day.

Joe walked briskly, following the man and trying to catch up. Casting his eyes backward, the man saw him and began to run, but it was too late. Joe launched into a flawless open-field tackle, slamming the man to the floor. Agent Pratt saw the commotion and ran up with his gun drawn.

"Freeze! FBI!" he warned both men as Joe pulled the man to his feet by his lapels.

"This guy's with him. He doesn't belong in *my* hospital." Joe pointed toward Ross, who was now in handcuffs, sullenly refusing to respond to Billings's line of questioning.

"OK, buddy. Let's see some ID." Agent Pratt had swung his Colt Detective to cover the man with the flowers. The KGB man only stared at Pratt and Black with contempt, angry to have been caught by such amateurs.

"Who are you here to visit? Give me a name!" Agent Pratt ordered. But the man was silent.

"Cuff him," Billings ordered as he walked up. He smiled at Joe Black. "Not bad police work for a black man," he complimented him.

"My mama raised me to be a *man,* not a *black man*!" Joe replied indignantly.

"Right!" Billings hated this racial thing. They were always changing their name. Sometimes they called themselves Negroes, and sometimes they called themselves black, sometimes colored. Now they'd added Afro American, or was that African American? No matter what a white man called them, they always got pissed, because a white man always got it wrong. Men—real men of any color—only wanted to be treated like anyone else.

"Well, thank you anyway, sir. You did some fine work, and your FBI is grateful. I'll need your name for my report," Billings added.

"Black, Mr. Black," Joe replied.

"Yeah, right!" said Billings. Why did they all have to be such smartasses?

Joe Black turned and headed toward the parking lot. It was time to go home. It was his day off. He could go home; his job was done, and *his* hospital was safe.

Steve Wainwright had watched the entire ridiculous thing. The CIA never would try anything that stupid. He had been casually wheeling the pill cart through the hallway as the drama had unfolded. He was so amused at the fumbling of these KGB men. The FBI could never stop a *real* professional. He wheeled the cart past Agent Billings, who ignored him as he entered Michael Orman's room. He glanced down at the snoring Orman, who was now heavily sedated. He pulled a syringe from his pocket and carefully removed the cap. He had to be careful because the evil tube held a soup composed of pneumonia, influenza, typhus, and botulism—the jolt that would collapse and destroy Orman's exhausted immune system, bringing his tortured life to an end.

Agent Murphy had watched Wainwright wheeling the cart, and he watched him inject Orman with the cocktail that would end his life. He watched because the excitement was over, and he watched because he was bored; he watched, but he would not remember. The whole thing simply had been too normal.

September 20, 1981
The Settlement; North of Bopolu, Liberia

On the way to the settlement, the young man talked constantly, happy to be returning to his tribe and happy to earn twenty dollars simply for speaking his native tongue.

Robert Hogan merely affirmed or agreed with everything the young guy said. It was a long drive from the coastal port of Monrovia to the jungle north of Bopolu. Finally, after a long, lean, tiring two hours, the jeep rolled into the native settlement and past the rusted-out flatbed truck and into what served as the town square. Hogan was glad he no longer had to deal with the young man's banal, insipid conversation.

The old chief was standing there, patiently waiting. There had been no plan and no notice of Robert Hogan's intention to visit or his need to find answers. But the chief knew he was coming; he knew Hogan would be here. It had been foretold.

Hogan and the young man dismounted the jeep. As the two men approached, Hogan raised his right hand in the Indian sign for peace. Chief M'kari smiled; it looked silly.

The young man already had begun his chatter, rapidly speaking to the chief in the local dialect. The chief continued to smile as he answered the young man's inquiries into friends and family.

Hogan interrupted. "Tell him who I am. Remind him I am the man who helped him with the soldiers."

The young man addressed Chief M'kari. The chief talked for a good six minutes, then motioned toward Hogan. The young man nodded; he understood and turned to Hogan.

"He knows who you are. You are the big, fat liar. You are the storyteller!" the young man replied. He was trying to convey this with the same gravity with which Chief M'kari had made the pronouncement.

"What!" Hogan shouted with amazement.

The chief noticed Hogan's confusion and angrily derided the young man for several minutes for his poor translation. Then the old man furiously directed the young man back to Hogan.

"Sorry, boss. I left here when I was but thirteen. Our words for 'big fat' and 'extremely important' are very similar. Chief M'kari wanted me to tell you that you are an important man, a man with a big job to do. You are a man with a destiny," he sheepishly apologized.

"Thank him for his courtesy, and thank him for talking to me. Tell him I need his help, and I won't lie to him anymore or tell him any silly stories." Hogan smiled at the old man as his companion explained this to the chief. First the old man was pleased, but then he flushed furious, shouting at the young man and deriding him until he turned meekly to Hogan.

"I apologize. I made more mistakes. He says you are neither a storyteller nor a liar. He says you write things, things that are real only within your mind, words that sing. He says you are *the Poet*!" the young man said. Still embarrassed, he stood with eyes cast into the dust. He hoped his bad performance wouldn't affect the promised twenty dollars; young men in modern Africa had expenses!

Hogan's jaw fell open, fairly striking his chest. No one knew he was the Poet. Only four men on the entire planet called him that. They were all friends and all within the CIA. It couldn't have been some bimbo either. Hogan never showed his poetry to anyone. Hogan wrote poetry strictly for himself, as an ode to God and an opus to his immortal soul.

"Why does he call me that? Who told him it was my name?" he asked the young man.

The fellow briefly addressed Chief M'kari and turned back to Hogan. "He says it is your *secret* name. It is the name written upon your soul. The gods of Bopolu told him that—they told him your secret name." As he finished this translation, the chief waved Hogan toward the monkeys chattering wildly in the trees, the gods of Bopolu.

Hogan ran his gaze through the forest, but he could see nothing; he had no clue as to what the chief wanted him to see. To a white man, the gods of Bopolu were usually invisible.

"How can I beat the evil man? Who can help me kill him?" Hogan asked.

The young man spoke to the chief for several minutes before he was ready for Hogan. "He tells you that you cannot beat this man. You cannot kill him. He is not a man. He is the essence of evil and cannot die."

Hogan was very confused. "I'm not talking about some phantom spirit. I'm talking about Emile Beaucroix. He's the man who murders your men and tortures your women!" Hogan needed specifics because as a spy, it was what he understood best.

The old chief and young man spoke briefly.

"Chief M'kari knows who you are talking about. You want to kill the *Monster!*"

Hogan was shocked. Only he and Max George called Beaucroix the Monster, and only between themselves. "Tell him I came here for his help, and tell him I need him to give me more information."

The young man spoke briefly to the chief and then turned back to Hogan. "He says he cannot help you. You must turn to the gods of Bopolu; only they can help. Only when you speak to the gods of Bopolu will you have your answer."

The old man pointed at Hogan and again waved his hand across the jungle, indicating the chattering monkeys, which were more agitated and excited than ever. Hogan followed the sweeping hand and frowned. He could see nothing. After reaching into his pocket, he fished out thirty dollars and paid the young man.

"Please thank Chief M'kari for me, and tell him it's always an honor to meet a king." With this, Hogan mounted and started his jeep. He was heading back to the medical station at Bopolu.

He had found no answer at the settlement, only a fog of confusion. He would ruminate later on what the chief had told him; perhaps time would distill the fog into clarity.

Chief M'kari waved as Hogan left the settlement. He continued to wave long after the jeep's whine had faded into the jungle. He stood alone, abandoned, as the young man had left to find his relations. Only the monkeys saw the sad old man waving in the middle of the settlement. They cried because they loved the old man; the gods of Bopolu would miss him.

Laughing, the Monster pulled out his organ in front of the terrified villagers and urinated upon the face of the dead chief, diluting the blood that leaked from the man's shattered skull. The young man watched in terror from his family hut and pushed his relations back into the dark safety within. No one would interfere with the Monster's pleasure because none of them wished to die.

Beaucroix had now finished his deed and zipped his fly. Soon he would leave. Soon he would need to find *new* recreation, because one could never have too much fun.

The monkeys were silent. The younger ones swung from their trees, swarming toward and merging into a huge, gnarled baobab tree. They turned as one and intently watched the eyes of one old monkey and the other four ancients that ruled with him. This ancient warrior looked into the eyes of his silent court. He looked into their souls. Then, solemnly, the old monkey frowned and nodded.

The gods of Bopolu steadied themselves, steeled themselves. They had just stood silent witness to the beginning of the end of the world.

CHAPTER NINETEEN
The Raging Wildfire

September 28, 1981
The White House

"I'm not going to waste my time or this nation's resources. Nor will I allow you to destroy this administration for the sake of a few faggots!" the president shouted furiously. The cowboy president didn't want to give up on Wildfire because he couldn't give up his dream.

Dr. Paxton was getting very weary of all this nonsense. He needed something, some way to impress upon the president the urgency of the situation.

"Mr. President, if we don't act today and act quickly with all our resources, it could very well be the end of all mankind. This is a virus for which there is no cure. It's an enemy unlike any mankind has ever faced. We were wrong to create it. We were wrong, and the time has come for us to fess up and do what we can to eradicate this great evil," Dr. Paxton pleaded.

The president cleared his throat. "Dr. Paxton, don't be such an alarmist. It's my understanding that this disease can be passed only through unnatural sexual—*homosexual*—contact. It is not, nor will it ever will be, a danger to the general population. Dr. Robles here is the world's leading immunologist, and he doesn't seem to be worried.

"Besides, if we admit to the presence of the disease, those commie media whores probably will figure out that we created the nasty little bugger. That will mark not only the end of this administration but also

America. Gentlemen, I won't allow America to be destroyed for the sake of a few fags."

The president of the United States meant to once and for all rid the world of communism. He intended to leave the world a legacy that would show the ex-actor had been America's greatest president. He would be a great president because he must. His entire life, he had hungered for his chance at greatness. In a film career that had spanned nearly thirty years, he had failed to achieve that greatness; he had failed to become the star he felt he rightly deserved to be.

"I ask you, in all God's infinite justice, who should survive—the commies, the homosexuals, perverts, and media whores, or this great land of ours, the United States of America?" The president delivered this with his pseudo John Wayne persona. He then surveyed the room with his eyes, seeking and then demanding consensus and affirmation.

Now it was Dr. Robles's turn to clear his throat. The president smiled and leaned back in his crested brown-leather presidential chair. He always liked it when someone interrupted on his behalf.

"Mr. President, Mr. Beaucroix, Agent Kendal, Dr. Paxton, before this turns into a debate, I think it's only fair that I be allowed to present my report in full before any portion is put up for question or ridicule." Reshuffling the papers before him, the doctor continued, "It seems that one Michael Orman of the CIA and one African national were accidentally bitten by one of the lab animals, a monkey, at our military research facility at Bopolu.

"This led to the introduction of the experimental virus known as Wildfire into their systems. This virus had such an unreliable effect on the primates that we were somewhat surprised how effective it was in attacking the human metabolic system. It virtually shuts down the entire immune system, making even a common cold deadly to the host."

"Host? What host is that, Doctor? What you're saying is that some Typhoid Mary or Typhoid Harry is going to spread this thing all over the planet," Dr. Paxton blurted.

"Dr. Paxton, take a sedative please," Beaucroix said flatly. "A little white pill or something to calm down. We need to hear Dr. Robles's entire report before we begin a debate. As for myself, I am a spy, so I can't understand your medical terminology, and I don't make pretense to. That would be ludicrous. But some of the answers do fall into the intelligence field, and as in expert there, it would be my pleasure to shed some light on those." Beaucroix smiled as he became very serious and professional.

"First," he continued, "we know is this disease can be spread only through sexual contact. We know this because the two men in question have had close contact with more than three thousand people, both men and women, and, with the assistance of the FBI, we have checked out every one of them. They have slept in the same hotels, eaten in the same kitchens, and bathed in the same pools with the general, normal, heterosexual population. So far, the only ones infected have been their queer lovers. This proves the virus is not a general danger to society as a whole—specifically, not a danger to our heterosexual society."

"Our best evidence—*my* best evidence—is that it's a danger only to...pardon me..." the Monster smiled broadly as he continued. "...butthole surfers. And now, with that established, we should allow Dr. Robles to continue." Beaucroix waved him on as the president covered his face to hide a grin. The phrase "butthole surfer" was hysterical. The president never had heard homosexuals called that before.

"Thank you." Dr. Robles rubbed his warty nose and reshuffled his papers again. "By 'host,' I meant a person carrying the disease. Significant concentrations of the virus are found only in the subject's blood and semen." The doctor shuffled more papers as he adjusted his thick glasses and continued. "Amounts in the urine, feces, saliva, and nasal passages are insufficient to pass the disease on to another human. In addition, the virus needs a transport into a new host. It cannot enter through unbroken skin, the digestive system, nasal system, or lungs. The skin must be broken, or the virus must be introduced into the rectum, and—"

"So what you're saying, Dr. Robles, is that when a queer with Wildfire has sex with another butt pirate, that fag is *really* fucked!" Beaucroix was ecstatic, and the president did his best to hide a grin by covering his mouth and pretending to cough. Hampstead and the two doctors weren't amused.

Dr. Robles scowled. "Mr. Beaucroix, was it not you who said I should not be interrupted?"

"Sorry, Doc. It was a joke no *heterosexual* man could resist." Beaucroix noticed with delight that the president was still fighting a grin.

Dr. Robles wasn't sure if perhaps Beaucroix was accusing him of something. Suddenly he hated Beaucroix.

"Thank you, Mr. Beaucroix, for your valuable contribution of insensitive bigotry. To continue"—the sarcasm shot over the Monster's head and bounced harmlessly off the ceiling—"once Wildfire enters the system, it confuses and destroys the human immune system. On the one hand, it prevents the body from defending itself against any foreign invaders such as pneumonia or the flu. This makes even a routine infection deadly. But we have discovered something else. The virus has a tendency to turn the body against itself, eating away at its own tissue, as if it were a foreign invader."

The president interrupted as he leaned forward. "Let's be clear on this point, Dr. Robles. Are you telling us this virus, Wildfire, serves no risk to the general population?"

"That's correct, Mr. President," the Monster broke in with a grin. "Only butt pirates need beware. The rest of society—normal heterosexual society—is safe."

Suddenly the president had an unpleasant picture in his mind's eye. "But Dr. Robles, isn't it also true that the virus may not be the real danger? What about all the dead homosexuals lying around? Someone will have to clean up the mess. Won't these corpses and emergency-room cases infect doctors, nurses, ambulance drivers, and morticians?" He didn't look forward to seeing images of thousands of dead bodies on the 10:00 p.m. news, at least not during his presidency.

"No, Mr. President." Dr. Robles was dead serious, and he spoke quickly to prevent any more outbursts. "Three to six minutes after leaving a human host, the virus dies. Twenty to fifty minutes after a host expires, the virus within them dies. This disease will confine itself to the homosexual population and then die out. Leave it alone, and it will quietly make itself extinct." Dr. Robles closed his folder and added, "As

I said earlier, this virus poses no danger to normal heterosexual society. Leave it alone, and it will burn itself out."

"Along with all the queers," Beaucroix happily added, and slammed his fist on the table.

The president smiled. "What if the press finds out? What if there's a leak?"

"Then it becomes my problem," Hampstead assured him.

"And my pleasure!" Beaucroix added firmly, much to the president's satisfaction. He felt he had a lot in common with this man. Perhaps the president would force Hampstead to retire and let a real American like Emile Darwin Beaucroix take his place.

The president addressed the two doctors. "How much time will it take to die down, to burn itself out and disappear?"

"Fags are everywhere. It could take some time," Beaucroix blurted.

"We won't know until it peaks." Dr. Robles was looking through his notes. "Once it peaks and begins to subside, we can predict with good certainty when it will, for all practical purposes, disappear. However, my best guess until we have that data is twenty-two years." Dr. Robles rubbed his warty nose as he flipped through his notes.

"Mr. President, we have no way of knowing whether this thing will stay in the homosexual population. Even if it does, a lot of innocent people will die. If we act now, we probably can save a lot of lives and an untold amount of human suffering," Dr. Paxton pleaded.

"Are you married, Doctor?" Beaucroix quizzed.

"Yes." The doctor saw no relevance in the question.

"To a girl? A female, I mean?" Beaucroix had gotten a hold of a bone, and he was going to chew.

"Of course a woman. Are you trying to imply something in your sleazy yet profoundly moronic manner? Perhaps you didn't sleep too well last night. Was the closet uncomfortable, perhaps too confining?" Dr. Paxton could play too, and he was very good at it.

Beaucroix's face red flushed with fury. "Are you trying to accuse me of something? Perhaps you should make yourself clearer!" The Monster's eyes narrowed into sharp daggers of hate and menace.

"This will immediately stop! This is my White House. I and I alone decide whose ass gets kicked here!" the president roared as he slammed his fist on the table.

"You're quite right, sir!" Hampstead declared as he coldly eyed a boiling-mad Emile Beaucroix. "There will be no more unprofessional outbursts. Will there, Emile?"

No one ever called Beaucroix by his first name, least of all Hampstead. He scowled furiously at the director, then immediately caught himself and instantly changed his demeanor. He turned toward the president. "I'm sorry, sir." The Monster smiled apologetically. He was devilishly clever, but he knew he must also be cautious.

"Mr. President, I truly apologize to you and all parties present. As a loyal American and a loyal servant of this administration, I see Wildfire as our most potent weapon in the war against communism. Dr. Paxton is correct and has a point, and we should use caution." Beaucroix turned to the president, who seemed to nod in agreement. "But we also should be careful not to deny America a great weapon because of a couple of glitches, a couple of bugs, and a few dead fags!"

Beaucroix noted Dr. Paxton's scowl, the audit of Hampstead's eyes, and the delighted interest of the president. "Once we iron out a few problems, it can be an effective weapon in the war against communism. The only thing we have to resolve is how to make it effective against a largely heterosexual population such as that of the Soviet Union. Once we perfect it, I believe it will be our best hope to rid the world of this evil scourge. I ask you all to pardon my callous, emotional outbursts. Perhaps some of you will understand my distress." Pulling out his handkerchief, the Monster wiped his eyes.

Emile Beaucroix couldn't care less if communists lived or died. He hated queers. He hated them because he was one of them, and it was a secret the world must never know.

As Beaucroix finished, the president solemnly nodded; he understood. The president also didn't want to lose Wildfire. He felt sorry for Emile Beaucroix and suddenly felt very close to the man.

Hampstead surreptitiously surveyed the room. He looked into the eyes of the two doctors, but doctors weren't real men. He looked into the eyes of Emile Beaucroix, but they were false shutters, their secrets well kept. Then he looked into the eyes of the cowboy actor, the president of the United States, the most powerful man on earth.

Therein lay the problem, realized Hampstead. The most powerful man on earth was no John Wayne, and no one in the room had the guts to tell him.

September 26, 1981
Vienna, Austria

The Steirer Restaurant in Vienna is Austria's gift to the gods of haute cuisine. Its beautiful art nouveau style boldly declared the Steirer family's belief that dinning, superior dining, was about more than great-tasting food, it was about the whole experience—the eyes, the nose, and the palate must all unite in a splendiferous symphony of pleasure. And with full appreciation of these truths, the fat man, the Shadow, never, ever failed to visit this culinary paradise when good fortune brought him to this wonderful city.

Kurnov was no small stranger here either, but it was the Shadow who suggested they meet today. The Russian pushed open the door and nodded as he walked past the reservations podium and worked his way to the Shadow's table past dining poets, statesmen, and kings.

Kurnov frowned as he walked up to the table and noticed the way the Shadow dug into the fantastic char cooked in beeswax with yellow carrots, pollen, and sour cream.

"My friend, I was starting to grow fond of you, but if you keep eating like this, you will not be around much longer." Kurnov took a seat and then turned and snapped his finger to the impeccably dressed waiter behind him.

"What do you mean?" The big man shoveled another mouthful of the delightful dish into his pie hole.

"You must admit, you are not in the best of shape. That must be ten thousand calories before you." Kurnov lifted his left eyebrow.

The waiter approached, and Kurnov pointed at the fat man's magnificent food array. "I will have exactly that, but first, bring me a wine list—the special one, the one you reserve for diplomats, presidents and kings."

The waited nodded, bowed respectfully, and then scurried away.

"Kurnov, your powers of observation are failing you today. Perhaps you need a vacation, some time off. To any unbiased observer, I am in perfect, flawless shape!"

"Perfect shape?" The left eyebrow shot to new heights.

"Round *is a shape*, a perfect shape. I am obviously a very well-rounded fellow." The big guy patted his belly.

"Please remind me never to play chess with you." Kurnov grinned as he lowered his head and raised both eyebrows.

"Why?"

"Because I hate to lose." Kurnov grinned.

The shadow shoveled another delightful spoonful into his mouth and only half chewed as he shook the spoon at the spymaster. "I have news for you, Slava Kurnov."

Kurnov leaned back in the chair. "Really?"

"This is what I have found out." The Shadow shook the spoon toward the spymaster as he surveyed the room and leaned forward toward Kurnov's ear.

September 28, 1981
Rabat, Morocco

"That bitch sure has a fucking attitude. She needs to find a new line of work," Max observed as he watched her tight, retreating ass.

"I bet she saves that entire attitude just for you." Hogan tracked Max's eyes, thereby confirming his suspicions.

Max put down his glass and turned to Hogan. "What do you mean by that?"

"I could tell you a secret." Hogan grinned.

"Like you know something about women I don't?" Max queried, surprised that any guy, especially Hogan, could possibly think he was qualified to give a stud like him advice about women.

"They only treat you badly if they want you badly." Hogan, the sage, delivered this snappy wisdom.

"Get real. She hates my guts. She always has." Max swung his gaze back to the waitress as she wrote upon the dinner ticket.

Hogan grinned. "She wants you, and you want her."

"Yeah, that's why she treats me like shit!"

"Think about it. Has she ever been this rude to anyone else?"

"Sorry, Hogan, but I'm not into whips and leather. I don't know about yours, but my ass doesn't glow bright red in the dark." Max's eyes were still locked onto her graceful body, which floated with a sexy wiggle from table to table across the crowded room.

"Are you wearing sticky eye liner, Max?"

"What the hell are you talking about?" Max's eyes were still locked onto the beautiful girl, a prisoner of that stupendous French ass.

"Well, since you really do hate her, I thought your eye liner wasn't quite dry, because when she was over here, somehow your eyes accidentally got glued to her ass!" Hogan offered this in the most casual fashion.

Caught and embarrassed, Max snapped his attention back to his drink. "I don't know what you're talking about, Bob."

CHAPTER TWENTY
The Knights of Saint George

December 28, 1982
Syracuse, Italy

Corporal Antonio Denetti was certain he was a young man with a destiny. Barely two months into his chosen field, he was already a corporal in Italy's elite national police; the Carabinieri. Only nineteen years old, he already had many of the skills and much of the insight and intuition that most Carabinieri spent a lifetime acquiring.

Patrolling through the crowded side streets of Syracuse, he alone had noticed the tall American in the greatcoat moving through the daily hubbub of merchants, gypsies, and thieves. It was the way the man moved suspiciously through the crowd with a fluid but unnatural care. It was the surreptitious skill with which this foreigner avoided attention that had awakened Denetti's curiosity and pulled him into the wake that soon would fulfill his destiny.

Quietly Denetti followed this man because he knew this shadowy individual must have dark plans, and when he broke the law and attempted his evil enterprise, Denetti would be there, and he would arrest him.

Surprisingly, the man in the greatcoat looked neither to the left nor right. Oblivious to his surroundings, he walked an ordinary pace with his hands in his greatcoat and with his eyes fixed solidly on the path ahead. This was most unusual behavior, thought Denetti, for someone who was clearly up to no good.

The man in the greatcoat turned sharply right into a narrow alley as Denetti quickened his pace. As the young policeman reached the alley and turned into it, the man was nowhere to be seen. There was a side alley about thirty meters ahead, and Denetti moved quickly toward it.

Pouncing from the shadows in an alley doorway, Emile Beaucroix grabbed Antonio Denetti from the back and, with his fine Sicilian stiletto, severed the young man's throat and let him drop bleeding into the dust.

Beaucroix looked down at the still-living but dying young man. One could never have too much fun!

However, the Monster had an appointment to keep and must not be late. It would not be sporting to allow Max George to plan his murder without him, but still he couldn't resist.

"How does it feel? Was it good for you too? It was sure fun for me. Choices, choices…so many choices. Do I have fun here or have fun there?" Beaucroix leaned over as his inner demons danced for joy within his rancid soul. The Monster grinned as he weighed all the options. He looked from the dying young man on the ground to his destination far ahead. He hated to leave behind so much fun. Reaching down, he removed the young man's wallet.

"Good!" he declared as he found the young man's address and photos of a very pretty young wife. "I hate to slit your throat and run, but I have a meeting to get to. I think I'll continue this conversation tonight with your wife!" The heartless Monster grinned over the dying man.

The young man looked up. Unable to speak and with his world ending, he pleaded with his eyes for the lives of his wife and young son.

"Don't worry. I won't slit her throat—that is, I won't slit her throat until I've stuck something inside it first." As Beaucroix grinned at the bleeding man, the young policeman's eyes still pleaded upward to the Monster, who had no heart to hear his plea.

Beaucroix glanced at his Cartier watch. Frowning, he kicked the dying man in the head as hard as he could and continued on his way. Moving swiftly up the alley and then turning right, he entered the rear service door of the magnificent Hotel Bellini.

It was a bit early in Italy for the noontime repast, so the kitchen was lightly staffed. One of the cooks moved to question Beaucroix as he passed through the kitchen, but the Monster froze him with a stare that terrified the man. The cook immediately dropped his eyes and frantically returned to chopping onions. He was remembering to forget that he ever had seen Emile Beaucroix.

Beaucroix cracked open the service door. He now clearly saw the two men talking at the table. The old hotel had great acoustics, and the Monster possessed great hearing. He would soon know their plan.

But the thing Emile Beaucroix didn't know was the fate of the chocolate éclair ten feet behind him. The fat man casually ate it as he watched Beaucroix peer through the service door; the Shadow delightfully sucked the rich cream from his fingers. With the delicious éclair now finished, the fat man passed within four feet of Beaucroix's back and quietly exited through the kitchen's rear door into the alley, unheard, unseen, and unsuspected.

The Shadow smiled as he walked down the alley to his waiting taxi. The plan to kill Emile Beaucroix seemed to be a bust now. Beaucroix would know the plan; Max would know; Hogan would know; Kendal would know. But now the Shadow knew, and that was always a very good thing. When the Shadow knows, interesting things can happen.

"You ordered ouzo?" Hogan indicated the clear liquid in front of him as he took a comfortable seat at the table and, quickly grabbing his waiting glass, swallowed a shot. He snapped his fingers to indicate to the waiter that he wanted something else.

"Anisette!" Max corrected as he raised his glass and took a long sip.

"It's the same thing. Armenians call it arak. Greeks call it ouzo. And Italians call it anisette. I call it this liquid licorice-flavored shit too weak for me." Hogan needed a bit more than ouzo to take on a monster like Beaucroix. "Waiter, I'll have a Napoleon brandy and a 7UP on the side, and a maraschino cherry in the brandy and in the 7UP," he instructed.

After surveying the empty glasses on the table and writing down the order, the waiter professionally melted away.

"Shaken, not stirred. You've seen too many James Bond movies." Max grinned. "Hey, when did you discover this weird taste in drinks? Are you pregnant?"

"What's up, Max? Afraid someone else is the father?" Hogan joked back.

"Hey, a man's got a right to know who his bitch has been doing," Max said with a laugh.

"Oh, hey. Here comes Kendal."

Kendal had entered the dining room and was briskly walking up to their table. "What's so gosh-darn funny, guys?" he asked as he took a seat.

"Nothing. We were just discussing Max's overactive sex life." Hogan grinned.

"Got a new bitch, Max?" Kendal asked. At this, Max almost fell over, holding his side and laughing hysterically. "What's with him?" Kendal pointed to Max, who was still quaking with laughter.

"He has too many fantasies," Hogan replied.

Kendal snapped his fingers for the waiter. After grabbing his attention, he pointed to Max's drink and held up three fingers. The waiter, a veteran of many tables, rapidly delivered three more drinks.

"Hogan, I've been wondering about something you said the last time we met." Kendal accepted the drinks from the waiter and tossed a tip onto the man's moving tray.

"Really?" Hogan asked, somewhat bored because he wasn't certain they'd invited the right man to this meeting.

"You said you joined the CIA in Korea. What were you doing in Korea?"

"I was in the army." Hogan had no desire to expand upon this.

"You joined the CIA in Korea? I thought they always brought you stateside to discharge you from the army." Something here wasn't adding up. Kendal needed to know if there was more to it than that.

"I wasn't discharged." Hogan again wasn't volunteering a story.

"How could you join the CIA if you weren't discharged from the army?" Something was definitely fishy here.

"There were circumstances," Hogan calmly replied.

"What circumstances?" Kendal pressed.

"Circumstances," Hogan finalized.

"Look, I have a right to know what kind of people I'm working with. For all I know, you could be another Emile Beaucroix!"

It wasn't wise for Kendal to compare Hogan to the Monster.

"What!" Hogan bolted out of his chair.

"Hold it, Robert!" Max rose and grabbed his arm, restraining him. "Kendal, you went too far!" he cautioned.

"Sorry. I just wanted to know what made you the man you are today and not a monster like Beaucroix. I didn't mean to offend you." Miles Kendal was sincere.

Hogan had calmed down and was blankly regarding the far side of the room as he downed his drink. He raised the empty glass and shook it at the waiter, indicating an urgent need for reinforcement. That day in Korea was a day he wished had never happened and had produced two weeks of nightmares he had feared would never end.

Max looked at Hogan, then indicated to the approaching waiter with a spinning finger that all the glasses on the table needed urgent redress. "Technically, Hogan is still in the military." After some thought, Max agreed with Kendal. They were all in this together and deserved to know the kind of men they were working with.

"How can you be in the military and in the CIA? Don't you have to report in to your commanders when you're in the military?" asked Kendal.

"Not if you're a deserter," Max said.

"What?" Kendal didn't like the smell of this; he was a loyal American. Loyal Americans didn't desert.

"Look, let's resolve this so we can move on to the subject of this meeting. Hogan was never discharged because he was in jail. He doesn't need to report to his commander because if he did, he'd be shot as a deserter. Does that answer your question?" Max wanted to move on; he knew this wasn't his best friend's favorite subject.

"Deserter? Then how did he end up in the CIA?" Now Kendal was both uneasy and suspicious.

"OK, I guess this meeting isn't going to go any further until I bend over and drop my pants for you." Hogan downed another drink and circled the table with his finger as he motioned to the waiter that all the glasses needed to be addressed again. His empty glass was the only one of this last round that had been touched.

"I was a sergeant in the Fifth Artillery Division, stationed in Korea," he said. "One night, around two in the morning, the military police dragged me from the barracks and into the stockade. They accused me of raping and murdering a thirteen-year-old Korean girl. I was innocent, but they thought they had more than enough evidence to convict me. One of the CIA's deep operatives had been following a Korean national who actually had committed the crime." His glass now refilled, Hogan took deep swallow.

"If you're innocent, why didn't the CIA exonerate you?" This whole thing was as clear as a London fog in Kendal's mind.

"Like I said, the CIA told me the man who witnessed the crime was a deep-cover operative. Blowing his cover would have endangered national security, so there was nothing the CIA could do to help me without compromising national security." Hogan swirled the drink in his glass as he peered deep into the shades and shadows.

"Legally anyway," Max added.

"What?" the fog was returning to Kendal.

"They knew I was innocent—that is, the CIA knew I was innocent. They offered to help me escape the military prison, but the only practical place they could hide me was within the CIA. They couldn't prove me innocent because the cost to American security would be too high. But they could set me free." A faint smile crossed Hogan's lips; he was grateful the inquisition was over, at least almost over.

"The CIA broke you out of a military stockade?" Kendal couldn't imagine this happening, at least not bloodlessly.

"Kendal, Hogan told you the whole story, the true story. So we need to move on. There's unfinished business to do." Max motioned for Kendal to move closer to him and closer to the table.

"The agency really broke you out? Was anyone killed?" Kendal needed to know; he needed the entire story.

"I'm sick of memory lane. It's time to move on." Hogan turned toward Max, who nodded.

"Let's get down to business." Max downed his anisette like a shot of whiskey. "Let's kill Emile Beaucroix!" He motioned for everyone to lean in closer.

"Murder? You called me here to plan a murder? What's the matter with you two?" When Kendal had agreed to meet Hogan to get rid of Beaucroix, he had assumed the three of them were getting together to issue some kind of joint petition or memo to Hampstead detailing the reasons Beaucroix should be fired.

"Why did you think we called you here? Did you expect Max and me to hold him down while you paddled him?" Hogan wondered if maybe he'd made a mistake inviting Kendal here. Max had voiced his reservations, and perhaps Hogan had dismissed them too quickly.

"I think he'd enjoy being paddled, but only in his tight fuchsia jumpsuit, the one with the pink ruffles and fluffy collar," Max offered, laughing.

"I don't know why you keep having these fantasies about Beaucroix being some kind of queer," Hogan said. "He's a psycho, end of story. He's a mad, deranged psycho who lives to serve only his evil ends." Just the thought of Beaucroix having sex with anything made Hogan sick; the idea of Beaucroix eating or sleeping was something Hogan never thought about either. He preferred to think of him as the Monster, devoid of any human needs or virtues. Hogan saw him as a modern-day Dracula, but without any of the count's manners, charm, or breeding.

"A lot of psychos are closet homosexuals. That's why they're so vicious. They're filled with self-hatred and an insatiable thirst for revenge, a thirst no amount of killing can ever quench." Max lifted his glass up to the light, almost as an eyepiece to God. He wanted to ask God why creatures like Beaucroix were allowed to exist.

"Wow! All these years we worked together, I was under the impression that you were a spy. You never told me you were a world-famous psychiatrist, Max. Was it Yale or Harvard medical school that you attended? I forget." Hogan returned his attention to his glass.

"Robert, let me tell you something about our profession. The average spy probably knows more about human nature than ten psychiatrists." Looking for support, Max turned to Kendal.

"Tell me, Dr. Spock, why do these fantasy homosexuals of yours need revenge?" Hogan inquired.

Max put down his glass. "For being born!"

"I didn't expect violence," Kendal said. "There has to be a better solution to getting rid of Beaucroix. I'm sure if the three of us got together and agreed on the facts, we could take those facts to Hampstead and get Beaucroix fired." It wasn't that Kendal was opposed to murder. Assassinating a foreign official was one thing, but the assassination of someone you knew was something else altogether. It didn't matter how evil Beaucroix was; the fact that Kendal actually knew him made the difference between a murder and a simple assassination.

"We'd be wasting our time." Hogan replied.

"Hampstead likes him. He'd do nothing," Max added.

"If Hampstead knew what Beaucroix was really like—what he was really up to—he would do something. He probably has no idea just how cruel Beaucroix can be," Kendal said.

"Hampstead doesn't care." Max held up his empty glass and shook it at the waiter across the room.

"How can you say he doesn't care? He works for the CIA, not the gestapo!" Kendal replied in amazement.

"Hampstead is the director of operations. The one and only thing he cares about is results. He never sees the bodies, and he never sees the pain, suffering, or violence, and even if he did, he wouldn't care!" Hogan turned to face the waiter, who had just brought fresh drinks.

"Bring two full bottles of Courvoisier cognac and proper brandy snifters, please, and we do not want to be disturbed. Do you understand?" Max tossed fifty dollars onto the waiter's hungry tray.

"Completely, sir," the waiter replied gratefully, and scurried off to fetch two bottles.

"Violence isn't always the answer, but it sure closes any issue with finality." Max quoted his favorite saying, one he had authored himself.

"Beaucroix is a hard bug to squash—harder than a steel-plated cockroach to kill." Hogan looked down into his glass, trying to divine the answer from the reflections.

"Not even Kurnov could catch and kill him, and God knows he wants to," Max added.

"We've got to keep this to ourselves. The agency must never know," Hogan said. "I need you to promise me, Max…promise you won't tell anyone else about our plans."

"Why would any of us speak to anyone? We can handle this ourselves," Max replied.

"I know about your meeting with Kurnov. We don't need him, and I don't trust him." He looked into his pal's Celtic-green eyes. "Max, we don't need Kurnov. Do you agree? I don't want him involved. This is strictly between us, OK?"

"I promise," Max solemnly declared, and that was good enough for Hogan, who moved on.

"The Monster has two main weaknesses: his ego and his love of torture, torment, and fear—that is, being on the giving end of torture and torment. We must find someone Beaucroix would love to kill then flaunt the idea that he could never catch him. That will be our trap."

"That could be either you or Max. Max could be the bait," Kendal observed.

"No, that would never work because Beaucroix knows we both want him dead. He'd never pursue either of us into a trap." Max said, explaining the obvious flaw in this plan.

"Then what about me? I'll take the risk, and I'll lure him into our trap," Kendal offered.

"I don't want to hurt you, kiddo, and smash your ego, but Beaucroix considers you an amateur and not interesting enough to kill," Max said in an apologetic tone.

Kendal felt hurt anyway and was in need of redemption. "Then where do I fit into the plan? I can take risk as well as any man. I'm as good a spy as either of you."

"Kid, your problem is a raging boner and too damn many hormones. The earth and the sea are filled with the bones of good spies, great spies. It's the lucky spies who survive," Max said with a smile.

"You're losing sight of the plan, Kendal. The plan is to kill Emile Beaucroix. If you want to get whacked, we can find you a suicide job another day," Hogan added.

Kendal smiled sheepishly. He was embarrassed but felt very much like family; he honestly liked these two men.

"Hogan, could I ask you one final question about what happened in Korea? And then I promise never to mention it again." He looked deep into Hogan's eyes.

"Kendal, the matter is closed. Hogan said everything he's going to on that subject." Max tried to close the door.

"Hogan?" Kendal needed an answer.

"Yeah?" He was a bit more detached, a bit drunker.

"Ever consider that maybe it was the CIA that set you up?" Kendal voiced the obvious.

"Look, Kendal, this conversation isn't doing any one of us any good!" Max said.

"Hogan, did you ever think the agency might have set you up?" Kendal pursued the question. Given that his own application process to the CIA had been nothing more exciting than clerical, he wondered how often the agency recruited through other means.

"Don't answer him, Robert. We're here to discuss the future of Beaucroix, not the buried past."

"Hogan?" Kendal pressed.

Max was getting irritated. "This isn't accomplishing anything."

"Hogan?" Kendal continued, but Hogan ignored the question and just stared into the depths of his glass. "Do you believe you were set up?" Kendal pressed on. "Hogan?"

"Yes, I found out later that they set me up," he finally said. "The young girl was murdered and raped by her own uncle. The agency just took advantage of it. Her uncle was a North Korean spy, so the CIA used her murder to blackmail him and turn him into a double agent. They needed a fall guy for the plan to work, so they took me," Hogan replied directly to Kendal's eyes, solidifying his answer with an intense stare.

"Good! Now that we've swapped naked baby pictures, it's time to move on and plan the murder of Emile Beaucroix!" Max turned the subject from serious matters long past to serious matters that affected the world around them.

"Then we're all in agreement. This is a job that needs to be done at any cost." Hogan surveyed the room. Satisfied the meeting wasn't compromised, he continued. "This, gentlemen, is how we'll end Beaucroix's miserable life. Here's the plan."

Beaucroix cracked the service door a tad wider and cocked his ear closer to hear the plan—and it was a damn good one.

December 29, 1982
Hotel Bellini; Syracuse, Italy

"You wanted to see me?" Slava Kurnov helped himself to a seat and sent his right hand into his vest, searching for a cigar. The fishing was good, and he produced two fine Cuban cigars and handed one to Max George, who gratefully accepted.

Producing a gold lighter, Max lit Kurnov's stogie and then fired up his own. These cigars were Fidel's favorites, his private brand. They were a personal gift from Castro to Kurnov, a small reward for many jobs well done.

"I need for you to find the fat lady. If you do that for me, I can make her sing!" Max leaned forward, peering into Kurnov's eyes. Kurnov had no intention of getting into a battle of wills with Max, because Max could surely win. This wasn't Robert Hogan the KGB man now faced. This was Max George, and he was a whole lot tougher.

"Why should I help you?" It was Kurnov's turn to feign disinterest and underplay his hand.

Max grinned at the theatrics and then slammed his fist on the table, sending his whiskey glass to the floor and startling Kurnov, a very hard man to upset or surprise. "Cut the crap! I intend to kill Beaucroix, and I need your help! You want him dead too. I'm offering to do *your* work for you. How can you pass up such an opportunity?" he roared.

Kurnov considered the matter. He would have to shelve his current plan. "Why should you want to kill your own man? I understood your company valued him highly. What happened to change their minds?"

The Russian took a deep draw of the delightful Havana cigar. Kurnov liked honesty because it was an enjoyable, if infrequent, diversion.

"Nothing has changed Hampstead's mind, and he has no idea I plan to kill Emile Beaucroix. I doubt you'll rat me out." Max grinned as he pulled upon the excellent stogie.

"Perhaps we should find out where Hogan stands on this." Kurnov was wary of a trap and needed to know what part Hogan was playing in this scenario.

"Hogan knows nothing and will be told less. He knows about my last meeting with you and has forbidden us to have any more." Max smiled into Kurnov's deep, probing stare.

"He has forbidden you? How nice. Is he your superior or your mother?" Kurnov joked. Joking and setting a man off balance improved the odds of his saying and revealing more than he might otherwise be willing to offer.

"Kurnov, you're sounding a little like that closet fag Beaucroix." Max took a long draw and shook his finger at the Russian.

"Never. You see, you and I can joke like this because we have nothing to hide. We are comfortable in our masculinity. Your enemy Beaucroix is serious, however—dead serious!" Kurnov had fought hard to make the KGB a professional organization and to keep it within the rules of the game. He had no place is his organized universe for men like Emile Beaucroix.

"You know he's queer?" Max raised an eyebrow. "Kurnov, I am finding myself becoming more impressed with you every time we talk." Max grinned; he was quickly starting to like Kurnov.

"We have psychologists in the Soviet Union too; we are not as backward as the United States press would like the world to believe. There is, however, no agreement among our experts to explain the inner rage of such psychotic individuals. Why repressed homosexuals hate gays is something that seems to confuse them."

"I am surprised at you, comrade Kurnov. Today you are a very important man, but in your youth, when sent deep into cover, didn't you ever act the fop, the coward, or the fool, just to hide your true purpose and identity?"

"Of course I did, just as you probably did. Rule one of entering the enemy's camp is to appear too ludicrous to be a threat. A fop, a spineless coward, or a gutless wonder is always a superb cover." Kurnov grinned. "Tell me more, this is very interesting."

"Kurnov, Beaucroix is queer. But he can never have a homosexual relationship. The very thought would tear him apart. He has always lived a life terrified that his secret would be discovered. Rabid hatred of homosexuals is a defense mechanism. If you shout and point at everyone else, there is less of a chance of anyone looking at you."

"Max George, you are a very erudite and interesting man, and I thank you. I will believe your explanation over these Kremlin fools. I can smell your explanation, and it has the odor of truth!"

"No normal man hates gays, Kurnov," Max continued. "We might think them funny or strange or perverted. But we don't hate them. The normal male world is a world of intense competition—competition for the ladies. All men will do more and go further for sex than for all other causes combined. It doesn't matter if that cause is wealth, health, power, politics, or even self-interest. Most men will toss aside these things readily, happily, in the pursuit of a beautiful woman.

"In the heterosexual world you and I are living in, gay men mean less competition for what we're truly after, the love and attention of a beautiful woman. To us, a gay person is no different from a sheep in a pasture, something of complete irrelevance to us—that is, unless you're from Montana," Max pointed out.

"Montana?" Kurnov failed to grasp the connection.

"Montana is a northern state in the western United States. They have a lot of cowboys and few women. It's the state 'where men are men, and sheep are scared'!"

"That's very funny. I need to remember that the next time I illegally visit your country," Kurnov said as he grinned broadly. "I agree, George. In my experience, the only men who hate gays are the men who hate being gay. The only time anyone shouts, 'Faggot!' is when that person is talking to himself; he's just too stupid to realize it. The big pity is that society as a whole is too ignorant to realize this. When society grows up, if it ever does, bigots will have a lot more critics and a lot fewer willing ears.

"But that is enough philosophy for now. Let's get back to business. Again, why would you betray one of your own agents and your own country? I understood all you agents were loyal to Hampstead's private, perverted agenda." Kurnov was trying to read him, but Max was a cleverly closed book.

"I don't have any politics, Kurnov. I follow my own agenda too." Max winked and then blew two smoke rings, one through the other. Beaucroix was proud of his own ability to blow perfect smoke rings. Max had learned to do it better, just to spite Beaucroux.

"How can I help you, and what do you require of me and my connections?" the Russian inquired. He liked this man, and he wished there were a possibility of getting him to defect. But then, perhaps he would defect at some future date. Who knew what really was in the mind of Max George? Slava Kurnov had seen stranger things during his long career.

"Beaucroix knows we plan to kill him," Max said. "Hogan is planning to have another meeting to discuss the details. I need you to leak to Beaucroix the details of when and where this meeting will take place. I need you to help Beaucroix *kill* Robert Hogan. I will do the rest."

"Your dossier says you and Hogan are very close friends. Why should I believe you intend to kill him?" Kurnov blew a smoke ring of his own and a not half bad one, either.

"Your dossier also says Hogan and Beaucroix are friends!" Max accused.

"That has been corrected, updated. Even your company makes mistakes!"

"Hampstead's days are numbered. Who's better qualified to replace him than I?" Max knew it was no less than the truth.

"In the meantime, how do you plan to deal with Hampstead? Surely after Emile Beaucroix is murdered, Hampstead will have questions and launch an investigation." Kurnov leaned back as he raised an eyebrow.

"I have no doubt there will be an investigation." Max grinned. "I plan to shift all the blame for the murder of Emile Beaucroix to the KGB," he said with a wink.

"Or the credit!" Kurnov lifted his glass in salutation.

"*Touché!*" Max grinned again.

"Now, what else is in this for me? What other favors do you plan to do for the KGB?" Kurnov asked, getting down to business.

"I'll give you a hearty handshake," Max offered.

"Not sufficient." Kurnov feigned a frown. In reality, if Beaucroix was murdered, it would be Kurnov who owed Max the favors. But as Russia's greatest spymaster, Kurnov always looked for the best deal.

"I like the frown. It's almost believable, Kurnov. But, you know, with Beaucroix dead and Hampstead forced out, I'm the likely choice to replace him. That would place me behind a desk in Washington and consequently out of your hair," Max said, smiling.

"In my failure to rid myself of you, I must admit that you are pretty good. It certainly might be in my best interests to have you off the field and out of the way in some bureaucratic capacity. But what do apples have to do with oranges?" Kurnov asked.

"Emile Beaucroix and Robert Hogan are also good choices, candidates for William Hampstead's office. If I can be rid of them both, the job is mine. There are no other logical choices to fill the position."

The Russian smiled; he thought it funny how these Americans were always plotting to kill their own. The KGB, he felt, handled their assets better. "Is that all?" He spread his hands, indicating that it was too simple. Max simply nodded. "Then, my fine capitalist friend, I will be happy to extend to you this little professional courtesy." With this said, he snapped his fingers. Two men carrying Russian machine guns emerged from their hiding place behind the room divider and headed for the door. Max didn't mind this little surprise. He had his own men hiding in the john.

Kurnov had planned to kill Max George. But getting rid of Emile Beaucroix *and* Hogan was better—much better. With Max in Washington, Kurnov could easily control the European theater, not to mention Africa. The Russian spymaster quickly searched the table with his eyes. Finding no more vodka present, he stood, and, without a word, the bravest, craftiest, and best the KGB had to offer quietly left the room.

CHAPTER TWENTY ONE
To Catch a Monster

February 2, 1983
Native Village; Twenty Miles North of Bopolu, Liberia

After several disjointed inquiries in bad Bassa dialect, Hogan was finally ushered to John N'tari's family hut. This was the young man who had helped him before with Chief M'kari. Hogan desperately needed the old chief to lead him to the gods of Bopolu.

"Hello, Mr. Hogan." John smiled as he walked up to Hogan and waved a greeting.

"Hi, kid. Need another thirty bucks? I need to talk to the chief."

The kid shook his head, sorry to lose thirty bucks.

"He's dead. The Monster killed him. I saw it all," an old woman shouted as she emerged from the adjacent hut. "The white devil flew down from the sky and raised his hand and chanted as the chief's head exploded. The Monster urinated on the dead chief in the very way devils show their contempt for all things mortal and good." The old woman quickly rubbed the fetish around her neck for protection lest the evil return.

"What she means is that two white men landed a helicopter in the village," John explained. "They questioned the chief for more than an hour, and when he wouldn't speak and tell them what he said to you, they shot him in the head with a pistol. Then one of the two men—the evil one with the eyes like blue steel—urinated on the chief's body, and then they both left, flew off into the sky." John turned to look at the old woman, but she was no longer there. After telling her tale, she had retreated into the safety of her hut.

"We have a new chief. We can talk to him." John needed those thirty dollars. If you think it's hard for a man to live in an American ghetto, you should try surviving in a native African settlement where cash money is as common as palm trees on Mars.

"So Beaucroix followed me here?" Hogan answered matter-of-factly to himself. He was sad for the old chief; he was sad for anyone who ran into Emile Beaucroix. He had liked Chief M'kari and would miss him. Hogan wanted to say a few words over the old man's grave; he felt responsible. It was, after all, Hogan who had led Beaucroix to the old man's door.

Hogan would leave a poem that he would compose graveside in the dead chief's honor. He hoped his simple Christian prayers wouldn't offend the old man's gods.

"Where is the chief buried?" Hogan inquired.

"He wasn't buried. His body was taken in the noonday darkness before we could bury him."

Hogan was amazed. What would Beaucroix want with the body? "Do you know where the white men took the body?" he inquired.

"The two white men—the killers—flew back into the sky in their helicopter. As soon as they left, darkness fell, and the entire world went black. Night began in midafternoon, and the monkeys left their trees and came into the settlement—they took the body." John repeated exactly what he had seen.

In deep thought, Hogan looked into the distance. He believed John's supernatural tale, so he made his decision. "Which way did the monkeys go?" he asked.

The young man answered by pointing east. After fishing out thirty dollars, Hogan paid him and then disappeared on foot into the sweltering jungle.

February 2, 1983
The White House

As Kendal left the meeting, he wasn't surprised to hear the double doors slam shut and seal in Beaucroix and the others behind him. He paused in the hallway outside the Oval Office, and, after reaching into his jacket pocket, he produced a fresh Montecristo. He was still irked that he was the only one in the meeting who didn't really matter. Why had they even invited him?

The CIA often did strange things like this. Sometimes you were invited to a meeting just so they could ensure that you couldn't be anywhere else.

The tall Secret Service agent guarding the hall stepped forward, offering to light the stogie. "Was it a rough meeting, sir?" the big guy asked with a smile.

"They're all rough, friend," Kendal replied as he accepted the light and then closed his eyes and drew willingly upon the verboten Cuban tobacco.

"I don't envy your job. That man—" He motioned toward the president's office.

"Has a bad temper and a worse memory." Kendal puffed frantically.

"I've never seen it, sir," the smiling agent lied. To keep his job, he had to be political. "But I think we'd both find out what kind of temper he has if he found an American smoking a Cuban cigar in the White House." As he said this, he indicated the antique French empire ash can that flanked the left double door. Kendal quickly complied by quashing the stogie in the knee-high brass. He fathomed the guard's intentions and, after a moment, decided he could trust him. The great cigar faux pas would be forgotten.

The agent produced a fresh Macanudo from his vest and offered it to Kendal, who gratefully accepted it, badly needing a smoke.

"It's not Cuban," the agent apologized. "But it's not bad either, and it gets you into a lot less trouble around here." He smiled as he lit Kendal's cigar and marveled at the fierceness of the agent's first two draws.

Kendal cast his eyes upward, noticing that the ceiling of the most powerful building of the most powerful nation on earth was badly in need of a coat of paint.

"Unbelievable," he professed through a wave of smoke. "It's unbelievable that a man who has two sons—one of whom is a drunken redneck and the other a ballerina—could rant and rave so much about fags and queers. Just because the president pulled strings and got his son a job photographing naked women for *Playboy* magazine doesn't mean he still isn't a q—"

A cold presence and a sudden involuntary tightening of his back muscles broke him off in midsentence. The Secret Service agent quickly lost his smile as he abruptly turned his gaze and stared past Kendal to a point behind him.

Slowly Kendal turned to see Beaucroix framed squarely in the doorway, burning through him with an icy, psychotic stare filled with animal rage. The Monster stood motionless, with hate bubbling and burning within him. Kendal tensed as he prepared to make a rapid grab for his gun. Quickly he checked the corner of his eye, as he needed to know if the Secret Service agent also was going to make a move to enter the game.

Then, suddenly and unexpectedly, the Monster's nose twitched. The Monster's demonic expression changed, it softened a bit. Beaucroix looked down to his right at the ash can. For several seconds, he merely stared at the barely abused Cuban Montecristo. Then, quite without warning, he flashed Kendal an evil smile and turned and reentered the president's office, quietly closing the double doors behind him.

Kendal took a deep breath. He couldn't believe he actually had been prepared to initiate a gunfight in the White House, right in front of the Oval Office. It was incredible; it was surreal, and he couldn't believe it actually had happened because it was impossible.

But Emile Beaucroix had that effect on people; when one faced him, there never was any other reality. Confronting him was like stepping into a fog of pure evil; everything else was but a wavering, flaccid haze.

But Beaucroix had been well and fully satisfied because, in his mind, Kendal was already dead, leaving the Monster only the pleasure and minor task of killing him. Emile Beaucroix loved few things, but one of the things he loved most was waking up every morning with a pleasant agenda. It was his favorite credo: "One can never have too much fun, or too many fun things to do!"

April 2, 1983
The Settlement; North of Bopolu, Liberia

Where he was going and why Hogan didn't have a clue. But something was guiding him and directing him through the maze of jungle trails. After about an hour and a half, he had managed to cover about four kilometers of trails and was beginning to notice something strange and supernatural in the world around him. It seemed that with every step, the jungle became more and more unworldly. Even the light seemed to change. It was as if he were walking into another existence, another dimension.

As he brushed aside the scratchy palm fronds, he found himself in a clearing. It was a large, flat clearing, empty except for the enormous baobab tree at its center. High in the branches sat more than a hundred monkeys, staring with solemn intensity at Robert Hogan.

Sitting regally at the base were five ancient, grizzled monkeys, all in a perfect row. These were the gods of Bopolu.

Hogan watched in amazement as a ragged monkey dropped from the tree to the ground and ran up to within seven feet of where he stood on the jungle floor. Hogan was glad he had come alone. The monkey had seated himself and was watching Hogan intently.

"How can I kill the Monster? How can I defeat him?" Hogan asked the monkey.

The monkey grabbed a handful of dirt, tightly crushed it, and held it out in front of him. There was a look in its eyes that told Hogan this was no mere monkey. Hogan watched carefully, trying to divine the meaning of its action. The monkey grabbed another fistful of earth and shook it furiously at Hogan, who frowned without understanding.

"Beaucroix is pure evil. He murdered Chief M'kari, and you know that because you took the body. Many men have tried to kill the Monster, and those many men are dead. It's as if the devil himself is protecting Beaucroix. Give me something I can use. Tell me how to kill the Monster!"

The monkey gripped its clenched fist of jungle dirt even tighter and took another step toward Hogan. Then he shook it furiously in front of Hogan.

"I must pick my ground!" Hogan finally understood, and the monkey jumped up and down, chattering furiously in congratulation. "But I can't trick him into a trap. He never would follow me, and even then, he's a hard man to kill. He's too wary, too tough, and too clever to be drawn into a trap. Many men—some better than me—have tried to lure him into dark places, but the only dark place they found was their own shallow grave."

Hogan was no longer speaking to an animal; he was speaking to an equal. The monkey quieted down and looked Hogan in the eyes as he pounded the ground twice. Two other monkeys quickly jumped out of the tree and joined him. One sat to the right, the other to the left. The monkey in the middle looked at Hogan, his dark eyes pleading for an understanding.

Hogan looked blankly at the monkey. The creature again hammered the ground twice, but Hogan still drew a blank. Then the monkey on the right hammered the ground three times as the middle monkey pointed at Hogan.

"I need to hammer him. You mean shoot him twice? Shoot him twice to be certain he's truly dead?" Hogan was having a hard time because this didn't seem to be very useful advice.

The monkey became more agitated and frustrated because Hogan was unable to understand. The creature paused and then slapped the monkey to his right. The monkey on the right looked at the center monkey then slapped him right back.

Hogan was still confused. "You mean I need to hit him with my hands, kill him with my bare hands so as not to make a noise?" Hogan was a strong man—he was a very strong man—but he had heard psychotics could exhibit incredible strength, and he'd never heard of a man who had struck Emile Beaucroix with anything and lived to tell the tale.

Now it was the turn of the monkey on the left. He lifted his leg and kicked the center monkey in the ass, sending him rolling in a ball across the jungle floor. The center monkey righted himself, returned to his place, and slapped the other monkey in the face. In defense, that monkey boxed the center monkey's ears and firmly pulled his nose.

This is ridiculous, thought Hogan. *It's like watching the Three Stooges, like watching a married couple fight.* He watched the silly antics, trying to glean the meaning of the pantomimes before him. It wasn't far different, he thought, from one of the many drunken squabbles he'd had with Max George.

That was it!

"It will take three men to kill him, so I'll need to involve two friends." The three monkeys jumped up and down, chattering excitedly. Hogan glanced over at the five elders, who watched solemnly and nodded.

"Where should we take him? Should we take him in Bopolu or on the road to Monrovia?"

The three seated monkeys stood and turned as one, and as one, all three pointed up at the huge baobab tree.

"Do I need to take him from above like a sniper? Do I need to kill him from a tree or a high place?" Hogan puzzled.

Normally a good sniper could kill any man. Most snipers would pick a high perch with the broadest field of vision and clearest field of fire. Usually they'd choose a high place that overlooked an open area, where they would wait for the target to pass. The problem was that Emile Beaucroix by habit always avoided open places.

The monkeys chattered louder and jumped up and down as they all pointed to the huge baobab tree.

Hogan lit up—he suddenly understood what they were trying to tell him.

"I need to kill him in my house, in my own home!"

The five elders nodded as one then turned and jumped back up into the tree. This meeting had ended. The gods of Bopolu had spoken and had given their sage advice, and the three young monkeys retreated and flew up into the high branches to join them.

"Wait—how will I trick him into coming into my house?" Hogan shouted at the retreating monkeys.

The last monkey paused at the base of the tree. He considered the question briefly and then turned his gaze up to the gods of Bopolu. The gods looked down from the heights of the tree and chattered as a dozen monkeys leaped from the tree and charged toward Hogan. The interview was over; the gods of Bopolu had nothing more to say.

Hogan turned and quietly walked away. The monkeys didn't follow, and with only half a plan in his pocket, he had much work to do.

January 3, 1984
The Safari Club; Nairobi, Kenya

Beaucroix raised his eyebrows at the Russian. "Why should I do your job for you?"

"As a courtesy, perhaps as a favor from one wolf to another, and besides, you hate the man." Kurnov grinned.

"I hate a lot of men!" The Monster addressed this comment to the ceiling, feigning boredom and disinterest. There was no fun in this for him, and Kurnov could not be trusted.

"You could choose to listen to me or not listen to me. Things are what they are, and things that will happen will still happen." Kurnov smiled as he looked into his whiskey glass and swirled the brown liquid within. "But if you don't kill him, it is possible you may regret it."

"I regret so few things, Kurnov, because men like me make so few mistakes!" In Beaucroix's mind, he had no equal. "But one thing I do regret is that I didn't take a good crap before I left the hotel this afternoon. A good crap would have been more productive than this meeting with you."

"You underestimate the quality and reliability of the information that passes my desk. I am, after all, a senior operative within the KGB." Kurnov was no simple operative. He was the biggest and best of the Soviet dragons; he was a legend throughout the KGB.

"You are not in my class. No one is. Don't insult me by trying to slither up to my level. Snakes are poor climbers."

"Snakes are excellent climbers. Perhaps you overrate yourself," Kurnov replied bluntly, somewhat surprised that someone who had spent so much time in Africa would know so little about snakes. In the Kremlin, you had to watch the shadows for snakes; in the jungle, you had to watch the trees.

"Perhaps I should kill *you!*" Beaucroix scratched himself, testing Kurnov to see whether his eyes would move.

"Hogan plans to murder you," Kurnov casually informed Beaucroix as he ignored these little games. The KGB knew all about such weird characters. Mental disease, instability, sexual deviation, and spying often went hand in hand.

"Really? When?" Beaucroix was somewhat interested now.

"On March first, Max George and Hogan will meet at Hogan's estate to plan your demise." Kurnov raised the empty bottle and shook it. The fat, jocular Greek bartender nodded and scurried off to fetch a fresh bottle.

"How do I know your information is reliable?"

"Kendal was supposed to join them, but a certain ballerina's father has made that plan most unlikely. Kendal has been reassigned, far away from his playmates. He has been sent to Guatemala." Kurnov proved what everyone already knew—that the KBG also had reliable men in the White House.

"What do I owe you?" Beaucroix reached into his vest.

"Pay for the next bottle, and we will be even." Kurnov indicated the fat bartender bustling across the room toward the table.

"Good!" Beaucroix pulled out a gambler's derringer and placed it against Kurnov's head as he pulled back the steel hammer, which responded with a sharp, echoing click. The fat bartender dropped the bottle, the crash almost drowning out the click of the now-cocked derringer's hammer.

"Today, however, shall be my treat," Kurnov replied absent-mindedly, ignoring the cocked pistol pointed at his temple. Beaucroix grinned and put away his toy; a mouse that wouldn't run offered little pleasure.

"Thank you. I'm a completely modern kind of guy, and I enjoy it when the *lady* buys the drinks." Having insulted the Russian's manhood, Beaucroix stood up, bowed, tipped his hat as if to a lady, and then worked his way to the door.

Halfway across the room, the Monster paused next to the frightened Greek, who was frozen in terror. Beaucroix grabbed him and roughly slammed him to the floor. One could never have too much fun!

Kurnov gloated because the dossiers were correct. Beaucroix was mental—a 101 percent psycho—and he was an idiot! Beaucroix probably would kill Hogan, and then Kurnov's man would kill Hampstead, and Max would be neutralized and neutered because Max would be given Hampstead's job and moved to Washington. That was where his skills would be wasted, and he no longer would pose an inconvenience to the KGB.

That was how Slava Kurnov hoped Emile Beaucroix would read his end and motive in the deal. But in reality, the great Slava Kurnov, the KGB's master spy, had his own agenda and a plan for his own very special kind of fun.

As the bartender lifted himself off the floor, Kurnov again raised the empty vodka bottle and shook it, this time holding up two fingers. This would be a two-bottle night. Things were going good; things were going great!

January 15, 1984
Kosovo, Yugoslavia

The Slav spymaster bolted up from his chair. This was his office, and he deserved some damn respect! "This is intolerable. There's no excuse for this sort of thing. It's just not done, Kurnov. I demand that you retire this player immediately. There is no room in our world for men like him." Alexi Yakovich stuck his finger into the chest of Slava Kurnov.

Kurnov looked down at the offending finger and then glanced into Yakovich's eyes. Yakovich quickly holstered the offending finger.

Kurnov frowned as he continued to regard the Slav. He was always amazed that these Balkan spies had such an inflated self-image. This man was only Alexi Yakovich, head of Yugoslav intelligence; he was certainly not a major player.

He, of course, was Slava Kurnov, the KGB's special operations section chief and one of the most powerful men on earth. Today wasn't a good day to try his patience or solicit friendly pats to a swollen ego.

"Perhaps it was an accident." Kurnov glanced at his watch, as he had other urgent, pressing matters to attend to. "Collateral damage happens in our business, and it's a risk we all take." Kurnov had no time for this idiot.

"There's nothing collateral here. That was a radio-controlled detonator, and Beaucroix had to know the agent's three daughters were in the car with him—he had to have known. There is no way, no possible way"—Yakovich was now screaming—"that he could not see those three young children get in the car!" He slammed his fist on the desk.

"Alexi, this matter is being attended to. Now, did you ask me here to tell me something important, or did you ask for this meeting simply because you wanted to kiss my pretty face? Whatever it is, please do so, and be done with it. I have to get back to Moscow and attend to things that are *actually important.*"

This wasn't the first time someone in the Soviet Socialist Republics had demanded the death of Emile Beaucroix, but he wasn't an easy man to kill. Kurnov was a master of his trade and knew a task like this would take time and careful planning. This useless, self-loving hack would be of no use in such a complex plan.

Thoroughly frustrated, Yakovich was also tired of Kurnov's constant assurances that Beaucroix would be taken care of. He also didn't care for Kurnov's contempt for Yugoslav customs; Kurnov wasn't fond of being kissed on the cheek. The Russian considered this old custom a throwback to feudal age. Kurnov preferred to save all his affections—including kisses—for pretty young ladies.

The spymaster wasn't really mad at the Yugoslav. He was just impatient with this narrow-minded idiot who had no global understanding of the game. The world was filled with bureaucrats so obsessed with one tiny screw that, if left to their own devices, their profound incompetence and tunnel vision would allow the whole machine to fall to pieces for the sake of one stupid screw.

Yakovich had also had enough. As head of Yugoslav intelligence, he thought he deserved more respect than this. "My patience is at an end, Kurnov, and this is a prime, exact example of why you must remove this player from the game. He has no concept of—or respect for—the rules, and I am tired of your constant delaying tactics. I demand he be terminated immediately."

"Happily and immediately I will do so, my friend, but first you must answer two questions for me." Kurnov grinned and leaned back in the rich brown leather chair.

"What can I tell you?" asked a confused Yakovich.

"Just answer two small questions, please." Kurnov leaned forward and jabbed his finger under the Slav's nose. "Just when did I die, and who the hell made you the KGB's special operations section chief?

"Alexi, you are an ignorant fool. There is a much bigger picture here, and as I am the KGB's special operations section chief, it is my responsibility and my responsibility alone to wield the palette. Beaucroix will be terminated, but only when the time is perfect and correct and not one second before.

"As I see it, Alexi, you play only one of two parts in this play. You can either exit through that door, or you can leave through that window!" Kurnov indicated first the faded oak door and then motioned toward the seventh-story window. "Either way, comrade, I want your arrogant, pompous ass out of my face immediately. I have a great deal of work to do!"

Kurnov snatched his briefcase off the floor and slapped it upon the desk with fury. He opened it and tossed through the coded papers. He had urgent need of a telephone number. The time had come to phone Max George in Africa.

Confused, ignored, frustrated, and thoroughly dismissed, Director Alexi Yakovich skulked quietly away. He would choose the faded oak door.

CHAPTER TWENTY TWO
The Great Groundhog Day Cleanup

February 2, 1984
Bopolu, Liberia

With a start, Dr. Oliver Tindal opened his eyes just in time to see the Tommy gun pass under the mosquito net and settle against his throat. A hand abruptly clamped over his mouth as the .45-caliber cold steel barrel pushed against his windpipe.

In a whisper, Kendal began. "Doctor, this is Kendal, and we're into some real serious business. I'm going to pull away my hand, but you mustn't talk for any reason. I'll do all the talking. Do you understand?"

The doctor nodded, and Kendal removed his hand and the cold steel.

Two weeks ago, Kendal had been recalled from Central America and told to report back to Bopolu to take over; he wasn't told why. Without explanation, Robert Hogan suddenly had been removed from his position of managing the camp's affairs and had returned to his Congo estate.

"Something bad is happening, because there are a lot of soldiers outside—way too many soldiers. Maybe we've been double-crossed. It's very important that you do everything I say without question. I'm going outside to check this out. No matter what happens, don't leave this room. And for God's sake, don't get curious and look out the window!"

Kendal cautiously worked his way across the room. Crouching as low as possible, he headed to the back window.

"You're leaving me here to die," Tindal whispered in a tone flavored with fear.

Kendal turned and crawled back to the cane bed. "I'm an American, and I'm CIA. It's my job to protect you. Failing that, it's my job to die covering your escape. You'll survive because it's *my* job to make sure you survive. Now, for God's sake, shut the fuck up and let me do my damn job." With this he turned, headed to the window, and, hoisting himself through it, he jumped out and dropped into the slurping mud.

Moving low along the veranda, Kendal worked his way around the side of hut and into the edge of the clearing. He deftly slipped under the large fern at the northwest corner of the house, almost slamming the fifty-round drum of the Thompson across the back of a bull snake.

With the instant reflexes of a survivor, he dropped the Tommy gun and brought his left hand down, grabbing the neck of the serpent barely a life-span short of those venomous fangs. Skillfully rolling onto his back with the snake still in hand, he slashed once with his Buck knife, beheading the serpent, and hurled its head toward the house. The spy then tossed the impotent, headless body away as it blindly wiggled its requiem upon the African duff.

Kendal now was able to silently crawl the remaining five meters under the low but concealing brush to where he could see most of the clearing and all of the buildings. He clearly made out five jeeps, and the fact that the troops hadn't dismounted was a serious reason for concern.

Against the dull glow of the jungle-filtered moon, the second jeep revealed a large silhouette in the passenger seat. This, he deduced, must be General Kutu, and if it was, this must be betrayal in a *very* big way.

The backs of the jeeps themselves looked funny in the dim jungle light. Instead of four soldiers sitting, each held two men who were apparently standing.

Then, like a charging avalanche, it struck Kendal square in the face. This was an assassination squad. In the back of each jeep, the dim light revealed the silhouette of a fifty-caliber Browning M2 machine gun, belt fed and pedestal mounted to the hard bed. The fifty-caliber BMG was the deadliest of John M. Browning's many contributions to the American war machine.

General Kutu had positioned all five jeeps facing his own barracks. He clearly was planning to kill his own men. Given the fact that he seemingly wasn't disposed to assaulting Kendal's hut or the doctor's hut, Kendal believed—temporarily, at least—that Kutu did not intend to kill him or Tindal. He would watch and wait.

More than two hours passed before the sharp light of morning began to slice a glorious path through the treetops, and, during that time, not one soldier had talked or moved. Even General Kutu, who was normally more talkative than a jaybird, sat silently in his jeep.

"General, what's going on here?" Lieutenant Howa inquired as he appeared from the east jungle trail and entered the central compound.

Jumping over the spare ammo canister, Private Benes, in the fourth jeep, swung the machine gun around and over the rear of the vehicle. Squashing the butterfly with both thumbs, he brought the Browning roaring to life, sending a tongue of flame and hot lead that disembow-eled the lieutenant in less than four seconds and sent the bloody, bullet-riddled mess crashing to the dust.

"Fire, you stupid idiots!" General Kutu screamed.

The soldiers looked at what remained of Howa and then at one another, collectively and completely confused. *Fire at what?* they thought.

Kutu clapped his hands and stood up in his jeep so as to give his men the full benefit of his awesome presence. Like a comedian, he smiled and placed his hat against his heart. Then he bowed and extended his left hand toward the barracks.

The soldiers were still confused. They turned their BMGs toward the barracks and looked blankly at Kutu. The soldiers inside the barracks had now armed themselves and were peeking through the windows to try to piece together what was going on. Never would they even consider firing upon their own general.

The lieutenant often had deserted at night to find a little social com-fort in a small native town about five kilometers away. The general obvi-ously must have warned the lieutenant about his actions in the past. As he had ignored the warning, the soldiers in the barracks assumed he had been rightly killed for desertion, with Kutu having caught him in the act of trying to sneak back into the compound.

"Well?" Kutu yelled, clearly furious and still extending his right hand toward the barracks. But his anger was poorly heard; it was drowned out completely by the sound of five machine guns roaring mightily to life, opposed only by grass, wood, and nine young soldiers who'd never again return home.

The five machine guns spat hundreds of 650-grain, metal-cased bullets into the ramshackle barracks. Within fifty seconds, there was no longer any sign of life from within the structure. The fusillade had driven the soldiers' bodies backward, pulverizing some and fairly disintegrating others. Kutu's soldiers kept their thumbs on the butterflies, knowing they must continue to fire until their ammo cans were empty, lest they too gain the general's displeasure.

Finally, the last smoking Browning clattered to a halt. The air was thick with the smell of gunpowder as the cloud of smoke slowly drifted off into the hungry jungle.

Kutu grinned and jumped agilely from his jeep, an amazing task for such a rotund man. He grinned even wider as he ran his gaze around the compound and walked in an absent-minded circle around the jeep, surveying all points within the compound, then grinning yet even more broadly. He paused as he faced Tindal's hut. This was truly a lot of fun!

"Come out, Kendal. Those bushes can't be that interesting," the general sang out with good humor. He had smelled Kendal from a full seventy feet away.

Still cradling the Thompson at the ready, Kendal stood and walked cautiously toward Kutu. The general's men were emptying five-gallon cans of petrol on the pulverized barracks.

"OK, general, what's going on here?" Kendal demanded as he cast his eyes to the right, noticing that three of Kutu's men were walking Dr. Emerson and Dr. Whitehead at gunpoint into the jungle.

"Relax, relax, my friend," the general happily said as he reached out to pat Kendal on the shoulder. Kendal took a few steps back, unwilling to take a chance at being disarmed.

Hurt by this affront to his gentle demeanor, Kutu pointed to the burning barracks. "These stupid monkey men were dirt, and they were bad soldiers. We're closing this base by orders of your president. We had to burn these buildings to protect your country's security." He motioned for Kendal to step closer; instead, Kendal backed up another half step.

"Look," the general continued, "I tried to reason with them, but when I told them they must leave Bopolu, they began firing. They forced me to fire to defend my men. I had to defend my personal staff."

Kendal looked blankly at Kutu. *Is this man an idiot?* Had Kutu forgotten he had found Kendal hiding in the bushes, watching the whole murderous affair?

By this time, Tindal had emerged from his hut and was approaching across the central clearing; Kendal spotted him immediately.

"Back! Get back to your hut, Doctor! I told you to stay in your hut!" Kendal swung the chopper back and forth, unsure sure what was really happening or who the enemy really was.

"No, no, Doctor. Come right in and join us," General Kutu said, beaming.

"What happened here?" Tindal pointed to the blazing barracks. The doctor had chosen the general's invitation and ignored Kendal, whom he viewed as an alarmist.

"Oh, we had a little accident. Some rebels came out of the jungle, but my brave men chased them off. Everything's OK now." General Kutu waved the doctor's question away.

The doc looked around and briefly wondered why Kendal was swinging his tommy gun around; someone might get hurt. Then, suddenly he realized he didn't recognize any of these soldiers.

"What happened to our guards?" Tindal asked as he stared at the burning barracks.

The general paused as he authored a clever story. "Oh, the rebels got them—my poor, poor men. They fought bravely, so their widows will get fifteen dollars and a medal for their husbands' courage."

Just then, in a trail of dust, Beaucroix and his driver roared into camp. The driver slammed on the brakes, bringing the jeep to a sliding halt. Beaucroix was upset he had missed the fun. Ignoring everyone else, he took giant strides directly toward Kendal, who was preparing to bring the Thompson roaring to life. Beaucroix stopped three feet from Kendal and squarely faced him off.

"You're wanted in Miami by Hampstead, and you're wanted immediately. You've been reassigned. These are Hampstead's direct orders!" Beaucroix growled.

Kendal wasn't going anywhere; either the general's men were going to kill him, or Beaucroix planned to shoot him in the back.

"Take my jeep," Beaucroix offered.

That was it. The jeep had been booby-trapped.

"I think I'll take the general's jeep," Kendal stated as he moved sideways toward the jeep, careful to keep his surroundings covered with the cold steel he waved before him.

"Do as you please," replied Beaucroix courteously and far too casually. The general had begun to voice his protest, but Beaucroix waved for him to remain silent.

Kendal mounted the jeep, and, pushing the starter button, he sent the motor to life. After placing the vehicle in gear, he spun the steering wheel as he floored the gas and, popping the clutch, sent the jeep flying out of the clearing and down the trail toward the fertile coast of Liberia.

After about a kilometer, he left the road by turning right onto a game trail. Then he stopped the jeep, dismounted, and searched the back of the vehicle. Two soldiers had left packs filled with rations. Smiling, he shouldered both and began his long walk to the sea.

Beaucroix had let him leave and let him choose a jeep, and that meant one thing: the danger and the trap were on the long trail that led to the sea. He could have taken the jeep across game trails; there were many of them, and most eventually went to the coast. But these might be watched, and a jeep was too large a target and too easy to see. A man on foot, however, could carefully slip through such traps unnoticed.

Back at the compound, Beaucroix glanced at Kutu. Knowingly, the general backed slowly away and motioned his men off far to the right. Tindal didn't notice and didn't care; he was glad to get out of there—glad to be going back to the States, where he could publish his results and cash in on his great adventure. To hell with the CIA, to hell with Africa, and Beaucroix could go to the devil. Tindal would be rich.

"It's time to go!" Beaucroix sang as Tindal turned toward the jeep, but Beaucroix hadn't moved. Tindal thought the Monster must want to play one more game.

"Well, are we leaving?" Tindal inquired.

"Yup, we're leaving," Beaucroix replied, still not moving.

"Well?" Tindal motioned toward the jeep.

"Aren't you going to ask me where we're going? Aren't you curious?" the spy asked as he tilted his head and lifted his right eyebrow.

"OK. Where are we going, Mr. Beaucroix?" Tindal decided to play the game. He had to if they were ever to get going.

Suddenly Beaucroix seemed to lose interest as he produced and lit a Camel cigarette. He slowly blew three perfect smoke rings and sent them climbing lazily upward through the humid morning air. He removed his brush hat and scratched his thick sandy-blond hair, seemingly trying to recall some small detail.

"I'm going to Cairo," Beaucroix announced, returning his hat to its proper place and carefully adjusting it. "And you are going to hell!" The Monster whipped out his Walther PPK pistol and, firing, shattered Tindal's right kneecap, sending the screaming doctor collapsing to the dust of Bopolu.

"Damn you, you dirty little sissy bastard!" Beaucroix shouted, and sent another pistol round into Tindal's left foot, causing him to shriek in pain and sending the birds of Bopolu scattering to the four corners of Africa to seek quieter abodes.

"So you think you're better than everyone? Better than me?" The Monster fired again, breaking Tindal's right elbow. The doctor was screaming so loudly that he fairly drowned out the bark of gunfire. "You and your fucking degree—you think that degree makes you better than me, don't you?" Beaucroix fired again, cleanly removing Tindal's right thumb. "Bastard!" the Monster screamed as he blew open Tindal's left hand.

Beaucroix was now completely out of control and becoming more deranged with each round. "You rich twit! You asshole! Why didn't anybody ever help *me*?" In a rage the Monster fired again, shattering Tindal's right thighbone. The Monster was now totally invisible to Tindal, who was surrounded by a fog of terror and blinding pain.

"Well, you wanted to go, asshole, so *go!*" Beaucroix screamed as he fired again, smashing through Tindal's skull and leaving his wonderful brain freely displayed to the gods of Bopolu. The monkeys jumped up and down in fury, chattering wildly in the tall, bird-barren trees that surrounded the central compound.

The Walther pistol had run out of ammo, and the slide was locked open. Beaucroix stood breathing heavily. Still filled with rage, he surveyed the compound. Kutu's men stood frozen as they watched this spectacle, shocked that any European could be so cruel. Beaucroix glanced at General Kutu, who was grinning broadly. The general never had seen such a good show in his life, and he was sorry to see it end.

The Monster turned to the soldiers, who were getting ready to run. Panting heavily, Beaucroix turned again to Kutu. The general had now stopped smiling and suddenly became very afraid; he began to count his options.

Looking Kutu in the eyes, Beaucroix pointed to what remained of Dr. Oliver Tindal. Kutu's hand began to slowly work its way down to his ivory-handled revolver.

"He forgot to say please," explained Beaucroix, who was no longer furious.

Kutu broke out laughing, and Beaucroix joined him as both monsters roared together. They were laughing so loudly that they almost fell to the ground in their joyful hysterics.

By now the soldiers were completely terrified. They could no longer identify which one was the greater monster, as one animal now appeared much the same as the other. For a full three minutes, the orgy of laughter continued until Beaucroix remembered the payoff and remembered the other reason he had come to Bopolu today.

The presidential order was not to close the Wildfire project, nor was it to close the base at Bopolu. The presidential order was for the CIA to erase any evidence—or trace of evidence—that they ever had existed at all.

Many involved could be killed: men like Tindal, the base guards, and the rest of the staff, who had been walked into the jungle to be executed.

Of the agents involved, men like Beaucroix, Hogan, and George were too valuable to kill. Even so, their knowledge of Wildfire made them a risk, which meant they were too dangerous to go free. They must remain in the agency, where they could be watched for the rest of their lives. For men who held such secrets, the CIA offered only two retirement plans: the choice of a steady, well-paying job or a fine, comfortably cool grave in which to rethink one's choices.

Having exhausted his laughter, Beaucroix remembered his mission as he fished in his pocket for a new clip, popped it into the warm pistol, and sent the slide snapping forward. Satisfied, he holstered the weapon. It was time to move on.

When the CIA closed such operations, sometimes others were involved who had possible future use and possessed less knowledge or believability. Such persons were frequently bought off with large sums of money. General Kutu certainly matched the criteria: possible future use and very little believability.

Emile Beaucroix walked over to his jeep and grabbed a heavy suitcase from the passenger seat. He had signed for this shit, and he wanted it where he could protect it. Through the drifting smoke, he headed across the compound toward Tindal's hut with General Kutu hot on his trail and following the suitcase. The general was grinning like a hungry puppy or a horny dog. He knew what the suitcase contained: the price of his silence and the price of his men's lives.

When Beaucroix gained the veranda, he paused to kick the door next to the hinges and shattered it. He knew Tindal had never locked it, but he enjoyed hurting things, even things with no soul. Beaucroix knew everything about his victims because it made killing them so much more fun. He entered Tindal's hut with the fat, greed-horny general trailing him.

But with Bopolu closing and Beaucroix leaving Africa, the general was in a precarious position. Damn the CIA; he was no longer necessary to Emile Beaucroix. As they reached the doctor's desk, Beaucroix swept his left arm across it, spitefully launching everything covering it to the floor. Kutu beamed broadly; he really liked men with balls, men like him, who feared absolutely nothing.

Beaucroix placed the suitcase on the clean desk and quickly popped the latches to reveal the serious, dour faces of one hundred thousand dead American presidents.

Kutu grinned as he touched the sacred Yankee dollars. "God, my friend, my wives will be so happy!" He lovingly caressed the bills on top, itchy to count the money. "I am so grateful! You are my best and dearest friend. I love you!" He gave Beaucroix an affectionate hug and then turned as he happily flipped through the stacks, searching for any small bills that might have been used deceitfully to fatten the stacks.

The Monster was in shock, frozen, and furious beyond reason. Had a man just said he loved him? Had the general just hugged him?

"You faggot!" Beaucroix exploded as he shouted with fury and five flavors of rage. "Nobody ever touches me!" he screamed and then whipped out the still-warm Walther and jammed it into Kutu's ample gut. He worked the trigger and fired the first round into Kutu's fat belly, driving his body backward with an involuntary spastic jerk, and sending its contents spattering to the floor. The money and the briefcase were now painted with blood and tissue as Beaucroix rapidly advanced, pulled by rage.

The Monster smiled and advanced some more, pushing Kutu toward the wall as he drove the pistol deeper into the general's gut and fired again with a blast that pushed Kutu even closer to the wall. With each shot, the Monster grinned wider and wider as he advanced, still shoving the pistol into Kutu's gut as he fired again and again and pushed Kutu into the matted wall, and with a metallic clack, the slide locked open and the Walther stood empty as Kutu's dead body fell with a thick, dull thud to the plywood floor.

Grinning with unrestrained delight, Beaucroix surveyed the bloody mess on the dusty floor with satisfaction. The Monster then popped in a fresh magazine and pocketed the pistol as he looked down with glowing satisfaction at what remained of General Kutu. He smiled even wider as he shook his head, shrugged, and casually headed for the door. One could never have too much fun!

February 22, 1984
Paris, France

"Tinker, tailor, soldier, spy, cross the line, and you shall die. But follow orders and obey, and rich you will retire someday!" Kurnov grinned as he snapped his fingers for the waiter and helped himself to a chair opposite the fat man. It was a beautiful day in Paris and a beautiful day to be alive.

"Clever ditty, Kurnov. Did you learn it in kindergarten?" The fat man grinned. He knew Kurnov had picked up this clever little piece from the CIA.

The Shadow had seen Kurnov across the room and divined that he wanted to speak. He saw no reason to stare him into the table.

"I didn't learn it in kindergarten. It's what they teach you spies in CIA spy school!" Kurnov raised his right eyebrow in feigned surprise.

"You surprise me, Kurnov. I thought you were a brilliant man." The fat man was mildly disappointed. He had hoped his confidence in Kurnov's abilities wasn't misplaced. "Surely you've had time to check me out. You know I'm not with the CIA. I'm no spy."

"That's right. You are my shadow!" Kurnov grinned as the tall waiter swiftly approached and rushed to attend. He was embarrassed that he had missed the spymaster's approach.

Rule one for waiters: You must attend!

"Good afternoon, monsieur. May I tell you about our delightful daily special?" The waiter smiled as the maître d' scowled from the shadows, irritated that the waiter hadn't spied Kurnov sooner.

"I would love to hear about your daily special." Kurnov turned and winked at the fat man. "You can tell me all about it after I order what I really want to eat. How is the duck today?" The Russian raised a questioning eyebrow.

"The duck, monsieur, is as tender as a newborn baby's bottom, and the skin is a golden brown and so crispy I cannot even describe it." The impeccably dressed waiter put two fingers to his lips and smacked them in absolute ecstasy.

"Fine. I will have that. Now go away. We do not wish to be disturbed!" Kurnov waited for the waiter to depart. The garçon nodded and scurried away.

The maître d' started to approach the table to offer his apologies. But when the waiter shook his head as he passed him on his way to the kitchen, the maître d' quietly retreated to his station.

"That's right! I had forgotten." Kurnov shook his finger at the big man. "You're no spy—you're my shadow. I remember now it's what you told me in Moscow when you broke into my headquarters!" Kurnov grinned, poking fun at the man.

"Come, come, Kurnov. I'm not with the CIA, and I'm not your shadow either." The fat man began his assault on the delicious crepes suzette.

"Then enlighten me and the rest of the KGB. Just whose shadow are you?" Kurnov leaned forward a little to emphasize the question.

"Evil…I am *evil's* shadow." The fat man grinned and chuckled to himself; it was an inside joke.

"I doubt it." Frowning, Kurnov leaned back as he puzzled the answer. "I would never take you for an evil man, and I am a stupendous judge of character. It's what keeps me alive!"

"I didn't say *I* was evil. Evil exists in the shadows. I exist in the shadows of the shadows. I'm the hunter. I hunt evil—evil may not fear God, but surely it fears me, because I get in its face. When evil turns, I'm there. It lunges at me, but I can't be touched. It chases me, but I can't be caught."

"Whom do you really work for?" Kurnov leaned back a little in his chair, regarding the big man with more than a little interest.

"I work for the American people, and I work to preserve American ideals!" the Shadow said with a smile.

"You're not with the FBI. The FBI always informs foreign governments before they involve themselves in any action overseas. If you worked for the FBI, I would know. Because just as quickly as the FBI informs foreign governments, I can tell you those governments surely inform me. Either you work for the CIA"—Kurnov smiled and shook his finger under the fat man's nose—"or you're insane and working alone, for motives known only to your imagination!" Kurnov slapped the table.

"I'm not with the CIA, Kurnov, and I'm not insane. If I were insane, I would've been invited to join this Wildfire mess. Politics in America is a lot more complicated than you think. There's more than one thought and more than one mind in America. Lately, the gap between American ideals and American government has been pushed apart by a few criminals in positions of power so that's it wider than the Grand Canyon.

"The American people, comrade, are better than the American government, and they want America to return to American ideals. I work for those few men in government who want America to return to American ideals."

"Then you work for the president of the United States?" Kurnov wondered just how much power the power players had.

"No, the president doesn't even know I exist!" The fat man wiped a bit of the delicious sauce off his chin with a crisp linen napkin.

"Then what is your purpose, my friend?" Kurnov inquired.

"My purpose is to save the world!" the Shadow replied in all seriousness as he placed his now-folded napkin on the table.

"I see." Apparently Fidel Castro's revelations were a good way north of pure speculation, perhaps even farther north than even Kurnov suspected. In a big way, Slava Kurnov would be drawn much deeper into the game.

February 23, 1984
Washington, DC

"What do you know about Nicaragua?" The president, having finished wading through the introductions, was ready to get down to business.

"Not a lot. I've been in Africa for some time." Kendal was completely taken by surprise. He wished Hampstead weren't so secretive all the time. Kendal should have been briefed in advance so he wouldn't appear so stupid in front of the president.

"We have a plan to defeat communism in Central America, and Nicaragua is central to that plan. Director Hampstead has offered your services behind the scenes to assist in the execution of this enterprise. Now, please continue, Mr. Hampstead," the president urged.

"I think the first step would be for your people, Mr. President, to quietly talk with some of the governments between here and Nicaragua. I need to know what kind of unofficial cooperation we can expect. The advisors will need staging areas, training areas, and access to logistics. We'll need a secure, protected air base." Hampstead could do all of this himself, but he liked to leave the boring, easy stuff to other governmental powers.

"I think we can take care of that. Mr. Weinberger?" The president turned to the secretary of defense.

"I'll get on it immediately." Weinberger grunted as he gathered his notes.

"Good! Now, Mr. Hampstead, what do you think we need to make this operation a success?" The president pushed forward; this covert little Contra war would be his baby.

"It's going to take a lot of money. More money than we can hide in the CIA budget." Hampstead wanted all the money he could get because he hated commies; he would enjoy snuffing a few out.

"What's your opinion, Casper?" the president asked as he turned to the secretary of defense. "Where could we find the money?"

Casper Weinberger shuffled through his notes. He was something less than an innovator and hoped a slight delay would prompt the president to look to someone else. The president searched the room, hoping someone—anyone—would volunteer some useful advice.

"What about the army, Mr. President? How much help can we expect from them?" Hampstead wanted his players to do the intelligence-related killing; for situations that required American operatives to die, he liked to use someone else.

"None. You will have no help from the army. We can't afford to take the chance that the Senate will find out. They audit the army's budget carefully," Secretary MacLauder interjected.

"That's not entirely true," the cowboy president interrupted, and every face in the room turned to hear his genius. "If you can give me a plan and *prove to me* that you can destroy communism in Nicaragua without creating a political fiasco here, then I can do this for you. I can request and obtain a couple of experienced and capable US Army or Marine Corps officers to be assigned to the White House. I'll then place them at your disposal, Hampstead. No one but me will know their true purpose. Is that acceptable?"

"That is very acceptable, Mr. President." Hampstead shot his eyes toward the door to ensure no one would enter undetected. That left only the question of money.

"Just one more thing, Kendal." The president suddenly flashed as red as a Macintosh apple. *"If you ever refer to my son as a ballerina again, I will personally kill you!* He's more of a man than you could ever hope to be. He works for *Playboy* magazine, and he photographs naked women for a living, for God's sake. What kind of a homo would do that! Now, you tell me, you little asshole—how could a faggot do that?"

"I truly apologize for what you might have heard, Mr. President. Perhaps something I said was misquoted or taken out of context. If so, I offer my full, unconditioned apologies," Kendal meekly replied, his eyes theatrically downcast.

Kendal had apologized, but *hell no*, he didn't mean it. To a spy, any politician—even a president—was nothing more than a turd no one would let you pick up and dispose of. You just sort of had to work around it. A president, to the CIA, was like that resident turd. It was something you really didn't like and didn't want to step on either.

The president nodded, grunted, and turned away.

It was true, Kendal thought, what the president had said. Kendal could never photograph naked women for a living because he'd be too distracted, fascinated, and far too excited to get it right. To photograph naked women and to be really, really good at it and to create the type of perfectly posed, sensuous photos that excite other men and make publishers rich, one would have to be queer.

February 23, 1984
Peshawar, Pakistan

Looking across the crowded tearoom, the Russian smiled; he wasn't nearly the idiot Kurnov considered him to be. The master spy had intimidated Sergei Makinov, and that was all there was to that; he was neither an incompetent nor a fool.

His sudden transfer to the embassy in Islamabad was certainly a punishment for his incompetence in dealing with the Shadow. But his unique skills had led him here, to this place, and he was hard on the trail to redemption. He lowered his eyes as Robert Hogan entered from the bustling Pakistani street.

"Why do you deal with these infidels and dogs?" Mustafa Al-Habib asked the sheik.

"Because the Russians are much bigger dogs, and to fight them, we need guns—money buys guns. When you are at war, the devil's gold spends as well as any other. Now go!" The sheik had just noticed the American entering the dimly lit tearoom.

Hogan quickly spotted the dark, piercing hawk eyes beneath the perfectly twisted turban of the tall man seated in the shadows. He knew at once this was his contact, Hampstead's reason for sending him to Pakistan. He recorded with interest the man who had left the sheik's table in far too much of a hurry.

"Please be seated. You must have tea." The Arab gestured toward a seat for Hogan and poured tea into a small cup and then half filled it with sugar. "Arabs always sugar their guests' tea for them, and you can mark the measure of your welcome by the amount of sugar your host places in your cup. You my, friend, Allah and I both welcome." The sheik smiled as he passed the cup to Hogan and with his hand indicated a blessing.

Hogan removed two coronas from his vest and offered one to the Arab, who politely waved it away.

"I'm a bit confused, Sheik. I was sent all the way from Washington to meet with the Afghan Mujahideen, and here I sit in Pakistan talking to a Saudi." Hogan leaned back as he underplayed his hand.

"I am a Saudi and of noble blood. Honesty is good ground on which to build the tower of trust. But you are not from Washington. You came to me from Liberia, so you have been less than honest." The Saudi smiled as he rubbed his chin.

"Then you have ears in Africa, Sheik. I am impressed!" Hogan hoped flattery might garner unexpected information.

"I do, but that is not where my information came from. I have ears in the KBG." The sheik pointed to the side of his head, indicating that intelligence was the surest way to acquire intelligence.

"Then you've planted a man in Kabul with the KGB? I think maybe we can do business." Hogan grinned.

"Not Kabul." The Arab smiled back.

"Really?" Hogan feigned surprise, hoping the Arab's pride and obvious ego would cause him to expand on this possibly useful information.

The sheik motioned for Hogan to lean closer. "We have someone in Moscow, in the KGB office of Slava Kurnov!" He pointed again to the side of his head and nodded.

Across the room, Sergei Makinov almost bolted. But quickly he gained his composure as he pretended to lean over his tea while inclining his ear to gain a sharper earshot of the information that may yet light the path to his redemption.

"That's impressive but not impressive enough for me to give millions of dollars to a Saudi when I was told I was meeting with the Mujahidin." Hogan started to rise, to end this chase of two-headed horses. The man was clearly a liar; no one could infiltrate the headquarters of the KGB. The CIA had tried and failed, many, many times.

Hampstead had led him to believe this meeting would change the fortunes of Russia in Afghanistan. It had been a wasted trip.

"The Mujahidin will follow me. I am their leader. You want Russians dead; we want to kill Russians. I can please Allah, and you can please your God. The Russian dogs are godless—we can both win. You only need to give me the money to kill them." The Arab folded his hands in blessing.

"What would I get for my money, another blessing?" Raising an eyebrow, Hogan had sat back down and now leaned forward.

"You want the Russians dead, yet you offer only money. We offer you blood, *our* blood. We are offering the United States a bargain you cannot afford to resist!" The sheik smiled again.

"Tell me, Sheik: why would a people as clannish and suspicious as the Afghans follow a Saudi?" Kicking the Russians out of Afghanistan was certainly worth more than ten million dollars, but it was way too much damn money to pay for one small pair of unproven ears inside the KGB.

"The Mujahidin—they would follow me. All of them would follow me!" The sheik placed his index finger to his temple.

"Why?" Hogan asked again. Why should he believe this Saudi had a dog in this fight or any followers?

"I can give them victory. That's why they would follow me!" The Arab again placed his right finger to his head, pointing to his wondrous, self-appreciated, ego-pure genius.

"You have to give me a better reason than that if you want this money." Hogan was ready to walk; he wanted to get back to Africa. Besides, he was horny as hell and needed to get some tail.

"They would follow me for many reasons." The sheik looked casually around the room.

"Give me one reason, one ten-million-dollar reason why I should give you this money."

The sheik scratched his beard in contemplation. Looking down at his dusty sandals, he was struck by the obvious answer to Hogan's question. He leaned abruptly forward as he smiled broadly and pointed to accentuate his reply as he pierced Hogan with a hawkish, self-certain, and confident glare.

"The Mujahidin need only one reason." The Saudi pointed proudly to his chest. "They would follow me because I am Osama bin Laden!"

CHAPTER TWENTY THREE
Dealing from the Bottom of the Deck

March 1, 1984
Hogan's House in the Congo

The great thing about working for the CIA was that you got to keep the incidentals, like the money you happened upon. Some men, as a cover, spent their whole CIA life as a *plant*, working a boring job for a seemingly legitimate company charged with nothing more exciting than to watch, listen, and take notes. Other agents, the lucky ones, were set up with a front. But all of them were allowed to keep the pay from their employer or some of the profits they made through their cover. It often supplemented their CIA checks rather handsomely.

Hogan's cover was being an expatriate arms dealer. To make his cover stick, he never quite said where he was an expatriate from. As an arms dealer, he was free to be seen with the scum of the earth, as well as any and every intelligence agency he chose, and it never raised an iota of suspicion.

That was what the agency got out of it—a superb deep-cover operative who could travel anywhere and always be under suspicion for something other than what he was. He could be suspected of being a cheat, a crook, and a double dealer, but never an operative. British intelligence could have a photograph of him shaking hands with President Ronald Reagan and never suspect Hogan of being a spy.

What Hogan got out of the deal was money and power, and more money. He was good at selling arms, and the agency had quickly learned the advantages of having a legitimate arms dealer who could move large amounts of arms to precisely the right places at the right time, without so much as one senatorial "Please, may I?" With the huge markups in the arms trade, the agency always recovered its cost, plus a sizable cash pool for expenses that couldn't (wouldn't) be reconciled—and Hogan happily got to keep the rest.

Arms dealing gave four great weapons to the CIA in the Cold War years.

One: It gave them a presence in all the wrong circles (however, the right circles for intelligence work).

Two: It gave them the ability to support military causes in numerous spots without official US government sanction (or, frequently, knowledge).

Three: Arms deals made a superb trap for those annoying little people you could get nothing else on.

Four: It made them a lot of money to spend on things the Senate thought they shouldn't.

Yes, thought Hogan, it worked out very well for everyone involved.

Hogan didn't have to turn in many claims for hotel bills because this huge Congo estate was his. He had paid for it in cash after only eight months as an arms dealer. Hogan had bought the estate in 1960 from a Belgian arms dealer who was cashing in on a bad heart. It was a double-walled estate with a guardhouse at the main gate and surrounded by eight-foot-high walls.

The main house was a magnificent building, built by that man in 1933 when Africa was still a great adventure. It was a wonderful masterpiece of old colonial European craftsmanship and was elevated somewhat to allow the upper levels a stupendous view of the Congo River, which lazily flowed below.

One of the best things the Belgian had thrown into the deal was his gardener, a terrified little man named Kurt Grostaldt. True, the man had been a Nazi, but then, everyone was in the Germany of the 1930s. You had little choice—you were either a Nazi, or you suffered the consequences; you either went with the flow or were drowned by the tide. Kurt had been a simple clerk, a paper-stamping nobody on Reichsfuhrer Heinrich Himmler's staff, and the Israelis had him branded as one of the

Holocaust's masterminds. Hogan had checked out his past and knew the man really was no more than a Nazi clerk. The only thing the poor man really had done for Nazi Germany was to show up for work on time.

Hogan, better than most, knew how it felt to be watched, followed, hounded, and tracked, and he didn't like it. So he got the man a new identity and an invented past. By calling in a few old favors, Hogan was able to get Kurt a decent-paying job in Nairobi booking safaris and greeting arrivals for four different tourist outfits; he thought that was the end of it. But Kurt the gardener wasn't exactly the good part of the deal. The really good part of the deal was who came knocking on his door in 1982 as payback for his unsolicited kindness.

Nearly Two Years Earlier; April 1, 1982
The Congo

Hogan was relaxing on the veranda when the guard walked up to inform him that a Mr. and Mrs. Gerber were at the gate with a private message for him. After asking a few questions and gaining a general description from the tall African, he directed the guard to bring in the message and to detain the couple at the gate.

The letter, he noted with surprise, was from Kurt Grostaldt. Three pages long, it detailed how happy he was and recounted every good thing that had happened to him. It seemed the only sentences in the letter that didn't thank Hogan, praised Hogan. Kurt ended the letter by introducing his daughter Tilde and son-in-law Walter and stating that he had sent them to work for Hogan to manage the huge house and expansive grounds. He closed by saying they would stay no matter what Hogan chose to pay them, even nothing, because he owed everything to Hogan, and his children were all he had to give.

Hogan sent the guard back to the gate to fetch the couple and bring them into the large study. He would thank them sincerely for the offer, give them a couple of C-notes, and send them on their way. He had just poured the last of the three schnapps when the guard ushered Kurt's relations into the room. Hogan was immediately impressed by the imposing presence of Tilde. She was no more than twenty years old, but she had that tall, square, Prussian build and a demeanor that commanded respect and obedience. If he had wanted a housekeeper, this was certainly what the doctor would have ordered.

Walter was a fine specimen also. At six foot two or three inches tall, he weighed perhaps 195 pounds. He had an easy smile and an honest face. Walter also displayed many of the admirable traits Germans were known for. He seemed polite and obedient, and, judging by his chest and arms, he was a man who understood what a good day's work was all about.

After pleasantries were exchanged, Hogan placed his hands on their shoulders and guided them into the two huge overstuffed leather chairs set by the great hearth. Softly he began. "I really have no use for a staff. The house might look large, but I actually use very little of it. Three times a week, two women come up from the village and clean it from top to bottom. Even then, it rarely takes them more than two hours. Please thank your father for me and tell him I'm quite fine living here alone."

Walter spoke up. "Sir, since you are a businessman, there must certainly have been times when it was inconvenient to have those village women around." He looked to Hogan for encouragement before he continued. "You know, sometimes silly native women imagine things to have happened that really didn't occur. Now, my wife never forgets to make the beds or cook the food, but when it comes to remembering faces, we both have terrible memories."

Hogan smiled as Walter went on. "There is more, I think, that you should know. When Tilde or I hear a conversation in English, we have a problem later if asked to repeat it, as we frequently cannot remember a word since it is not our native tongue."

Hogan really liked this man, and he had a point. There had been situations when locals had been in a position to see or hear things that might later have returned to haunt him. He especially liked the part about their *native tongue*. These two Germans had been raised in British East Africa and spoke perfect English. Hogan was sure he would regret having to turn down this offer, but sometimes things just had to stay the way they were, and that was that.

Tilde now broke in. "Walter is an excellent mechanic, and he is the only driver to take you into the jungle. More than this, he is an excellent bushman. Twice he has won the races at M'roya. Where there is a Land Rover and no road, no one can catch him."

Hogan broke her off. "I want you to thank your father for me and tell him he never will know how deeply this has touched me." Hogan really was touched, but he was also a master actor. "Tell him the offer alone is more than enough to repay his debt. I want him to consider that debt paid in full." *There—that was pretty damn good dramatics*, thought Hogan.

Tilde became more stolid. "No, we must stay. My father's debt must be paid. To do less than repay the debt would be less than honorable."

Walter smiled in agreement.

Gosh, Hogan thought. *That's some woman you have there, Walter.*

"I'm truly sorry, but I don't need any help. Tell your father that sometimes an old soldier just needs to be alone. I think he'll understand." *There, that should do it.*

"That won't be possible," Tilde replied with finality.

Hogan lifted his finger as he stood up and stepped toward the writing secretary on the far side of the room. "Then I'll give you a letter to take to him explaining it." But he wasn't destined to gain the hand-rubbed mahogany desk.

"He died," replied Tilde.

This bit of new information froze Hogan in his tracks. Tilde closed her eyes and swallowed as Walter stood and squeezed her shoulders from behind.

"He wrote the letter Monday night, and when we woke up on Tuesday, we found him. You gave him everything, sir. For thirty-nine years, he lived in terror like a hunted rat accused of crimes committed by others—crimes he had no knowledge of and no part of.

"Sir, you allowed him to live like a man. You gave him his life, and now, in poor payment, we give you ours. Neither of us has any relatives left; the war took care of that." She wept openly as she begged. "Please let us honor my father's memory. What more could you ask for than servants who have no interests beyond your walls?"

Damn, thought Hogan. Tilde unfortunately made as much sense as Walter did, and he would have to dance gracefully to get out of this one and avoid hurting either of these people—or the memory of Kurt Grostaldt, for that matter.

Walter had walked over to the open window facing the tall river wall and was staring at something far away. "Do you like buzzards?" he inquired.

Shit, more talk about honoring the dead, Hogan thought.

"I hate the vermin," Hogan said as he walked over to the window, following Walter's gaze. Then he spotted them—three large black African crows sitting atop the river wall about eighty yards from the house.

Walter motioned toward the first gun rack by the door. "Can I use one of these?" He pointed at the assorted military and hunting rifles.

"Help yourself," Hogan replied. Since he was an arms dealer, people were always trying to impress him with their shooting prowess. But few could outshoot Hogan with a rifle, and no rifleman to his knowledge had ever outshot Max George. He watched Walter check the breech on a Mauser.

"They're all loaded, every single one," Hogan said as he watched in amazement as Walter removed a Winchester 1895 from the rack. To do so, he passed by four modern automatics, two custom Mauser rifles with fine Swiss optical scopes, and a mighty Nitro Express in favor of the primitive lever action. This was the very gun Theodore Roosevelt had called his Big Medicine because of the powerful, bone-crushing effectiveness of the .405 Winchester on African lions.

Walter returned to the window, raised the gun, rapidly hammered the lever-action, and fired. In less than four seconds, he had emptied the five rounds in an earth-shaking barrage—a barrage certain to bring the bells of Saint Mary into anyone's ears.

"Nice four-o-five. Teddy Roosevelt's Big Medicine, I believe." Walter smiled broadly.

"Thanks, Walter. You surely know your rifles; as a matter of fact, that exact rifle did belong to President Roosevelt. It was a gift from TR to the father of a man I knew. When his father passed on, he made a gift of this rifle to me for sorting out an old squabble," Hogan replied as he advanced to the window to take the smoking Winchester from Walter's hands. "With all the noise you made, I don't think those damn crows will ever be back."

"I don't think Walter scared them." Tilde pointed across the yard toward the wall.

"What? A deaf elephant couldn't stand that kind of racket." Hogan's eyes followed Tilde's finger and froze as he counted two dead crows in front of the wall. Shit! Hogan had seen three. Two out of three shot and killed that fast was incredible!

"Not bad, kid! You killed two out of three—and greasy fast, too!" Hogan was impressed.

"Sorry. I hit five out of five," Walter politely corrected as he took the Winchester rifle from Hogan's hands and carefully returned the famous gun to its rack.

"There were three, and I count two down. Still, it was damn fine shooting."

"You will find the others behind the wall. I saw them fall, sir," Tilde chimed in.

"You got any children?" Hogan demanded as he planted himself in front of Walter.

"We have none. We are only just married," Walter stammered. He was surprised by the severity of the question.

"It doesn't matter either way," Hogan said. "You'll take the three rooms closest to the front door. They're yours, so do what you want with them. You're hired. I'm going for a walk."

Hogan had to see those crows. Nobody—nobody—could convince him they had been shot from the house, not with that kind of greasy-fast speed. He headed out the door as Walter embraced Tilde. It was the first of a great many embraces they would share in Robert Hogan's great house above the broad and gentle Congo River.

March 1, 1984
Hogan's House in the Congo

Having found a fresh bottle of cognac, Hogan plopped into the overstuffed chair. He had used the secret river entrance to enter the estate. Tilde had gone by boat to Morocco to buy new wool Berber carpets for the house, and Walter was fast occupied on a very special errand for Hogan.

Hogan was totally and delightfully alone. Even the guards at the front gate didn't know the house was occupied, nor would they. Hogan had trained them so well that, without his summons, they wouldn't even approach the house if it exploded. They weren't employed to protect him; they were only employed to deter the curious and to announce visitors.

A man of Hogan's experience knew that only he could protect himself against the caliber of killer who would be set upon him. Guards would only give him more bodies to bury when the fracas was over.

But this was the life. Hogan rubbed his back against the thick burgundy leather of the deep, high-back chair in the game room, much as a bear would rub its side against a favorite tree. He laughed as he realized how childish it must have looked. He was glad he was alone. He yawned, stretched, and then scratched his neck. Life was good; yeah, life was real good.

Tomorrow was the day Hogan had promised himself back in Bopolu in 1963. Tomorrow was the day Max George and Miles Kendal had agreed to meet and to help him plan the murder of Emile Beaucroix. Only now, it would just be Max George joining him through the secret river gate. Kendal had fallen from favor and banished to Guatemala. Miles was on very thin ice, and if he wanted to live, he had to be very careful whom he was seen with. Hogan and George would have to be enough because there was no one else to trust.

Hogan looked with peculiar interest at the massive masonry edifice before him. The soft stone of the fireplace extended from the hearth clear to the ceiling. The heavy jungle hardwood crackled and burned in the fired-brick hearth. The iron grille on the hearth was flanked on each side with a six-foot width of soft Egyptian limestone running floor to ceiling. Tonight, Hogan wondered if perhaps these stones had brothers or sisters on the Egyptian pyramids at Giza.

Closing his eyes, he inhaled deeply and slowly through his nostrils, savoring every flavor and nuance of the warm, log-scented air. He couldn't understand why anyone would want an electric heater. It offered the air a nasty, stale odor and gave any room an unnatural feel. Most of all, though, how could people survive without the wonderful scents and warm feeling generated by a burning log fire?

Hogan felt surely that in ancient times, when mankind had been both smarter and more basic, great wars certainly had been fought over fires. He chuckled to himself. *Yes, log wars,* he thought. The great log war of 4001 BC, which led to the price-fixing of clubs and the two head-clunk law for honeymooners. He laughed inwardly at his ludicrous thoughts. God, things must have been simple back then.

He kicked up his feet on the ottoman as he leaned back in the big chair. He took another sip of warm, delightful Courvoisier XO from the snifter and then set it down on the serving table to his right. He quickly snatched the snifter just as he started to loosen his grip. He raised his head and turned to the right, seeking the offender. Quickly it revealed itself—not Hogan's usual drinking partner, at least not in his own home. He almost had set the snifter directly on top of the loaded Schmeisser submachine gun. He slid the weapon six inches farther away to allow the snifter its rightful and usual place on the side table.

In his castle, Hogan had guns—or gun racks full of guns—in every room, never farther than two seconds from his grasp. As an arms dealer, he had enemies; and, as an arms dealer, he was more than a rich and tempting target for robbers and thieves. But today called for a lot more caution than usual, because today he needed a gun at the ready. Even the thought of plotting to kill Beaucroix made him nervous. The Monster had a way of knowing about these things before they happened, and Hogan had every intention of seeing Beaucroix dead and not vice versa—ergo the Schmeisser and taking no stupid chances.

Between the smoke, the warmth, and the delightful nose of the superb French cognac, Hogan was feeling pretty good. He loved Africa, and he enjoyed his job. He never would quit the CIA; he didn't need to. One of the things people never thought about when they joined the agency was retirement. A spy who stepped out of the cold was a real security risk. After a year or two, you might not know enough about current operations to hurt the agency, but you always had the past. There was always the danger that an ex-spook would spill to the papers. So suicide—slightly assisted suicide—was the number-one cause of death among ex-CIA men.

But Hogan had it dicked because he never had to retire. He would continue as an arms dealer until the day he died, just like the Belgian who had sold him the estate. If the CIA no longer wanted to pay him, that was OK. He would continue to do favors for them and provide them with intelligence, thus assuring himself a long life and hopefully a natural death.

He toasted himself by lifting the brandy snifter high in the air, marveling at the spirits' glint of gold and flashes of fire as the liquid reflected the leaping flames dancing joyfully in the hearth in front of his comfortable chair.

Suddenly, the Irish Waterford glass was shattered with a blast as his hand was knocked forward by the force of the 7.65-mm round as it passed through the glass and into his wrist on the way to the fireplace mantel. Hogan's right hand shook in pain as he turned to face his assailant. But his right hand was now crushed and impotent. Damn, the Schmeisser was sitting on the table to his right side.

"Do you want your gun, Hogan?" Beaucroix had moved over to the right and into Hogan's view between him and the fireplace. The Russian Tokarev pistol was still playfully smoking in his steady hand. "Why don't you pick it up—pick up your little Schmeisser? It's right there on the table." Beaucroix motioned toward the submachine gun.

Hogan wondered how Beaucroix had known about Max's plan to kill him. Perhaps he had tortured, then killed Kendal for the information.

Beaucroix pulled up a chair and grinned as he sat facing Hogan. "It looks like I'm a day early for my assassination, so we shall have a full day to get to know each other."

With this, Beaucroix removed an evil-looking steel razor from his jacket and regarded its edge with interest. God, Hogan wished Beaucroix hadn't sat down. Hogan had two weapons within three feet of him. First, there was the Schmeisser to his right. But his right hand was useless, and the grip on the Schmeisser was facing the wrong way. Besides, the Schmeisser was between him and Beaucroix. The second weapon was the Beretta nine-millimeter hidden under his ammo vest in his left shoulder holster. But it was almost impossible to draw a gun from a left shoulder holster quickly with your left hand. He appeared helpless, and the Monster Beaucroix certainly knew it.

"Prince Vlad the Impaler of Wallachia used to skin his victims alive. He was the source of all the Dracula legends." Beaucroix continued to mark him with the 7.65-mm Tokarev as he held the razor toward Hogan for his inspection. "Tell me the truth. Haven't you wondered how it might feel? That is, to be skinned alive?"

Hogan knew Beaucroix planned to torture him before the kill, but any sudden movement would instigate a reply from the 7.65, and Hogan needed time. He tried to make as little movement as possible as he surveyed the area within his reach for a possible weapon. His futile efforts became of sadistic interest to Beaucroix.

"Just what are you looking for, Hogan? You're a lousy host," the Monster accused, and the gun barked again, shattering Hogan's left knee and causing an involuntary spasm that knocked his leg off the ottoman and sent his heel painfully crashing to the floor.

"Gosh, that was fun." Beaucroix smiled as he gave the pistol a gentle kiss and then leveled it back on Hogan. "Was it good for you too?" With his other hand, he continued to play with the straight razor, swinging it back and forth carefully so as to catch the dancing reflections of the fire. "We're going to have lots of fun together. I really mean it." He tossed Hogan a fiendish wink.

Hogan's leg was in a lot of pain—not from the bullet hole, but from the way his lower leg lay twisted after it was knocked off the ottoman. The angle of his leg held the shattered bone in his knee directly against the nerve. More than anything in the world, he wanted to reach down and shift his left knee. Right now, he wanted to do that even more than he wanted to kill Emile Beaucroix. The pain was making the sweat roll down Hogan's forehead, but he knew if he reached for his knee, another blast from Beaucroix would sever it completely. The Monster could be so predicable sometimes. Hogan briefly wondered through his fog of pain why so many men had found Beaucroix so difficult to kill. The Monster must be protected by the devil himself.

"You're sweating, Hogan. Is it that hot in here, or are you a tad under the weather?" As he said this, he again offered the razor for inspection. "Maybe a nice shave would make you feel better. What do you think?" The Monster raised an eyebrow and grinned as he rocked the razor back and forth, causing its reflections to dance across the beads of sweat rolling down Hogan's face.

The pain had reached the point where there was a real danger of Hogan passing out. He knew his only chance was to take everything Beaucroix had to offer and play for time. He hoped he could stay conscious. Shit, he wished Beaucroix hadn't sat down.

"I've always wondered what your house looked like." Beaucroix nodded as he surveyed the room. "Tell me, do you suck Max George's dick right here, or do you two go into one of the bedrooms?"

Beaucroix was trying to rile him, to get him to reveal Max's whereabouts; obviously Beaucroix didn't know. If he did, he would have taken the safe route. He would have killed Max first and then come for Hogan.

"What?" Beaucroix said. "Aren't you going to threaten me with Max?"

The gun barked again, tearing through Hogan's left boot and severing the tip of his big toe. Anticipating the blast, Hogan took the opportunity to jerk his left leg. Now, even though his left foot was burning in a pool of blood, his torn knee was no longer cutting through the nerve. He felt much better—a strange thing for anyone to think after being shot for the third time.

"Don't be so shy, Hogan. I know George is meeting you here tomorrow. Even Kendal is considering slipping out of Guatemala to join you, although it would mean his life."

At least now Hogan knew Kendal was alive, but that left the mystery of how Beaucroix had known about the plot. Kendal was now eliminated as the one who had talked, and, despite Beaucroix's inflated self-image, Max was too tough to break.

"George has his clever moments." Beaucroix talked as if nothing had happened. "But you—I've always known you to be a coward and a wimp. You're one of those worthless mice with neither the courage to kill nor the courage to die. Well, it's too late for you to learn how to kill, so how about I teach you how to die?" Beaucroix leaned forward and winked. "But not before we have had some fun—a whole lot of fun."

Beaucroix stood and circled away from the fireplace, keeping the pistol well poised and the razor still gleaming. His new position placed him squarely in front of Hogan instead of to the right, where his last vantage point had been.

"I'll bet ten British pounds that I can blow your dick off in one shot," Beaucroix offered.

Now Hogan was at the end of his rope. It seemed there was nothing more to do but to die.

"Hey, why don't you answer me, Hogan? Is it a bet or not?"

Beaucroix was too far away to lunge at, and Hogan's leg wouldn't support any weight even if Beaucroix had moved closer.

Beaucroix shrugged. "I guess you don't have ten pounds. Well, that's OK. You can owe me." The Monster pointed the pistol at Hogan's crotch and tightened his grip. A loud blast sent a bullet whizzing through the air. It made a loud smack as it hit tissue, bone, then tissue again, ending its journey in the fireplace facade.

When Hogan heard the blast, he rolled from the chair and onto the floor in time to see Max George framed in the doorway with the receiver of his Walther PPK just setting back into position as the pistol loaded another round.

A loud crash announced the opening of the service window louvers as Walter appeared with the massive .600 Nitro Express. Walter jerked both triggers, thus cutting loose both huge barrels in a simultaneous discharge, instantly disemboweling Beaucroix and slamming his lifeless body against the mantel slightly to the right of the fireplace.

Walter didn't have time to lean into his shot, and the powerful double-barreled elephant thumper sent him flying backward into the kitchen and onto the floor. The fourteen-pound express rifle flew backward out of his hands and slid across the floor, making a loud clang as it stopped against the right iron leg of the gas oven.

Not missing a beat, Walter bolted up, grabbed an 8 mm Mauser off the rack by the kitchen door, and ran into the game room.

Beaucroix had just now bounced off the mantel, leaving behind a paste of blood and tissue. He lay on the floor about three feet from the fireplace in a widening pool of blood. Max had tracked his fall with the sights of his Walther. He was sure Beaucroix was dead when his pistol delivered the brain shot, but when Walter halved him with the double cannon, it ended any doubt.

Max and Walter had seen the whole thing: Beaucroix playing his psychotic mind game with Hogan. But when Beaucroix had taken his seat, he was out of view of both Max George in the kitchen and Walter at the serving window; there was nothing they could do. They had to listen helplessly until Beaucroix stood and moved into a safe line of fire.

Max slipped as he stepped toward Hogan to help him stand. He looked closely at the floor as he righted himself. "Robert, you are one clever son of a bitch," Max told him with a grin.

Hogan managed a little smile as he looked at the floor. Several days before, Tilde had coated it with three thick layers of wax and then sealed it with silicone and waxed it again. Tomorrow, after she stripped it and lightly waxed it again, no test on earth would be able to find a trace of blood. This wasn't an official termination, so to protect the guilty, it must be an official disappearance, and it must remain a mystery.

Walter had put the Mauser back in the rack and brought out a surgical kit. As he wrapped Hogan's wounds, Max examined Beaucroix just to be sure.

"Well, Robert, you were right." He walked over and placed his hand on Hogan's shoulder. "He was one predictable SOB. You were right about the limestone, too. It caught every bullet." Max had moved over to the mantel and was examining the wall. Tomorrow, Walter would throw the limestone blocks, along with Beaucroix's weighted body, into the Congo River, thus revealing the original, undamaged blue marble fireplace beneath.

Beaucroix's death would remain a mystery. The mighty Congo River was filled with accommodating critters that would be pleased to eat the evidence. The agency would assume the Soviets' best player had eliminated him, and the CIA would do its best to forget he ever had existed at all.

Walter had just finished his quick patch job on Hogan and was on the phone to the town doctor, telling him what he would need to bring.

With a weak smile, Hogan regarded the fireplace. "Walter, do you think we could use the undamaged stones to make a new fireplace in my study?"

Walter took his ear off the phone and covered the mouthpiece. "I will make you the best and warmest fireplace in Africa, and Tilde will bring you warm soup and cognac to sip by the fire." He returned to his conversation with the doctor.

Hogan turned to George. "A great evil has died. *Comedia finita est*: The play is finished," Hogan quoted, repeating the very words the great composer Ludwig van Beethoven had said as he lay dying and shaking his fist at the gods above.

"That sounds a bit melodramatic!" the intruder declared with a broad smile.

Slava Kurnov somehow had entered the room unseen with five soldiers of the Soviet Special Forces behind him. The men quickly fanned out into the room, marking all present with their assault rifles.

Kurnov surveyed the scene before him: the blood-and-tissue-smeared mantel, the blood-soaked body of Emile Beaucroix, and the pain-painted face of a now well-bandaged Robert Hogan.

"You gentlemen have had a hard day, and hard lives. We are all going to take a little plane trip to your new homes. You will enjoy your new lives. You will not be bored, as we have so much to talk about." Kurnov motioned to the door. "Please, gentlemen, step this wa—"

But Kurnov was cut off by the sensation of cold steel at the back of his head, and the player who now had entered the game was certainly no friend of the Americans either.

The latest intruder snapped his fingers, and a dozen of his armed escorts entered the room and roughly disarmed the Soviets. He grinned broadly as he slowly tracked his weapon away from Kurnov, and, pausing his swing, he leveled the Colt 1911 pistol, marking a point between the eyes of Max George, and, with a sharp click, he pulled back the hammer.

www.ingramcontent.com/pod-product-compliance
Lightning Source LLC
Chambersburg PA
CBHW070800180626
46818CB00001B/33